CW01067337

About the author

David Hair is a New Zealander living once more in Wellington, New Zealand, after nearly four years in India. He is the author of *The Bone Tiki* (winner of Best First Book at the 2010 NZ Post Children's Book Awards), and its sequel, *The Taniwha's Tear*. David is also the author of the *Return of Ravana* series, a four-book teen-fantasy set in India. David is married to Kerry, and has two children, Brendan and Melissa. He has a degree in History and Classical Studies, and a passion for football (real football, played eleven-a-side with a round ball).

THE
LOST
TOHUNGA

DAVID HAIR

HarperCollins*Publishers*

HarperCollins*Publishers*

First published 2011
HarperCollins*Publishers (New Zealand) Limited*
P.O. Box 1, Auckland 1140

Copyright © David Hair 2011

David Hair asserts the moral right to be identified as the author of this work.
All rights reserved. No part of this publication may be reproduced, stored
in a retrieval system or transmitted in any form or by any means, electronic,
mechanical, photocopying, recording or otherwise, without the prior written
permission of the publishers.

HarperCollins*Publishers*
31 View Road, Glenfield, Auckland 0627, New Zealand
25 Ryde Road, Pymble, Sydney, NSW 2073, Australia
A 53, Sector 57, Noida, UP, India
77–85 Fulham Palace Road, London W6 8JB, United Kingdom
2 Bloor Street East, 20th floor, Toronto, Ontario M4W 1A8, Canada
10 East 53rd Street, New York, NY 10022, USA

National Library of New Zealand Cataloguing-in-Publication Data

Hair, David, 1965-
The lost tohunga / David Hair.
Sequel to: The taniwha's tear.
ISBN 9781-86950-827-2
1. Maori (New Zealand people)—Juvenile fiction.
[1. Maori (New Zealand people)—Fiction. 2. Tohunga—Fiction.
3. Warlocks—Fiction. 4. Good and evil—Fiction. 5. Fantasy.]
[1. Pakiwaitara. reo 2. Tohunga. reo] I. Title.
NZ823.3—dc 22

ISBN: 978 1 86950 827 2
Cover design by Louise McGeachie
Cover images: Tapotupotu Bay at dawn by Tony Pleavin/ The Travel Library/
Photolibrary.com; Greenstone hand club by Focusnewzealand.com/ Frank
Gasteiger, Jade carving by Ross Crump/ JadeGallery.co.nz
Typesetting by Springfield West

Printed by Griffin Press, Australia

50 gsm Bulky News used by HarperCollins*Publishers* is a natural, recyclable
product made from wood grown in sustainable plantation forests. The
manufacturing processes conform to the environmental regulations in the
country of origin, New Zealand.

Acknowledgements

Many thanks must go again to my wonderful wife Kerry for reading the manuscript many, many times over! Also a big 'kia ora' to Arama for his comments and feedback, which were as always very much appreciated. Thanks also to 'The Family Stone' (Kate and Liz) for edits and keeping me on task, and Eva, Bonnie and everyone else at HarperCollins New Zealand for your continued support for, and belief in, this series.

Namaste to all the friends Kerry and I made during our Indian sojourn, especially Mike and Heather, Simon and Bettina, Harshal, Catherine, Melanie, Kelly, Tanuva, Vidhi, Stella and all the fabulous folk at the New Zealand High Commission in Delhi. We miss you all.

This book is dedicated to Hirini Johnston, whose cheerful courage is inspirational to all of us lucky enough to know him.

Contents

Prologue — the girl with the porcelain doll

Auckland, 1956

Whenever the girl heard the crunch of boots on the gravel path outside, she imagined that her father had come to take her away. So when she heard the telltale sound, she picked up her one-eyed porcelain doll, smoothed its perfectly combed hair and tea-stained christening gown, and took it to the window. Brushing aside the mouldy lace curtains, she wiped a hole in the condensation on the glass, then gasped as a big eye peered through the circle she had made.

'Mummy!' she squealed, leaping back, letting the curtains fall. 'There's a man at the door!'

That eye kept following her.

'I'm sure it's not Father, Rose,' she told the doll as she backed away. 'Father is a soldier.'

Rose looked doubtful. *You don't know that*, the doll whispered. *Mummy never said he was a soldier.*

'He is too,' the girl insisted. 'He's a captain!'

The horrid eye continued to follow her.

She heard Mummy bustle through the house from the laundry, the floor creaking beneath her feet. 'Who is it?'

Mummy asked crossly. 'I'm in the middle of my laundry. Go and put your underwear through the wringer!'

The girl's face fell. She hated doing washing. The grey soapy water that came off the clothes when they were wrung looked horrid and it made her feel that all of her clothes were coated in grime. She only pretended to go to the laundry, then crept back, wrinkling her nose at the cigarette smoke that trailed her mother. The tiny downstairs apartment off Ponsonby Road always smelt bad, like cooking fat and damp rot. The girl hated it.

She watched her mother primp in the cracked hall mirror. *Mummy is ugly*, Rose whispered meanly.

'You shouldn't say that,' the girl whispered back.

She is too. She's fat and ugly and not really your mother. She's just a cleaner and the priest says she has 'low moral character'. I heard him. We should run away.

The girl quivered a little. 'Shhh!' she told Rose, not wanting her mother to overhear. She had been thinking a lot about running away, but she wasn't quite ready yet. The little shopping bag she had filched from Mummy's cupboard had only a few copper coins that she had found in the gutters, a pair of shoes she had stolen from a girl at school, and three ribbons. She would need more for her escape. 'Soon, Rose,' she told the doll placatingly, watching her mother undo her top button.

Maybe it was a new man-friend who would leave money.

Her mother rallied her tired face, and tilted her hips as she fumbled with the deadbolt. 'Hello, who is it?' she called through the mail slot, in *that* voice.

'Nessie,' a man's voice purred, just like that frightening cat in the 'Alice' book the teacher was reading aloud at school. The girl felt a quiver of fear and excitement, a tremble that tickled the whole of her spine. She watched in fascination as her mother suddenly clutched the wall, her whole frame wobbling.

'Asher … ?' Mummy breathed in a strangled voice. She took two steps away from the door, pressing onto the wall as if her legs were failing.

'Mummy?' the girl whispered.

Her mother threw a look back over her shoulder. 'Edith, go to your room.' Her voice was frightened, but the instruction was normal. Whenever a man-friend came to give Mummy money, she had to go to her room. Why did Mummy sound so scared this time?

She tried to scuttle past her mother, when the key turned in the lock of its own volition. Her mother whimpered, and she grabbed her daughter, dragging her back towards the kitchen. The girl squealed in protest, her heel lashing against her mother's shin. 'Lemme go! Lemme go!' Her mother cried out, and dropped her. Then the key turned, and the door flew open.

The man in the doorway looked like an actor from a stage show. He wore a velvet robe and cloak, and a floppy plumed hat. In his right hand was a long wooden cane, polished ebony with a crystal knob.

The girl's mother stopped moving. 'Asher? Asher?'

The man smiled, his lined face lighting up although his eyes remained cold. 'Nessie. It's been a long time.'

The girl watched her mother's face drain of colour. But she struggled to her feet. 'What do you want?'

'Only what is mine, sweet Nessie.' He pointed his finger at the girl, who stared at that crooked talon with its overlong nails and almost wet herself. 'I've come for her.'

'No,' Mummy breathed. 'No! You have no right. Not after eight years!'

The man reached out his ring-encrusted hand to the girl. 'Has it been so long?' He shrugged and looked at the girl directly. 'Hello, child. What is your name?'

Mummy jerked the girl to her breast and wrapped her arms about her, as if she wanted to crush her. 'Don't answer him. Don't ever talk to him!' The girl struggled, frightened and fascinated, peering out at the man as he bent closer. 'She's mine!' Mummy gritted in a voice the girl had never heard. 'Get away from us!'

The man straightened, and then gestured with his cane. Mummy dropped her, and she fell to the floor with a squeal. Another sweep of the cane, and Mummy flew backwards through the air, slamming into the back wall. She didn't fall, but hung there, her mouth open and eyes pleading.

The girl clutched Rose, too scared to breathe.

'Please, Asher,' Mummy pleaded.

She's pathetic, Rose whispered in her ear.

The girl was too scared to acknowledge the doll's opinion. She just stared up at this elegant creature towering over her, as her brain made connections. 'Father?'

His eyes turned to her. 'Yes, child. You are my daughter.'

Mummy sobbed, still held invisibly pinned to the wall. 'Asher! Please! You ruined me. My family threw me out. I've raised her on my own! On my own! She's mine!'

Asher made a flicking noise with his hand, and her mother reacted as if slapped, her face jerking aside with an audible crack. 'Silence, Nessie. She is my daughter, and I claim her.' He lifted a single finger and made a zipping gesture. The girl watched as her mother suddenly lost the power to open her mouth, although she visibly tried, her cheeks and eyes bulging.

Don't feel sorry for her, Rose told her. *She deserves it. She has loose morals.*

'Are you really my father?' the girl asked.

He bowed floridly. 'I am,' he said grandly, and handed her a rose that appeared in his hand. 'My name is Asher Grieve.' She took the rose and sniffed it, but it had no smell.

'My name is Edith Madonna Kyle,' she replied proudly. 'But Edith is a horrid name. Rose calls me Donna.'

'Then Donna you shall be,' Asher told her. He reached down and offered her a hand.

Mother tried to move, as tears spurted from her eyes.

'Say goodbye to your mother,' Asher Grieve told her. 'You will not see her again.'

The girl straightened. 'I don't need to. She's *pathetic*.'

She turned away, and didn't look back.

They stood in a clearing in a forest that she had never seen before. The air was so clean, without even a trace of smoke, and the pool was fed by a stream so clean she felt she could drink it all night. The moon hung overhead, and it was the strangest moon ever, because if you looked at it out of the corner of your eye, it had a face in it like a native carving. She thought it weird but pretty, and Rose liked it, too.

Asher Grieve sat on a fallen log, watching her as she washed Rose's dress. *No more grey water*, she thought with satisfaction. *From now on, everything is going to be* clean.

Then the frightening native came. She didn't see how —

one moment he wasn't there, the next he was. He had a mane of silver hair and his whole face was black with the horrible face carving the natives did. Donna wanted to hide her eyes, but she didn't, because Rose told her not to. *Be brave*, she whispered.

'This is she, I presume?' the man rumbled in the Queen's English.

'Aye, she is my daughter,' Father told the native. 'She calls herself Donna Kyle.'

'And does she have the potential?' the native asked.

That's odd, Donna thought. *This man behaves as if he were my father's master, but natives are lesser men; everyone knows that. And my father is* important.

'See for yourself,' Asher told him. He smiled wryly, and called in a soft voice. 'Rose, is Donna special?'

The doll's head turned slowly and her one eye flickered towards the man. *She is very special*, she told the two men. *She is the cleverest eight-year-old in all of Auckland*. The doll's out-loud voice was tinkling and clear. Donna felt very proud to be spoken of so, although Rose was her friend and would always say nice things about her.

The native's eyebrows raised fractionally. 'Ahhh,' was all he said. Then he stood, and offered her father a handshake. 'Then we have a bargain,' he said in a resonant voice.

Asher Grieve stood and took the larger man's hand. 'Yes, Master. That we do. She is yours.'

There was something in his voice that Donna didn't like.

Her father crouched beside her. He lifted her chin. 'This man is Puarata. He is the master tohunga. You belong to him, now.' He put a hand on her head, stroked her blonde curls briefly, then he straightened. His face lost all interest in her. The earth seemed wafer-thin suddenly, and for the first time she felt truly frightened. She reached out a hand to him, but all at once he was gone, simply not there.

The waters of the stream trickled onwards as if nothing had happened, but she stood there blinking, her mouth open. It occurred to her that she was dreaming all of this.

Then the heavy hand of the native grasped Rose and tore her from Donna's grasp. She screamed, and then felt a sickening wrench inside her as the man tore the doll's head off, and flung the two pieces to the ground. She found herself grovelling in the grass, shrieking in horror and pain at a sensation like having her heart ripped in two.

The tohunga was impassive as he picked her up with one hand, his strength horrifying. *Crack!* His hand slapped her, making her cheek burn and her skull ring. 'SILENCE!'

She was frightened mute.

His alien face filled her vision. 'The doll was a prop, dangerously weakening over the long term.' He regarded her coldly, dangling in his grasp like a specimen for inspection. She was too frightened to struggle. 'I do not tolerate weakness.'

He lowered her to the ground, and cupped her face, holding her eyes locked in his gaze 'My name is Puarata. I am going to break you down and re-make you, Donna Kyle. I'm going to mould you and fire you like pottery, and when you emerge, you will be everything I want you to be. And you will be utterly mine.' He dropped his voice to a whisper. 'There is only one thing of your past life that I desire you to remember: *that it was your own father who sold you to me.*'

Taupo

Saturday

Matiu Douglas fidgeted as the kilometres rolled past, taking him ever closer to Taupo. His father, Tama, hummed tunelessly to an FM signal that came and went as they wound through the hills. The spring rains lashing Hawke's Bay that morning were well behind them. On this side of the Kaimanawa Ranges the skies were silvery grey, and a stiff wind swept the aisles of verdant pines on the final approaches to Taupo. He hoped it would be blue skies for the next two weeks. School holidays were meant to be sunny. It was the first Saturday of the September break, and Dad had insisted on driving Mat to Taupo, hoping to see his estranged wife for a while.

The Napier–Taupo road held many memories for Mat. His mind drifted back to almost exactly one year ago, and the terrifying chase that had changed his life totally. He held his breath at the spot where he and his new-found friend Kelly had been run off the road by the minions of Puarata, the evil tohunga. But Puarata was dead now, and Mat had survived and grown. Nine months ago at Lake Waikaremoana he had been duped by one of Puarata's former allies and almost died in a flood, but he had got through that, too. He was now almost seventeen.

Dad glanced across at Mat, a strangely uncertain look on his dark, pugnacious features. 'Mat, do you know if your mother is still seeing that Neil fella she was dating back in June?'

'Dunno.' Mat shrugged apologetically, feeling bad for Dad. Since that Christmas holiday in Gisborne, it felt like Mum and Dad had hit another brick wall in terms of them ever getting back together. Dad was pretty low, and on the few occasions he saw Mum, he tensed up and said the wrong thing. His parents seemed further apart than ever. Dad still worked his law practice in Napier, and Mum still taught at her school in Taupo.

The pine forests that fed the central North Island's logging industry gave way to thick brush and tussock, and then a lake appeared through the folds of the land, shining like a sheet-metal plate. Lake Taupo, a water-filled crater left after an explosion thousands of years ago that had matched the famous Krakatoa eruption for power. Or if you went with the Maori legends, a great dry basin, until the legendary tohunga Ngatoro-i-rangi had flung a tree from the top of Mount Tauhara, which pierced the basin causing water to erupt from below and fill the lake.

Remembering this naturally led Mat to thoughts of Ngatoro. Since his adventure in Waikaremoana at New Year, Mat had been in intermittent mental contact with the supposedly dead tohunga. It was eerie — sometimes the old tohunga's thoughts would spill into Mat's mind. They managed conversation occasionally. All Ngatoro could tell him was that he was floating weightless, in complete darkness and silence. It sounded awful.

On impulse, he called in his mind. *Ngatoro?*

The dry, ancient voice responded almost at once. *Matiu? What is it?*

Oh, nothing really. I just wondered whether you actually created Lake Taupo or not?

I'm an old man, Mat. The last thing I need is this trivia! You know how these things are: in your world, it was formed by a volcanic eruption, but in Aotearoa …

It was made by you. Yeah, sorry. I just kind of thought of you, and called without thinking.

The old tohunga tutted. *I must preserve my energies, poai. I feel so weak …*

Mat winced as the contact faded. 'Uh, sorry,' he said aloud.

His father threw a look his way. 'Huh?'

'Oh, nothing,' he replied. Dad knew about Aotearoa, but if he knew Mat was in mental contact with a missing tohunga, he would flip.

Jones and Mat had a mini project going trying to trace those brief mental contacts so they could find Ngatoro and free him, but they had made little progress. He was looking forward to seeing the Welshman again. This would be his fourth holiday in Taupo since he had met Jones. He would divide his time between Mum's house, and Jones's cottage in Aotearoa, the Ghost World. Just thinking about going to Aotearoa had him smiling again. Sure, he had to study and Mum would ride him hard over the exams that were coming up next term. But most importantly, he wanted to see Jones, and renew his REAL training. His fingers carved little patterns in the air as he remembered lessons and movements … *Mat Douglas, apprentice Adept of Aotearoa!*

The township of Taupo lay on the north side of the lake. It was base camp for those wanting to ski the mountains, boat or fish the lake, go bungee jumping or white-water rafting, or try any of the loads of other adventure activities. It was also a geothermal area. He liked Taupo. Mum and Jones made it special, even if they didn't get on with each other.

Mum's house was on a quiet side street several blocks from the lake and the shops. It wasn't the same house Mum had lived in a year ago, where Puarata had kidnapped her and attacked Mat. She had left that place almost immediately, unable to feel safe there again. Dad peered up the driveway, sighing in relief that only one car was parked there. Mat agreed. Not that he didn't like Neil, but Mum's recent boyfriend didn't feel like family. Mat hoped he was off the scene, too.

Mum greeted Mat at the door with a warm hug, her red hair tumbling over her shoulders and into his face. Her voice still held a soft Irish lilt. There were a few strands of grey, and a few more frown lines, but she still felt the same when she hugged him.

Mum hugged Dad, too, but it was brief and businesslike, a glorified handshake. Dad agreed to stay for lunch, and the two adults headed for the kitchen while he deposited his bag in a bedroom that still didn't feel like it was his, with its cheery yellow curtains and sky-blue walls. He propped his practice taiaha in the corner and stared at an old easel and some paints by the window. A half-finished girl's face stared back at him from the canvas: Lena, painted from memory. It wasn't a bad likeness, but it didn't express all he wanted to say about her. Recently they had been learning some Art History and he had tried out adding symbolism to the picture, little coded messages. A taniwha coiled in the waters in the background, and Lena's finger was raised to her lips, urging silence. He regarded it for a while, until his parents called him for lunch.

The table was awash with bowls of salads and tins of fish. Mum only ate fish and vegetables at the moment — no red meat. As usual they talked about Mat as if he wasn't there. His father gave a rundown on Mat's recent school test results. Mat was in his second-to-last year at high school, and had big NCEA exams in six weeks or so. 'They're doing mock exams in his first week back at school, so keep him focused,' Dad told Mum.

Mat rolled his eyes while Mum nodded firmly. 'That means you'll not be spending all your time at that Welshman's place,' she told Mat. 'I'm expecting some good marks to justify those fees we're paying.'

'If he goes on to university, then the costs are only just beginning,' said Tama. 'The fees are going up more than ten per cent again next year. Those varsity heads are bigger crooks than most of my clients.' He immediately coloured, clearly wishing he hadn't put it quite that way.

'I got pretty good marks mid-term,' volunteered Mat, to head off the old 'protecting criminals' argument. It worked. They went back to picking over his results, which at least they agreed upon. Finally, it was time for Dad to go, and Mum shooed him off. They all hugged again awkwardly, then with a gentle surge the Mercedes was gone.

That could've gone better, Mat reflected sadly. He noticed a pile of letters on the bench addressed to 'Ms C O'Connor'. Mum was using her maiden name then. She had told him she would be doing that, but it didn't feel real until you saw it written down.

Mum frowned, and visibly put her ex-husband from her mind. She reached up and ruffled Mat's hair. 'Well, you've grown, to be sure. You're taller than me. And handsome, too. You breaking those Napier girls' hearts?'

Mat grimaced. 'Other way round, more like.'

Colleen looked intrigued. 'Really? Have you got a sweetheart then?'

'We don't have "sweethearts", Mum. We're not living in the 'fifties or 'sixties or whenever you last dated.'

'Oh, that's harsh, Matty. I wager I get as many dates as you do. More, probably, with you being at an all-male school, and under your dad's thumb at home.'

Mat grunted. 'It's like a prison camp sometimes.'

'Well, after this year, you've only one to go, and then you'll be off to university. You'll have to leave home then. Which university do you want to go to? Victoria in Wellington, so you can stay with Wiri and Kelly and Fitzy?'

'Hopefully. Wiri says that Wellington rocks.' Just thinking of Wiri and Kelly brought a smile to his face. They had married in March at a Hawke's Bay vineyard, announcing mid-ceremony that Kelly was already four months pregnant, which was kind of obvious when she arrived looking like a puffball. The baby was nearly due.

'Come on, lad, let's go for a walk down by the lake. You still haven't told me about your sweetheart. Or whatever you want to call her.'

They walked down to the lake, where holidaying children were shouting and running, and tourists were peering out across the water wondering how the sky could be so blue when the air was so cold. Southerlies in Taupo carried fresh mountain-top air, direct from the snowfields.

The only unhappy faces were two Maori women, sitting beneath a tree, crying and hugging. The younger one looked strangely familiar to Mat, so much so that he caught himself staring. When she saw him watching her, she mouthed something rude and he looked away, feeling guilty.

His mother pulled his arm. 'Don't stare, Matty. Whatever it is, it's their problem, not yours.'

They left the two women to their crisis, and bought an OJ and a coffee from a café on the edge of the shopping area, and took them down to the shore to sip. The lake's surface was dark grey-green, small waves being whisked by the stinging wind into little white-tops. Gulls tacked their way across the wind like airborne yachts.

Mum sipped her coffee appreciatively and smiled at him. 'So, how's my boy then?'

He didn't mean to tell her much, but as usual he ended up telling her everything. He was OK at school, and he was basically popular, but he felt like an outsider at times. He didn't drink, smoke, attend church or play rugby. Cross all those off, and he felt like he had no common ground with anyone. Not when his mind was filled with Art and Aotearoa. Riki was still his best friend of course, and they were planning on getting together in the second week of these holidays, after

Riki's taiaha camp in Rotorua was over. But Riki also hung with the beer-and-dirty-jokes crowd, who treated Mat like he was a radical Mormon.

'It's like, everyone I know smokes and drinks,' he found himself saying to his mum. 'They've *all* got girlfriends, and spend all their time talking about them. Even the jerks have girlfriends. In fact, they get the girls before anyone else does. And the guys with cars can take their pick ... Are all girls really that stupid?' he grumped morosely.

Mum smirked. 'If you mean, is it stupid for girls to want to hang out with popular alpha males with visible wealth and status? Well, I wouldn't call them stupid. Life is like that. In the animal kingdom—'

'Mum, I'm not a chimpanzee! I just want to fit in.'

'Well, you're the one going off with that mystic Welsh weirdo, and spending all your time and money on art equipment and antique weaponry. Don't you think you're isolating yourself a little?'

'If you saw the things I've seen in Aotearoa, you'd—'

Mum flinched. 'Matty, I have no desire at all to see that awful place ever again. This world is hard enough without going to another place that's worse. I wish you could just put it aside. It's not safe, and it's taking you away from your family and friends.'

Mat looked at her. Mum never spoke much about what had happened a year ago, about her kidnapping by Puarata, and what they had seen up at Cape Reinga. He sometimes thought she was trying very, very hard to forget it had ever happened. He couldn't blame her. They fell into an awkward silence.

Finally, Mat looked up and asked, 'So, are you still seeing Neil?' Dad always said attack was the best form of defence.

It was Mum's turn to colour. 'Sometimes. No, not really. Sort of. Don't you like him, then?'

'He's alright, if you like cars and rugby. He's just kinda … *ordinary*.'

'Well, ordinary is nice sometimes. And Taupo can be a bit of a man-desert, for sure.'

'Why live here then?'

'Well, life is not just about finding a fella, Matty. I like my job here; I'm Deputy Head at the school now. I like the skiing and the hot pools, and there are a whole bunch of us single women I've buddied up with. It's close enough to Napier that I can see you regularly without bumping into your dad all the time.' She looked at him frankly. 'Your dad and I aren't going to be getting back together again, Matty. You need to let it go. I'm happy enough. I like my life here.'

It was distressing how matter-of-factly she said it. He felt a deep ache inside, and didn't know what to say. His mum looked at him sadly, then gazed out over the water. 'Look, Matty, there's a big log floatin' in the water out there.'

He looked, and sure enough, a dark shape bobbed amidst the waves, perhaps fifty metres from shore. He let his eyes mist slightly, and refocused the way Jones had taught him. Now he saw a serpentine shape sliding through the water. He blinked it away and shivered slightly.

'They do say that there is a taniwha in the lake,' said Mum, as if she were a mind-reader. 'They say it appears like a big log floating in the water, and it's seen before disasters.' She glanced at him anxiously.

'It's just a log, Mum,' he lied. 'Probably washed in from the forests.'

She smiled sadly, then reached over and pulled out his necklace. It was a greenstone pendant on a string cord. Really, it was two pendants, a Maori koru and an Irish knot, designed to fit together. He had carved them himself, from kauri, but in Aotearoa they had been transformed into pounamu, or greenstone. He had intended them as gifts for his parents, but they had seen the two pieces as implying they would be reconciling, so he had ended up with both the pendants after all. Maybe it was meant to be that way. It wasn't a bad thing — together, they seemed to augment his abilities. Another pendant hung beside the koru–knot now: a tear-shaped piece of jade. The tear of a taniwha: Lena's tear. It was cold and strange to touch.

'I suppose you'll be going off to see that Jones fella as usual, then?' Mum asked, in disapproving tones.

'Sure. He's expecting me.'

He watched her bite her lip, trying to find a reason for him not to go. Finally, she gave it up. 'Well, best you go then, so you can be back in time for dinner. But you tell him from me that he's to cut you some slack. It's trying to live up to what he wants that's setting you apart from your friends. A boy has to have some fun, too. You tell him that.'

Mat left Mum and walked southeast along a muddy little shoreline path leading away from town. To his left, the holiday homes were coming alive as their families arrived. To his right, the dark shape of the log flowed through the water, closer and closer. He glanced over his shoulder to check he was alone, stopped and then drew out his koru–knot pendant.

He closed his eyes, and shut out the smells of the lake, the distant traffic, and the chill touch of the wind. Inside himself he could feel a thin coil of verdant fire. He grasped it, visualized Aotearoa, the Ghost World that existed parallel to the real world, the place where legends lived and the dead went. It took seconds, as energy surged then left him shaking and perspiring. He opened his eyes, and looked about. The time-shares had vanished, replaced by verdant forest. The town had been replaced by a Maori pa and a collection of colonial houses. He exhaled with satisfaction, and then the lake boiled about his feet, and with a rush, a massive water-serpent towered over him, its teeth bared.

'Kia ora, Horomatangi!' he shouted, as a wave washed over his knees and made him stagger.

The taniwha hissed, and its fishy breath hit Mat like a cold blast of steam. Massive filmy eyes took turns at regarding him as the serpent turned its head first one way then the other. Lake weed slid from its oily black flanks, and clung to the twisted folds and ridges of its massive skull. If a mythical dragon had mated with a massive eel, it might have resulted in this creature. But it was far more than a big fish. This was the lake-god, and the world seemed to bend around it. Mat could feel throbbing skeins of power that emanated from it. It was both in and of the water, bound to both worlds at once.

Horomatangi lowered its head back into the water, half-submerged, one huge opalescent eye watching him. Its tongue flickered out. On it was a stone the size of a compact disc, grey slate washed smooth by the waters of the lake, presented as a gift. Mat reached cautiously into the taniwha's mouth, between fangs the size of his hands, and took the stone. In the great reflecting eye, he saw an image flicker of Jones, and he nodded. Then a pulse of energy made him gasp, and the pale disc of stone seemed to fizz with light. Further images formed. A blonde woman with a scarred face and a tattooed chin: Donna Kyle! His heart beat faster. More images followed. A hollow-eyed tramp limping down a gravel road. A shape like a woman, composed entirely of birds. A giant pounamu stone that pulsed like a heartbeat. Then darkness. His vision cleared, and he stared up at the taniwha.

Horomatangi reared again, towering above him, then swirled away into the depths with a mighty crash of water. Mat barely kept his footing, his clothes were sodden. He stared after the taniwha, hoping for more, but it was gone. He was left wet and shivering. He slopped back to the shoreline and sat on a tree stump, shivering.

The face of the blonde woman still haunted his dreams. Donna Kyle, Puarata's former apprentice. The last time he had seen her was an instant before the waters had swept him away in Waikaremoana. He had hoped she had drowned, but her sneering, cold-eyed face never left his nightmares. Why did she feature in the taniwha's message?

Standing, he began to run down the trail. Under the pallid sky, if seen out of the corner of the eye, the sun seemed to be a huge carved face — only the most obvious sign that he was in another world. He reached an old jetty, then turned up a short path through bush that thrummed with insects and birdsong, to an old wood cabin that lurked among towering kauri trees.

'Jones! Jones!'

An old man stepped from the front door, a bony figure with lank, grey hair and rough white stubble. He wore faded brown cotton pants of the sort worn by colonial settlers, and his checked shirt was stained and threadbare. A grin adorned a leathery face that had something of a wolf about it.

'Mat! About time!' Aethlyn Jones strode down the path and hugged Mat, his warm embrace reeking of pipe smoke. He still spoke with a Welsh burr, despite having left Wales two hundred years before, fleeing a Church-led purge of the remnants of druidism and witchcraft. Eventually, he had settled in Aotearoa. Since New Year, Mat had become 'wizard's apprentice' to the old man. Which was fine, because he liked Jones hugely, whatever Mum thought.

'Let's be lookin' at ye, laddie,' Jones said, holding him out at arm's length. 'You smell like a swamp and you're wet through. What on earth have you been doing?'

Mat held up the stone disc. 'I saw Horomatangi! He gave me this, for you!'

Jones raised an eyebrow. 'Well then, best I have a look.'

On the day Puarata died ...

One year ago ...

Parukau

In the seconds after Puarata fell at Cape Reinga, a dog on a dirt road near Hawera, far to the south, jerked to its feet and barked furiously. It was a bony, feverish creature with diseased yellow eyes, and belonged, if that was the right word, to Old Mac, a tramp steeped in his own filth. They had been together for seven years, and sometimes the old wanderer puzzled over how the dog still breathed. It smelt like week-dead road kill. Bare patches festered on its hide, it walked like a drunken sailor, and there was nothing healthy about it. Or its appetite — it ate carrion, bugs and whatever it could scavenge.

'Lil' bugger won't last a week,' Old Mac remembered thinking as he had kicked it away from his pack, all those years ago. But it had hung around, begging scraps, and he had been lonely. He had never even named the vile mutt. But they were well matched. Old Mac was no whitewashed saint. He had gone bush after attacking a nun in Levin back in '83. By the time the case had gone cold, he had forgotten how to live in the normal world.

The barking woke Mac, confused and bleary-eyed from the rot-gut he had been swilling. They were beneath a stand of pine, amidst the sheep shit but out of the rain. 'Shut up, ya mangy bugger!'

The dog turned and growled. Something flickered in its eye that had never been there before. Before Mac could move, the dog leapt on him, both forepaws on his chest. A weight like a boulder crushed him, emptying his lungs. 'Get off me! Ya feckin' … ugh … get off.' His voice changed from threat to choking plea as the dog's weight intensified. Its eyes seemed to grow. Mac went rigid with fright as a spiral of unlight poured from the dog's mouth and coiled like a snake, a serpent made of smoke which poured into his mouth, choking his final words. He couldn't speak, not even to beg. He tried, though. He writhed and twisted, but the dreadful thing on his chest neither moved nor relented. His heart hammered like an overstressed engine, until the world fell away.

The tramp sat up and stared at the dog lying cold and dead beside him. Although the tramp wasn't Old Mac any more: he was Parukau. Parukau, first among Puarata's servants, before the tohunga had imprisoned him in the body of that filthy mutt.

But I'm free now … Puarata must be dead …

Puarata dead! He could taste it! He was free! 'FREE!' he shouted aloud, his first words in over a century. He shouted for sheer joy, half his outpourings mere barking and gibberish, but he didn't care.

An hour later he was hobbling down an eastward road.

Puarata's fortress was in the Ureweras, and there was a very special place there, known to only one other being: himself — Parukau! A secret place they had made together, that they called Te Iho, 'The Heart'. It was where the true power lay.

I'll be damned if I let someone else gain control of it. Quite literally damned.

Kurangaituku

When Puarata fell from the bluff at Cape Reinga, birds rose from the trees and streamed south, shrieking the news. Deep in the bush near Hamilton, hundreds of sparrows, pigeons, starlings, magpies, water birds, gulls, all manner of birds, began to swirl madly together, swarming like insects. They spun in tighter and tighter knots, blending in a blur until an observer would have sworn they were trying to form a shape: a blurred outline amidst the sight-defying movement appeared vaguely human.

The birds flew closer still, their wings beating against each other, fouling each other's flight, sending feathers flying as blood spattered the ground. Still they meshed closer, their calls deafening, until suddenly they turned inwards and with a sickening crunch collided, ramming into each other, breaking spines, rending bodies, shattering each other. The bloody mess collapsed in a heap of feathered, quivering, red-stained flesh.

The mass of dead and dying seemed to dissolve, their last calls growing plaintive and thinner as each succumbed, and then the whole ghastly heap was still. It remained so for some minutes, as red fluids fed the roots of the trees. Then it quivered.

Gently shaking, and then more violently, the ghastly pile bulged from movement deep within. The top corpses slid to the ground with wet little thuds. Something was beneath, struggling to rise through the deathly debris. Then a skeletal arm broke through, brittle-looking, tendons glistening, downy feathers sticking to bone. A head emerged, somewhere between human and bird, with a long beak sticky with gore. The pile of debris deflated as this new thing stood, and raised its arms. Brown skin formed slowly to cover the sinew and flesh. Bluish veins pulsed. Grey hair sprouted from the skull, and fatty globules formed buttocks and breasts. It was female, muscular and athletic, with the strength to power through the air, although the bird-like face, whose nose and chin almost touched, was aged and gaunt. She stretched and sighed, dreaming new dreams of freedom.

A tui called from the trees. She answered in a lilting voice, wordless, everything conveyed in the pitch and tone. She let the tui alight on her hand. She was Kurangaituku, the Bird-witch. The tui paid her homage and brought her news.

Puarata was dead, it sung. She had suspected this, sensing the release of bonds that bound her, compelling her service. She closed her eyes, opening her mind to her children, whose eyes were everywhere. She focused on the north, witnessing the aftermath of Puarata's fall. She recognized Wiremu, the tohunga's warrior-slave, now also free, it seemed. She noted the face of the half-caste boy who had stolen the tiki. Puarata had commanded her to find the boy for him, but she had failed him. She didn't regret that, now.

She turned and looked southeast. To the Ureweras, where his lair lay unclaimed.

I must get there first. I must be the next power in the land, the one who inherits his mantle.

I refuse to serve another Puarata.

Donna Kyle

Donna Kyle was dreaming of a time before it all began. It was a dream she often had, of a porcelain doll in a yellowed christening gown. Sunlight was shafting through curtains, and men were singing as they staggered home drunk down Ponsonby Road. The six o'clock swill. Footsteps crunched down the gravel path and she wondered who it could be …

Daughter!

The dry voice in her head made her flinch, and her eyes sprang open. *That voice! Surely not …*

'What's happening?' she murmured aloud to the empty room.

Get up, Donna! Puarata is dead! They're coming for you now!
Father's voice? Impossible — he's dead!
They're both dead …

She remembered. She had been watching Puarata's end, in a scrying glass. She saw him die, and didn't know whether to laugh or scream. She should have run then, but she was still so weak. The drugs dragged her down, back into that same dream she always had. Of that last hour of childhood …

She tentatively raised a hand and touched her swollen face, wincing. She had been beautiful, until Wiremu's blow had broken her nose and split her face. Her head was swathed in bandages, so that she felt partially embalmed. She had been wondering if Puarata would discard her, like others he tired of. *That's irrelevant now. You're on your own, girl …*

And now that voice ... *Father? No. Impossible ...*

Then it really hit her ... *Puarata's dead! My God, he's dead!* She had never thought Puarata could fail. Not against a mere boy, or anyone else. The images in the scrying glass had seemed like some foolish television show. But he really was dead, truly finally gone. *And I'm next ...* Jeff Rothwell was outside, ostensibly to help her home, but Rothwell belonged to Sebastian Venn, like so many in the organization these days. *Rothwell is here to kill me ...*

When Wiremu struck her down it had felt like death, but she had woken to nurses and bandages and drugs. Puarata had been there, speaking comforting words as drips fed her veins with a pale fluid he said would heal her. She had been afraid that he knew what she had said to Matiu Douglas; those words about escaping his control. But the tohunga had said nothing of it. Did he know? Sometimes it was all too much, being Puarata's lover. It was like being in a cage with a panther. She was over sixty, despite her youthful appearance. Puarata had been tiring of her, she suspected.

Donna, that voice whispered again. *I have had a nurse place a gun under your pillow.*

She spun, but there was no-one there. 'Father?' she breathed, her heart hammering. A cellphone rang outside, the conversation was terse, and then footsteps approached her door.

She tried to reach for her power, that flame inside her that Puarata had found and taught her to use. But it was weak, barely flickering after the beating and the drugs. *I can't do it ... I'm losing it ...* She fumbled frantically under the pillow and found the gun where Father's voice had said it was. It felt

34

heavy and reassuring in her hand. Outside Rothwell spoke in his flat voice. 'Miss Kyle?'

She lurched to her feet. The room swam and her head felt like it would burst. Rothwell opened the door. She didn't wait for him to speak, just raised the gun and opened fire. She was so dizzy her first shot missed, but the second knocked him off his feet. She staggered over his twitching body and out. A nurse appeared and she couldn't risk that she wasn't one of *them*, so she fired and watched the woman clutch her belly and fold up, her face stricken. She tottered down the hall, firing at every movement, as panic erupted about her. Red-stained walls and floors marked her trail.

Finally she made the shift to Aotearoa, although the effort dazed her. She crumpled to her knees in wet grass, outside a smaller, older building made of wood and whitewashed plaster. A man and woman turned towards her, clad in colonial garb, and their faces swelled with concern as they reached out …

She couldn't be sure. So she raised her gun again.

Click!

The transition had destroyed the powder. The man took the gun from her shaking hands. 'My lady!' He looked up at the building behind her, then pulled her to her feet. 'Come, we must leave. Venn is coming. I will see you safe.'

Well done, daughter, her father's voice whispered. *But do not forget to whom you owe your life.*

Guardian devil

Saturday

Hine Horatai hurried from bed as the tide rose in her belly, and a vile taste invaded her mouth. On the bed, Evan Tomoana stirred then lapsed back into sleep. Hine pushed the door shut and teetered dizzily down the hallway, through the discarded cans and spilt ashtrays, into the tiny toilet cubicle. It already stank and hadn't been flushed, but there was no time for that. She opened her mouth with a little cough and vomited.

She huddled there for what felt like hours, her head pounding. Then she heard a warm voice, and Ko's kind, fleshy face loomed over her as she flushed the toilet and wiped Hine's face with a wet flannel. 'Jesus, girl, you look terrible.' She pulled Hine into a sitting position. 'There, lovey. Better now?'

Hine nodded weakly, embarrassed and ashamed. 'Think so. Sorry, Ko. Can't hold my drink, huh?'

'At least you made it to the bog, lovey. More than bloody Brutal managed. He just chucked up in the lounge and then took hisself out for a smoke. Guess who had to clean it up?' They exchanged hopeless looks. The Saturday morning come-down. Last night the house had been rocking, but now it slumbered in a silent haze. Hine gazed back down the hallway she had crawled along, to where the front door was ajar. Some guy was there, unconscious. She wondered blearily how many others were lying about the house amidst the trash and empties. 'What's the time, Ko?'

'Just gone midday, lovey. Ronnie's gone to work, bless him. Brutal's out back, and everyone else is taking off as soon as they wake up so's to dodge the cleanin' up. Evan awake yet?'

Hine hoped not. 'Don't think so.'

'Amount of rum he knocked back last night, he should be out cold 'til Christmas.'

'You want a hand in the kitchen, darl?'

Ko looked back at her wearily. 'Nah. I need some fresh air. Let's go for a walk, eh?'

'But there's gonna be another bash tonight. Evan'll want—'

'You worry too much 'bout what he wants, girl. Let's go for a walk. Brandi-babe needs to get outta this house. And Filli, too.'

Hine got unsteadily to her feet, and crept back to her bedroom, which echoed to Evan's snores. She slipped in, grabbed clothes from a pile in the corner, and crept out. Evan's hard face was softened in repose, his mouth open and dribbling into his spiky goatee. His bare chest was covered in heavy-metal tattoos, all spikes and swirls. He said he was part-Maori, but he looked Pakeha. At twenty-nine, he was eleven years her senior. The man who had rescued her. She prayed she hadn't woken him.

She dressed in the bathroom, eyeing the stranger in the mirror uneasily. She had been slim and pretty once, she vaguely recalled. Her tummy had been flat and her limbs taut. Her skin had been clear and her hair shiny. All the boys at Rotorua High School had wanted to date her. She had been happy, and dreamt of Olympic swimming medals and modelling.

Her stepfather had changed all that one night, when he had held her face down on the mattress, sobbing that it was her fault. *Glenn Bale* ... He had done it again whenever her mother turned her back, so she had run away. Bale had tracked her down, but when he had tried to drag her into his car, Evan had stepped in, bashed 'Gentle Glenn', and taken Hine home. She had been so grateful for her rescue she had not noticed that all she had done was swap jailers.

Now she had aged, and her hair looked like a rat's nest. Her eyes were sullen. She hugged herself and shook silently, trying to stop the girl in the mirror from crying.

Finally, she dressed. The tee was too tight and the trackies were baggy. *I look like a tramp.* She dragged her fingers through her hair, pinched her cheeks, and slipped out. A half-empty pack of ciggies lay in the hallway, and she pocketed them. The man at the front door had gone. She glanced into the lounge: cigarette haze and empties everywhere. The stained carpet squelched as she picked her way into the kitchen, where Ko was dressing her children. Three-year-old Brandi was sitting on the floor fiddling with an empty beer bottle. Filli, who was eight months, was lying on the table while Ko finished changing her nappy. Ko's partner, Ronnie, was Samoan, and the two kids took after him. Ko passed Hine a huge hoodie, about five sizes too big for her, which she burrowed into. 'You 'kay, lovey?' Ko asked. 'Grab the pram and we'll do a runner, eh.'

They made it past the main bedroom without Evan's snore faltering. Whoever was awake was in the back yard so the coast was clear. They wedged Filli into the old pram, and Hine carried Brandi as they made their escape. The sun was horribly bright and she hadn't remembered her sunglasses, but she wasn't going to risk going back.

A southerly stung her cheeks, and for once the three mountains were faintly visible, the low, snowy mass of Tongariro in the foreground, the cone of Ngauruhoe behind, and then the snow- and shadow-streaked Ruapehu hunched behind and dwarfing them both. It was a fine sight and gave her back a little heart. They ambled down towards the lake, Brandi holding Hine's hand now, while Filli burbled happily in the pram. Ko's waddling gait meant they moved slowly, and Hine snuck a look back every few seconds to make sure they weren't being pursued, to be dragged back and chained to a mop. Finally, they were out of sight of the house and she let out a long breath she hadn't realized she'd been holding.

They walked in silence to the main road, and crossed to the lakefront. The water lapped at the shingle and sand. A few windsurfers were out, and far to the south triangles of sail unfurled from sleek yachts that swooped like gulls in the stiffening breeze. Brandi ran to the water's edge to look for shells, while Ko and Hine found a spot under a tree to watch over her, nurse their headaches and puff on a ciggie. Ko took Filli from the pram and let her roll on the ground, gurgling blissfully. She was a happy baby, which was a miracle considering the squalor she was being brought up in. Evan owned the house, left by some dead relative. Hine shared his room, and Ko and Ronnie had the second room with their kids. Brutal had the third room, and Hine refused to go near it, it stank so bad. A bunch of other itinerants came and went. 'Soul brothers,' Evan liked to call them. *Parasites* was Hine's word for them.

'So, how's Ronnie doing at his new job?' she asked Ko.

'Yeah, good. Been there two weeks now. Hasn't stolen nothing.' The word 'yet' stayed unspoken. 'Hopin' this'll last, an' we can maybe get a place of our own.'

'Yeah, that'd be sweet. Well, for you guys.' *No bank would ever give you a mortgage, but dreams are free.*

'He tries hard, does my Ronnie. Tries to do his best, mosta the time. When he ain't drinkin' an' talkin' trash with Brutal and Evan.'

'It's Evan,' said Hine. 'If it wasn't for Evan, Ronnie wouldn't do half the stuff he does.'

Ko looked at her intently. 'Evan been smackin' you 'bout again, hon?'

You couldn't hide stuff from Ko. 'Most ev'ry day now,' Hine admitted in a whisper, her eyes on the distant mountains, her lower lip quivering.

They stared out across the water. Ko was talking, but it wasn't easy to listen when all the thoughts crowding her head kept welling up. She had been a little golden girl when she was younger. She had been tall and athletic, and she wasn't dumb. Her teachers had told her she had a 'future' and spoken about university. None of her family had gone past fifth form, but for her the sky had seemed the limit.

'Then what happened?' asked Ko.

Hine started, and realized she had been thinking out loud. 'Mum got tired of being on her own. So she took up with Glenn Bale, this Pakeha ex-miner from Huntly.' The thought of 'Gentle Glenn' made her feel nauseous. After Evan had punched Bale, she had been so grateful she would have given him anything. In fact, she had. He had got her away from home, and for a while it had seemed like paradise. She had thought herself safe. Ha! 'Evan treats me like dirt now. Just another source of welfare money. He's always angry, an' ev'rthing's my fault. I've got to get out, Ko.'

Ko reached out and pulled her in as she began to shake. She clung to the fat woman and bawled like a baby, while Filli stared confusedly. 'I've got to get out. But I don't know how. What'll he do if I run, Ko?'

'Lovey, there are people who can help you. You go down to the Women's Refuge. They's good people. I know them, cos of my sister, y'know. I could take you there, when the boys are out.' Ko's voice betrayed what she really thought, that no social worker or cop could stop Evan if he went after Hine. They might catch him later, but by then Hine would be smashed up or dead.

'I don't know what to do, Ko. Some days I just want to walk out into the lake and never come back.' She had dreamt it, dreamt of swimming in deep water, while dark shapes swam below. She stared out across the lake. There was a log floating there, but somehow it seemed like a huge black eel, circling and waiting. She shuddered and looked away.

A young Pakeha or maybe part-Maori boy was walking past, with a redheaded woman who looked like his mother. Their clothes were clean and neat, and she had her arm around his shoulders. There was something about him that caught the eye, something subtly strong. He was probably only her age, but he seemed a world apart. He looked straight at her, with concern in his eyes. She felt a sudden flash of resentment and shame, to be seen like this.

I bet he's never been smacked over. I bet nothing bad has ever happened in his prissy little life.

Piss off, she mouthed, then buried her face in Ko's shoulder. She stayed there a long time, and when she looked up again, mother and son were gone.

'What shall we do, lovey?' asked Ko. 'You want to take a walk down to the refuge?'

Hine almost agreed. But then she thought about Evan and she wasn't so sure any more. He kept her safe from all the other dark things. He needed her, she made him calmer, she made him happier … he told her so. Her place was with him. He was her Guardian Devil. She loved him, didn't she? 'I dunno, Ko. I … I need to think on it a bit, y'know. I don't want to do the wrong thing. You know what I mean?'

Ko looked at her sadly. 'Okay, deary. I gotta get back and put Filli down for a sleep. You stay here if you want. I'll get Ronnie to help clean up when he gets back, eh.'

Hine nodded, and bowed her head. She kissed Brandi and waved them off, then just sat and stared at nothing. Time passed and she couldn't remember a single thought crossing her mind. People probably went past, maybe some of them looked at her, but nothing registered.

Finally, a gentle wuffling intruded on her thoughts. There was a dog, a black-and-white sheepdog like Dog from the *Footrot Flats* cartoons, worrying at something that lay in the tidal sands. Then it looked up and trotted towards her. She shooed at it half-heartedly, but it came right up, nuzzling her gently, so she relented and let it curl up against her. 'You better not have fleas, boy,' she told it.

It looked at her indignantly, as if it found her remark offensive.

'Okay, sorry!' She smiled and patted it. It licked her face, and she felt herself relax for the first time that day. So she hugged the dog, and before long, the gentle waves of the lake and rhythm of the traffic had blended into a lullaby.

She woke suddenly, and found the sun was dipping towards the western horizon. The dog was still with her, and it tugged at her sleeve, as if trying to persuade her to follow it home. She shook it off. 'No, fella! Go home! I'm going this way!' It took a long time to convince it that she was not going to follow it. *Crazy dog! I wonder who owns it?*

She hurried home — there was another booze-up tonight and she should have been helping Ko get it ready. *Shit! Evan's gonna be mad as!*

When she arrived, one of Evan's Rottweilers charged down the path to meet her, scaring her to a halt. The door slammed open and Evan strode down the path towards her, teeth gleaming through his goatee. She began to stammer an apology that turned into a yelp of pain as he seized her hair and pulled her behind him. She shrieked, trying to keep on her feet.

'Where the hell have you been, you lazy little bitch? What gives you the right to piss off and leave the rest of us to clean up for Deano's party? Do you live here on my charity or not?' He half-dragged her towards the house. 'Where were you? Who were you with?'

'I was down by the lake! I was alone! Don't hurt me! Please!'

At Jones's cottage

Sunday

Mat woke early on Sunday, made a coffee for his mother and headed for Jones's cottage, his mother's instructions ('Be home by three') ringing in his ears. Mat hurried along the track. Yesterday afternoon, Jones had clammed up after seeing the vision-stone Horomatangi had brought. They had chatted, and Mat had gone over his magical exercises: fire, water, earth and air — the basics. They still left him dizzy, but he was getting better at them. He could now light fires, produce gusts of wind, and create any manner of small subtle effects. This break they were planning to work on the basics of mental communication. It was heady stuff, and he wished he had more time to devote to it. School work was such a drag compared with magic.

He ran up to the house, where Jones was smoking his pipe. 'You're late,' the Welshman grumped. 'Give me one good reason why I shouldn't send you off for an hour's run as punishment.'

Mat hung his head a little. 'Actually, I had a nightmare, and slept through my alarm. Not much of an excuse, huh?'

Jones frowned. 'Actually, it's a very good excuse. Dreams are important, laddie. I've told you that before. For folk like us, they can be the voice of the spirit world. Pay them mind, Mat. You can tell me about it later, after you show me where you're up to with this.' He threw a taiaha at Mat, who caught it deftly. 'Show me what you've got, and make it good.'

Mat twirled the taiaha, and went into a crouch. He went through the preparatory movements while Jones settled back into his easy chair, and then leapt into a full routine. The taiaha swished and whistled about his head, and he began to perspire as he jabbed, swung, lunged and thrust in a crabbing dance back and forward. He finished with a shout and crouched, pulling a face with his tongue out, part in challenge, part panting like an overheated dog.

Jones got up, tapped out his pipe. He looked cross. 'Well, laddie, that's all well and good. No doubt your kapa haka teacher thinks you could be lead dancer in a feckin' cultural party. But you're supposed to be learning to *fight*, not twinkle-toe about like a prima feckin' ballerina!' He walked up, and tapped the taiaha. 'Yer Maori had no metals, just stone, bone and wood. So they mostly used impact weapons, not edged ones. That thing you're waving around like a *rhythmic gymnast* is a CLUB. It's for bludgeoning people to death.' He picked up a heavy basket-hilted sword. 'So now you can show me if you've learned how to *fight* with it.'

Mat flushed as Jones lunged with a speed that belied his years. Mat beat the sword away and countered, but the blade was already snaking at his stomach, and he was forced to defend again. On the old man came, making the air sing as the blade chimed off the taiaha, sending little chips from the wooden blade. Mat fought desperately for a way to get control. Their two fighting styles were entirely different: the taiaha was a two-handed long-club, wielded like a samurai sword, whilst Jones's heavy sword was from the musketeers' era, a thin springy blade that searched for gaps but had enough weight to parry the heavier taiaha. Another thrust and then a feinted jab, and Mat found himself slipping in mud, landing heavily on his back, only just parrying an overhand cut that gouged the taiaha blade. The steel caught in the wood, and he kicked out, trying to tangle Jones's legs, but the old man's stance was strong. He wrenched his blade free and flicked it against Mat's chest.

'Ach!' Mat looked up along the blade to Jones, his lined face a little flushed, frosty breath billowing from his mouth. 'I'll yield ...' Jones grinned, and Mat suddenly swung at his legs, ' ... later!'

His blow connected with air, and then Jones's foot came down on the taiaha, jamming it into the turf. He flicked his wrist and Mat had to flop to avoid being skewered. He lay in the wet grass, looking along the polished blade. 'You'll be yielding about now, then?' Jones enquired, jabbing the tip of his sword into Mat's chest.

'Ow! Yes!' He let go the taiaha and shoved the blade away. 'That hurt!'

Jones stepped back, out of reach of another surprise blow, and brought the hilt of his sword to his lips in a mocking salute. 'Not bad, laddie, you're improving.'

Mat sat up and glared at the wet patch of grass. 'If it wasn't for that mud ...' He looked up at Jones accusingly. 'It wasn't muddy earlier in the fight! Did you ... ?' He made a 'magical' gesture, fluttering his fingers.

Jones grinned wolfishly. 'Of course. You'd stopped noticing

your footing. Easy enough to summon a little water and back you into it.'

'That's cheating!'

'No laddie, it's winning. All's fair in love and war, don't they say? Now, let's see you with a patu.' He retired to the balcony and exchanged Mat's taiaha for a bone-carved, thin, sharp-edged hand club, a patu. It was light, a cutting weapon as much as a club. Mat moved with grace and made the air about him hiss, while Jones smoked his pipe. He made Mat stop and go over certain moves again until he was satisfied. Then he tossed Mat a heavy stone hand club, a mere, thicker and blunter, made to smash bone. Mat tired quickly using the heavier weapon.

Jones raised a hand. 'That's enough, lad. I think the taiaha will always be your main weapon. You're small for a warrior, so you need to fight at a distance. Get in too close, and a big man will take you down through bulk alone.'

'So I'll need a gun, too, for that real fight-from-a-distance vibe?' hinted Mat meaningfully. Firing the antique guns Jones owned was his favourite training.

'Indeed. Come on out the back.' Jones led Mat around the house, where his yard backed onto denser bush. He had evidently cleared the ivy that winter, as last time Mat had visited there had been a curtain of it falling over the back veranda. On the back-porch table lay a flintlock with a walnut-inlaid handle and embossed plates proclaiming it the workmanship of 'Williams & Powell' of Liverpool. Jones had a room in the stables full of old-style guns, all shining like new and perfectly maintained. Only antique guns worked in Aotearoa, which was curiously resistant to modern weaponry. 'Show me,' the

Welshman grunted, leaning back and puffing his pipe.

Jones had Mat load the gun with black powder and a lead ball, then discharge it at an old keg thirty paces away, over and over, until the lawn was wreathed in sweet, acrid smoke. The recoil was wrist-breaking, and the gun became progressively heavier, but Mat was a fair shot, and soon the old keg was shattered.

Jones laid a hand on Mat's shoulder. 'Good, lad. But too slow. A good pistolier can fire a musket or a flintlock four times a minute. You're not doing much better than two.'

Mat scowled, reproaching himself. 'It's the cleaning. I'm worried about leaving a spark in the barrel that'll make it explode.'

'That's fine, lad. Care is good. But you're not being deft enough. Here, I'll show you.' Jones picked up the flintlock, turned and fired. From then, his hands were a blur, as he ram-cleaned the barrel, recharged from the powder flask, inserted a ball and whirled. The last remnant of the barrel flew to pieces as the clearing reverberated.

Mat had been counting the seconds. 'Seven! Wow!'

The old man shrugged. 'It's just practice, lad. And there are ways of using our powers to speed the process. When you've got the basics right, I'll show you how.' Jones tapped the embers from his pipe. 'The real question with any weapon, lad, is: are you prepared to use it? In World War Two, the American military found that most soldiers didn't even fire at the enemy. On old American Civil War battlefields they found muskets that had been loaded a dozen times or more and not discharged. Killing is abhorrent to most people.'

Mat frowned, struggling to reconcile this with movies and

television and books. He had been in some deadly fights. Yet now he thought of it, he had never deliberately tried to kill, although sometimes those he fought had died. He wasn't proud of that.

Jones refilled his pipe. 'Remember Waikaremoana? You all just fought to survive.'

Mat nodded slowly.

Jones patted his arm. 'It was training that got you through. And luck.' He sighed and took the gun from Mat's hands. 'Let's have some tea, and you can tell me about this dream of yours.' He opened the back door with a strange smile on his face, as if harbouring an amusing secret. Mat looked at him, walked inside and gaped in surprise.

Cassandra Allen was sitting at Jones's table, surrounded by a tangle of wires and boxes and gadgets, an open laptop beside her. 'Cassandra?'

She looked up at him distractedly, her eyes flashing through her thick-rimmed glasses. Her mouth glittered with a full rail track of braces. She looked no less odd than last time he had seen her. Her hair was in a 'Sideshow Bob' pile of ginger semi-dreads, and her clothes appeared to have been stolen from Pippi Longstocking. 'Hiya, Mat!'

She wasn't supposed to be here until next week. 'What're you doing here?'

She grinned up at him with a wry smile. 'Great to see you, too!'

He reddened. 'Uh, yeah, sorry ... hi!'

'Dad decided at the last minute to come to Taupo early this year,' Cassandra said. 'I thought I'd bless Jones with my skills and genius.'

'Apparently it's an honour,' Jones drawled.

'Are you kidding? I normally wouldn't go anywhere that doesn't have full wi-fi access, an Xbox-360 and an espresso machine; you haven't even got electricity! You bet it's an honour!'

Jones just shrugged imperturbably. 'I can wait 'til Aotearoa provides. I'm in no hurry.'

Cassandra sniffed, and turned back to Mat. 'We only got in last night at about eleven.' Since the adventures on the East Coast at New Year, Mat, Riki, Damian and Cass had contrived to spend at least a week together each school break, whether in Napier, Gisborne or here in Taupo. This time around the plan was for everyone to get together in the second week, once Riki had finished his taiaha class and Damian got back from a fencing tournament in the South Island.

'How'd you actually get here?' Mat asked curiously. Normally he had to bring his friends across to Aotearoa.

'I hacked my way in,' Cassandra laughed. Then she glanced up at Jones a little warily. 'Actually, last time I kept an eye on the trail and figured out how you use that big kauri to get here. Three times widdershins! Nothing stays secret from me for long.'

That's true enough, Mat reflected. Cassandra could take a person's cellphone number and find out their history and secrets inside an hour. She was like a character from *The Matrix*, only without the fashion sense and the slo-mo kung-fu moves.

'Whatcha doing?' he asked as he sat at the table, while Jones put the kettle on the hob.

Cassandra looked down at the wires and clamps and

screwdrivers, and nibbled her lip thoughtfully. 'I'm trying to hook this place up with a telephone that links to the real world.'

Mat glanced at Jones. 'Isn't that, like … impossible?'

Cassandra gave a one-shouldered shrug. 'Jones says you got a car to transition across without fritzing it out last year. There must be a way to do it.'

'But even I don't really know how I did it,' Mat confessed. It had been Donna Kyle's car, and he had somehow got it through a transition to Aotearoa without it missing or failing. It was something he had puzzled over with Jones, but they had not solved yet. 'Ngatoro helped me with it. And maybe it was something to do with the car itself.'

She pursed her lips, her goldfish-bowl eyes thoughtful. 'Anything doable is repeatable.' She handed him a thing that looked like a spanner with a speedometer on it. 'Grab the pincers and give me a current.'

He stared at her, feeling a little silly. 'Huh?'

She rolled her eyes. 'This is an ammeter. I thought boys knew stuff like this! Let's see how much electricity you can create.'

Mat glanced at Jones. 'Uh … I've never created electricity … Not consciously anyway.'

Cassandra fumbled in the pile of gadgets. 'You don't know electricity? I thought you were supposed to be some kind of apprentice wizard.'

'I can do fire and water and stuff,' he offered.

'I want electricity!' She handed him another wire attached to some kind of power pack. 'Hold the metal clamp at the end.'

He grasped the metal clamp, and she twisted a knob on the power pack. He yelped. 'Oww! You electrocuted me.'

She giggled. 'It was only a few volts, Mat! Come on: duplicate it. Come on!'

Mat glanced at Jones, who nodded, his face curious. Mat closed his eyes, and tensed himself as Cassandra trickled electricity into his hand. He concentrated in the same way that he had for Jones when learning fire and water and the other elements. Time slowly passed, as he learnt the sensation, feeling it build and tingle and course through him. Cassandra murmured something about the level of volts, so that he could measure the levels of input and what he could deal with.

His concentration suddenly shattered, as a black-and-white dog bounded in the open back door, woofed happily, and leapt into his lap. There was a sudden crack, the dog's fur shot up, and he spun, jerked and landed on the floor, wuffling indignantly. 'What the hell?' Godfrey the dog growled. He shook himself, while Jones, Mat and Cassandra struggled not to laugh, and failed. Mat doubled over, holding his stomach, while Cassandra vented her loud, horsey laugh that could clear restaurants. Even Jones chuckled.

'Uh, sorry, God!' Mat offered finally, wiping his eyes, while the little shape-shifter earthed sparks into the floor as he stood.

'I should bloody think so,' Godfrey muttered, lowering his tail and rubbing himself against Jones's legs. 'Don't come near me again.' God was 'Godfrey Llewellyn III', who, like Fitzy, was a turehu shape-shifter; only Mat supposed God wasn't really a turehu because Jones had brought him from Wales, which probably made him a bogle or pooka or something similar from Celtic mythology. The dog settled in the corner and glared at Mat.

'So I guess there is electricity between us after all,' Cassandra observed slyly, making Mat blush.

Jones sat down with them, poured the tea, and then lit his pipe. 'You'll get lung cancer,' warned Mat, to change the subject.

'I've been smoking for centuries, boyo. Walter Raleigh himself lit my first pipe.' Jones took another puff. 'Come out the front, Mat, and tell me about this dream.' He nodded apologetically to Cassandra. 'I'm sure you don't need to hear what teenage boys dream about.'

Cassandra wrinkled her nose. 'Yeurch. Take him away!'

Mat and Jones took their tea to the front porch, which was now in sunshine. He plunged right in, no longer shy about such conversations. 'I've been having bad dreams for weeks, now. They start in a familiar place, like home, or school, but I know something is wrong. There's a girl ...' He stopped suddenly. 'I saw her! Yesterday by the lake!'

Jones lifted his shaggy eyebrows. 'You know her?'

Mat shook his head. 'Never seen her before. In the dream, she's running ... not from me. I go after her, across a garden or park or whatever, and then suddenly she turns into Donna Kyle. She chases me. I hit a dead end, and she comes round the corner ... then there's a man behind her, in dark clothes. He looks kind of medieval ... he calls out to her, she turns, and I wake.'

Jones tapped his finger on his pipe. 'Mmmm ... do you know the name "Asher Grieve"?' Mat shook his head. 'Asher was

53

Puarata's main rival for a long time, and then they formed an alliance. He used to flounce about in medieval attire, quoting Milton and Dante. Eventually Asher got above himself, and Puarata killed him. He was Donna Kyle's father.'

It was hard to imagine that Donna Kyle had a father. There was something so hard and unfeeling about her that she was scarcely human to Mat. 'Why would I dream of him? I've never heard of him before.'

'That's the beauty of watching your dreams, laddie. If your mind is open, Aotearoa speaks to you. And right now, it's sending you a warning that Donna Kyle is back, and that she hasn't forgotten you. Although what it has to do with Asher Grieve I don't know. She hated him passionately and had a hand in his downfall.'

That Donna Kyle would aid Puarata against her own father sounded entirely in character to Mat. The thought that she might be near was chilling. 'Is this to do with Horomatangi's message?' he asked.

'Perhaps. Between that and other information, I'm beginning to believe that the struggle amongst Puarata's warlocks is renewing, and maybe coming here.'

'Here?' yelped Mat, sitting up.

'Maybe. Calm down. You know that since Puarata fell, his warlocks have been fighting each other. At Waikaremoana, Bryce and Kyle's alliance failed. Bryce has retreated south, and Kyle went into hiding. It all went quiet a few months ago. The American, Sebastian Venn, controls Puarata's old base at Waikaremoana, and most of his real-world assets.'

Mat had heard of Venn, but not seen him. 'What's he like?'

Jones curled his lip. 'Rich. Arrogant. Smug. He's not a big

talent magically, but he's ruthless and resourceful. And his wife is some kind of ninja.'

'Don't tell Damian, he's nuts on Asian swordswomen ever since seeing *Kill Bill*,' Mat laughed. 'But what about that tramp I saw in the stone? Who is he?'

'I don't know, but I have my suspicions.'

Mat peered out the window, half-expecting to see sinister shadows lurking. 'What if they're here for me?'

Jones shook his head. 'It may be a blow to your fragile teenage ego, but you're still a relatively small fish in this pond, despite Reinga and Waikaremoana. These warlocks have bigger fish to fry — each other.'

'Then why are they all coming here?'

'It's not certain they are. I've not seen any of them.' He blew a ragged smoke ring.

'What are you doing about them?' Mat asked.

'Me? I'm staying out of their way. Let them kill each other, and we only need contend with the winner.'

Mat pursed his lips and leant forward. 'But where are all the good guys? Why do the bad guys have free run of this place? Where are all the heroes? Maori legends and settler history have lots of heroes. Guys like Maui and Hatupatu. And there must be heroes among the settler soldiers. Aren't they some-where in Aotearoa?'

Jones tapped his pipe. 'Maui was a demigod: the gods don't really come here. As for the heroes of legend … well, some have died in Aotearoa — been killed that is — and are gone. Others have vanished. And the more modern soldiery don't have the mystique of legends — those who remember them, remember them as men not magical beings. So they're

55

ordinary people. Not everyone who dies becomes a ghost in Aotearoa, Mat. Probably fewer than a quarter of those who die in the real world come here. Maybe fewer. We don't know why.' Jones looked at him. 'You have to remember that Aotearoa is, for most of its inhabitants, a form of afterlife. People who are reborn here have their own priorities, usually to do with the life they just lived. They are looking for peace of mind and to resolve internal conflicts. Wars and politics are things they have left behind. Aotearoa doesn't have an economy, and its people seldom organize. As long as the warlocks don't openly assail the larger communities, such authorities as there are avoid them.'

Mat grimaced. 'But you've told me before that they are killing Aotearoa folk in more isolated places all the time. And that if we weren't getting in their way, they'd be strong enough to attack the larger places.'

Jones nodded. 'And that's true. Aotearoa teeters on the brink of a war, but most who dwell here are oblivious. Here, most folk are only concerned for their own afterlife.' He took a puff on his pipe. 'The warlocks have the upper hand, for now. They are cunning, and they cheat. But they aren't invulnerable, as you know. I'm beginning to believe there is a very real way we can stop them, or at least hurt them badly, and you may be vital to it.'

Mat put his tea down so that he wouldn't drop it. 'Me?'

'Don't sound so eager, boy!' He grimaced, as if reluctant to speak. 'It's about Ngatoro. You say he describes a floating sensation, and the feeling of being drained … it reminds me of an old spell that I once found being performed by a witch in the Waikato. Must've been 1911. She had kidnapped another

Adept, and was bleeding him of his magical energies. The poor fellow was only nineteen, but he looked sixty when I rescued him. He described similar sensations.'

'Do you think Puarata was doing that to Ngatoro?'

Jones nodded. 'Yes, I think it is possible. Ngatoro, instead of being dead, may have been Puarata's prisoner for centuries, and a major source of his power. If so, we've got to find him before Bryce, Venn or Kyle do.'

Mat stood up, clenching both fists. 'Yes! We've got to help him!'

Jones blinked. 'I meant "we" figuratively, Mat. "We" as in myself and various other Adepts; not "we" as in "you and me". This could get very dangerous.'

'But—'

'No "buts". It was bad enough how close to death you and your friends came in Waikaremoana. You've been lucky, boy, but you're only half-trained.'

'You've got to let me help,' Mat insisted. 'It's me he talks to! I'm the link!'

'I know that,' Jones agreed reluctantly. 'Otherwise I'd not even mention it. But I don't want you and your friends endangered this time. I mean it!'

'Okay, okay. I get it!'

Jones slapped the table. 'I think that's enough for today. Let's have us some lunch, and then you can get your friend out of my house before she burns it down. Best you don't neglect your mother, too. I dare say she's not happy at your visiting me.'

'She believes that if I spend time with you then more bad stuff will happen.'

'Well, she might be right. No-one said I'm safe to be around.'
Jones led him back to the kitchen. 'Clean up, Cassandra!
Lunch time!'

Over a pleasantly plain lunch Jones questioned them both, but
principally Mat, about life. How was school going? How were
things with his family? Jones didn't comment on much, which
was a relief. He sent them home with the usual instructions
for Mat. 'Don't forget: no coffee — it's bad for bones and
nerves. No soft drink—'

'Because it's bad for teeth and stomach,' Mat interrupted.
'No alcohol or dope, because they're bad for everything. No
fast cars or fast women, cos they're just bad. And above all,
no fun.'

Jones beamed. 'Excellent. I knew you'd turn out alright in
the end. Now, off you go, laddie. I've got things to do. Keep
watching your dreams, keep listening for Ngatoro, keep your
nose out of trouble, and …'

'No fun!'

'Aye. You've got it.' They grinned at each other, and Jones
waved them off.

Mat and Cassandra walked back around the track that led
to Taupo, spinning three times around a certain kauri tree to
return to the real world.

Mat had never really been alone with Cassandra before.
Usually, there was one or both of the others around, except
for odd minutes here and there. He realized that he had been
kind of avoiding being alone with her. Riki had told him that
Cassandra fancied him and, well, he didn't really feel the same

way about her. Not that he didn't like Cassandra, but she wasn't what he pictured when he thought of girls. In his mind she came under a category labelled 'One of the guys'. And also 'Kinda kooky'. And she had no magical abilities — she was an ordinary person — so what future could there be anyway? Best just not go there.

'What have you been up to?' he asked, to fill the slightly awkward silence.

'Oh, y'know. School. Night-class in 3-D animation. Part-timing on the Telecom Xtra helpdesk. And training for a half-marathon. The usual.' She paused. 'Oh, and I've taken up judo and karate.'

'Judo and karate?'

'Yeah. After all that wacko stuff in Waikaremoana, I figured I needed to be able to defend myself a little. Damian keeps trying to get me to take up fencing, but … nah.'

'Are you and Damian … ?'

She pulled a disbelieving face. 'No! I believe that relationships are kind of pointless 'til you're eighteen,' she told him in a lofty voice. 'I'm going to marry when I'm old, say twenty-eight. Kids maybe. I should have a house by then, and have a bit of OE behind me. Guys can just kind of fit in around that.'

Mat frowned. He had enough trouble figuring out what to do from one hour to the next; that much forward planning couldn't be natural. 'How do you just decide not to have boyfriends? I mean, what if you meet someone you really like?'

She cocked an eyebrow. 'It's just prioritization. It's not like hanging with some acne-ridden dweeb is so rewarding that I can't put it on hold for a while. And if I meet someone so totally special it can't wait, well hell, I'll just change the rules. They're my rules. Anyway, kissing with these braces on kills the insides of my lips. I'm left using Bonjela for weeks like a teething infant. Embarrassment city.'

He remembered kissing Lena with a sudden flush. Cassandra saw the look, and seemed to read it straight off. 'So, seeing as you're a hopeless romantic, have you got a girlfriend?'

He pulled a face to hide his blush. 'No. Not really.'

She fixed him with her full stare, her eyes huge behind her glasses. 'Does it bother you, then?'

'Uh, I guess.' He suddenly wished they could talk about something else.

'Then it's counter-productive. Chill, you're sixteen. Anyway, what are you doing this arvo?'

'Homework,' Mat grumped. 'I promised Mum. If I'd known you were gonna be around ...'

'Yeah, well, it was a kinda spontaneous thing. An' my Dad doesn't tell me anything,' Cassandra muttered. 'I only found out last night.'

'Why don't you just hack into his computer and check out his calendar?' Mat laughed.

Cassandra grinned. 'One: he doesn't use an online calendar. Two: his computer is locked down harder than the Intelligence Service. Um, apparently.' She shrugged. 'Anyways, wanna go to the AC Baths and check out the waterslides and stuff later this arvo; around five?'

He hesitated, then smiled. *Why not?* And it seemed she didn't want entanglements either, so it should be fine. 'Yeah, sure!'

She beamed. 'Cool!'

They walked together to the northern foreshore, and then parted — Cassandra's father had a time-share not far away. Mat carried on towards town and his mum's place. People were sunbathing and picnicking, locals and tourists enjoying what sun there was. He was just about to cross the road when he glimpsed a girl in a hoodie sitting under a tree; he stopped with a thumping heart.

It's the girl from my dream ... Should I talk to her? What if she's like me, a potential Adept? Maybe she's like Lena, and I'm meant to help her ... He wavered, chewing his lip. She was staring across the waters, her face a void. She didn't look like she wanted company, but her head swivelled and she saw him. He couldn't read anything in her sunglasses and stony face. *Nothing ventured ...* He screwed up his courage, and walked towards her. He couldn't think of anything clever to say, so he just said 'Hi'.

She lifted her shades and jerked her head around as if afraid to be seen with him. He was struck by how unhappy she looked. Her eyes were puffy and bloodshot, her mouth hung down at the ends, and there were tear tracks on her face. Her hair was tangled and appeared slept-in. She looked tired and run-down and hung over, although she remained a natural beauty.

'Hi. I'm Mat,' he offered. 'Well, Matiu actually,' he added, as she was clearly Maori.

She dragged on her cigarette with a shaking hand. 'Matiu? Picked you as Pakeha.'

He let that pass. 'This is going to sound really weird,' he said, 'but I saw you yesterday afternoon, and ...'

61

He was going to say 'You looked sad. Is there anything I can do?' but something happened to his words on the way out of his mouth, and what he found himself saying was: ' ... I dreamt of you last night.'

Oh, for Chrissake! He turned scarlet and tried to sink into the ground. He stared at the grass between his feet and waited for her to laugh at him and tell him to get lost.

The next cell

Déjà vu, Hine thought as she threw up over the toilet floor. She couldn't remember anything about the party except that there had been truckloads of drinking. Now she couldn't stand up and her stomach felt like an eel farm. Even the dim light in the hall was enough to set off shafts of white noise in her skull.

She struggled to the basin and splashed cold water over her face. Her body was starting to voice some really loud complaints. The stomach was the worst, but she had painful welts all over, too. She wanted to curl up and die, but not here. She reeled into the lounge, grabbed that old hoodie of Ko's, some cash and sunnies, and crept out the front door.

It felt like the world was spinning, but she managed to steady herself. *Come on, you loser!* She fumbled the gate latch open and set off down the road towards the nearest petrol station. Although the petrol fumes on the forecourt made her want to chuck all over again, she managed to order a coffee and doughnut to go. She cradled the coffee like a newborn baby as she nursed herself to the lakefront. Her watch said quarter to twelve. The wind was easing and the sun was trying to break through; she hoped it failed. She found a tree, and lay against it, sipping the coffee. The doughnut could wait till her stomach settled.

This is killing me.

The night before, Evan had laughed loudly and praised up Deano, who was a nice kid, long may he remain so. No doubt Deano was headed down the same path as the rest of them, though. Anyone who fell in with Evan ended up dead, in prison, or trapped on Loser Street. He had also thrashed her, but still had the gall to act like everything was sweetness and light afterwards. His friends all thought he was so cool. He had joshed with the guys, all matey, but if one of them got too close to her, she could feel his eyes lasering through her.

I used to think girls who stayed with guys who beat them were pathetic. Now I'm one of them. Different perspective, huh!

I gotta get out.

I've gotta go where he can't follow.

God knows where that might be. The only folks she knew here were Evan's mates. None of her rellies believed her about Glenn Bale. No-one would take her side.

There had been a girl that had run out on Brutal, and word had it she had gone to Auckland but ended up on the streets. *If I don't do this right, that'll be me.*

It was too much to think about, and she was too tired. So she set her head against the tree, and blanked out everything. Despite the caffeine and the sugar, sleep came like a rising tide, and pulled her under.

She started awake. She looked at her watch: *Jaysus!* Quarter to four! But she felt so much better ... the gnawing in her stomach had settled, and she wolfed the doughnut in three big bites. It was sickly sweet and vaguely unpleasant, but she felt better for it. She caught a whiff of herself: *like a ciggie stubbed out in a puddle of beer.* She felt utterly wretched.

She was suddenly aware of scrutiny. A young guy was standing nearby, watching her. She realized it was the same kid who had seen her crying the day before. She lifted her shades and jerked her eyes about, scared that Evan might be around, but no — tourists and all sorts were everywhere, but no-one she knew. It was as if she and the young guy were totally alone.

'Hi', the guy said hesitantly. 'I'm Mat. Well, Matiu actually,' he added.

She considered ignoring him, or telling him to get lost. But instead, found herself drawling offhandedly, 'Matiu? Picked you as Pakeha.' She puffed her half-forgotten ciggie to buy some time. He must be only part-Maori, with his paler skin, and that reddish hair must come from that mother of his. He was kind of cute, in an over-serious way. *Maybe he's a bloody Mormon, trying to save the sinner.*

He looked at her intensely. 'This is going to sound really weird, but I saw you yesterday afternoon, and ...'

She waited. *Here we go ... Is he a Jesus-freak or just chatting me up?*

'... I dreamt of you last night.' Then he seemed to realize how disastrous he sounded, and went redder than a Santa suit.

She was suddenly cross to have wasted even a second of her life on him. 'Yeah? Piss off, kid.'

He took a step back. 'Yeah, look, sorry, I deserve that. Sorry to intrude ...' He seemed to be berating himself silently.

She turned away, when suddenly the black-and-white sheepdog from yesterday came up and nuzzled the boy affectionately. She stared. 'Hey, is that your dog?'

'Yeah, this is God,' the boy told her, ruffling his fur.

'God?' *Definitely a Mormon!*

He grinned. 'It's short for Godfrey. He's a friend of mine.'

She felt herself unbend a little. 'He's everyone's friend, kid. He was all over me yesterday.'

'So, aren't you going to introduce us, Godfrey?'

She smiled at him suddenly, feeling an unexpected liking. *He's just an ordinary kid.* He was respecting her, and didn't have a dirty mind. *How long since I met someone nice?* She had to look away again, to compose herself. Then she stared. *Oh, shit!*

Evan was striding across the grass towards her, with Brutal and Ronnie at his heels. She leapt to her feet and hissed 'Run, kid! Run now!'

But the boy didn't run. He set his jaw and stepped forward instead.

Heads turned towards them and then the crowd on the foreshore seemed to melt into a circle of bystanders, not wanting to get involved — or miss a moment. Hine felt that 'aquaplaning-towards-a-power-pole' sensation she got when trouble was inevitable.

Brutal was snarling something, but Evan didn't say a word. His face looked like a gestating murder. He towered over Mat, his tattooed shoulders muscled like the flanks of a racehorse and his chest straining his tank top. He bared his teeth, cradling his right fist in his left hand.

Ronnie dragged Hine aside. 'What are you doing, Hine? Evan hates you talkin' to other guys.' His pudgy face was torn between concern for her and eagerness to help Evan.

'We were just talking,' she told him, straining at his grip. She yelled at Evan. 'We were just talking!'

Evan didn't listen, just eyeballed Mat, who stood his ground, his face pale but not overly scared. Brutal was circling on the far side, his teeth bared. He looked about to thump his chest like a gorilla. Ronnie gripped her shoulders. 'Go home, Hine. This is between him and us now.'

Evan said something in a low voice, and Mat answered him back in similar tones, his face calm despite his pallor. A tall blond man yelled 'What is happening?' in a foreign accent, and pushed through the circle of onlookers. He tried to brush past Brutal, who shoved him back and squared up.

Evan put his left hand on Mat's chest and snarled something, a knuckle-duster gleaming on his right fist. He spat in Mat's face, then pushed him. Mat staggered, and visibly restrained himself, as though he was doing Evan a favour by not hitting him. Hine marvelled at his stupidity, and was suddenly terrified he would get knifed for his bravado. She pulled out of Ronnie's grip. 'Evan, he didn't touch me! We were just talking! Let him be!' She lurched towards him, off balance. 'Evan!'

The air turned to water, and she was swimming through it in slo-mo as Evan's right hand swung up, back-handed, and his fist connected. 'Shut up, bitch,' he said, without even looking at her. Light exploded inside her head. She fell backwards, arms flailing, until her skull smacked the hard ground, and she lay dazed as everything unfolded about her.

The blond man tried to push past Brutal, who punched him in the head. Mat tried to step towards her, his eyes leaving Evan for a crucial second, but Evan's left hand snagged his collar, and his right fist bunched, knuckle-duster glinting. Mat's shirt tore as he twisted under the blow, kicking out at Evan's knee in the same motion. He might as well have tried to kick a telephone pole. Evan grunted, and then launched a kick of his own into Mat's ribs as he tried to pull away. It connected and Mat doubled over.

Ronnie loomed over her. 'Hine, you okay?' he asked, blinking stupidly. She felt a hot sting on her torn cheek and tasted blood in her mouth. She tried to speak but couldn't remember how. Sirens blared from the direction of the shopping precinct half a kilometre away. Ronnie looked up, and then flung himself in the way of a long-haired youth who had launched himself at Brutal. All three went down in a rolling, flailing flurry.

She sat up, her vision swirling. Evan followed Mat and kicked again, but this time Mat rolled aside, and sprang to his feet, moving like an athlete. Evan's fists flailed, but Mat ducked away. Beside them, the blond man cried out and fell to his knees, clutching his face. Brutal spun and surged toward Mat from the other side. Someone in the crowd yelled 'Watch out, kid!' and Mat glanced just in time as Brutal closed in, arms spread. He dropped low and kicked out. His sandshoes connected with Brutal's groin, and the big man grunted and fell towards Mat like a toppled building. His big hand fastened on to Mat's jeans, pinning him tight. Evan closed the distance and smashed another boot into the small of Mat's back, connecting solidly. Mat's body arched as if he had been shot.

Hine tried to stand, but a middle-aged woman with a sunburnt face grabbed her. 'Stay down, girl. They aren't going to stop for you.'

Evan kicked Mat again, and again, while Brutal got to his feet. He roared and lifted a huge boot, poised to stamp down on Mat's midriff as the boy writhed beneath him. Suddenly a black-and-white dog erupted out of the crowd, and sank its teeth into Brutal's leg. The big man howled and toppled. The dog, Godfrey, Hine realized, darted away and showed his teeth.

The sirens blared louder now, and tyres screeched on the road. Ronnie stiff-armed the long-haired youth, clambered upright and grabbed Evan's shoulder. 'Cops!' he yelled. Evan glanced back, then down at her. 'Come on, let's go!' he yelled at her.

She sat there, utterly numb. The face she had kissed, the man she had given herself to, the devil she had sold her soul to, demanded her obedience. Her body moved to obey, but the woman holding her didn't let go. 'Stay here, girl. Don't go with that animal.'

'Get up, Hine!' Evan took two steps towards her and reached down.

The woman holding her looked up defiantly. 'You stay away from her,' she snapped, like a school teacher. Hine was frightened Evan would deck her too, but then he looked towards the cop cars, and backed away. He pointed his finger at them both.

'I won't forget this,' Evan told the woman, then looked

69

down at Hine. 'See you soon, Hine. See you at *home*.' Then he turned and ran, Ronnie and Brutal pelting at his heels. A huge Alsatian swept past, and Godfrey seemed to yip advice to it. Light-blue uniforms filled the lawn around her.

Evan and the others fled along the lakefront. Four cops were sprinting after them, and, as she watched, the Alsatian brought down Brutal in a flurry of limbs. Blue shirts dived onto him, and the police dog surged on again, past Ronnie who had turned to see what had happened and then thrown up his hands in a gesture of surrender. The Alsatian closed in on Evan. At the last moment, Evan stopped and turned. The dog stopped also, and circled behind him. He raised his hands in surrender also, too cunning to resist arrest.

A policewoman fell to one knee beside Hine. 'What happened here? Are you okay?'

Hine took a deep breath, suddenly feeling that this moment was crucial. She felt her nerve cracking. If she lied or said nothing, Evan would probably get away with it again, and then he would beat her, and punish her, and life would go on. But at least it was a life she knew.

'Those guys ...' Hine waved her hand towards where Evan was being cuffed, along with Brutal and Ronnie, '... they attacked him.' She pointed to where Mat lay, a medic kneeling beside him. More medics were tending the blond foreign guy and his mate, who both looked pretty bad.

'Why did they do that?'

She hung her head. 'For talking to me.' She looked up at the policewoman, hating the pity she saw there. 'Because Evan, the bearded guy, he's my man.' She looked at the ground. 'It was my fault.'

The sunburnt woman let her breath out and shook her head. She and the cop exchanged glances. 'What's your name?' the cop asked.

'Hine.'

The woman looked Hine over, taking in her bleeding cheek. 'Did Evan hit you, Hine?'

She turned her cheek away, and didn't answer.

The cop touched her shoulder. 'I'm Police Constable Robyn Partridge. We need you to come down to the station and make a statement. And then I'd like you to come with me to the refuge. Just for the night, so you can think things over. Okay?'

Godfrey was looking at her with big soulful eyes, and he trotted up and licked her bloody cheek. It stung, and she shoved him away, but her cheek felt better immediately, as if he had wiped it with anaesthetic. She reached out and cuddled him. 'I'll be okay,' she told them. 'I don't need no refuge.'

Godfrey whined mournfully at her.

Taupo Police Station was on Story Place, behind the Rose Gardens. The police loaded Evan, Brutal and Ronnie in a van, but they took Hine in a cop car. She wished Godfrey was there, but they wouldn't let him come in the car. He had wagged his tail and darted away, as if on a mission.

They took her through reception and down a corridor, past the holding cells, to an interview room. The closest cell was empty except for a dishevelled tramp, whose eyes followed her as she walked past. Although he looked like a broken old man, there was something malevolent about him. His reek reached her through the open doorway, and he smacked his lips as he watched her walk past. Shadows clung to him, as though light refused to come too close.

'Revolting man,' muttered PC Robyn as she led Hine into a bare room. 'We picked him up last night, urinating in a drinking fountain at one in the morning. Some people you feel sorry for, but there's something about him ...' Her voice trailed off, and she glanced at Hine as though embarrassed to have said so much.

PC Robyn went for tea, while Hine tried not to think how badly Mat and those two tourists might have been hurt. Sometime during those few minutes, she lost her remaining courage. When PC Robyn came back, she said as little as she could, before asking to see Evan. PC Robyn made an exasperated noise, and ignored her request. 'Do you know this Matiu Douglas? We took him to A&E — he has broken ribs.'

'No, I've never met him before. We'd only said a few words, see. I'm sorry he got hurt,' she added truthfully.

'What about the two Germans? One has a broken nose and both have concussion. Do you know them?'

'No, they just wanted to help, I guess. Pretty dumb, huh?'

'It's not dumb to help a person in need, Hine,' PC Robyn told her in flat tones. 'Evan and his associates will be bailed, you know. They'll be out in twenty-four hours.'

A vague hope he might be locked away for a while vanished. *Which means I've got to make it up with him.* 'Let me see Evan!' she pleaded. 'He's my boyfriend. Ain't it my right?'

PC Robyn rolled her eyes. 'Very well,' she said grimly, standing up. She hit a buzzer, and a big Maori cop came in. 'This is PC Tamati Richards. He'll take you through. Your *boyfriend* is in the middle holding cell.'

Hine nodded and got up. They took her back down the corridor to the holding cells, a room full of cages just like in a movie. The room fell silent, and she felt that horrible tramp watching her. Then Evan leapt to the front of the cell.

'Hey, baby! I'm sorry! I didn't mean nothing! Are you okay?' He looked sincere, repentant.

She nodded numbly, unsure now what it was she wanted to say.

'I still love you, baby,' he said in that voice he always used to melt her heart. 'I'll be out tomorrow and we'll make it all okay.'

Suddenly a bizarre noise froze her. The tramp had got up and stalked to the front of his cell. A wave of putrid air washed the room as he began to ululate like an American Indian; slapping his mouth and whooping, his eyes locked on her. 'It's you!' he shouted, his tones incredulous. 'It's you!'

Everyone stared, and then Evan lunged through the bars from his cell, grasped the tramp's jacket, and wrenched him face first into the bars. 'Don't look at her, you stinking ape!' Evan bawled, his face centimetres from the tramp's. The officers in the room converged, but the tramp's face just split into a huge grin.

'She's *your* woman?' he asked, his eyes bulging. *'Excellent!'*

Suddenly the room went black, then dazzlingly white, and black again, as though a massive strobe light was flashing on and off. Faces and expressions changed with each flash, but Hine's gaze was fixed on the tramp and Evan. She saw the tramp exhale, and a cloud of shadows seemed to well like a serpent from his lips, and pour into Evan's open mouth. Evan's face went wide in sudden panic, and he tried to tear himself away, but the darkness kept flowing into him, and then he was reeling away. She screamed and suddenly everything stopped and reverted to normal, the room reverberating to her cry.

The tramp turned and looked at her, his expression vacant and lost. He fell against the bars, tried to grip, then toppled backwards. She screamed again as the officers leapt towards his cell. 'It's just a power fluctuation,' PC Tamati told her, although his face looked haunted.

Evan had fallen between Ronnie and Brutal, who peered down at him in bewilderment. Then he sat up, and looked straight at her. She saw darkness gather behind his eyes, felt that serpent baring fangs at her, and found herself trying to push her way backwards through the wall. 'Nooo! Nooo! It's in him, it's in him! Don't let him out! Evan! Evan! Noooo!'

The Evan-thing began to laugh, blowing her kisses from where he sat on the floor. In the next cell the tramp convulsed, gurgling. Constable Richards took her in his huge arms and dragged her towards the door. The tramp went rigid with a rattling noise in his throat. Then Evan slowly turned his head, raised his finger and pointed at her. Right at her, right at the spot between her eyes, and he smacked his lips, just like the tramp had earlier.

She swallowed a sob as PC Richards pulled her away.

When next she was aware, she was in a car outside Evan's house. *Her house.* It was twilight. The dark was creeping through the city, street by street. PC Tamati Richards was driving; PC Robyn had her arms around her and was cuddling her like a mother. 'Shhh, Hine, we're here now. We're going to go in and collect your things.'

She let the cop hold her; she was frightened of being let go. 'Did you see it?' Hine whispered. 'Did you see the snake? It went into his mouth!'

She saw Tamati and Robyn glance at each other. 'Easy, lass,' said Tamati. 'It's a shock to see someone die, but you're okay now.'

'But the lights flashed … and the snake, the snake …'

'There was no snake, Hine. There's no snakes in New Zealand. It's okay. We'll get you in and out of here as soon as possible.'

They had seen nothing. There hadn't been anything. She was hallucinating. She was mad. And they seemed to be acting like she had said she would go to the refuge after all. *I never said that* … But the thought of being home when that Evan-thing returned appalled her. She nodded meekly.

The front door opened and Ko came waddling out, concern all over her face. Robyn helped her out of the car, and Ko gripped her in a huge bear-hug, tears running down her face. 'Lovey, lovey, oh lovey, are you okay?' She touched the wound on her cheek. 'What's happened? Deano came running and said you was all arrested. Is Ronnie with you? Is Ronnie okay?'

'Ronnie's okay. But I've gotta go, Ko. Like you said: I've gotta go.'

Ko's face widened. 'Tonight? Oh my …'

'I gotta, Ko. Evan caught me talking to this guy, and beat him up.'

'Oh, honey, you shoulda known better. Evan's so jealous.'

So it's my fault? She felt a sudden anger at her friend, had to stop herself from shouting something she would regret. 'He was no-one, Ko. Just a kid who said "hi". Nothing was going

75

on. But now Evan's gonna do me for it.'

Ko wrapped her arms around her, and that nearly started her crying again, but she must have used up all her tears for now. She felt hollow and chilled to the bone.

PC Robyn laid a hand on Hine's shoulder. 'I'm sorry, but we need to keep moving.'

Ko glared, but slowly let Hine go. They all went inside, and she stopped, wondering what to do. They had to lead her into her room. It was a pigsty, as usual. Unwashed clothing and tangled sheets strewn about. Unwanted memories of her and Evan together surfaced, but she pushed them away. Robyn followed her in, sniffed with distaste, and gave her a plastic rubbish bag. 'Pile your things into here. I've got plenty of them. Do you have possessions in other rooms? What can I do to help?'

It didn't take long to empty the two drawers she used, and clear her side of the wardrobe. She took a tiny jewellery box and tucked it into a pocket, her toothbrush from the bathroom, the dregs of a perfume bottle. 'That's all.' She hung her head. 'I ain't got much.' She realized she still had Ko's hoodie on. 'Ko, this is yours …'

Ko wouldn't look at her. 'You keep it, lovey. Is too small for me now. You keep it, eh.' Brandi came out, looked at the cops, and shrank against her mother's legs. 'Brandi-babe, you give Aunty Hine a hug, there's a girl. Aunty's got to go away for a while.'

Brandi shyly hugged Hine, who felt her tear ducts recharging. She squeezed the girl and prayed Brandi would never have to go through this herself.

Tamati looked at his watch. 'We've got to go, Robyn.'

PC Robyn nodded, running fingers through her hair then replacing her hat. 'Okay, Hine?'

Ko seized Hine and squeezed her tight, crying again. 'I'll be in touch, Ko,' promised Hine. 'I'll see you again, I will.' She wished she could tell Ko about the tramp-thing, but how could she explain it? She dropped her voice, and said only, 'Evan is evil. You and Ronnie have got to leave, Ko. Please!'

'When we can, honey.' Her voice sounded hopeless. 'You take care, lovey. You take good care.' She looked at Robyn and Tamati. 'I'm holdin' you two personally responsible, you hear? Anything happens to her ...'

The two cops fidgeted awkwardly. Hine backed out the door, her hands trembling so much she had to stuff them in her pockets. She needed a smoke, badly.

Robyn walked with her to the car while Tamati talked into his radio. She looked back at the house, at Ko and Brandi silhouetted in the front door, the light behind shrouding them in shadow. She waved hesitantly, and then allowed Robyn to help her in. Everything seemed fluid suddenly, as if the ground were an illusion cast over a huge dark lake, and she was about to be swept beneath the surface. Into the deep water.

They took her to the Women's Refuge, a big old house only a few blocks from Evan's house. It didn't seem far enough away. Robyn was speaking but all Hine could think about was that she had only tonight in which to find somewhere to hide before that Evan-thing came looking for her.

When she stepped from the car, in front of the refuge, her heart fluttered. She shouldered her bag of things, while Robyn went ahead. The street was empty. Tamati was bent over his cop radio. She took a few steps, then looked around as a small *woof* sounded in the shadows of the building. Godfrey was there, his tail wagging. She went to the dog, unnoticed by Robyn who was knocking on the door. She knelt, stroking his fur.

'Hello, lass,' said a quiet voice, English-sounding, throaty and down to earth, melodious and resonant. 'I'm Aethlyn Jones. Godfrey and I have come to take you home.'

She looked up. Standing back from the dog was an old man with a rough whiskery face, a pipe hanging out of the corner of his mouth, shapeless clothing, and unkempt grey hair. He held out a hand. Godfrey rubbed against her leg, and then walked to Jones and licked his other hand. That decided her, somehow.

She held out her hand. He took it in his callused but gentle grip, and they walked away down the side of the building, and were gone.

Robyn and Tamati searched for her all night. They tried every street, every known place that the girl could have gone to, to no avail. At dawn they issued a missing persons report before getting dressed down by the local police chief for letting the girl out of their sight. But Hine Horatai was gone.

Asher Grieve

Sunday

Donna Kyle stared at the mirror, mourning all she had lost. Her once-perfect nose was crooked and scarred; a puckered reddish-pink ridge cut a jagged line across her face. Her skin felt like old paper. The moko on her chin had faded to grey and her lips were bloodless. She turned from the looking glass, unable to bear the beaten visage it held.

She was in a war, and she was losing. She hadn't realized how much she had depended upon Puarata's gifts. He had given her a stream of little trinkets and potions that did this or boosted that. She had once thought it was her skill that had brought her to his side, elevated her above the others. She had imagined herself his most powerful acolyte, but now she knew better.

I was just his favourite whore.

When he died, his trinkets had also begun to fade. What did she have left now? The binding words to enslave a few fairy beings of limited power. A little influence among the tipua tribes. The mana of having been Puarata's woman, such as it was. Little else. She now knew her talents were no better than the others', no more than even that pig Sebastian Venn's. *Venn!*

79

Damn the man! He had taken everything. All that was hers by right, he now held. And damn all those vile men, clubbing together against her. He had bought the loyalty of everyone, turning her into an outcast.

She had fought tooth and nail, but it had been hopeless. She was no general. She had no money. The bikers and mobsters she managed to woo were nothing against his mercenaries with their fat contracts. Even her supernatural allies failed her. She sent hau hau or tipua, but he countered with settler soldiers, armed with guns and well disciplined. Her forces had disintegrated. Those few apprentices of Puarata's circle that had joined her were dead. Bryce had fled south after that debacle at Waikaremoana. *Weak bastard!* Only Kurangaituku still stood by her, and she was mad and utterly untrustworthy. The Ureweras were lost. Venn controlled the Lodge she had once thought of as home. He had legal title to all of Puarata's property and the manpower to back it up. His pre-eminence among the northern warlocks was undoubted. Bryce still held the South, but he was refusing to aid her. Unless she swore service to him. *Never!*

The war went on covertly, nevertheless. Information and clues were traded or stolen, murders arranged and carried out. Most thought her defeated. But she knew of one way back. Te Iho … her last hope.

Venn didn't even know! He thought this war was all about property and wealth. But Puarata had been more than rich and influential; he had been the mightiest tohunga makutu ever known, and Venn was no Puarata, not in the field of makutu.

To truly inherit Puarata's mantle required Puarata's secret

lair: *Te Iho, The Heart*. Puarata had told her of it, but had never taken her there. Without Te Iho, victory or defeat was incomplete. She was now certain it wasn't in the Ureweras. Best of all, Venn did not even know it existed. *Venn can rot in the Ureweras*, she told herself. *Let him think me defeated. I shall return, possessing might undreamt.*

A flicker in the mirror caught her eye, and she turned in fright. There was a man there, in the glass, staring back at her. A man clad in velvet with a foppish hat and furs at his throat, like some Renaissance potentate. His furrowed, clean-shaven visage was framed in long, silver hair that floated strangely, as if underwater. 'Hello, Daughter,' he said laconically. 'Feeling sorry for yourself?'

Her world lurched. '*Father?*' She had tried hard to forget that mental warning that had saved her from Rothwell a year ago. She had almost convinced herself she had imagined it. Almost. '*Father?*'

'Donna, my dear. You look anxious. Let me help you.' His voice sounded pained, sympathetic. 'Let me restore you to what you once were.'

Too many emotions flooded her: hatred, for what he had done to her; betrayal, that he had failed her; contempt, that he had been so foolish as to go up against Puarata; anger; bitterness. 'What are you? Some kind of ghost?'

'No ghost, Daughter, for I did not die. I am merely a prisoner, here in the darkness.'

'A prisoner,' she breathed. Her fury at him welled up. 'The mighty Asher Grieve, trapped? I hope you rot there for eternity!'

Asher's eyes narrowed. 'Trapped, aye,' he hissed.

81

'Imprisoned and bled dry by your *lover*, because you betrayed me, you ungrateful little sow. After everything I gave you.'

'Everything you gave me?' she echoed derisively. 'You gave me away! *I was eight, Father*. You gave me to that bastard, and he *destroyed* me!'

His lip curled. 'Destroyed? Fool! We *made* you, my girl. You were ignorant of your potential. We freed it! You were to be co-ruler of this world when I became king! As I would have if you hadn't turned on me. You sided with *him*, and condemned me to this prison!'

'Why should I have sided with you, you monster? You *sold* me! Did you expect to get me back for free? For some kind of deluded family loyalty?'

Asher Grieve's face twisted nastily. 'Loyalty? Yes, I expected loyalty from my only acknowledged child! Especially as I sought to free her from the man she claimed to hate so much! I had every right to expect a daughter's loyalty. I took a bed-wetting cry-baby and gave her the tools to *rule*. But poor little Princess Donna didn't like getting her hands dirty, and didn't have the guts to seize her chance — *our* chance!' He leant towards her, as if straining against some invisible bond. 'I would have made up for every hurt he inflicted upon you, but you didn't have the courage to see it through!'

She flinched at each word, her legs wobbling. 'Did you have a point to make?' She wished her voice didn't sound so quavery.

He lifted his right hand, clutching a walking cane with a crystalline lion's head on the tip. 'Yes, my daughter, I do. You are seeking Te Iho. You cannot be victorious without it.'

'I know that,' she replied scornfully.

His face floated closer, until it almost filled the mirror. 'You cannot find it without my help.'

She felt her skin become slick. 'You, help me?' Her voice betrayed her desperation.

'Yes, Daughter, you cannot find it without me. I wish to help you. But how can I trust you, you who so thoroughly repudiates me? No, there is only one way I can trust you.' He smiled. 'Pledge your soul to freeing me, and I will guide you to The Heart itself!'

She backed away and sat on the bed. It was that or fall to her knees. A *Pledge* … she knew what he meant. This was no empty promise that could be broken. This was an oath that harmed the swearer if broken. The sort they all swore to Puarata. The breaking of that Pledge had been part of the fatal weakening that enabled Puarata to defeat Asher's revolt.

Not to you, Father! She straightened, and raised a hand. 'Burn in hell or rot in prison forever, Father. Just don't talk to me again.' She exerted a little force, and the glass shattered. His cry of pain sweetened the feeling of vindication.

But in the hours afterwards came the fear, and then the certainty, that she had just doomed herself.

Parukau

Monday

Parukau sat with his back to the wall all night, unsleeping. He was learning the mind of his new host, Evan Tomoana, and especially examining his memories of Hine Horatai. *Hine* ... Parukau had seen her for what she was immediately. All those years trapped in the dog's body, he had carried one clue regarding Te Iho: *Blood of the Swimmer* ... He had wondered about who or what 'the Swimmer' might be. It was obvious now, as the answers to riddles often were. He would find Hine Horatai, and she would open the path to Te Iho.

His mind reeled with the possibilities. Beside him, Tomoana's friends slept; a mindless mountain who called himself Brutal, and a lamb in wolf's clothing called Ronnie. This evening they would be released, and he would find Hine Horatai. Then Te Iho would be his.

It had been more than a century ago that Parukau's attempt to supplant Puarata had failed. Puarata had punished him by imprisoning him in the body of a dog. In pre-contact days, Parukau had been a tohunga makutu serving Puarata, one who had learned body-jumping as a way of living forever. Unlike most, he had embraced European settlement, enraptured with these alien beings and their elegant trappings. Plush clothing and foreign women had been his addiction. Literally enduring a dog's life had nearly destroyed him. Only one thing had kept him going: Te Iho, The Heart. He had helped design and create it. One day, he would claim it and overthrow Puarata.

However, that dog body could get into places a man could not. Parukau had watched and learned. He had seen the rise of successive favourites and pretenders, and laughed as they all fell. When Puarata died he had gone straight to the Ureweras, and slipped into the hidden caves which led to Te Iho … and found them blocked and disempowered. Puarata had closed the gateway. He had panicked for a time, but he clung to the fact that Puarata had *needed* Te Iho. It must be merely hidden. They had designed it with no fixed abode, a pocket of space and time independent of both worlds. The gateway was movable, and of course Puarata would have moved it from time to time. He just had to find the new door, and the new key.

So he had ignored the war, and hunted for the gateway instead. The longer he used a body the better he controlled it, so he had kept the tramp-body despite its shortcomings. But now he was ready for a new phase. He was ready to enjoy this powerful younger frame, and make 'Evan Tomoana' a feared man.

At dawn, the shifts changed and a new pack of uniforms swaggered in. His 'friends' slept on. Let them; he didn't need them yet. He had plans to lay, a new world to explore. When last he had worn human guise, aeroplanes and cars were undreamt of, electricity a foreign rumour. Old Mac had gone bush decades ago; he had been an ignorant loner. So Parukau feverishly shuffled through the memories of this Evan Tomoana to educate himself.

Eventually the police took statements. He feigned regret. A lawyer came and talked about bail. It was easy. He laughed inwardly at the pathetic amount tendered for his good behaviour as, exactly twenty-four hours later, he walked free. *Free. In a body worthy of me ... I am Parukau. I am back in the game.*

Monday evening

The girl was gone when Parukau returned to Evan's home. He needed to find her. But he was starving, needed to refuel. So they ate pizza and drank beers on the back lawn as evening fell, a scarlet sunset with clouds gathering to the north. He savoured every mouthful of food with relish. Life felt good, and was about to get better. The fat waddling creature that Ronnie was shackled to, Ko, kept the beers coming. She was afraid to meet his eye. He would talk to her later ...

'What's happening, boss?' asked Brutal. 'What we gonna do?'

'Yeah, what we gonna do?' Ronnie parroted.

Tomorrow, I will find other men to serve me. Better men than these cretins. 'First thing, I want you to know that I am going to take a Maori name. "Evan" is a Pakeha name. I renounce it.'

The two thugs looked at each other in surprise. Evan was basically Pakeha, for all his pretensions. But neither argued. 'Sure thing, chief,' said Brutal. 'What should we call you now?'

He let it roll off his tongue. *'Parukau.'*

'Parukau?'

'Yes, Parukau.' It was a joy to hear his name spoken aloud

after all these years. 'Secondly, we will enlist some men tomorrow. Then we're going to get rich.'

'Rich?' they chorused myopically.

'That old tramp at the police station whispered a secret in my ear as he died. He told me where he had buried his money.' He leant forward conspiratorially. 'It's in Rotorua. So that is where we're going, tomorrow night. To dig it up. But first, tomorrow morning, we're going to enlist some allies.'

'Allies?'

Are these fools going to echo every word I say? 'Indeed.'

He got up, indicating he was going to pee, and swaggered across the lawn to the back door. The toddler was there. She saw something in him that frightened her, made her flee into the house. He stalked into the kitchen, where that obese creature Ko was cooking. The other baby looked at him and began to cry. *Children have such good eyes.* 'Where is Hine, Ko?'

Ko didn't look at him. 'I dunno.'

'I think you do, Ko. You were here when she came for her clothes. You're her only friend. Where did she go?'

'I dunno, I swear.'

He picked up a carving knife. 'Where is she, Ko?'

The baby screamed, like a torture victim. He watched Ko shake, too scared to move.

'Don't you want those little brats to just *shut up* sometimes, Ko? Don't you just want to cut their tongues out sometimes?' She looked at him with her big pleading-cow eyes. He stroked her cheek with his left hand. 'Where did Hine go, Ko?'

'To the refuge. She went to the refuge.' Ko began to weep, rivulets flowing from both eyes. 'Don't you hurt my babies.'

He put the knife down. 'Of course not. I love children.'

In Aotearoa

Monday

Hine opened her eyes, and realized with mild shock that she didn't have a hangover. She peered cautiously out from under the musty blanket, and guessed from the angle and hue of the sunlight that it was still early morning. She was on an old sofa in Aethlyn Jones's lounge. Godfrey lay on top of the blanket, snuggled against her, with a nice clean dog smell like warm rugs and pine needles. The ceiling above her head was open-beamed, with cobwebs in the corners.

She huddled under the blanket, clad in an old nightgown that Jones had handed her on arrival. He had been grandfatherly and gentlemanly, and she had trusted him right away. She liked the offhand way he talked, and the concern he showed without being over-solicitous. He had made it clear that they would talk, but only when she was ready. That suited her fine. She couldn't remember the exact impulse that had caused her to abandon the cops and run off, but it still felt like she had done the right thing. If she had gone to the refuge, Evan would know exactly where she was.

Evan … or whatever he is now …

She found to her surprise that she had no trouble

88

believing that Evan was possessed by some evil thing. She had grown up believing in good and evil, in religion and magic — this was just an extension of that. That tramp had been possessed, and now the demon was in Evan. It was horrible, but conceivable. It didn't really change things: she had already decided to leave. It just made it more imperative. She couldn't even mourn Evan: there weren't enough good memories to cling to.

Jones was fussing in the kitchen, and Godfrey got up and scratched at the door. It opened a crack, and the smell of bacon and coffee welled into the darkened room. 'You awake, lass?' Jones called.

'Yeah! I'm coming out! You got a dressin' gown'll fit me?'

'Aye, I've got one warming by the stove. It's a cold morning, lass. You wantin' coffee or tea?'

Her mouth watered. 'Coffee, please.' She got up, marvelling briefly at the antique cotton nightie she was in as she dragged fingers through her curls and rubbed the grit from her eyes. She felt refreshed as if after her best sleep ever. She fingered the scab on her cheek and found it almost gone, which was weird. Godfrey had licked it, she recalled.

The kitchen was warm and redolent of pipe smoke, cooking bacon and rich coffee. There were two chairs at a table, and she wrapped herself in the dressing gown hanging by the stove, and sat. The room had no electricity, at least that she could see, although there was a muddle of electrical wires and gizmos piled at one end of the table, looking out of place.

Jones turned and smiled. 'Did ye sleep, lass?'

'Yeah. What time is it?' Her watch seemed to have stopped.

'Oh, about nine I'm thinkin'. Don't hold much with time

here. Although I can't abide lateness,' he added with a wry smile. 'I keep a sundial out the back.'

She peered out the window onto a sunlit back yard surrounded by trees. Their shadows stretched towards her, so she guessed the back yard must face east. The grass was long and there were two sheds, a small one that contained a toilet she had used last night, and a bigger shed containing two horses and the cart they had ridden in to get here. It had been a strangely silent journey; *no street lights*, she had thought dimly at one point, but then she had fallen asleep.

Jones fixed some eggs while she took the coffee pot off the element and poured the black liquid into two old mugs. Then she wolfed down the best breakfast she could remember for a long time, while Jones picked at his, feeding half of his bacon to Godfrey.

'You're probably wondering a few things, lassie,' he remarked finally. His accent was definitely British, and had a rough honey texture she warmed to. 'Like maybe "Where am I?", "Who's the old guy?", and "What am I going to do?" perhaps?'

She smiled despite herself. 'Yeah, I guess. What was the first one: where am I?'

'We're on the lakefront, a little south of the Napier turn-off.'

'I thought it was all time-shares and hotels down here? Your house must be worth a packet, eh? You hanging out for some rich dude to make you an offer?'

'Something like that, lass.'

'So, who's the old guy?'

'I'm Aethlyn Jones, once of a hamlet near Abertawe, in Wales. But that was a long time ago — I've been in Aotearoa longer than I ever lived in Wales.'

'Don't sound like it.' The old man had a pommy accent worse than she had ever heard.

'Don't I?' He raised an amused eyebrow. 'Perhaps the way we learn to enunciate as a child stays with us.'

Enunciate? She had not heard words like that since high school. 'What do you do? Are you on the pension?'

'The pension?' He laughed. 'I've never really thought to apply, to be honest. Maybe I should: I'm sure I've got papers somewhere saying I'm over sixty-five.' He chuckled, as if he found the thought inordinately funny. 'No, I guess I'm something of a trader and fisherman, and a man who gets things done.'

She asked the last question. The serious one. 'What am I going to do, Mister Jones?'

'Just "Jones", lass.' His eyes were suddenly serious. 'That's the real question, isn't it? What are you going to do? Because you sure as hell can't go back to *him*, can you?'

She caught her breath at that, and wondered whether he somehow knew what had happened to Evan. 'Can't I?' she asked, just to see what he would say.

'No, you certainly can't.'

She tried again. 'What's happened to him? I saw ...' Her mind flicked back to what she had witnessed in that cell, and she shivered suddenly, as if someone had opened the door and let the cold inside.

'What *did* you see, lass? Tell me.'

For a second she didn't want to, but she made herself do it. He didn't once scoff, or even interrupt, as she described the horrible vagabond, and the dark shadow-serpent, and what had happened to Evan. She found herself talking about Evan, even though her eyes welled up with salty tears that stung as they flowed out and down her cheeks. She talked about Evan and what he did to her, which took her back to how he had been at first, which led further back to Glenn Bale and her mother. By then she was just crying, soaking the shoulder of this kind old man who knew how to listen and not question or accuse or condemn. It seemed like hours until she ran dry of tears and words.

He talked softly in her ear. 'Lass, the world is a little more uncanny than you can know. The thing that is in your Evan now is something that I've been hunting for a long time. I'll tell you about him later, when you're up to it.' He wiped her eyes. 'Go and shower, now. I've laid out some clothes for you in the bathroom. They're a bit old-fashioned, but they'll be a novelty for ye 'til I can take you shopping.'

She dutifully plodded to the bathroom. He told her there was hot water through a wetback on the wood burner. Enough light came through the grimy back window that she could see what she was doing. The shampoo packaging looked like something from a country fair, but there was a toothbrush and toothpaste by the sink. She locked the door from habit, although she was sure she was safe. The shower was divine, hot and bracing, and she spent ages in there without the hot water faltering.

Finally, Jones knocked. 'Come on, lass, ye can't spend the whole day in there! I'll be getting you to cut me more firewood if you do.'

She called out an apology, got out and dried off in a huge thick cotton towel. It was wonderful to feel clean. The dress and underwear that Jones had laid out made her laugh aloud. There were baggy white cotton bloomers with lacy edges and embroidered roses, and an ivory-coloured camisole. The full-length dress had a front-lacing bodice. *Jaysus! What century does this stuff come from?* It was like a dress-up party. Everything was too big, although the bodice fitted about her boobs nicely after a bit of fiddling with the lacing. When she combed her hair out, she looked like one of those Maori women from early colonial photos in the museum, servants or wives of the early settlers.

I wonder where he got it all. Weird stuff for an old guy to own. Be careful here, girl.

When she went out to the kitchen again, he stared a little and his breath seemed to catch, as though remembering someone else. 'Where'd you get these relics, Mister Jones? I feel like a museum exhibit!'

He handed her one of her own ciggies, and tapped out his pipe. 'Come on out the front and I'll tell you.'

He led her down the hallway, which led past the one bedroom and the lounge to the front door. They went out onto the small veranda. The front lawn was smaller than the back yard, with two goats cropping the grass, and the lake was only about fifty metres away, partly obscured by willows. There were a few dark shapes on the water, canoes or something, but she didn't look closely. The dark shape of the hills loomed beyond the water, out towards Acacia Bay on the far side. She went to sit down, and then her eyes registered what she was seeing, and her brain flipped.

Where are the houses across at Acacia Bay? I oughta be able to see them from here …

And while we're at it, why are there only Maori waka out on the lake?

She got down off the veranda and walked through the trees

to the jetty. She heard Jones follow, but her eyes were drawn to the gradually unfolding view of Taupo. She felt her knees quiver. She turned back to Jones and the words fell out of her mouth. 'What have you done to Taupo?' She turned and looked again, just to make sure she wasn't mistaken. She wasn't. Taupo was gone.

In its place was a pa, a fortified Maori village behind rows of wooden palisades. There were wooden European buildings too, outside the pa walls. She could make out people walking and riding, and black-clad soldiery filing along the waterfront. On the shores, clumps of women of both races were washing clothes, and children ran along the shore. Men on horses ambled along the road where there should have been trucks and cars, and the road seemed to be a ribbon of pounded dirt. There were no telephone poles or power lines or street lights, either. Smoke billowed from chimneys. Only one boat wasn't a waka: she only recognized it because she had seen it before — it was the sleek white *Barbary*, a 1920s fifty-foot yacht once owned by Errol Flynn, which operated as a lake cruise attraction by a local company. Evan had promised to take her on it one day.

She turned to Jones. 'Where's Taupo gone?' she asked, unsure whether this was some prank or something a whole lot stranger.

He rubbed his chin. 'Well, lass, it's a long story ...'

The sun was past its zenith, and her stomach had gnawed away breakfast, but she listened as the old man talked about the 'Ghost World': Aotearoa, where legends and the long-dead walked. It seemed impossible, but she could see the waka and the pa and everything else. Her eyes couldn't lie! She had no choice but to believe.

'When can I go back?' she asked tentatively, suddenly afraid that he might never let her go, like some hermit who kidnaps a princess in a fairy story.

'Oh, soon, lass. Godfrey and I just thought it best to get you off the streets for a while, to somewhere your man can't reach. Don't worry,' he added as though he had been eavesdropping in her head. 'I'll take you back when you want to go.'

Godfrey the dog looked up at her with sincere eyes, and her doubts melted.

'This is so weird,' she said, shaking her head. Bizarrely, amidst all this strangeness, the one thing she did feel was *security*.

Suddenly she heard a body brushing through foliage, coming from the direction of the Taupo settlement. She got to her feet apprehensively as two shapes appeared at the edge of the trees and walked up to the cottage. One was a teenage girl she mentally christened 'Freakshow': a geeky creature with a mop of ginger dreads and a skeletal body clad in garish and unflattering clothes. Her face was all braces and glasses.

But the other one … was Matiu Douglas. He had a blue-black swelling about his eye and his hand was clutching his ribcage as he breathed awkwardly. She remembered that he knew Godfrey. They both stared at each other and blushed. Freakshow peered at her, looking put out.

'I believe you know each other,' said Jones, with a dry chuckle.

Jones's guest

Monday

Mat woke stiff and sore, but he was in one piece, and over breakfast he reassured his mum that it was just one of those things. The doctor had told him his ribs were 'probably just cracked or bruised', and sent him away. They didn't strap ribs any more, just prescribed rest. Three months and they'll be fine, the nurse had said, as if this was good news. *Three months!* That was halfway to forever! And the really annoying thing was that if it hadn't been so public he could have taken down those goons in seconds, but, with so many people watching, using magic was out. 'Some idiot thought I was chatting up his girl.'

'Were you?' Mum responded, as though this was more important than his ribcage.

'No, Mum, I wasn't! I didn't even know she had a boyfriend. He was a skinhead arsehole, with mates who looked like Uruks from *Lord of the Rings*. They beat up some German guys who tried to help me, too. Poor fellas; they kept saying they didn't think this sort of thing happened here!'

He managed to convince Mum that gangland thugs weren't lurking outside waiting to get him — something he was by no means sure of — and then told her he had to go tell Jones that he couldn't train. He called Cassandra along the way and met her by the kauri tree. He had texted her from the hospital and said he couldn't go swimming, but hadn't said why, so his beat-up look was something of a shock to her. He was telling her what had happened as they walked, but seeing Hine on Jones's veranda stole his breath away.

She was in a colonial dress, and she looked ... breathtaking. She was a vision, out-of-time, luminously beautiful. He wanted to take her hand and kiss it and tell her exactly how lovely she seemed to him. Unfortunately, before he could get that elegant thought processed, another less cultured part of him gasped, 'What the hell are you doing here? Uh — I mean: "Hi".'

She suppressed a laugh. 'Jones found me, and brought me here. And Godfrey, of course.'

Cassandra looked at Jones. 'Really?'

'Yes, really,' said Hine loftily. 'What are you two doing here, anyway? Do you know Jones?' she demanded, as though Jones was *her* friend alone.

Jones came to the rescue. 'Mat, Cassandra: Hine is my guest. She needed rescuing from her former boyfriend, and Godfrey suggested we do the rescuing. Hine, Mat is my pupil.'

She looked at Mat with renewed interest. 'Your pupil? What do you mean?'

Mat went to answer, but Jones interrupted. 'Just a few skills I happen to know and he has an affinity for, lass.'

Hine looked at Cassandra. 'And you, too?' she asked, still struggling to take the girl seriously. Her eyes flicked to Mat. *Surely they're not dating?*

Cassandra shrugged a bony shoulder. 'Just a friend,' she said coolly. She patted a satchel overflowing with wires and cabling, and looked at Jones. 'I'll get busy then,' she told Jones, pushing past.

Jones peered at Mat. 'Let me take a look at your ribs, lad. You look like you need a poultice and some strapping.' He took him back to the kitchen and made Mat strip off to the waist so he could examine his ribs.

Mat was burningly conscious of both girls' eyes on him, but mostly of Hine's. She was no doubt comparing his battered torso with that of her neo-Nazi-super-he-monster ex-boyfriend. 'The doctor said that they don't do strapping any more; it's old-fashioned,' he told Jones.

The old man grunted. 'Mmm. So am I.' He laid a big thick bandage on the table, then began pulling out clay pots from his herb shelf. 'So, we'll be wanting some arnica for the bruising, comfrey for bones, and cloves and camomile for the pain. Maybe some aloe vera, too. What do you think, God?'

Godfrey barked thoughtfully, and Jones pulled out something else and added it to the pot. 'True, an antibiotic wouldn't hurt … echinacea perhaps?' He turned to Hine. 'As for you, do you know how to operate an old colonial-era washing machine and wringer?'

Hine shook her head.

'Well then, as soon as this poultice mix is on the stove, I'll take you out and show you. You didn't think you were free-loading here, did you? Guests have to earn their keep!'

Cassandra smirked as she wired up a clock.

Jones took Hine out to the wash house, while Mat stroked God's head and daydreamed. Cassandra was talking about electricity again, but he was thinking about Hine's face. Eventually Cassandra rather huffily went silent. When the old Welshman returned, he got Mat to recount the previous day's events. He had already had to tell Cassandra all about it. Mostly he was worried for Mum. 'I don't want Mum threatened for something I've done,' he told Jones.

'That's not the real issue, lad. The girl told me something that makes me fear much more than some gangland thug with a grudge. Do you remember the tramp we saw in the stone the taniwha sent us? Well, I think I know who he is.' He told Mat about the vision that Hine had had in the cells, of the dark serpent shape that seemed to move from the tramp and enter her former boyfriend, Evan.

'I believe that what she saw was an evil spirit moving from the tramp to a fresh host. That evil spirit is an old enemy of mine called Parukau. Do you know the name?'

'Parukau?' Mat shook his head. 'Never heard of him.' He noticed Cassandra was listening intently.

'He was Puarata's right-hand man, centuries ago. I was on his trail at one stage, and found out his history. Do you know the tale of Peha?'

Mat shook his head again.

'Peha was a famed carver,' Jones said, sitting down and lighting up his pipe. 'Of course he was more than an ordinary carver — his carvings had power. He had an enemy, though; a man from a neighbouring tribe called Parukau, who practised makutu. One day Peha was in the forest seeking wood when the forest fell silent, and he heard sinister laughter. He found himself pursued by a disembodied head floating above him. Parukau's head! He didn't panic, though. He went to Parukau's pa, and found it deserted. But he found Parukau, buried up to his head in the earth, seemingly dead. He dug him out, thinking to bury him properly. But as soon as he was free of the earth, Parukau leapt up and fled.

'It was near dusk, so Peha slept in the deserted pa. Next morning, Parukau was outside the whare door, looking up at him. As their eyes met, he felt energy surge into him, and then Parukau fled, and was never seen again. Peha returned to his tribe and ascended to supremacy soon after, as all could see that he burned with new vibrancy and power.'

'Weird story,' Cassandra put in. 'What does it mean?'

Jones started, as if he had forgotten she was there and might not have spoken if he had. 'Well, many interpret it as a positive story, that Peha overcame Parukau's sorcery, and became stronger. But I think what really happened was quite the opposite: that Parukau's spirit entered Peha's body — especially in light of what happened next.'

'Which was what?' asked Mat.

'Well, it seems Peha had a long and prosperous life. He was a virtuous man, and a powerful tohunga. He was able to master Parukau's spirit. Parukau struggles to control good people. He can only truly control those of similar nature to himself. But when Peha died, another tribesman, a nasty piece of work, took to calling himself Parukau. The tribe cast him out, and he vanished. Soon after, a new warlock entered Puarata's service, also called Parukau. He would change body every few years. I believe it is Parukau that has taken possession of Evan, Hine's former beau.'

'He's no-one's "beau",' said Mat, bitterly. 'Beau means "handsome", but he was an ugly bully, and from what you're saying that's before this makutu spirit got into him.'

'Then Parukau will have found an apt body to house himself in,' Jones commented grimly.

Hine came in, and Jones gave Mat a cautionary look, then set the girl to preparing lunch whilst he steeped a poultice of clothes and herbs, drained it, and strapped it tightly to Mat's chest. Then he sat back and looked at the three of them, clearly making the decision to include Hine this time. 'Listen, I'm telling you this because you need and deserve to know. What you thought you saw at the police station was real. Evan Tomoana really is possessed by a body-jumping spirit. He is called Parukau. He will likely stay in that body for some time if he can. And you should all avoid him. If you see him, stay away — you hear?'

Mat nodded, while Hine looked at the floor, nodding slowly. She didn't display any shock, which surprised him. He wondered how she was feeling. Although she had left Evan to go to the refuge, she must have felt something for him once.

Jones prodded Mat's strapped chest. 'No exercise today, lad. I recommend you go home and rest. But I'll expect you here tomorrow to check progress. My medicine works quickly. Now, let's have lunch.'

Jones made it clear he wanted more time alone with Hine, so after lunch Mat and Cassandra said farewell. Hine followed them out the front door and onto the lawn. 'Hey,' she said softly to Mat, 'I shoulda said this already, but thank you for standing up to Evan like that. I think you're really brave. Dumb, but brave.' She leant in close, and kissed his cheek.

He flushed scarlet, beamed and backed away, feeling like a child. He floated on air all the way home, his cheek tingling all the way, and the pain of his ribs forgotten. Cassandra trudged beside him with a funny look on her face he couldn't quite pick.

Hine watched Mat go with a wistful smile. He seemed so young, even though they were the same age. But he had grown up surrounded by love, even though he had mentioned over the meal that his folks were divorced. He had not had to go through any of the shit she had. He was just a kid, really. She envied that, she realized suddenly.

Jones appeared at her shoulder. 'Have you thought up any more questions yet, lassie?'

'Uh, yeah, plenty!' Hine answered. 'Why me? Why did I see that thing, and no-one else in the whole police station? Why did Godfrey come and help me? And who is Mat really? What did you mean about him being your pupil?'

Jones smiled. 'You're thinking about it all; that's good. Pull up a chair — I've got a lot more to tell you.' They sat down, but instead of answering her questions immediately, he asked her one. 'Tell me about what you dream.'

'What I dream?' she puzzled whilst lighting up. 'Well, I'd like to be a nurse or, well, anything really so long as I can earn some money and …'

'No, lass,' he interrupted softly. 'I want to know what you *dream*. About the visions that you see when you sleep. As Bromel once said, "Dreams are the windows of the soul".'

She put the weirdness of the question aside, and took a

drag on her ciggie. 'Water. There's always water in my dreams.'

He nodded slowly. 'I thought you'd say that, lass. Tell me about it.'

So she talked again, wondering at herself because normally she was so quiet. Maybe all her words had been storing themselves up, waiting their chance. She told him about her dreams of swimming, and of freedom, and breathing water and revelling in weightlessness. She also told him of the horrible shark dreams, and the drowning ones, and the ones where the deep water followed her onto dry land. She seemed to re-live them as she spoke, and her cigarette went out in her hand without her realizing it.

'Aye, aye,' was all Jones said when she finished, and he patted her hand gently. 'I thought so.' Then he sat back, and began to tell her more about Aotearoa, and the more he told her, the stranger it seemed.

Embodiment of a legend

After they left Jones's cottage, they walked in silence for a while. Cassandra had promised to come over and help Mat with a maths assignment that afternoon, although she wasn't really in the mood. But she dutifully walked back to his place, where they set up on the dining-room table and she walked him through it, feeling like a teacher with an airheaded pupil.

It's not like I fancy Mat that much. Really! It was just annoying how his tongue hung out whenever he looked at that Hine chick. It was times like this when boys didn't seem worth the effort.

'Hi, you two!' Colleen, Mat's mum, bustled in with an armful of grocery bags. 'How's the maths going?'

'Okay,' Mat said desultorily. Cassandra smiled; she liked Colleen, who had a bit of sparkle to her, not like Mat's dad. Colleen paused to stare at her, take in her latest look, and went through to the kitchen. A burly, balding man followed her a second later: Neil, her boyfriend. He peered at her suspiciously, nodded at Mat and went into the kitchen.

Mat was going hard out on some algebra, so Cassandra left him to it. 'Thanks, Neil; catch you later,' she heard Colleen say, and glimpsed her pecking the man on the lips before he left via the back door.

Cassandra slipped into the kitchen. 'Can I help with the groceries?'

'I'm fine, Cass,' she replied in her lovely Irish lilt. 'But a coffee would be grand.'

'Okay.' Cassandra organized some cups, and filled a plunger with some ground coffee. She had taken to coffee herself this last year, black and sweet. Dad had a cool espresso machine.

Colleen stacked her shelves, eyeing Cassandra up. 'You know,' she commented, 'when I was your age, I was a little punkette, and only dressed in black leathers.'

Cassandra grinned. She couldn't picture it. 'Nah!'

'Oh, 'tis true. I can show you.' Colleen lifted a finger. 'Wait here!' She was back with an old photo album a minute later. She flicked it open to some Polaroids of white-faced teens wrapped around each other in close-knit presses. 'There!'

Cassandra peered at a skinny girl with vivid red hair swept up in a wind-tunnel 'eighties style, clad in skimpy Goth-like leathers and fishnets. Her face was dead white with violent red lipstick, and she was smoking and drinking. The boy she was draped over had a Mohawk and pierced lips. 'Wow!' she breathed.

'Total tramp, huh?' Colleen smirked. 'I was into The Cure and The Mission, and drank like a fish.'

Cassandra flicked over a few sheets of posing teen Goths, and then suddenly there was a serious-looking redheaded girl in a ball gown on the arm of a young Maori in a tuxedo. 'Wow! You just changed your look overnight!'

Colleen nodded, her eyes faraway. 'Yeah. I met Tama at a

bar, and he was fun to talk to, and I really liked him. He never said so, but I could tell he thought I was nice enough, but too freaky to actually date.'

'So what happened?'

Colleen looked at the roof wistfully. 'I dropped everything. The look, the crowd I hung with, the works.'

Cassandra felt offended at the thought. 'You just changed everything for a guy?'

Colleen laughed softly. 'It was more complex than that. It was the last year at teacher's college that I could mess around before it got serious. There were standards of appearance required. I wouldn't have been allowed to carry on as I was and still graduate. And the drugs and the drink were hurting my results. I needed to grow up. Meeting Tama was the catalyst.'

'Did you miss it?'

Colleen laughed. 'Oh, heavens, no! The next few years were the happiest of my life. Tama and I fell madly in love, we both graduated and set up a life together. It was grand!' She smiled sadly. 'Although I still can't listen to "Friday I'm In Love" without wanting to suck on a clove cigarette!'

Cassandra looked at her warily. 'Are you trying to tell me something, Mrs O'Connor?' she asked suspiciously.

Colleen blushed, just like Mat when he was caught out. 'No! Well … I do see a little of myself in you.'

'I'm totally happy,' Cassandra told her, gently but firmly. 'And I don't need any fashion advice.'

'Oh, I know, dear.' Colleen looked at her thoughtfully. 'When are those braces due off?'

'First week back at school!' she replied, brightening. 'It's been three years. I was a chronic thumb-sucker,' she admitted.

'Hmmm. What are you doing tomorrow morning?'

'Why?'

'Well, Neil is an orthodontist, and I'm sure two weeks isn't going to make too much difference. Shall I give him a call?'

'Could you?' Her eyes went wide. 'Really?'

Colleen smiled. 'Let's see, shall we?'

Tuesday morning

Jones was waiting for Mat in the real world, under the willows on the lakefront, puffing his pipe. Mat's ribs felt twice as stiff and sore as yesterday, a fact he wasn't slow to mention to Jones. 'Well, we'll see, laddie. That poultice may not be recognized by modern medicine, but it's never let me down.'

The old man was wearing a long coat and he had his sword buckled on, a flintlock pistol in his belt. The walking stick he was leaning on was iron-shod. 'Are you expecting trouble?' Mat asked.

Jones frowned. 'There's a little too much going on to wander about unarmed right now. Godfrey is nervous, which makes me edgy, too.' He looked about. 'Anyway, that's not why I met you halfway. I just want to let you know something important.' Mat put on his most attentive face, wondering what it was. Jones's face was as serious as he had seen him. 'Mat, Hine is not an ordinary person. I know you're quite taken with her, but you shouldn't get your hopes up in her direction. She's been through a bad time. She needs to get herself together, not start a new entanglement. Are you hearing me?'

Mat sucked on his lower lip. *I only want to talk to her*, he wanted to protest. 'I guess ...'

Jones twirled his walking stick at a dandelion head. 'There

is something you need to know about her. But you must never tell her what I'm going to tell you.'

Mat nodded, surprised. 'I promise.'

'One of the quirks of Aotearoa is that sometimes it throws up some strange things that are reflected in the real world, instead of the other way around. I call it the "avatar phenomenon". In mythology, an avatar is the shape that a god takes when on earth. Sometimes a person is born in the real world who is an embodiment of a mythic being. Hine is like that. She is associated with Hinemoa, the legendary woman who swam to Mokoia Island on Lake Rotorua to be with her lover, Tutanekai. Hine dreams of water, has nightmares of water, thinks of things in terms of water, tries to act like water even — to flow about obstacles instead of confronting them. Water is tied to her destiny. I've met three other Hinemoa-avatars. They all looked exactly like Hine, and were born in Rotorua.'

'Are you saying that she's not a real person?'

'Goodness, no! She is as real as you or me. But she is also Hinemoa, the embodiment of a legend, and one day, that part of her will claim her. It is a type of destiny.'

'Am I an avatar too?' Mat asked, not really wanting to know the answer.

'No, lad. You're an Adept, someone born with the abilities to manipulate the fabric of the two worlds. You're like me.'

'So are you saying that because of this "avatar" thing, I can't be … um, friends with her?'

Jones shook his head. 'Think about the Hinemoa legend, boyo. In it, she swims Lake Rotorua to meet her *lover*, Tutanekai. His role in the tale is as crucial as hers. Somewhere out there, Tutanekai is waiting to meet her. Her destined lover, the *only* man who can make her happy.'

Mat felt his tiny half-formed hopes wither away. Aotearoa seemed needlessly cruel just now. He had been looking forward to seeing her. Her kiss still played on his cheek, and had kept his mind straying all through the maths homework, and through the night.

Hine was waiting on the veranda, smoking. She was wearing her own clothes, including the oversized hoodie. Mat wondered if Jones would try to nag her to stop smoking. She had a very serious, faraway look in her eyes, but when she met Mat's eyes, a slow smile blossomed on her lips. He wondered if Jones had warned her off him, too. He smiled back, and the world seemed to shrink to just him and her.

'Hi, Mat. Uh, where's Fre— uh, Cassandra?'

'She's off doing something with my mum,' Mat replied. He found himself looking at her differently, looking for signs of her 'avatar' status. How could you tell?

Jones coughed for attention. 'You, milady, have some floors to sweep, I believe? Mat, you need that poultice changed.' Jones bullied them apart, muttering to Mat: 'You're not going to make this easy on yourself, are you?'

Beneath the strapping, Mat's ribs were yellow and purple, as if a huge bunch of violets were flowering beneath his skin. Jones looked pleased, saying that the poultice had accelerated the healing process, and he set about boiling up another one.

After the new poultice was bound on, warm and damp against his skin, Mat went out the back to see what Hine was doing. He heard her singing a pop song as she churned the laundry in soapy water. 'Crappy old pile of junk,' she muttered, looking up at Mat. 'It's like being on an old-time movie set. I can't wait to get back to dishwashers and television.' She eyed Mat up. 'I guess Jones must've told you about me?'

'A little,' he replied, not sure what she meant.

She leant against the door. 'I ran away from home, cos my stepfather … well, anyway, I ended up living with Evan … Now I'm running away from him, too. So, I didn't really get to be a teenager — not like you,' Hine told him, her tones slightly resentful. 'All the people I know are like me. Runaways and from broken homes, life in the shit lane. Never had money, left school young. I don't know much about anything, really, 'cept being kicked around.' Her voice almost cracked, but her eyes were dry and watching him. 'I think you're really sweet,' she said. 'But you're just a kid, really. I like you, but we ain't even from the same planet.'

You don't cut corners, do you? 'Sure. That's cool,' he replied as nonchalantly as he could. He told himself he already knew all this. He just wished it wasn't so, because when she forgot about being a tough gang girl, she was really nice. 'You should stay here with Jones. He won't hit on you, and he'll look after you. No-one can reach you here.'

She gave a small, bitter laugh. 'I can't stay in this backwater. I mean, Jones is nice an' all, but I'm a city girl. I gotta have people round. I'd go nuts here.'

'But there's Taupo — I mean, the Taupo here in Aotearoa. Taupo-nui-a-Tia. Soldiers come through, and the local tribe. And … well, I'll be round every few months.'

She shook her head. 'I don't wanna live in a bloody pa, or settler village. I want movies and TV an' stuff. I gotta learn some skills, get a job.' She looked about her. 'This is like that

Neverland place. You can visit, but you can't live here. Well, I can't.'

'But here is the only place where you can learn this.' Mat held up his hand. It was an impulse, and he wasn't sure it was a good one. He had become suddenly worried at never seeing her again. Or maybe he just wanted to impress her. He let a small tongue of fire burst from his palm, a pale red-yellow tongue that hovered above his hand, warm but not burning.

She gasped and backed away.

'You want to learn how to do this?' he asked her. 'Maybe you could, like me. This is the only place I know where you can learn how.'

Her mouth was wide as her eyes as she backed out the door, then turned and fled.

Oh, hell …

Finally, Jones came out. He sat down beside Mat, and ruffled God's fur. 'Maybe you want to stay away for a couple of days, lad. She's a bit "freaked out" or so she says.'

'I'm sorry. That was really dumb.'

Jones pursed his lips. 'Aye, it was, boyo. She's scared, and dealing with too much at once. Abusive boyfriends and leaving home are no picnic. Alternate realities, demon possessions and boys who can conjure fire — well, that's way too far. She's resilient but she needs rest, or she's going to go backwards fast and we'll be dealing with a nervous breakdown. So, let's just tread carefully, okay?'

Mat put his head in his hands. 'But she's one of us! She has to stay!'

'No, she doesn't *have* to do anything. And avatars are not Adepts — there is no saying what she can and can't do! She might have the potential, if trained. Or not. Some do, some don't. I'm just going to listen a lot, talk some, and then give her some choices.'

Mat exhaled guiltily. 'Sorry. I hope I haven't messed things up too much.'

'Remember what we said before, Mat: she's not for you. I know you want to meet the perfect girl, like any teen. Be patient! Learn from the Lena experience! The universe provides, if you give it time.'

They walked back through the house, and out the front door. As he was going, Hine slipped through the door, red-eyed and fragile-looking. 'See ya,' she said, and put her arms around his shoulders, pressing her cheek to his. 'See you in a few days.'

He hugged her back, then reluctantly disentangled himself. He backed away, his eyes only on her.

Suddenly he was flailing for balance as he tipped off the veranda, landing on his backside in the long grass. The two goats peered in bemusement, while Hine giggled, then bent over and roared. Jones joined in, with a burst of throaty guffaws. Mat tried to be cross and failed, and soon all three of them were laughing so loud the clearing echoed. The strapping about his ribs hurt, and he was reduced to clutching his sides in pain.

Eventually he clambered to his feet, and bowed. 'Thank you; you've been a wonderful audience. Good night, and good luck!' He bowed again, and walked away, feeling both foolish and good at once.

Roadhawks

Tuesday afternoon

Evan Tomoana,' said the big man opposite him on the bench, his deep resonant tones rumbling from a wide belly, muscle turning to fat. 'Or "Parukau" if you prefer, although I remember your mother as white, and I never knew your father at all.' He sipped his beer, watching Parukau carefully. 'Tell me why I should listen to you. You ain't a patched member. You're nobody to us.'

Parukau leant closer, nibbling battered fish and sipping a beer. To all the world, it could have been a meeting of friends, just another gathering in a back yard in Taupo, enjoying some late afternoon sunshine after the overnight rain, a gentle northerly stirring the trees and breathing warmer air over the volcanic plateau. There were fish and chips laid out, and beers aplenty. They were behind a tidy four-bedroom house in west Taupo, Acacia Bay, amidst the holiday homes of the wealthy. The setting was private and unpretentious, with children's play equipment scattered about the lawn. But the undercurrents of threat were tangible.

The night before, the cops had come past, claiming Hine had vanished. Parukau couldn't trace her, even using scrying spells. He was beginning to feel perturbed. But he had pushed ahead, setting up this meeting to gain extra hands. Ronnie and Brutal and Deano were eating greasies at another table, watched by seven rough-looking men in filthy black leathers with *Roadhawks Taupo* emblazoned on the back, and a hawk head wearing a Roman legionary helmet.

The Roadhawks were one of the motorcycle gangs, modelled on the American biker gangs, that had proliferated in the 'sixties. The Roadhawks only rode Nortons. Its membership included Pakeha, Maori, Pacific Islanders and Asians, and was notoriously criminal. Given the smallness of New Zealand, they could never aspire to the sheer size and aura of overseas equivalents like the American Hells Angels. They were only minor players, but players nevertheless. The Roadhawks were notorious for rumours that escalating levels of petty and violent crime culminating in rape were required of gang prospects, although their leadership denied it.

The man opposite Parukau was one such leader. Robert Heke, like many of the early leaders, was pushing sixty now, with an affable smile and a rumbling laugh. Even with the gang patch on, he looked like somebody one could trust. But he had done time for killing a man — the charge had been reduced to manslaughter on appeal. He didn't have to break laws now: he had troops to get their hands dirty for him. He had a pretty young wife and a new child, to go with three children from earlier marriages. His second son, Arama, was among the seven Roadhawks present. Heke was the number two here in Taupo. He was considered 'old school' when it came to settling grievances.

Parukau waved a hand. 'I've got a plan; I need some muscle

to help me out. I know you've got muscle, and I thought that it could be mutually profitable.'

Heke half-smiled. 'A plan? From the likes of you? When is the last time you made a plan, Evan "Parukau" Tomoana? I hear your plans don't run much past dealing pot to tourists and playing with that pretty little woman of yours.' It was Heke's way of saying that he knew where Evan lived, how he made his money, and how to get at someone he cared about. Which might have worked if Heke had actually been talking to the real Evan Tomoana.

'Do you know the name "Ranginui Puarata"?' said Parukau quietly.

Heke's eyes widened, then quickly narrowed. He took a slow swallow of beer. 'I hear he's dead. What does the likes of you know about Puarata?'

Or, indeed, the likes of you, Heke? Puarata had dealt a whole way further up the food chain than Heke, and when Puarata recruited muscle, it wasn't from among undisciplined gang members. Puarata went for ex-army, and got fighters a whole lot scarier than anyone Heke had, however tough they walked and talked. Parukau kept his face expressionless, though. 'They say he was rich, and that his old inner circle are fighting among themselves to claim it all. A secret war. Have you heard of Sebastian Venn?'

Heke frowned. 'Of course. But Venn is nothing to do with us. The Hawks don't deal with Puarata, or Venn, or any of that organization. What has this is to do with you, Tomoana? All you've told me is that you know names that it isn't good to know.'

'Sunday night, I got some cell time with an old man, a

geezer who'd hiked in from the Ureweras. He was pretty sick, and died in the cell after we talked. He told me that he'd broken into Venn's HQ at Waikaremoana, and learned where old Puarata kept his secret stash. Gold, art, antiques, money ... anything you can think of.'

'He told you that? Why would he talk to you?'

Parukau shrugged. 'I think his mind was going. He thought I was someone else. I just played along, teased it out of him. Wasn't hard. An' then he died.' He chuckled.

Heke looked unimpressed. 'So where is it? What's it worth? And why come to me?'

Parukau feigned hesitation, then finally said. 'Well, it's in Rotorua. Old guy reckoned it was worth more than twenty million.' He took another sip of beer. 'We need muscle because the old guy says Puarata has men safeguarding it; men loyal to him and not to Venn or any of his other old lieutenants.'

Heke raised an eyebrow, seemingly interested now. 'Still loyal even though the old man is dead?'

'The old guy reckoned these boys were hanging tough, hiding out until a winner emerges. That day could be soon. Venn has sewn things up in the bush, pretty much. Just one rival to stomp out, I've heard.'

Heke licked his lips. 'The Kyle woman,' he murmured.

Not so ignorant of all this after all, are you, Heke? Parukau shrugged. 'I need men to storm the place, before they throw in their lot with Venn and the opportunity is lost.'

Heke leant back and drained his can, waved a hand, and waited until another was opened and put in his hand. He was silent for a long time, stroking an old Rottweiler that lay at his feet, its throat and flanks scarred. The veteran of many a pit fight, Parukau guessed. A lot like its owner.

Finally, Heke spoke. 'We never liked Puarata's outfit, but they don' cross our path, so we jus' live and let live.' He spat. 'They're a weird bunch — too much superstition and "Godfather" crap. We got their number.'

Parukau could barely keep the derisive smile off his face. *'Got their number'? You'd have kissed Puarata's tattooed arse if he'd come calling.* Keeping from laughing out loud took an effort.

'We don't need no small-timer coming to us like we're some sort of hired security firm for you to hide behind,' Heke went on. 'So, I'm going to give you my sort of deal, *Tomoana*. You can tell me where this treasure is, and then walk out of here with your balls still in your scrotum. Then, if and when we find anything, we will give you a reward for services. That's the deal. Don't waste your time bargaining, because I don't bargain.' Heke didn't look like anyone's kindly dad any more.

Parukau met his eye. *Heke, you bag of blubber. You think you can intimidate me, who has lived for centuries and learned at the elbow of Puarata himself?* He kept his voice level and his face neutral. 'I thought you'd say that, Robert. I ain't stupid. But when you see what I've got to show you, you'll want to keep me in on the deal, and reach a better split.'

Heke belched contemptuously. 'Will I? I told you: I don't bargain, Tomoana.'

Parukau ostentatiously looked about them. 'Do you have somewhere more private we can talk?'

Heke looked at him. They had been patted down and disarmed on arrival. He shrugged, and gestured to the most muscular of the patched men standing around the garden, who happened to be his son. 'Arama, come with us.' Arama Heke drained his beer and stalked over.

'Looks like his father,' observed Parukau. He did — a younger, slimmer version, bred for violence, an athlete of mayhem.

Heke slapped his son on the back. 'Arama's twice the size of your man "Boo-boo" or whatever you call him.' He said it loud enough for them all to hear, and the Roadhawks boys laughed while Brutal scowled into his beer.

Heke led them through the garage to a windowless room with a stained and empty pool table in the middle, and a beer fridge in the corner. Old sofas lined the walls. Heke shut the door behind them, and locked it. Arama grinned at Parukau as he picked up a broken pool cue. Holding the narrow shaft, he slapped the heavy metal-ringed handle into his palm meatily.

Subtle, thought Parukau. He turned and looked at Heke across the table. 'Want a game?' he asked drily.

Heke shook his head, placed both hands on the table and leant forward, whilst Arama circled behind Parukau. 'I'm through with games, Tomoana. Tell me where this place is or we'll smash you into pulp.'

Parukau grinned at him, and felt the serpent within him rise. He met Heke's eyes. The man was confident, complacently secure, and though his will was strong, he was an innocent in the way the world really was. The world he lived in had such *ordinary* nightmares. He raised a hand, and reached out with the shadows that dwelt within.

To Heke it seemed that Parukau's whole form wavered, like a stone dropped in a pool, and then his eyes went black. The ceiling lights flickered, and then blew with a loud crack and the stink of burnt dust. The room was plunged into darkness.

'Arama!' he yelled, and he heard his son begin to reply then gasp. Something heavy smashed into the pool table, once, twice, like meat slapping the counter at a butcher's shop. Someone slithered to the floor heavily.

The room fell silent. Impossibly, the broken light bulbs flared; for a second. Parukau was looking at him across the table. Then darkness. Then they flashed on, and Parukau was crawling across the table. Then the image was gone again, but not before it was burned on his retina. He backed away, mouth opening to scream.

Hands clamped his skull, and an unseen mouth closed over his. He shrieked into it, trying to pull away, a reflex of terror and disgust, but it was as if he were caught in a vice, and then something slithered inside his throat. He fell to the floor, choking.

The lights came on. Parukau stood over him, a tender look on his face. From his mouth a thin stream of smoky shadow seemed to run down to his own mouth. He froze, beyond panic, rigid in terror as the being above him smirked, and bent over him. 'Hello, Robert. What are you doing down there? Aren't you well? Have you caught something perhaps? Or perhaps something has caught you!' He laughed vilely. 'Do you know the old saying *"There are more things in heaven and earth, Horatio, than are dreamt of in your philosophy."* It's Shakespeare, you know. Asher Grieve used to like to say it — do you know *that* name, Robert?'

Heke shook and lost control of his bladder. The stink of hot urine filled the room. Parukau sniggered, and spoke again, but this time his mouth didn't move and the words spoke directly into the Roadhawks' boss's mind.

'The rules have changed, Robert. Parukau has returned! I'm going to take everything Puarata once had, and I am going to destroy Venn and Kyle and whoever else stands in my way. And then I'm going to turn on the gangs, and those that do not pledge to me will be *flayed*. Do you hear me?'

Heke nodded mutely. He glimpsed Arama, lying senseless but still breathing. He could not remember feeling such terror ever before.

'Yes, I'm speaking into your head, Robert. I can get there whenever I want to. So you think that Puarata was all just superstition and secrecy, do you? Wrong! His power was real and I spent six hundred years at his side. I am the heir to his kingdom. Only those that are with me will be spared.'

He smiled, and offered his hand to the fallen man, palm down. He spoke naturally this time. 'Pledge yourself to me, Heke. And believe me, I *will* know if you are insincere. That will not go well for you, your son or your wife. Or your pretty little daughter.' He held out his hand, where a silver death-head ring gleamed dully. 'Kiss it, Robert.'

The big man did so, and only then did Parukau swallow that thread of darkness. He watched the older man shudder as he was released.

'You are mine now, Robert.'

Deano drove them home after Heke had been given his orders. He would lay hands on guns and ammunition, and the whole chapter would muster. Although before they could go to Rotorua, they needed to find Hine Horatai.

'Heke looked like he'd seen a ghost, eh. Whitest brownie I've ever seen,' chortled Brutal. 'Can't believe they're gonna follow your orders, boss,' he added. 'I thought they'd beat the crap out of us.'

Parukau just smiled. 'You gotta know the right strings to pull, Brutal. That's why I am the boss, and that is why we're going to come out of the next few days very rich.' He had told them a little of what was going on, essentially the same story he had spun to Heke. They laughed and joked as they wound their way through town, but his mind was elsewhere. *Where are you, Hine Horatai? When I find you, you'll regret running away. I want you even more than Evan Tomoana did. How are you hiding from me?*

He sat up suddenly. And slowly smiled.

Of course! I know where you are, you little bitch!

It was the only place that made sense, here in Taupo.

Aethlyn Jones's house.

Patupaiarehe

Donna Kyle stared from her hotel balcony, swirling a cognac. The evening was chill but she scarcely felt it, or the sweet, strong spirit. She was numb. Everything seemed grey, as if she was going colour-blind. It was a sensation both physical and spiritual. Her skin didn't register pain or pleasure the way it used to. Emotions that should have been intense were dull and distant. All that kept her going was the refusal to lose, to succumb to Venn or Bryce or the others. Doubts and fears gnawed at her like maggots.

Father … Asher Grieve, back from the graveyard of her memories. The thought of seeing him in the flesh petrified her, unless it was to drive a knife through his poisonous heart. And yet … did he really hold the key to Te Iho? Could she afford to turn her back on him?

She blinked those thoughts away. Lake Taupo was darkened now to a rusted metallic sheen as the sun set. The volcanoes were hidden in cumulus gathered in the south, brooding and ominous. It would be bleak outside tonight, and bitterly cold. She tossed off the cognac in one swallow, waited for the alcohol to hit her, but felt nothing. None of the hotel staff saw her leave in her grey Toyota 4WD. The streets were almost empty, the houses were dark hulks with curtains faintly aglow. When she left the city limits, the darkness felt like a cave.

It took her thirty minutes driving through stony back roads to reach the foot of Mount Tauhara, where she parked the Toyota in a place Puarata had shown her, between two old totara, their roots deep in both worlds. Tauhara leant over her like a watchful giant. A half-moon peered through the shredded ghosts of clouds, and half-lit the clearing. She unlocked a shrouded cage that sat on the passenger seat, and pulled out a young tabby cat. It thrashed about, but her grip never flinched as she carried it into the middle of the clearing, knife in her hand.

She could have chanted some 'magical' gibberish, but it would have been just ceremony and nonsense, a fancy way of saying: 'Here I am, look at me.' She had no stomach for that tonight, just wanted to get it over with. She raised the knife, and slashed. For an instant, she wanted to swallow the hot fluid. Blood was what she dreamt of now, ever since that life-saving fluid Puarata had fed her. But the thought turned her stomach, and worse, it would insult those she summoned.

She lowered the dying cat to the ground and backed towards her vehicle, still holding the knife. Shadows seemed to melt together and swim across the clearing. There were four of them, two male and two female. Pale-skinned, wild hair coloured like rust, eyes feral. They were clad in a motley collection of Maori and colonial attire. Their movements were feverish and jerky. The tallest male had a sword at his belt, a medieval broadsword. He looked at her warily as he lifted the cat to his mouth. He made a slurping noise as he drank, blood spilling down his chin. One of the women licked his face clean, then fed second. The other two waited hungrily, and took their turns, while the first two, their faces slowly turning ruddy, regarded Donna watchfully.

They were patupaiarehe, vampiric fairy creatures from the darkest places of Aotearoa. Tauhara was known for them. They usually lurked on the fringes of isolated settlements, content to steal babies or cattle from the denizens of Aotearoa. Many were harmless, but these ones weren't. She knew their names, imparted by Puarata, and she named them now, secret words that bound them to her will. They hated that. She felt the names twist like rope about their souls. She held up her hand, and from it four silvery cords now extended, one each to the centre of their chests. She yanked the cords and watched them flinch, their hackles rising, eyes glittering with malice.

'Why didn't you drink, lady?' the chief male called her, trying to break her composure. He had tattoos, but they were Celtic ones that writhed weirdly across his face. He spoke English, with an Irish accent. All their true names were European, oddly. 'We know you wanted to. We could feel your hunger.'

The thin-faced lady at his feet held out the cat to her. 'There is still a little wine left, lady. A few dregs at the bottom of the flask,' she giggled.

'Nearly one of us, you are,' observed the lesser male, a scarecrow with his skinny limbs hunched like a roosting bird. 'Your blood is tainted, like ours.'

Only the fourth didn't taunt her. A quiet one, that looked barely into puberty. She stood on the verge of flight, but tethered by the cord wrapped around her heart. Donna drew herself up. 'Silence! I command you now. You will not question my authority.'

'Oh, your authority is undoubted, Princess,' sneered the chief male wearily. 'We are your humblest servants. You have our names, you have bound us.' He reached up and tugged gently on the half-visible cord of light that ran like a leash from his heart to her hand. His smile was ironic. 'All I wanted was to be free. I crossed the globe hundreds of years ago, before it was even known that it was a globe, to escape witches like you. Arcane slave-keepers, and murderous priests. But here at the end of the world, there is nowhere else to run. So I shall be a slave after all.'

He bent his knee with a haughty toss of the head. The other three mimicked his movements. The four cords in her hand felt oily and untrustworthy, like vipers, with fanged heads that could twist and lunge in her grasp. But short of binding a taniwha to her will, there were no better servants for the conflict to come. She needed them.

'I will give you use-names, as I cannot use your true names openly. You, I will call "Stone",' she told the leader. He nodded disinterestedly as he fondled the hilt of his broadsword.

'You, the hunched male, you are "Heron".' The scarecrow patupaiarehe nodded casually.

'Give me a pretty name, lady,' said the elder female, the one at Stone's feet. '"Isabella", perhaps?'

Donna studied the girl, her ribs showing beneath her tiny breasts, her teeth glittering, and her lips vivid. 'You are "Thorn",' she replied spitefully. The skinny girl pouted, muttering under her breath.

The last female had hung back a little, had fed last and only briefly. Clearly she was the lowest in the nest. She looked barely fifteen, and reminded Donna suddenly of herself, before Asher came for her. 'You, the quiet one, what is your preference?'

'Call her "Sow Face" or "Cow Breath",' suggested Thorn with a cold snicker. 'She is our servant. She licks our feet to cleanse us after we journey. She can lick yours, too, if you like,' she added with a cold titter. 'She has no pride left. We took it away from her.'

'Shut up, Thorn.' Donna stared down at the skinny being briefly and then returned her gaze to the dark-haired girl. Her hands were clasped as if in prayer, her head bowed. She still seemed to cling to some kind of innocence, despite her state. She found herself moved unexpectedly. 'I will call you "Rose",' she said with a faint softness in her voice that she instantly regretted. *Why that name?* The other three looked at each other conspiratorially.

She reasserted control, jerking the silver heart-cords. 'These are my commands. Stone, you will go to Rotorua, to the tipua goblins that haunt the northern shores, and tell them that Puarata's heir commands their obedience. I will join you there in two or three days. Be discreet, and do not kill unless assailed.'

Stone bowed deeply. 'As you command, Princess,' he growled, his voice laden with resentment.

'And you, Thorn, go to the tipua chief to the west of Taupo and demand a war-party be sent here to serve me. I shall expect its arrival tomorrow, ready to fight.'

Thorn spat blood. 'The tipua are worms.'

'Then you should get on famously. Both of you, go! And do not forget who holds your souls.' She twisted the cords in her hand, sending a lash of pain before releasing them. 'Go! Go and do not tarry.'

Stone and Thorn fled into the night. She turned to the remaining two patupaiarehe. 'Heron, you will be my eyes and ears here in Taupo. I have sensed presences, people of power. Identify them for me. Move unseen. Observe their actions. Report to me before dawn. Understood?'

Heron cowered obsequiously. 'I hear and obey, O Princess. Do not hurt me. I am your servant, loyal and true.' He lifted, and soared away before she changed her mind.

Rose stood watching her, huddled in her cloak and shivering. When she turned towards her, the girl bowed her head, awaiting the lash. She looked like an abuse victim. Donna fought a pang of kinship. 'Come, Rose.' She turned and pulled her along by her silvery half-seen leash. 'You will serve and guard me. You will do as I say, nothing more or less. Do I need to whip you also, to teach you your place?'

'No, mistress,' the girl breathed. 'I already understand my place.' She looked at Donna sideways through a curtain of tangled hair. Up close she smelt filthy, of rotting leaves and fetid mud, and her breath was foul with blood-taint.

'Then come with me.' She took her to the Toyota and showed her how to get in, then drove back to the hotel. Rose was terrified of the great mechanical monster in whose belly she sat. She clung to the seat initially, then she slowly sank to the floor and huddled, whimpering. Donna had chosen this hotel because she could come and go without being observed, and was glad of this as she led the girl inside. The young patupaiarehe whimpered in terror as the lift ascended.

Inside her rooms, Donna led the girl immediately to the bathroom, and showed her the shower and toilet. 'If you are going to be of use to me, then you must be clean. You can't

127

be seen as you are.' She held up a bar of soap. 'Do you know what this is?'

Rose's face lit up. 'Soap,' she said in wonderment. 'It is soap!' She clutched it to herself girlishly. Donna felt another strange emotion, an almost motherly pang that infuriated and frightened her. She hastily showed Rose the toothpaste and toothbrush and how to use them, and what to do with shampoo, conditioner and mouthwash. What the hairdryer was for. Rose took it all in like a child in her favourite class at school. Her mouth hung open and her eyes were wet with unshed tears. 'I do want to be clean again,' she whispered, her face glowing. 'Like I used to be.'

Donna half-turned away, caught her own eye in the mirror, thinking, *I used to be clean, too.*

She watched the patupaiarehe pull off her stinking cloak and loin cloth, her lean body all flat planes and jutting bones. She was unsettling to watch, alternately timid and bold, old and young, wild yet vulnerable. Donna left her, returning to the balcony with another cognac, and lit a cigarette. The night air was cold and stars glittered, callous as fairy eyes in the ebony sky.

It seemed clear now: Puarata had fed her patupaiarehe blood to speed her healing, careless of the long-term effects. Another sign of how little he had truly cared for her. What is it doing to me? *Colonizing me, that's what* … Tiny particles of alien matter taking her over. She could feel it, the urges, the new strengths and weaknesses. She was changing, inexorably. Unless she could find a path through this maze, she would slowly degenerate into one of these half-feral beings.

Her hand trembled and ash spilled from her cigarette, a

tiny comet plunging into the darkness below. She shook her head and went back inside, her legs hollow, her belly strained with tension. The shower pumped steam through the bathroom door, and she heard Rose singing softly as she washed. She sounded like a child. Then it went quiet, and she smelt blood again.

She opened the bathroom door. Rose was kneeling on the floor, crooning softly, her back to her, black wet hair cascading down her back. The patupaiarehe's song faltered, and her face turned upward. Her skin was clean and white. The window was open, and the girl held a pigeon in her hands, bloodied and torn. Feathers and blood clung to her chin. Her violet eyes widened slightly, and then she pulled back her wet hair shyly, and offered her throat. For a second an abyss opened at Donna's feet, and she saw herself bite, saw herself surrender to the thirst that would damn her. Vertigo seized her and she staggered away, slammed the bathroom door and threw herself onto the bed, trying not to vomit.

I will never become like that.

After minutes or hours or days or years, she recovered herself. Rose was on the floor beside the bed, staring at her curiously. There was a dark shape perched on the railing: Heron. She slid the glass door open and stepped outside. Her breath steamed about her like a cloud, something noticeably missing from the air about Heron's face.

'Did Rose please you, O Glorious Princess?' he smirked in a low voice.

'Shut up and report, before I rip your heart out.'

He bobbed his head. 'To hear is to obey, Gracious Princess. I have flown above the city, and sniffed the fragrant air. There

129

are several people of power here. Foremost, a young man, asleep in his bed, troubled by dreams. His mind is half-trained, easily read. Matiu Douglas, he is called.'

She smiled.

Heron continued. 'There is a dangerous old man walking the lakeshore, whom I feared to go near. Also two old women, sisters in a big house, with feet in both worlds. A fortune-teller asleep in the fairground caravans. But most interesting was a skinhead thug, who called himself by an old name ... *Parukau*.'

She felt a thrill of fear. She knew the name. *Isn't he dead?*

Heron twisted his neck, and looked at her. 'Have I done well, Princess? Have I earned a reward?' He licked his lips hungrily.

She pulled on the cord about his heart. He jerked and tumbled at her feet. She twisted and yanked while he shrieked silently in agony. 'You will obey me for no reward but the gift of continued life!' she hissed. 'Go, watch this Parukau, and report again at dawn. We will strike him tomorrow night.'

When the patupaiarehe was gone she sat thinking. The old man ... she remembered that the Welshman Aethlyn Jones dwelt here. He had been part of that debacle at Waikaremoana. There were scores to settle. She knew the two sisters, weak talents and meddlers, not to be trusted. The fortune-teller could be anyone.

And as for Matiu Douglas ... Jones's protégé ... her hand went to the scar on her face.

Revenge was overdue.

Flintlocks and blades

Wednesday

Hine woke. She had been dreaming of Evan and felt hot beneath her blanket even though the air was cold. The sofa was too short and her neck was sore. Godfrey was pressed against her, and light crept under the curtains. She could hear Jones in the kitchen, and could smell coffee, but she needed more time alone, to think.

Was that demon-thing still inside Evan? Was he looking for her? The heat drained from her body in a rush. She shivered, pushed Godfrey off the sofa and sat up, trembling. Thinking didn't seem such a good idea all of a sudden. Godfrey gave her a reproachful look, and walked out with his head in the air.

She talked with Jones again over breakfast, and all through the day. He walked her a little along the lake to better view the town, but he wouldn't take her in. 'It is best no-one knows you are here,' Jones told her. 'Gossip spreads, you know, even in small mythical towns.'

Well, that sounded about right: gossip was universal. It surprised her how much she could just accept all this. It was as if she had always known this place existed, and had just been waiting to find it. She had to also admit that what she had seen Mat do, making fire dance in his hands, was holding her here. Could she really do that, too? Or shift between worlds as he could? If she could learn that, well that was an education worth having! No maths and history and boring shit! To learn magic, and be able to protect herself! That was worth knowing! That was worth living like a hermit for a while. That was worth any sacrifice.

By dusk, when they sat smoking on the back porch, they had reached an accord. When Jones had made sure the Evan-thing was gone, he would help her find a place to live nearby, in the real world. But she would come here every day, and he would teach her: stuff she had need to know to get by, like how to manage money and do numbers and stuff. And maybe, if she had the aptitude, he would teach her *magic*. Make her into a witch, a good witch, so she could look after herself and her whanau. It was a good deal.

'But you'll need to make some sacrifices,' he told her.

'Sure, whatever,' she agreed casually, her head swimming with possibilities.

'No smokes, no drink. No coffee. No drugs. No mentioning me to anyone. No meat would be preferable. And no sick days.'

'You hypocritical old bastard,' she told him. 'Look at you, you smoke that ghastly relic of a pipe, you have a whisky still in the shed, you drink coffee like it's ya mother's milk, and don't think I can't recognize marijuana in your garden either!'

Jones smiled agreeably. 'Guilty on all counts, lass. And you didn't even mention Widow Calder down the road. But it's not me we're talkin' about. It's all about you, lass, and learning during your *formative* years. I've been through all that — it isn't important now: I'm fully formed. You still have to become *yourself*.' He jabbed the pipe handle at her. 'T'will do you good, some clean living for a change.'

'Clean living!' She swore at him, passionately, called him nine kinds of bastard, and he responded in kind, in a totally genial manner that nevertheless wound her up. It turned into a profanities competition, which became more inventive and hilarious as the evening progressed. The sun fell below the tree line, and shadows stalked towards them. The air cooled, and somewhere a morepork hooted.

She suddenly shivered for no reason. Godfrey woke, and sniffed the air. He growled a little.

Jones looked down at him. 'Aye. Let's go in,' he said.

Hine looked at him with sudden concern. 'What is it?'

'Just a smell in the air, lass. Best we're inside.'

'I thought we were safe here?' she asked.

'No more than half a dozen people in Aotearoa could find this place without me wanting them to,' Jones replied. He opened the door for her. Godfrey slunk off into the night. 'God'll have a look round, don't you worry.' She noticed he kept that heavy walking stick close by, and felt a queasy sense of foreboding, the bush suddenly a gloomy and grim place. They seemed awfully alone. But the cheerful lamp in the kitchen drove the shadows away, and although she jumped when there was a scratch at the back door, it was only Godfrey wanting to come in. He yapped a couple of times, then went to the empty food bowl, which he stared at in apparent disgust.

'Don't worry, Godfrey, dinner soon,' she told the turehu.

'What does he look like in his real form?' she asked Jones.

'Like a goblin,' the Welshman answered, stirring some stew. 'Ugly little bugger.'

Godfrey growled at him, but Hine swore that he winked as he did so.

They had just sat down to eat when suddenly Godfrey began to bark furiously, and then the cottage shook as something smashed against the front door.

Hine screamed as Jones leapt to his feet, snatching up the walking stick, and ran to his room. He emerged a couple of seconds later, armed to the teeth. A big sword was in his fist, and he thrust an old pistol, like something from a pirate movie, into his belt before hefting another.

The house shook again.

'Take this!' shouted Jones, thrusting a long, sharp kitchen knife into her hands. She stared at him, then cried out as a dark face pressed against the kitchen window.

Mat had slept poorly, unable to get Hine's face out of his head. Finally he woke, well past dawn, when Mum battered on the door. 'Mat, are you awake? Have you done any study at all yet? Get yourself out of bed, and have some breakfast.'

He looked at the clock, and realized it was nearly midday. She's right, he acknowledged, and resigned himself to a day with his books. They went to Mum's school and she did some prep for next term, and he took his maths books. He couldn't get his head into it though, and hours passed without any new facts imprinting themselves on his memory.

Finally it was time to go. He had agreed to spend the

evening with Mum. 'I don't see why your friends should monopolize you,' she had remarked tartly when he had floated the idea of going round to Cass's place to play video games. They shopped for groceries and rented a DVD, something called *The Usual Suspects*, which Mum said had a cool ending. For once, he would rather have watched a romance, with a sultry dark-skinned lead actress, like Jessica Alba maybe. Someone who looked a little like Hine ...

'You're very quiet,' Mum remarked when they got home. 'What are you thinking about?'

He affected nonchalance. 'Oh, you know. Maths, exams, career ... you know.'

She smiled. 'Mmmm ... so, what's her name then?' She laughed when he blushed. 'Mat, you're a treat! You've been mooning all day, and it can only be a girl. Anyone I know?'

'No ... ah, yeah.'

'So there *is* one!' she leapt on his words triumphantly. 'Not this girl you were chatting up with the nasty boyfriend, I hope?' she said sharply.

'No! Okay, yes, her ... but I wasn't chatting her up!'

Mum frowned, looking somewhat put out. 'Well ... so, what's her name, then?'

'Hine.'

'Is she pretty? Where does she go to school?'

'Ummm ... yeah, I think, well, she's kinda left school.'

'Really? How old is she?'

'Eighteen, I think.'

Colleen frowned. 'Hmmm, well that's not so good. She should be getting the most out of her education. It's sad when a young person drops out of school early, and doesn't make the most of themselves. You take care, Matty. A girl like that mightn't be very suitable.'

Suitable? He felt a swell of annoyance. 'You don't even know her.'

'But I know lots of girls just like her, and I know you can do much better than a dropout,' retorted Mum.

'That's not fair! You know nothing about her!'

'Oh, Matty, hush. I was a teenager too, you know, and not so long ago. I'm not saying anything but "be careful". You don't even live here. What's the point of getting mixed up with a local? Especially with someone whose boyfriend beats people up! The police called today and said he got bail, so if you see him around, you're to call them.'

'Yeah, I know.' Right now, he wouldn't mind him showing up, makutu body-jumper or not. He felt cross and edgy.

Then the doorbell rang, and Mum answered the door. It was some friend of hers with orange spiky hair and black leathers on. She looked kinda Gothy, and said 'Hi' without introducing herself.

'We're just putting a movie on,' Colleen announced for the benefit of the newcomer.

'Sure.' The voice was vaguely familiar.

Mat was still simmering over Mum and what she had said about Hine. *What does she know, anyway?*

The movie was about halfway through and he was making no sense of it, which was apparently the point. Mum's friend was bugging him because she never said a word, flashed her teeth a lot, and seemed to be watching him out of the corner of her eye, while stroking her fishnets as if she had never worn them before.

Mum paused the movie. 'Shall we have a coffee?'

Mat sighed. 'Yeah. I'll get it,' he offered, before he was told to anyway. He stood up. 'What'll you have, Missus … um?' He realized he still hadn't been given a name for Mum's friend. He peered at her, and then several tumblers fell into place and the safe-box marked 'recognition' dropped open. 'CASS???'

'It took you long enough,' Cassandra told him tersely.

To say it had seemed like a good idea at the time wasn't really true: it had sounded naff. But Cass was so pleased to have the braces off, that it seemed a small thing. She was due a haircut anyway, and she was over the dreadlocks. Too stinky and people assumed it meant she liked reggae (ugh!). Besides, she liked to change her look regularly and keep people guessing. So she let Colleen's hairdresser cut them off, and somehow got talked into a spiky thing like Colleen had had in the 'eighties. After that, well, here she was in Colleen's old leathers that she had never thrown out, wearing make-up for the first time ever.

Colleen had looked almost tearful when she let her in the front door. 'Oh my!' she had said, putting a hand to her mouth, then tracing Cass's cheekbones with her fingers. 'You look so …'

Cassandra put a finger to her lips. She didn't want to know what she looked like, and this was beginning to feel like a silly game. She was only going with it because she liked Colleen.

When she was young, the doctors had told her parents she was ADHD and autistic, and her mum had left soon after. *Join the dots on that one*. Somehow it had gone round school, and she was The Freak from then on. So she had embraced it. Being Different had become who she was. Let others deal with it.

And now … Mat was staring at her like she was Exhibit A, having taken an hour to recognize her. She hated it. She felt like she was dressed up in lies. 'Get an eyeful, Mat, cos I'm wearing my own stuff for the rest of the hols.' She tapped the armrest impatiently. 'I'll have a cola.' She glanced at Colleen, who was studying them both. *Colleen wants Mat to like me, instead of that Hine. Too bad. He's a lost cause.*

Abruptly she stood up. 'Look, this is silly; I feel ridiculous. I'm going home. I'll bring you these clothes back tomorrow, Colleen!' She suddenly felt close to tears and she had no idea why.

'Cass, wait!' Mat blurted. She half-turned. Colleen looked upset, and was opening her mouth …

They all heard it. The dull but distinct sound of a window being forced at the back of the house.

Mat froze, and looked at his mother, then Cassandra. 'Ring the police,' he hissed above the movie soundtrack. Cassandra — *Jeez, she looked different!* — nodded curtly, reaching into a pocket, then she scowled and cursed softly.

'Not my jacket,' she hissed. She looked suddenly helpless. He looked at Mum.

'Mine is on the recharger in the kitchen,' Mum told him.

'I'll go out the back and check it out.' He slipped out of his chair, and peered down the hallway. All he could see was the open kitchen door. To the right, out of sight, was the bathroom and toilet. Something rattled in the bath, and he thought

138

immediately of the shampoo bottles on the window ledge above the bath. He slipped across the hallway and retrieved the taiaha from his bedroom. Mum came to the lounge door, chewing her lip, her knuckles white. Behind her, Cassandra was peering out a window. He wished she wouldn't: she was too visible and exposed.

He met Mum's eye, and nodded at the phone, which was on a shelf by the front door. She tiptoed towards it, while he went the other way, to the far end of the hallway where it turned a corner. Something smelt up here, like an animal, musky and earthy. A shadow moved in the kitchen. Had they left those windows open too? Behind him he could hear Mum begin to dial. The noise filled the silence.

Suddenly there was a deafening howl, and a dark shape erupted from the kitchen. As it came, the light stripped it of size. It was shorter than him, wiry and pale-skinned, a narrow hairless skull with a moko carved into its face like a mask. Its eyes were slitted amber, and triangular teeth flashed as it charged, flailing a sharp-edged bone patu. It was a tipua, a goblin of Aotearoa.

It clearly expected him to be paralysed by fright. He wasn't. Stepping in, he jabbed with the taiaha, slamming it past the patu and into the twisted little face, bracing his feet as it came. The wooden shaft smashed the creature's nose, shattering it in a splash of black-green blood. It arched its back as if shot, and fell backwards, but another sprang from the bathroom. Windows smashed on both sides of the house, and the glass panel on the front door cracked under a sudden blow. Mum screamed and he heard the receiver drop and hit the wall. In the lounge, he heard Cassandra swear as glass shattered.

He didn't take his eyes off the newcomer, but he was terrified at the sudden silence behind him. 'Mum?' She didn't reply as he backed down the hallway. The oncoming goblin kicked its fallen colleague aside, patu slicing the air. He parried, reversed the taiaha and thrust the handle at his foe, catching it in the throat. The sharpened tongue of the taiaha struck the tipua's throat and tore. It dropped, gurgling, spraying blood between its fingers. Mat spun, sensing movement on either side, dark shapes pouring into the lounge and his bedroom. 'Mum, the phone!' He retreated past both doors, putting himself between the goblins and his mother. But he couldn't be on both sides of her. And where was Cass?

The glass panel in the front door shattered as a fist punched a hole. There was no option: he spun, pushing against the wall, reaching inside himself. His mother stared as a narrow stream of fire poured from his fingers and burst about a pale arm that was reaching through the hole in the glass. Something female shrieked and the arm snatched back, charred.

'Mum — call the cops!' He saw her shake herself, and begin to dial again. Then he spun as wiry shapes poured through from the lounge, where a series of strange sounds suddenly broke out, like a giant aerosol discharging, and tipua shrieked angrily. *Cassandra! Where was she?* He met them head on, swung overhand and felt a satisfying crunch on the skull of a goblin. Another grabbed at his weapon, and he swatted the hand, shattering the fingers against the wall. He blocked another blow, and let fire pour along the blade of the taiaha and into the largest goblin so far, a gruesome creature with a scarred face; it staggered away clutching its face. He felt a wave of dizziness from the exertion of magic. That amount of fire was far beyond what he had practised. Another goblin pushed through and swung. Its blow was fortunately obvious, and Mat blocked and jabbed, swiping it across the temple. It fell, fading into thin air as it did so. The remainder of the goblins scuttled backwards, eyeing him malevolently.

His mother shouted down the phone. 'WE'RE BEING ATTACKED! GET SOMEONE HERE!!!' Then she dropped the phone as a thin blackened arm reached through the broken door again, and twisted the handle. Mat felt a wave of dizziness as he tried to summon more flame, feeling the sudden backlash of the energy he had already expended. He couldn't do too much more of that.

'Cassandra?' he called despairingly. No reply came. His throat tightened.

The door opened, and a different type of creature stepped into the light. It was female, clad only in a thin, dirty shift. Her face was half-lost in the thick red hair that fell to her waist. His mother edged back down the wall. 'Matty,' she gasped, 'Matty, watch out.'

'Yes, watch out, Matty,' smirked the newcomer, pulling the hair from her face, like opening a curtain. Her face was thin and pointed, like an albino rat. 'I've come to get you.' Her teeth were fanged like a snake.

He stepped between her and his mother, and set his jaw. 'Patupaiarehe: get out before I burn you up!'

'Oooo, big scary boy,' the patupaiarehe giggled. 'My mistress, Donna Kyle, sends her final respects. She says I can eat you, and your mother, too.'

He shouted defiantly, and slammed the blade of the taiaha at her face. Her hand blurred and caught the weapon, while her other hand smacked across his face, throwing him against the wall. He staggered, wrenched the taiaha from her grip, and backed away. Beside him, Mum clutched the wall, staring in mute horror. Behind him, more tipua growled. They were trapped, and doomed unless he did something fast. He threw everything into another burst of fire, but the patupaiarehe somehow half-faded, as if moving partially to Aotearoa, and it washed through her harmlessly. He reeled, almost utterly spent.

'Is that all you've got, boy?' she taunted, stalking forward.

Her name is Shonagh, Ngatoro murmured into his mind. *Bind her!*

I don't know how! But he tried. 'Shonagh, stop!' he shouted, hefting his weapon again.

For just an instant, she froze, her eyes suddenly afraid. He slammed the tongue of the taiaha at her, and it punched into her chest. He felt more than heard her shriek as the wood pierced flesh, and then the creature flew backwards, smashing against the inside of the door. *Got you!*

Something exploded behind his left shoulder, an arc of pain as an edged patu cut through cloth and flesh. He heard himself cry out, and then his mother shattered a vase over the skull of the tipua who had hit him. It faded as it fell, glassy-eyed. Mum looked around for another weapon. He snatched the patu from the grasp of the fading goblin, and put it in her hand, then turned back to the patupaiarehe at the front door. Shonagh had her back to the door, and a look of shock on her face. Her hand was pressed to a wound below her left breast, thin red fluid on her hands and chest.

'You evil little boy,' she hissed. 'Look what you've done!'

He reversed the taiaha again, and readied himself. 'Get out, *Shonagh!* Get out or I'll do it again. Only I'll split your heart next time.' He advanced slowly down the hallway, praying the thing would run, because his last burst of fire had just about done for him.

She hissed and raised her talons.

She's going to come straight through me ...

Sirens blared in the distance, filling him with sudden hope. 'Get out, Shonagh!'

Almost involuntarily, she half-turned away. He swung at her skull, an all-or-nothing blow that would have had Jones cursing him, because if he missed he would be off balance and dead meat. But before the weapon struck, there was a sucking sensation. Shonagh exploded backwards through the door, howling dismally as she went, a banshee wail that echoed in the suddenly empty hallway. He overbalanced and fell against the wall, barely keeping his footing.

He turned tiredly, but the goblins were fading, slipping back into Aotearoa, hissing disappointedly. He stared dazedly into the silence, and then abruptly staggered into the lounge. 'Cass! Cass?'

Every window was broken, the curtains half-torn and flapping in the breeze. The corner suite was covered in white foam. Everything else was utterly still. 'Cass!'

A red-topped head poked up from behind the corner arm-chair. ''S okay. I'm here.'

He ran to her, staring at four parallel slashes on her right arm. 'What happened?'

She shrugged, although her face was white. 'When they came through I grabbed the fire extinguisher, and I kept

143

squirting any that came near me. I had to bash a couple with the canister, too. Then they ran away.' She panted, and forced a grin. 'Are you and Colleen okay?'

'Yeah.' He threw his arms round her bony frame and squeezed. 'I thought when I couldn't hear you that ...' He swallowed, and released her. She seemed suddenly fragile and precious.

Mum came in, looking pale and furious. 'Little buggers,' she kept muttering, her hands shaking as she sat down heavily, all the vigour going out of her at once. 'That was my best vase,' she whimpered, as if that were the worst thing that had happened.

She's in shock. Mat wrapped his arms round her.

By the time the police burst in, the tipua were long gone. The thin blood of the patupaiarehe woman had soaked in like a tea stain, and the blood of the goblins had faded to smears of ash. The violence done to the house remained, but the attackers were gone without trace. The police milled about, with looks of bafflement, staring at the burn marks on the inside of the door in confusion. Neighbours had heard violence, seen shapes moving. 'Was it Evan Tomoana?' a policewoman asked.

Mat shrugged as nonchalantly as he could. 'Maybe.' He glanced anxiously at his mother.

For a moment he thought she would tell the truth. She seemed to waver, then met his eyes and swallowed, before turning back to the cops. 'It was a gang of kids, with hoods and balaclavas,' she told the policewoman. 'We'll go to my friend Sue's place. Can someone guard the house, please?' Security guards were called while they packed bags. Mum talked to Sue on the phone, and yes, it was okay for them to stay.

Mum pulled him and Cassandra aside. She was visibly struggling to keep herself calm when all her nightmares were coming true. 'Mat, what's happening?'

'I don't know, Mum. I have to warn Jones, and see what he says.'

'I'll come too!' Cassandra said determinedly.

Mat bit his lip. 'No — please! Could you stay with Mum? Please?'

Cassandra looked at him hard. 'The danger's passed here. You don't know what you're going into.'

He leant close and whispered. 'Mum needs someone with her, Cass. Please?'

The girl stiffened. 'Okay,' she relented. 'Just this once.'

Mum looked like a frightened girl, but she didn't argue over it. 'Then you must go,' she said, in a sombre voice. Her eyes were moist. 'You were very brave, Mat. I'm proud of you. But if this is something that Welsh bastard has brought on us, I'll kill him myself.'

Mat shook his head, aching to be gone. 'Jones is one of the good guys, Mum. If he hadn't shown me what he has, I'd never have been able to protect us.'

Colleen nodded reluctantly. 'If he'd not, maybe they'd have left us alone. I'm so scared I'll lose you. Ever since that dreadful man and that Kyle woman came. Is she behind this, Matty?'

He remembered what the patupaiarehe woman had said. 'It looks like it,' he breathed. 'Jones and Hine might be in trouble. I've got to go and see them.'

Colleen's eyes narrowed. 'This Hine is mixed up in this, too?'

145

'Jones is looking after her, to protect her from her ex. Mum, I've got to go!'

She pulled him into a hug, and then pushed him away. 'Then go, Matty. Go as fast as you can, and then come home faster, you hear? Come home!'

'I promise, I promise,' he said. He snatched up his taiaha, walked through the debris to the door, and out into the shadows. The policemen stared at him curiously, and one started towards him, but he turned a corner, and let himself fade into Aotearoa before he could be stopped. Then he ran.

The kitchen window shattered, smashed by the butt of a gun. Hine flattened herself against the cupboards as glass sprayed the room. Then the gun was reversed, while massive blows shook both back and front doors. Godfrey snarled and ran to the front door, while Jones cursed and raised his flintlock. Before he could fire, the gunman at the window vanished.

The lock shattered and the back door swung open. A Roadhawks man in a leather jacket whirled into the room, pulling the trigger of the gun cradled in his hands, even as Jones corrected his aim. The mobster's gun clicked impotently.

'Wrong toy, boyo,' snarled Jones. An explosion boomed in Hine's ear as Jones's pistol spouted fire. Blood erupted from the biker's chest, the impact throwing him backwards out the door. A second man came through, bellowing in rage as his gun also failed. Jones placed his smoking pistol on the table, his hand waving, and drew the second pistol. The second man tried to turn, but Jones's shot shattered the side of his skull. He pitched sideways and fell to the floor.

Another gun roared, but this one was in the hallway. There was a canine howl, and a thump. Hine realized what it was instantly, and gasped. She stepped towards the door, her hand raised, a kitchen knife in it. Jones grabbed her. 'No! It's too late. Stay with me!'

He stepped to the back door, his hands a blur as he gestured and a cloud of fine dust and ash flew from the barrel, then gunpowder streamed into the weapon, followed by a lead ball. She looked back at the table and saw that the first gun was also loading itself. Jones waved a hand and the door to the hallway flew shut and locked. The first pistol finished loading itself and flew into his grasp. He gave it to her.

A voice called from behind the hallway door. 'Hine! Where are you, bitch?' Her legs nearly gave way. *Evan!*

Jones blew out the kitchen lamp, sidled to the back door, and aimed the reloaded second pistol towards Evan's voice. His sword was in his right hand. 'Come through that door and you're dead, Parukau.'

An evil laugh sounded from the hallway. 'Dead like this mutt, Aethlyn?'

A tiny sob bubbled from Hine's mouth, and she clenched the pistol and knife tight. They felt alien, but by God she would use them!

'Dead like your friends out the back here, Parukau,' said Jones, gesturing Hine to his side.

'I have plenty more, old man. And you know me: I can't die at all. So why don't you just throw down your arms and surrender. I might even let you live. You can watch me take Hine back.'

She raised the pistol, pointing it at the hallway door. 'Not yet, lass,' murmured Jones. He peered out the open back door. 'There's more of them out here, and others in the real world,' he told her, biting his lip. 'But I've got a few tricks up my sleeve.' He winked at her. 'We're not done yet.'

The handle of the hallway door turned. Jones nodded urgently, and she backed towards him. 'At my word, follow me out, lass. Don't shoot until you can't miss. You'll only get one shot, so make it count.'

He murmured something that made all the lights dim and the air fill with misty smoke, then pulled her out onto the back porch, over the two bodies that lay there. Both were Roadhawks, young men she half-recognized from around town. More stupid than evil. A strange haziness filled the air. She expected a burst of gunfire, but none came.

She heard the kitchen door rattle, and then there was a storm of shouting, and dark shapes erupted from both sides. She whirled in time to see Jones empty his pistol at a man whose face exploded like a rotten pumpkin. Then the old man's sword flashed out in a straight-arm thrust. The man he had stabbed stared in disbelief at the thin metal blade in his chest, then slid sideways to the earth. All about them, the trees seemed to come to life, wrenching and tearing at the intruders. Men shouted, scattering.

A knife flew at Jones's back, but veered and hit the wall instead. Brutal loomed out of the shadows, but Jones's sword flashed around and slashed him across the belly, making the big man roar like a wounded boar. Jones flicked his hand, and an invisible force hurled Brutal back, his mouth widening in shock. Then Ronnie burst through the back door, and Hine raised her gun. His big face widened in recognition and terror as her finger tightened on the trigger.

Time froze. She thought of Ko and her babies, and found she was paralysed. Ronnie blundered towards her, and wrapped his arms around her, pinning her arms to her side. He began to cry. 'Hine, Hine, Hine …' She twisted in his grasp helplessly, as Jones whirled and took aim.

'No!' she shrieked. *Not Ronnie!* Jones looked at her with furious eyes. 'Run!' But he turned back. Evan stepped onto the porch, with a pistol like Jones's in his hand. He raised it, and fired.

The ball punched a hole in Jones's chest, and his body jolted backwards. Fires that had begun to materialize in his hand flickered, like a spent Roman Candle, and the sword slid from his suddenly frail grip. He fell to his knees, holding the wound, muttering a stream of words. Brutal loomed over him, bloodied and enraged, and drew back his right boot. Hine screamed as Ronnie gripped her tighter. She closed her eyes to be blind, praying not to hear the death blow …

… that never came.

She heard Brutal curse in disbelief, and opened her eyes again. Jones was gone. Evan strode over, cursing. He raised a hand, and seemed to flicker, vanishing momentarily then reappearing, a look of bafflement on his face. 'Where's he gone? Where's the old bastard gone?'

Ronnie prised the pistol and knife from her hands. She looked up at his big stupid face, as a sense of hopelessness engulfed her. *I did nothing … I did nothing and let him grab me … and got Jones killed … maybe.* She hung her head, staring at the patch of earth where the old man had fallen, praying.

Ronnie took her back into the kitchen. Evan was shouting

about grabbing something, and clouds of men were throwing all Jones's spare muskets and pistols into a heap on the porch. She saw Evan gesture and all the weapons vanished. She could hear the monster in his voice. Couldn't they all hear it? The mocking glee as he pretended concern at Brutal's wound. The scorn as he congratulated Ronnie on recovering her unharmed. Outside there were angry voices, and she heard Evan go to the door, cocking two pistols.

Someone shouted from outside on the back lawn. 'Hey, Tomoana. Our bloody guns didn't work! An' the boys in the trees … half o' them are dead!'

'So, Arama? What of it? They're your guns, not mine,' said Evan, coolly. He raised his voice. 'Hurry that packing, Deano!'

The voice of this Arama rasped. 'But you knew! You brought them old guns an' they work! You bloody knew!'

'Be prepared, Arama. Be prepared. Scout's motto, eh? Guess you weren't never a boy scout.'

Arama pointed out into the night. 'The hell with you! What about Joe and Henare? And Si and his cousins? You knew! You knew them guns weren't goin' t'work! An' where are we anyway?'

Evan sniggered. 'In the backwoods, that's all. Thought you boys would be tougher than this. You better be more use in Rotorua, eh?'

'We ain't goin' to Rotorua! Not after this! I'm tellin' Dad about this!'

Rotorua! Hine fell to her knees on the kitchen floor. Let Ronnie think she was fainting. And she reached out, to the pool of blood welling about the dead man in the doorway … her fingers dipped in the cooling fluids, and she scrawled blind, onto the side of the cupboard: $R - O - T - O$ ...

Strong hands pulled her away, but there was no cry of discovery. Her message was overlooked. Ronnie wrapped about her, crooning like a lost baby. The argument continued outside, and she could feel it simmering towards blows. *Come on — fight each other*, she willed them silently. *Kill each other!*

Suddenly there was a choked cry and Evan swore. Ronnie looked up, and called out in a scared voice, 'Wass happenin'?'

Someone cried out in shock, and then the night was filled with howls, like a pack of hunting hounds descending on their prey. She heard Evan shouting, cries cut off. She was pulled to her feet as the back door slammed shut behind Evan, his face livid. Something smote the door behind him, and a big brown hand reached in the kitchen window. She peered out, and saw a biker, his eyes bulging with fright. Then a small, pale, hairless face appeared behind him, and a thin club split his skull.

'Tipua!' Evan bellowed. 'We've been tailed! It's a trap!' He lunged for Hine and pulled her to him. 'Ronnie, Brutal — grab my arms!'

'Wha—?'

'Do it!!!'

A man wrenched open the back door, pale hands snagging him. Hine recognized Arama Heke, a Roadhawks man, son of the gang boss. His face was bloodied and frightened. 'Tomoana, get us out of this!'

Evan laughed, then he gasped and tore at a dart that had flown from the window and gouged his neck. A thin white face, a blowpipe in its mouth, peered in, eyes lit with triumph. Evan's eyes bulged, and he staggered. But he recovered enough to chant a phrase, and the whole room seemed to shiver. The kitchen faded slowly.

But before it did, she saw Arama Heke stagger as pallid shapes flew at him out of the darkness. He vanished beneath naked white bodies that spilled over him, scrawny little nightmare figures that ripped at him with teeth and nails. His face was the last thing she saw, his mouth open, as his skin split and his insides bubbled out. Then the blood-spattered room where she had felt so safe those last few days faded from view, to be replaced by a bewildering press of people, gunfire, and shouting. A ghastly pale thing flew at them, then vanished when Evan shot it with one of those old pistols. Cars revved, doors slammed. Then it all fell away.

Hine woke in Ko's arms, in Evan's lounge. Ko looked totally bewildered. Ronnie and Brutal were slamming clothing into bags, while Deano was loading loot from Jones's house — old guns and barrels from the shed — into the boot of the car. Evan was snarling at them, keeping them moving. They were leaving, going somewhere. All she wanted to do was crawl into a hole and pull something over the top. The face of Arama Heke as he was being torn apart would not leave her.

She wrapped her arms around Brandi, tried to stop the scared child from crying, and in doing so found something to deflect her own rising panic. Evan moved like a stoned dope addict, clearly still affected by the poison on the blowpipe dart, but when his eyes crept over her, she felt utter dread.

'Hush,' she whispered to Brandi and herself, shutting her eyes. 'Hush, it's all okay,' she repeated, although she knew nothing would be okay ever again.

It seemed to take hours, but by dawn they were all in Deano's car, driving north towards Rotorua.

Mat crept up the front lawn, but the house was silent. Fog from the lake had trapped the reek of gunpowder and violence. A small black-and-white shape lay in the hallway, the rug black and wet. The little body was cold. Mat extended his senses and sensed the lump of silver in the turehu's heart. The attackers had known what they were facing. Godfrey was gone, forever.

The lounge was undisturbed and so was Jones's room. No-one had plundered the house. The only room with anything out of the ordinary in it was the kitchen. He lit the lamp, picked it up, and looked about him. His heart was hammering, but he told himself to be calm. Observe. See what was to be seen. He squatted over a ravaged corpse, a man, half-eaten where he lay. The tipua goblins lay around him.

Beyond him, on the back porch, another six men lay. Three had gunshot wounds and another had been stabbed. They had all been ripped at by teeth and claws. Small piles of tipua lay about them. He walked further out, raising the lantern. More gang men, more goblins. The men had been outnumbered, he surmised, but they had fought desperately. And died horribly. What they had been doing at Jones's cottage he didn't know. But he could guess … two parties, the bikers coming first, the goblins second. An ambush, the hunters becoming prey.

Jones's shed had been raided and all the old guns were missing, bar a few that had been right at the back. There was no sign of Jones and Hine. But there was a pool of blood soaked into the turf outside the back door, and Jones's favourite weapons lay there. The air crackled with the afterburn of some magical energy, but he had no idea what had been done. He crouched there, fighting tears, trying to sense what he could of what had happened. It took time, and he was close to exhaustion, but he managed. A blurred vision struck him behind the eyes, of Jones falling, and then … nothing …

He opened his eyes, as the air quivered, a silent roar of power. The bloody ground boiled and the grass somehow drank the blood away. He reached out, trying to sense what was happening, and for an instant it seemed he saw Jones above him, bound to a tree, with creepers covering his body, piercing his skin, pumping his own blood back into his veins. Then it was gone.

My God, what was that?

He backed away, unsure whether to be reassured or frightened. He shifted to the real world, found himself in the back yard of an empty time-share, utterly still. The grass was torn up, and he smelt blood, but someone had removed all the bodies. He flickered back to Aotearoa again, and sagged to his knees.

Eventually he found the strength to act. He found a shovel and buried Godfrey, trying not to think about that mischievous, fun-loving and wise little spirit. The other corpses could rot forever, as far as he was concerned.

Godfrey, I hope you soar and find a new place where you can wait for us all to join you.

Eventually, he went back inside — and then he saw it, smeared blood on the side of a cupboard: R – O – T – O …

He knelt and tentatively reached out with his senses, tried

to catch the after-images of what had happened. He saw flashes … Hine, writing in blood … *Rotorua*, surely. The vision faded. *Rotorua.*

I will find you and protect you, Hine, he promised her. *I'll find you.*

He stopped for a moment, and put his remaining strength into a call, a silent plea for help. *Ngatoro, can you hear me?*

There was a faint stirring, and then a voice, distant but clear. *Mat?*

Ngatoro! We've been attacked! I don't know where Jones is, but he's hurt! Hine's gone! She's an avatar of Hinemoa. It was Parukau … he paused … *or maybe Donna Kyle.*

He thought he felt the old tohunga groan. *Parukau? Beware of him. Be very careful …*

What do I do? Jones might be alive: I don't know where to find him. Please, help me!

I will … try … Mat … be careful— The link with the old tohunga, so tenuous already, suddenly snapped.

Mat rubbed at his face. He felt shattered, bewildered. But there was so much to do. He straightened, and threw himself into what had to be done.

He dragged the bodies outside and mopped the floor. He took Jones's sword and pistols, and some powder and shot from a stash in the cellar. He boarded the broken windows and locked the door, in case someone came. Then he walked away, not looking back, not wanting his last memories of the place to be like this. As soon as he knew it was out of sight, he broke into a run.

It took no time to convince Mum that he had to go to Rotorua. He had to find Hine and protect her. There was no-one else. She cried and held him, but didn't try to change his mind. He put his and Jones's weapons into a sports bag with a few changes of clothes. He phoned the police anonymously and told them he had seen the missing girl, Hine Horatai, in Rotorua. Maybe it would make life difficult for her abductors. Then he collapsed onto the sofa, and stared at the ceiling.

'Mat?' Cassandra slipped into the lounge, where he was sleeping. They were at Sue's house, and the night noises were all wrong. Whenever he closed his eyes he saw some horrible tipua, or that ghastly patupaiarehe, crawling towards him.

'Hi,' he murmured. Cass was still in those leathers, and looked alien; too 'everyday' to be the real her.

She knelt on the floor, leaning over him. 'I want to come, too. Jones is my friend.'

'Then stay here and find him.' He hadn't meant it to come out so brusquely. He reached out and grabbed her bony shoulder. 'He's here somewhere, Cass. It's a puzzle. And you're the best person at puzzles I know.'

He thought she would argue, but she didn't. 'Okay. But I'll be on call. Any time, day or night.' She put her hand on his chest, bent over him and kissed his cheek. She smelt of Mum's perfumes.

He wanted to pull her close, but his imagination kept suggesting what might be happening to Hine and he felt like throwing up. 'Sorry,' he said, unsure what for. Cassandra just nodded, stood reluctantly, and tiptoed to the door. 'It's weird,' he said to her back. 'Your clothes, I mean. You look strange.' He didn't know why he said it, it was the least important thing that had happened that night, but his mouth just kept babbling.

'I was supposed to look normal,' she said, slightly tartly.

'Sorry.' He felt numb and stupid. 'I'm tired.'

She nodded, and slipped away without another word. For a moment he wished she had stayed. But sleep stole in and snuffed out his candle. He dreamt of Jones, caught up in the arms of a giant tree, his face slowly turning to bark, his eyes to knots in the wood.

Rotorua

Thursday

The Rotorua bus left at twenty to eleven. Mat had slept until after eight, when the unfamiliar house noises broke through his exhaustion. He'd called Wiri and Kelly, a short and anxious conversation. They were in Wellington, five hours' drive from Taupo and further from Rotorua.

'Wiri is going to drive up,' he told Mum at the breakfast table. 'I've asked him to call past on the way through, and check on things. They'll have left by now. The last text I had said they would be in Taupo by two.' He wished he had thought to call last night, but his brain hadn't been working too well.

At the bus terminal, Mum pulled him into a fervent hug, and Cassandra — still in Mum's old leathers as she had not yet gone home — hugged him, too. He realized as he let Cass go what it was that he didn't like about her new look: with it, she was no longer 'one of the boys' or 'kinda kooky'; she no longer had a pigeonhole, and he didn't know how to react to her. He didn't have the energy to explore that just now. 'Take care,' he whispered in her ear.

'I wish I could have the police lock you up, to keep you

out of this,' said his mother in a shaky voice. 'Don't you do anything stupid, Matiu Douglas. And come home.' He nodded obediently. 'I love you, Mat.'

'Love you, too. Gotta go, Mum! Bye!' He boarded the bus, and waved until they were both out of sight, then pulled up the hood of the tracksuit top, and wrapped himself in thought. He pushed the violence of last night from his mind, and picked up his cellphone. He texted Riki, letting him know that he was coming. He felt he ought to be making plans, but he was too exhausted to think. Instead he closed his eyes, and let it all fall away for a while.

He jerked awake when another passenger tapped him on the shoulder. 'Hey, mate, wake up. We're here.' The bus was pulling to a halt in a parking space off the main street. He could smell Rotorua's sulphurous tang in the air. Rain was falling in a light mist.

Rotorua is around eighty kilometres north of Taupo, built on the south shores of the largest of a cluster of lakes. The skin of the Earth is thin here. Hot mud pools and geysers bubble and gush through the rock. 'Roto-Vegas' the locals sometimes call it, for its tourist-trap culture. There are replica Maori villages and nightly kapa haka displays, theme parks where visitors can view the geysers and hot pools, and lots of hotels. Rotorua has a long history, by New Zealand standards. Whakarewarewa has been a pa site from the fourteenth century, growing into the fortress of Te Puia. Europeans did not arrive until the 1820s, when traders and missionaries established stations. European settlement changed Rotorua drastically, as the Europeans brought guns, cloth, alcohol and the trappings of the British Empire. Rotorua became a spa town, a tourist destination even then.

Mat had been here before, of course, but not since he had learned of Aotearoa, and how to move between the worlds. He knew no-one here. The Maori of Rotorua are sub-tribes of the Te Arawa, whereas Mat was Ngati Kahungunu on his father's side and that wasn't going to help. These distinctions are important, especially in Aotearoa.

And if Parukau was here, maybe other warlocks were too: John Bryce. Donna Kyle. Sebastian Venn. Who knew which others? *I've got to find Hine. But how ...?*

He walked down Tutanekai Street, the taiaha jutting from his sports bag attracting a few looks, and turned into the main shopping area, where cafés, pubs and souvenir shops serviced the tourist market. Foreign faces and languages were everywhere. It felt strange, as if he had wandered onto a tourism infomercial set. He found a café and lunched while trying to make a plan. First up, he needed a place to stay. Wiri might know people here, but they would date back to his servitude to Puarata, and be of no use now. Wiri had texted him to let him know that he had left Wellington at about nine in the morning. They wouldn't be here until mid-afternoon. Kelly was coming, too. Mat guessed Wiri wasn't too happy about that. Weren't pregnant women supposed to be confined to bed or something?

After eating, he walked down to the lake and booked into a big hotel, one that looked out over the lake to Mokoia Island, a dim shadow in the misty rain. Mat thought about Hine, and what Jones had said about her. Why had she been kidnapped? Was it mere vindictiveness or was she significant in ways they didn't realize?

The hotel staff seemed anxious that a teenager staying alone might trash his room or try to slip out without paying, because they seemed at pains to lecture him on behaviour, and to get payment in advance. Mum had credited his account so he had plenty of funds. The room was pleasantly nondescript. Mat had just laid his stuff down when his cellphone rang.

'Hi, Riki,' he answered, trying to keep his voice light. 'Are you on the island?'

'Yeah, man! Cold and wet! Your text said you're coming to Roto-Vegas? How come? Your mum sick of you already?'

'I wish it was just that, man.'

Riki was silent for a second, and his voice became sombre. 'Wassup?'

Mat quickly told him about the attacks on Mum's and Jones's houses, Jones's disappearance and the kidnapping of Hine. 'I think … I hope … that Jones might be alive. But I can't reach him … and I think Hine is important somehow. I'm going to try and find her anyway, and get her back. I can't just let some bastard run off with her.'

'I'll be there by two o'clock, dude.'

'You don't have to. We're just looking round at this stage, and—'

'Are you kidding? Jones is my mate! You, too. Anyone that comes at you guys is comin' at me. Simple. I'll get my stuff together and grab the next ferry to the city from this here island.'

'You're on Mokoia Island, the place Hinemoa swims to in the legend, right?'

Riki paused. 'Yeah. Why?'

'Oh, just reminding myself.'

Riki grunted. 'Huh. Anyways, dude, I'll be on the next ferry, so you meet me on the lakefront a bit after two, and we'll work out what to do.'

Mat sat on one of the lakefront benches, watching a sleek white powerboat glide through the other watercraft and pull in alongside the jetty. Riki, a long sports bag over his shoulder, was already at the railing of the boat. Tall and stringy with wild hair, his normally laughing face had a hard and serious edge that Mat hadn't seen since that night at Waikaremoana. He leapt to the dock as soon as the boat touched the dock, to the annoyance of the ferrymen, strode up to Mat and threw his arms around him. 'Mat. Good to see you, bro. Any news?'

It felt so good to see Riki that Mat almost forgot his guilt at dragging him into danger. 'No. But I've got an idea. We've got to keep things moving. Wiri is on the way. He'll be here any time now.'

Riki chewed his lip. 'Sure, what's the plan? And have you called Damian?'

Mat shook his head. 'No. He's in the South Island at that tournament. I feel bad enough dragging you into this.'

Riki shook his head. 'Dame'll be gutted if we don't call him, man.'

Mat shook his head. 'Don't, please. This could get much

worse than Waikaremoana. But I promise I'll talk to Wiri about it.' Riki looked mollified for now. Mat's anxiety for Hine and Jones dissipated a little — just to have Riki here to talk to was great — but there was work to be done. Although part of him wanted to wait until Wiri got here, he had a horrible feeling that every minute could be crucial.

They made small talk as they hurried back to the hotel, but then Mat got down to business: 'I've got a plan to try and find Hine.' He rummaged in his bag. 'We need something of hers.'

Riki raised his eyebrows. 'Got anything? A heart-shaped locket she gave you, perhaps?' he added slyly.

'No! She went to Jones's with just a few bits of clothing … and this!' Mat held up a small metal disc on a ribbon. 'Swimming medal. It's dated 2006 and she's kept it. I found it in the room she was using. I think it'll do the trick.'

Riki looked doubtful. 'A swimming medal? What's special about that?'

'Well, when she talked about her swimming she was really proud. And … well, she's an avatar.'

Riki snorted. 'She's a seven-metre-tall blue alien?'

'The blue aliens were Na'vi, it was the—' Mat peered at Riki, who was winking at him. 'Dork, why did I call you in again?'

'To cheer yourself up. So, she's an avatar: what does that mean in the mysterious and spooky world of Mat Douglas, Apprentice Wizard?'

Mat exhaled, seeking the right words. 'In Aotearoa, it refers to people who are born in our world, but are like legendary people reborn. Kind of.'

'You're lucky I don't already know you're nuts … A real person, but also legendary?'

'Yeah. See, Hine is the avatar of Hinemoa, from the Hinemoa and Tutanekai story. Her fate is tied up with water. Or so Jones reckons.'

'Jones is a very strange man,' Riki observed. 'Okay, what do we do?'

Mat frowned. 'I think I'll need to concentrate on it. I haven't done this before, but I know the theory. Can you give me some privacy?'

Riki got up. 'Sure.' He threw his sports bag on the second bed, and stretched. 'Man, they worked us hard these last few days at the taiaha camp. Got some good new moves, though. Anyhow, I'll go take a shower.'

Mat barely heard the shower, or Riki's clattering around. He just sat, cradling the medal, and let his mind reach out, focused on the face of the girl he had known for only a short time but to whom he felt so close. *She's not for you*: Jones's words echoed in his mind. He knew that, but it wouldn't stop him trying to save her, though. *Hine! Hine! Can you hear me? I'm here, here in Rotorua. Where are you?*

The minutes flew away, and all there was were those words, a mantra, hanging in the air.

Once, he thought he might have felt her presence. Her breathing. A fluttering of awareness. But it was gone before he could focus. He fought a wave of tiredness, laying back and blinking to stay awake.

'Any luck?' Riki came back in, wrapped in a towel. He was

skinny enough that you could count his ribs, but his shoulders were muscled and his belly flat.

Mat shook his head doubtfully. 'I don't know …'

'You look whacked, bro,' Riki commented. 'You need to rest up? Wiri and Kels'll be here soon.'

It was very tempting … But the feeling that time was slipping away persisted. 'No, let's go get something to drink, then I'll try again.'

Ten minutes later they were down by the lake, sipping milk-shakes on a park bench. The sun was battling successive waves of clouds from the south. Wind gusted and whipped up some white-topped waves. It wasn't peak season, but there were still lots of tourists, mostly Japanese, wrapped in bright parkas and photographing everything.

Riki turned to him, about to speak, when he froze, staring over Mat's shoulder. Mat followed his gaze to where a gull had landed on a railing a few feet away, looking at them with button-like eyes. 'It's watching us, man,' Riki whispered.

It would be easy to scoff, but Mat didn't. The gull was too intent, too focused. 'Maybe we should go back to the room,' Mat breathed.

Another gull swooped to the other end of the bench, mere feet from them. This close, its familiarity was overlaid with menace. It looked big and vicious. Then a sparrow landed beside it, calmly ignoring the bigger bird, its beady eyes on him and him alone. Others came, until the two boys were sitting in a circle of silent, cold-eyed birds.

'Jeez, I always hated that Hitchcock movie,' Riki groaned.

Mat looked up, glancing along the lakefront, where someone was walking towards them, through the crowds. A brown-skinned woman, in a long coat, with a mane of grey hair. She walked like a stalking heron, with an uneven bobbing gait. Her eyes fixed on his face, and the ground seemed to quiver silently with each step. Her coat floated behind her like a feathered cloak, or wings. A name from legend entered his mind, from conversations with Jones and Wiri … *Kurangaituku*. The Birdwitch.

'Riki,' he breathed. His friend was already on his feet. Mat stood and looked about him. The gulls squawked threateningly, fluttered about them, wings thumping the air. Suddenly they were in a sea of beaks and wings.

'Poai,' the woman called, in a harsh voice that seemed to come from the throat of every bird about them. 'Poai, stay right where you are!'

Parukau felt a tentative touch on his shoulder, and woke with a jerk. It was Deano, the young man puppy-dog, eager to please but frightened to disturb him. He grimaced, his mind groggy. *Damned drug-dart … tipua scum …* It felt like someone had poured glue into his veins then encased him in cotton wool. It took him several seconds just to focus his eyes. His watch read nearly quarter past eight in the morning.

'Where are we?' he managed.

'Roto-Vegas, chief. We just hit the city. Where you wanna stay?'

Must I do everything? 'I don't give a shit, Deano. Any ol' dump … No, hang on … It's gotta be side-by-side twin-shares with an adjoining door. Find a tourist info.' He dredged Evan's memories. 'There's a bureau by the lakefront. Get someone there to find us a place.'

In the back seat, Brutal was staring out the window, having lapsed completely into silence since the fight last night. He looked like he was in shock, and he had his hands pressed to his bandaged belly. Evan had stitched his stomach wound before leaving. Brutal had blubbed throughout. The girl, Hine, was asleep, leaning against the opposite window. Ronnie was in another car following them, with Ko and their little girls. He wanted them all under his wing. With the Roadhawks cut down or deserted, he needed them: the men to fight; Ko and the babies for leverage. Ronnie would fight or his family would die — it was that simple. The other two men, Deano and Brutal, he would just have to keep his eye on. If they could handle some weird shit, they would be of some use.

Deano found the tourism desk, and sorted some accommodation at a place on the east side. They detoured into the industrial zone, and he stashed the guns on the Aotearoa side, barely managing the transition. Then they found the motel: a low-rent place across the main road from the lake, off Te Ngae Road. The units were simple, each a big lounge-dining bedsit with side-by-side double beds, plus a separate bathroom and kitchen. Original 'seventies decor, as tired and bedraggled as its guests. But the units had connecting doors, so he could keep an eye on everybody. It would do for now.

He put Ronnie, Ko and the babies in one unit, locked the main door and pocketed the key. He left the connecting door open, so that Ronnie and his family could only exit via his unit. Brutal took one bed, clutching his slashed belly silently. Parukau took the other. Just before he passed out, he remembered the handcuffs, and gave them to Deano. 'Take Hine and cuff her to the railing in the bathroom, Deano. Then stand watch. I gotta sleep. She gives you any grief, smack her one.'

Deano took the cuffs, and then went to the corner, where Hine sat like a zombie. He pulled her upright, and dragged her into the bathroom. The click of the cuffs were the last thing Parukau heard before he succumbed to exhaustion.

Much later, a voice woke him, not with sound, but a prickling in his mind.

Hine! Hine! Can you hear me? I'm here, here in Rotorua. Where are you?

A mental call, amateurish but loud. He shook his head, and sat up, feeling a little refreshed. Brutal was asleep on the bed, snoring gently. Deano sat across the bathroom door, his head on his chest, eyes closed; *useless!* He felt a sudden panic, and stumbled to the bathroom door, but the girl was still there, cuffed to the pipes of the basin, asleep. Her hair was a dark pillow, and her chest rose and fell.

He opened himself to the mental call and got a vision of the little shit that had caused half this mess: the kid he had smacked up in Taupo. Matiu Douglas, the cops had named him during questioning. He was in a hotel room somewhere. He looked fragile, a twig to be snapped. He repeated the call, and Parukau heard Hine stir in her sleep. He pulled back slightly, and orientated himself, tracing the point where the call originated … *Ahh, there you are … I think we owe you a visit, kid …*

He dragged himself to a sitting position, fought for energy. 'Brutal, Deano, get up, you lazy bastards!'

The two men groaned and stirred. He kicked Deano's leg. 'Asleep on duty! If this was the army you'd be up for a flogging! Brutal! Get your fat brown ass outta bed. We got work to do. Get Ronnie!'

Within half an hour, they were wending their way through the traffic, back into town. Deano drove, while Ronnie sat in the back. Brutal he left at the motel to guard the women. He didn't trust Ko not to try to bust Hine and do a runner.

'What are we doing this kid for?' Deano asked, timidly.

Ronnie grunted. 'Cos we didn't get to finish the job back in Taupo, an' he got us arrested.'

It was only half the truth. *You don't really want to know what I'm going to do to him …* There were various ways a fellow Adept could be butchered so that his power flowed into his killer. *Doing this kid is gonna give me a big nasty boost, right when I need one.*

'How'd you know he's here?' Deano puzzled.

You don't wanna know that either.

They slipped into the hotel lobby. He stole a master key from an oblivious Asian cleaner. He was feeling better and better — getting his full array of tricks and treats working again. But when they entered the boy's room, the little turd was gone. His weapons were still there, and his clothes, but the room was empty. There was another sports bag on the second bed. Whose? He glared about in frustration, then gave a tired shrug.

Where is he? He closed his eyes. The image came quickly: the boy was quite close, in a café ordering food, down by the lakeside. He probed his surface thoughts, and then chuckled. 'They's jus' refuelling, boys.' He sat by the window, and put his feet up. 'Rest up, fellas. The little sucker will be back soon enough.'

Donna Kyle owned a house near Rotorua airport, which Puarata had given her. Like her home in Auckland, the house opened onto both worlds. She didn't like this house, though. It creaked, and was full of bad memories. She lay on the big four-poster bed, and watched the slowly shifting half-light that penetrated the drapes play across the old oil paintings and antique furniture.

She had come here that morning, before dawn, and slept away the day. She was becoming a night creature, was forced to be, so that she could direct her nocturnal minions. The patupaiarehe lay in lightless cellars below ground, awaiting the sunset. They could walk in daylight, but it left them weaker. She had fed them on cats she had bought from a pet shop after the journey from Taupo. Thorn and Heron were both wounded: Thorn had been burned and stabbed by Matiu Douglas, and Heron grazed by a silver ball fired by Parukau. They would heal, though. Stone had returned bearing messages of loyalty from the nearest goblin tribe. Waka were coming, he told her, full of eager warriors. Well, they couldn't be less useful than those Thorn had roused in Taupo.

She had lashed Thorn mercilessly when the skinny wretch had returned in failure from attacking the Douglas boy. One half-trained Adept and she couldn't handle it! *He knew my name!* Thorn had wailed. That brought her up short. *How could the boy know Thorn's true name?*

And then there was her own failure. Despite trailing Parukau in his raid on Jones's cottage, she had been unable to destroy her rival and take the girl he was so interested in. She had no-one but herself to blame for that. *Only a bad carpenter blames their tools … It is I who is failing …*

She got up, pulled a gown around her and sat in the cane chair beside the curtained window. The remains of a bottle of red wine stained the bottom of a crystal glass. The digital clock that Puarata had always said marred the colonial decor told her it was just after three in the afternoon. She left the curtains closed, more comfortable in the half-light. *And let's not think too hard about that …*

Too many unanswered questions. Who was the girl Parukau had gone to so much trouble to take back? How had the Matiu Douglas boy known Thorn's true name? Was Te Iho here? Most of all: why had her father reappeared and what does he really know?

He promised to help me — why? Instinctively she rejected the thought of seeking him out. She would never be able to control him … *God, I hate this game! But there is no way out of it.*

A harsh voice crackled inside her mind, startling her. *Mistress Kyle,* Kurangaituku called. *I have found the Douglas boy. Shall I seize him?*

She clenched a fist. Second chances were all too rare in life. 'Strike,' she replied, aloud and psychically. 'Take him alive if you can. I will come and collect.'

It was still daylight. The patupaiarehe were of little use to her until sunset. She decided to let them recover. She rose quickly, dressed and was gone, while her servants slept, oblivious.

Mat pulled his arm over his head, and ran for the hotel, yelling for Riki to follow. The birds erupted in a cloud around him. Talons and beaks tore at him, feathers billowed, then he burst into clear air, Riki a few steps behind. The towering old woman seemed to flow towards them. A few people stared at the birds, but no-one came to his aid. A couple shouted something, but the words were inaudible to him, lost in the beating wings and shrieking beaks.

'The hotel!' he shouted. 'Run!' The building loomed ahead, towering over the lakefront green. He glanced up at the sheer wall of glass, as a gull veered and smashed into the bank of windows with a sickening smack, bounced and then plummeted in a broken tangle. A cross of broken glass smeared in blood and feathers marked the impact point. He saw the outline of a man, right where the bird had struck, and just *knew* that their rooms had been found already.

'This way!' he shouted, swerving left towards the main street, with no plan but to find people, lots of people. Birds smacked against his back and shoulder, tearing cloth and skin. He staggered. Behind him, Riki gasped and swore. Mat couldn't look, he was too tangled in beating wings and flashing claws and beaks. Then Riki fell, and Mat spun, his heart in his mouth. Riki sprawled beneath the Birdwitch. She had leapt on his back and forced him to ground. Mat raised a fist, fire leaping to his command, and hurled it. Birds shrieked and veered aside, but with a feral grin, Kurangaituku vanished, with Riki limp in her claws.

'No!' Mat tore at the air, shifting himself to Aotearoa. The world lurched and he stumbled and half-fell on an expanse of well-trampled earth amidst a cluster of settler buildings, outside the walls of a huge pa. Clumps of settlers turned with startled eyes. Voices shouted, calling the witch's name. Children stared mutely. Men snatched up weapons. There were hundreds of eyes on him, but his were on the Birdwitch, already forty metres away and bounding at an insane speed. He tore after her, ignoring the shouts of the locals, and plunged into the bush that rimmed the settlement. Kurangaituku bounded away, through marsh and water, her every step ten of his. He howled a challenge, threw fire — but it burst impotently over the bush. She moved like a jumping spider; he couldn't even get close.

Within a few minutes, he had lost her entirely. He stopped, breathless, furious and frustrated.

Idiot! You've brought your best friend into this and he's been taken inside two hours! Some Adept!

He stared about him, desperate for something he could do. The forest was utterly silent. Rotorua-Aotearoa was lost somewhere behind, and there seemed to be no pursuit. Not even a bird sang. There were birds, though. Thousands of them. He stared at them and they stared back.

Suddenly he heard someone, someone with no bush sense,

stamping through the brush and undergrowth, following him. He dropped from sight, and crawled behind a fallen log. But not before he caught a glimpse of a pale woman whose face regularly filled his nightmares. He tried to muster the strength to slip back to the real world, but knew she would still sense him if he did. Her footsteps stopped, a mere dozen metres away.

'Matiu Douglas!' Donna Kyle called in a low hard voice. 'Come out! I know you're there!'

Once a warrior

Thursday afternoon

Deano sat at the window of the hotel room and stared out at the lake. They had been there nearly an hour and still the boy hadn't come back. Evan — no, 'Parukau' — wouldn't let him light a ciggie, because he said the boy might smell it out in the hallway and run off. As if anyone had that good a nose! Outside, the shadows were lengthening across the green. Evan — he couldn't get the new name into his head — was staring down at the park intently. It was starting to freak him out.

So he fingered his pack of fags some more, and played with the gun in his pocket. A nice little piece that Evan had given him; a Glock, just like real gangsters might use. Christ, he had never even held a handgun before, but he felt like a proper LA boy in da hood now ... *But why can't I have a smoke?*

The temptation got too much and he stalked over to the bathroom door. Ronnie was lying on the bed, holding a taiaha they had found in the boy's gear. Evan had grinned when he found the two old pistols, and had loaded them up. Old relics, but kind of cool. Ronnie wouldn't touch any of them, wouldn't even look at them. He was still freaked from what he had seen the night before. For Deano it had just been a blur, of stacking guns, and then Evan had touched him and the guns and they were somehow, somewhere else. He refused to think about that.

Bugger this — I need a puff!

He shut the bathroom door, lit up a ciggie and had a quick puff, to stop his hands shaking. Not that he was scared or anything, but the waiting was getting on his nerves.

Parukau stared down at Matiu Douglas and his friend, wondering if he should wait or move. Then he saw the way the birds were hovering, and realized what was happening. Kurangaituku, he guessed immediately, even as the Bird-witch stalked into view, the same flowing hair, the cloak, the heron-like walk. Old Cootface! They had hated each other from the start. She was an ugly, primitive thing. A jealous, carping old harpy. Maybe this time he could take her down forever.

Kurangaituku!

He hadn't meant to shape her name out loud, but it just fell from his mind. She glanced up at him, her eyes flaring, then her arm jabbed towards him. Suddenly a gull veered from the flock in a sharp arc, and flew straight at him. He flinched as the bird hit the glass and broke itself. Blood and feathers smeared as it rebounded and fell away. The plate glass cracked in a great cross. Kurangaituku glared up at him, and then turned back to her prey.

'Holy shit!' yelped Ronnie, gaping at the cracked window. 'What the hell was that?'

Parukau shook himself, and then gave a hoarse laugh. 'Jus' some stupid ol' bird.'

He watched the boys run, first towards the hotel, and then veering away. He cursed under his breath. *What the hell? Damnit, safety is here!* Then Kurangaituku leapt like a deformed Amazon and landed on the back of the other boy in a tumbling whirl. Matiu Douglas turned and flames washed through the press of birds — *Impressive!* — but the witch was already gone. In a heartbeat, the boy was too, as the birds rose and flapped away. A couple of people were staring at the dissipating flock of birds, as if wondering whether what they thought they had seen was real or some stunt.

Damn! Cootface got to him first … Damn!

Deano came out of the toilet, reeking of smoke. Couldn't these idiots do anything he asked of them? 'What happened, Ev— Parukau? What broke the window?'

'Just a dumb bird.' He peered down, trying to think clearly. *What did it matter if Cootface got the boy? But why did she want him? Was he just another meal for her? Or was he another piece in this puzzle after all? What had Jones confided in him?*

'Boss?'

'Shut up,' he snarled. 'I'm trying to think. Deano, check the hallway. And put out that bloody smoke!'

Ronnie said nothing as Deano slunk out the door, which for a dumbass was pretty smart.

Parukau turned back to the cracked, gore-smeared window, and chewed his goatee, clenching and unclenching his fists. There were more important questions to ponder, about Kurangaituku and whose side she was on. And where was Donna Kyle? Surely it was her behind the goblin attack

177

last night! Where was she now?

He felt like a child at a footy game — he could see some of the moves, but he wasn't understanding them, didn't know the rules, wasn't able to play ... *Blood of the Swimmer; Hine's blood ... I know it's vital! But where? How? Why? Damn this!*

Ronnie got up, and fingered the cracked glass, his soft face lost. Suddenly he giggled incongruously, and pointed down into the street. 'Jeez, look at that thing!'

Parukau peered incuriously down to the street, where a Volkswagen, an original Beetle by the look of it, was turning into the hotel car park. It was vivid pink, with bright floral patterns and some sort of clown face painted on it. 'Heh, gotta be a clown to drive an ol' heap like that!'

Couldn't the moron stay focused for two minutes? 'Sit down, Ronnie. An' shut up. I gotta think ...'

Deano waited in the hallway, in a little alcove just down from the door to Mat's room. Some old biddy walked past, looking sniffily at the ciggie in his hand. He puffed it defiantly, meeting her eye. *So what you gonna do 'bout it, lady?* He wished they could just go and get on with finding this loot that Evan — Parukau — *whatever* — kept talking about. Where was it, anyway? Why weren't they working on that?

His mind went back to the motel where they were staying. That was a bad scene, too. Hell, he liked Hine, thought she was damned hot, true thing. Chaining her up was extreme, even for Evan. And whatever had gone down in Taupo the other night had seriously freaked Brutal and Ronnie. Those few seconds when Evan had vanished and then reappeared with the boys and Hine had been savage, he could sense that. He had never seen those guys scared, but they had come back all torn up and shit-scared. And how did Evan do that?

He shied from that question, instinctively.

If Evan hadn't been in such a foul mood, he would have demanded some answers, for sure! But ever since that overnight in the lock-up, he had been weird. Deano wanted the old Evan back, the laid-back, cool dude. He dragged on his ciggie, working up the nerve to go back inside that room and get some answers. He wanted to hit something. Or shoot the gun, and feel that hard, heavy thing buck in his hands. *Where's that stupid kid? I hope he shows up, so we can take it all out on the little jerk.*

The lift chimed and a man got out, with a pregnant woman and a big golden Labrador. The man was Maori, tall and rangy. He moved like a runner, or a rugby player — strong, loose strides. He was wearing jeans and a loose polo shirt, and his face was handsome, clean-shaven, with curly black hair cropped close; just one blemish — a scar on his temple. Deano felt a surge of resentment, for his looks, for his confidence. Wasn't right, him stepping tall like he owned the place. The bitch with him was Pakeha, waddling like she was about to drop a sprog. She had dyed-pink hair and looked like she had an attitude, but both of them seemed tired, like people who had come a long way with bad news to tell.

The Labrador looked up at him and he returned its stare. There was something strange about its gaze, something too focused. He looked away first, then back at the man. 'Hey, bro,' he said, unsure why. He felt truculent and nervy.

The man nodded at him, and their eyes met. Clear, strong, timeless eyes that looked like they had seen just about anything, and faced it down. Deano dropped his gaze, feeling suddenly small. He looked up again only when he knew those eyes had moved past him. They had stopped outside the door to the boy's room. *Jeez, now what do I do?*

The man raised his hand and knocked twice. The woman was still looking back at him, and so was that mutt, wary and hostile. *Maybe they're friends of the boy.* He slid his hand into his pocket, gripping the Glock. 'Hey! That ain't your room.'

The Lab growled. The door opened a little. He held his breath, everything paused … and then it was like someone yelled 'Go!' in his head. He pulled out the gun.

Parukau sat bolt upright as someone knocked on the door. Ronnie looked at him for guidance. 'Dat the boy?' he asked.

The boy wouldn't knock, you idiot. It's his own room, and he's got the key. Nor would Deano … Room Service? Where was Deano? Shit! What if it's another ambush, like those *tipua* that came flooding out of the trees last night? There was only one other way out of this room, through the window — but they were three flights up. He swallowed, his skin going slick.

He picked up one of the antique pistols and rammed it into his pocket, then cocked the other one and put it in his left hand. If it was another attack, he would cross to Aotearoa, so best he had guns whose powder worked there. In his right hand he palmed another Glock, one of those he had got from Robert Heke in Taupo. 'Get the door, Ronnie,' he hissed. 'Take it slow.'

Ronnie stared at him, his left hand holding the taiaha like a kid's softball bat, then he dropped it and pulled out his own Glock. He looked like he was crapping himself as he fumbled with the handle and pulled the door slightly ajar. He peered through the crack, blinked and growled, 'Who da hell are you?'

Even as Deano advanced, he saw the man flick his head forward, forehead neatly cracking Ronnie's nose. Ronnie howled in pain and staggered backwards into the bedroom.

Bastard! I'll fix you! He hefted the gun, began to shout a challenge.

The Labrador was already moving, coming towards Deano in two accelerating bounds. Its muscles bunched and then all he could see was teeth as it leapt. He pulled up his hands to shield his face, and then the hot wet mouth closed over his gun-hand wrist, and rows of teeth punctured his skin as the weight of the dog hammered into him, pitching him backwards. The sudden agony of the bite shocked through him and he heard himself screech, and his fingers lost all grip as bones snapped in his wrist.

He hit the ground with a pulverising crack. The gun spun off down the corridor. Shots went off inside the room and bullets tore into the hallway ceiling. The pregnant woman shouted something, but he was under the Lab as its jaws snapped at his head. He tried to roll, but the thing was heavy and there was no leverage. His left hand beat weakly at its flank, his legs flailing for purchase, and then those huge jaws opened above his throat, and plunged down.

Parukau saw Ronnie's head suddenly cracked backwards, and Ronnie lurch, trying to aim his gun at a man who had burst through the door, slamming him sideways against the wall. Ronnie howled and fired, but the newcomer had already caught his gun hand and forced it upward so the bullets spat high into the ceiling of the hallway. Then the newcomer butted his forehead once more into Ronnie's face, and Ronnie fell backwards onto the bed with a choked cry, his gun spilling as blood splattered from his pulped nose. He cried out like a child and crabbed backwards.

The newcomer saw Parukau and moved instantly, diving sideways through the bathroom door even as Parukau's gun trained on him. A wide, shorter shape — *a pregnant woman?* — was silhouetted in the hallway door, but reflex took Parukau's aim towards the man, and the Glock coughed two bullets between the two targets, puncturing the bathroom wall. He jerked his aim back to the doorway, but with surprising grace the woman at the door was gone. He heard her voice call 'Wiri?', and his mind whirled.

Wiri — WIREMU! THE IMMORTAL!

He knew Wiremu, Puarata's spirit-warrior, one of the tohunga's two bodyguards, his hit men when all other coercion failed. Two immortal warriors he had conjured somehow: Tupu, the unstoppable force; and Wiremu, the silent killer. He recalled hundreds of council sessions with those two flanking Puarata, reminding them all of his power and reach.

And now Wiremu the Immortal was here. But he had never been one to dodge bullets back then — he hadn't needed to — and he had heard rumours whilst skulking about in the Ureweras that when Puarata had died, things had changed for Wiremu too ...

Boots thumped outside in the hallway, then went still. He heard a wet canine growl. Shadows moved beside the door. *Deano must be down. Useless kid.* He cocked the pistol, and kicked Ronnie. 'Get up, Ronnie,' he whispered. Then he raised his voice. 'Hey, Wiremu! Is that you?'

'Who's asking?' came the reply from the bathroom.

'An old friend,' he called out, stalling for time. 'What're you doing here?' Although he could almost guess — the Douglas boy must've called him. 'I hear you ain't so immortal now ... an' your woman out there is either a fat cow or you got a kid on the way. Not so invulnerable any more, are you?'

'Parukau,' answered Wiremu, a few seconds later. 'I recognize your voice ... and your stink. I was warned you were back in circulation. How was the time spent as a dog? Did you pick up any manners?'

Ronnie was on his knees behind the bed now, clutching his face like a woman. He would be no use, except as a distraction. More distantly, he heard shouting, and he could bet the sirens would sound next. He wished Brutal were here, to throw at Wiremu whilst he escaped. 'If you gonna come out that door and settle this, you better do it soon, "Immortal",' he taunted. 'Otherwise the cops are gonna be all over this place.' He put the antique pistol down on the bed, and gripped the Glock with both hands.

'Doesn't bother me,' Wiremu returned. 'I think you'll have more to explain than we do.'

Parukau heard a noise from the bathroom, like a knife

scraping glass, and wondered what it was. 'Maybe.'

The bathroom went silent. Sirens blared in the distance, muffled by the hotel's soundproofing — which meant they must be pretty close. Parukau eyed the door to the hallway. The woman was out there. There had been no sound since the dog had growled. Deano must be out of it: did the woman have Deano's gun? Did she know how to use it? Where was the dog? If it had taken down Deano, then it was a factor.

Time to gamble.

'Throw your gun out, Wiremu, and I'll let your woman live.' He looked at Ronnie, and pointed to the door. The big man nodded, and levelled his gun shakily. He was guessing Wiremu had a gun, although he had not seen one. 'Deal?'

A heavy black metal object spun out the bathroom door. He grinned.

Coiling himself up, he sprang towards the bathroom. He was firing even as he lunged around the corner. The gun bucked as bullets exploded from the muzzle and ripped holes in the walls, shattered the mirror, and flew straight through the window — which had no glass, just a gaping hole: the panel had been removed, and laid neatly against the wall.

He whirled, and looked straight down the barrel of Deano's Glock, gripped steadily by a pink-haired Pakeha girl in floral maternity overalls. She was still in the hallway, perfectly placed to cover him while remaining out of Ronnie's field of fire. *Well played, bitch!*

Her trigger finger squeezed; a bullet smashed into his left shoulder and spun him round. A second tore across his back, missing his spine by centimetres and slashing a rut across his right biceps. He shrieked, and desperately began to shift.

More bullets tore his flesh even as he began to fade. Out in the lounge he heard glass shatter inwards, and Ronnie bellow in terror. He pulled the whirling forces around him, and dived into Aotearoa. Empty air embraced him, and he had just a second to remember that he had shifted across from a point three storeys above ground level, before he was falling through tree branches. The ground flew up at him, and the world went out.

Armed police were swarming about the building within minutes. Seven police cars with sirens blaring surrounded the hotel, and uniformed men set up a cordon, herding the curious back. More police were guiding the staff and guests out to a staging area down the street. Sirens clamoured deafeningly. Through the chaos, hard-faced men with walkie-talkies strode about, creating a clear zone around the building, keeping the media back as they arrived, calming frightened guests. White vans disgorged a dozen black-clad Armed Offenders Squad officers with face shields, Kevlar body armour and automatic weapons.

It took a few minutes to secure the ground floor, and get men onto the back stairs. By then all apparent violence had ceased. A shattered window alongside a missing one identified the likeliest location, and a sharpshooter was racing to get to a vantage point across the street.

A hand appeared at the shattered window, holding a handkerchief. It wasn't white, in fact it was brilliant orange, although the intent seemed clear. Guns and cameras trained on it as a woman with spiky pink hair appeared.

'Hi, everyone!' she called anxiously. 'We've apprehended a criminal. Can you come up and give us a hand, please?' She smiled hesitantly, and waved at a news camera. 'Hi, Mum!' Then she exchanged a couple of words with someone inside, and turned back. 'Could someone give Tim Spriggs a call, please?'

The witch's cage

Thursday evening

Kurangaituku dropped the limp form into the cage she kept for just such a purpose, and then sat back on her haunches and watched the unconscious boy, occasionally reaching through and greasing her fingers in his blood, then licking them clean.

She hadn't meant to snatch this boy — it was the other one she was after — but when this one fell into her talons, instinct had taken over. And the Douglas boy had almost burned her. She shuddered.

I hate fire!

Mistress Kyle will want me to keep this one alive, for leverage … but I'm ravenous.

The boy groaned, and rolled over. He opened his eyes and peered through the gloom. He wasn't one to hide his face and pretend things hadn't happened, this one. Not like most of them. She liked that. But there wasn't much fat on him. Maybe he wouldn't make much of a meal after all. He looked up at her, through the wooden bars of the cage, with wide eyes. The room was dim. All he would be able to see of her would be a silhouette. His nose wrinkled as he inhaled the fetid air.

'What is your name, poai?' she asked.

'Riki,' he replied tentatively.

'You are a friend of the Douglas boy?'

He nodded. 'Yeah,' he said huskily. 'What do you want with us?'

She leant closer, measuring the fear in his voice. He was worried, but not terrified. And he didn't seem shocked by her appearance. What did he know of Aotearoa? Was he an Adept, like Douglas? Another fire-wielder? 'Do you know where you are?' she asked, ignoring his question.

'Aotearoa?' he replied, after a pause. 'You've gotta be that Birdwitch, that gets parboiled when she's trying to catch Hatupatu.'

She scowled at the reminder. 'Don't think that you'll escape me like that,' she growled. She shook her grey mane. 'Don't think you'll escape me at all, Riki.' She stood, thinking. *Kyle will want to question him.* She sighed, abruptly bored. 'Sleep. I will return in the morning.'

She stalked outside, into the night air. Most of her children were settling to sleep, but the night birds were waking. She called a morepork to her, filled its tiny mind with a message for Donna Kyle, then tossed it into the air. 'Tell her I have one of them,' she told it. 'But not the one she wants, so he's mine.'

Thursday afternoon

'Matiu Douglas! Come out!' Donna Kyle pirouetted slowly, watching every angle. 'Come out — I know you're there!' Nothing moved in the shadowy bush. Insects buzzed lazily, a gentle breeze stirred the leaves, and those damned birds just kept on watching her. She fought the desire to lash out at them. 'Matiu — come out! I only want to talk.'

She had followed as swiftly as she could, but had quickly lost sight of him in the dense bush, apart from a glimpse ten minutes ago, labouring up a slope half a kilometre ahead, just a chance sighting through the woods. But now … his elusive presence hung in the air.

'I know you think I'm the enemy, Matiu,' she called, fishing for contact, listening with every sense she possessed. 'But I'm not — I'm not really your enemy at all. I'm not even that different from you: I'm just fighting to survive!'

Her words echoed and faded about her. Nothing stirred. But the birds cocked their heads intently.

'I was *eight* when my father sold me to Puarata — can you imagine what that was like? What chance did I have?' She tried to put all that old pain into her voice. 'Mat, we don't have to be enemies.' She raised both hands. 'I just want to talk!'

She panted slightly, feeling very, very strange. This had begun as a ruse, to try to lure him out. But somehow, speaking these words aloud felt dangerous, and gave them a life of their own. And she couldn't stop talking suddenly. 'What happened to me could have happened to you, Mat. If Puarata had won last year, you would be *his* now. We would be allies.' Nothing moved. 'But he didn't win. You did! You freed me!'

A huge old crow turned and faced her from a branch in the nearest totara, with eyes like a camera.

'I'm the least of your enemies, Matiu. Venn is a foreigner — he'll rape this place if he wins! John Bryce: you know what a bastard he is. And Parukau … he's the worst of them all.' *Except for Father.* 'Parukau has the girl, Mat. The girl you're hunting. Together, we could find him and get her back. He can't hide from me, not when the Birdwitch is my servant! Not with all these birds looking for him.'

I bet Kurangaituku knows where the boy is … Crooked bitch …

'I'm not what you think, Mat! I'm like your friend Lena. I've had to swim in dark waters, but now I want to come back, into the light — and I need your help to do that. I can't give myself up to the authorities. Governor Grey would have my head on a pole in seconds — if my enemies didn't get to me first. So I've got to keep fighting. But with you beside me, vouching for me, helping me … I'd have a chance. People would listen. Please! Give me that chance!'

The silence mocked her.

She spat suddenly, and said a word that made every bird visible drop dead from its perch. It would not do to have this one-sided conversation reported to Kurangaituku.

Damn you, Matiu Douglas.

She had run out of words, and nothing stirred. Emotions she had forgotten boiled inside her, frightening her, so she pulled the darkness about her, and faded back into the real world.

The local constabulary

A tall, thin man with sandy hair and a dapper moustache ambled past the holding cells in the Rotorua Police Station. He wore a long trench coat, yet looked nothing at all like a policeman, or even a detective. But he had the right papers, and doors were opened for him. He was well connected, rumour said.

An eccentric appearance and manner, combined with favour in high places, should have made him an ostracized, resented figure who would be undermined at every turn out of sheer territory-protecting bloody-mindedness. But he wasn't. The fact that he talked like an old-world British army colonel should have made him a figure of fun. Which he was, but not in a mean way. Because it was impossible to dislike Tim Spriggs.

It was something about the way he chatted with everyone like they were good friends. He made others feel likeable. He was friendly with no hint that he was currying favour. He treated everyone with equal respect and esteem. And he operated with calm precision, despite his idiosyncrasies. The station officers had quickly learned to trust him. They occasionally wondered where on Earth he came from, but ghost worlds of the mythical past didn't figure in the speculation. Spriggs was one of a number of the Aotearoa constabulary that had some semi-regular contact with modern real-world police, but they kept it off the record.

So when he walked into the station, someone called out in a pantomime voice: 'I say, chaps, it's Inspector Timothy Watt-Ho from Scotland Yard!' Greetings showered down around him as he returned their smiles and waves.

'Good evening, young Anne. How are you this fine evening?' Timothy Spriggs beamed at the young policewoman behind the desk. 'I hear you have some friends of mine staying with you.' She smiled up at him, and directed him to the door to the interview room. 'Thank you, my dear.' He sidled past a couple of Armed Offenders Squad officers, who looked at him curiously, and into the narrow hallway beyond. He took the second door on the left, entered the spartan room, and sat down. Opposite him was a frayed-looking Maori police detective, a handsome man growing old quickly, with grey forming at his temples, and hands that seemed to be smoking a non-existent cigarette. His name tag read: *HOLLIS, T.*

Hollis looked up and smiled bleakly. 'Gidday, Tim. Coffee?'

'Gracious, Tu, you know I only drink the finest Ceylon tea. Purifies the mind, you know.' Spriggs smiled at the man opposite him. 'You married yet, Tu? Surely some lovely wahine is just waiting for you to drop on one knee and pop the magic question?'

Hollis rolled his eyes. 'Not you, too, Tim. I get enough of that at home. Haven't met anyone likely for a while ... and not likely to in this bloody job,' he added ruefully.

'It all comes to us in time, Tu. So, what's the problem then?'

Hollis frowned. 'Well, these friends of yours — I take it you do know them? — are the problem.'

Spriggs smiled reflectively. 'Wiri and Kelly are very close friends, Tu. What's the matter? I heard they caught someone you were looking for?'

Tu Hollis rolled his eyes. 'Hmph! Either they're just unlucky people in the wrong place at the wrong time, or they are vigilantes on a revenge spree. And I can't work out which.' He looked at Spriggs with a serious expression. 'Nothing in their background suggests too much trouble: a part-time entertainer and a security guard looking for their friend — and yes, their friend was staying in that room — and they seemed to have no idea what they were walking into. But hell, Tim, they're just too damned competent for people who are supposed to be innocent passersby.' He looked at Spriggs with a look of exasperation. 'Your friends — an unarmed man and an unarmed pregnant woman — and a dog, lest we forget — took down three armed men without a scratch. What are they — ex-SAS?'

'Goodness me, no. Just good citizens, Tu. You say they weren't hurt at all then? Thank heavens!'

'Hmmm. I believe the man — Wiremu — might have grazed a knee when diving *into* the *third floor* window of the suite. Otherwise, nothing. But their dog almost killed the kid in the hallway, and the big guy in the bedroom is still out cold.' He leant forward. 'Tim, there are clearly connections here. They claim they came to meet a Napier schoolboy called Matiu Douglas, but instead found three men in Douglas's room. None of the hotel staff saw the men arrive and have no idea how they got into the room. The manager wants it hushed up because it implies the hotel isn't secure. Fat chance! There were more cameras flashing than at a Peter Jackson premiere.'

Spriggs waved a hand airily. 'I understand one got away?'

'Yeah. A lowlife from Taupo called Evan Tomoana.' Hollis frowned. 'Which is where it gets interesting: last Sunday, two of these guys were done for assault in Taupo — Tomoana and Ronnie Symes, the big guy who was KO'd in the bedroom. They got bailed from Taupo, and then failed to show up at the station on Thursday. We got an anonymous tip that they were in town, having kidnapped a missing girl, Hine Horatai. Know the name?'

Timothy Spriggs shook his head, and motioned for Hollis to continue.

'The person they were arrested for beating up was the same Matiu Douglas, son of a Napier lawyer, who was visiting his mother in Taupo. These names familiar, Tim?'

Spriggs grinned. 'Everyone knows Tama Douglas.'

Hollis rolled his eyes again. 'Indeed. The lowlife's lawyer of choice in the Hawke's Bay. Anyway, it's the Douglas kid's room. He hasn't come back, by the way. But wait, there's more! The assault that Tomoana and Symes got done for was apparently over Tomoana's girlfriend, who is — you guessed it — the missing Hine Horatai! She went missing Sunday night, right after the fight. It seems our colleagues in Taupo misplaced her while delivering her to the women's refuge. And this morning Taupo station got an anonymous message telling us the Horatai girl was in Rotorua. But nothing is truly anonymous anymore: the call came from the telephone of

Colleen O'Connor, Matiu Douglas's mother.' Hollis rubbed his eyes. 'So, it's nearly midnight here in Roto-Vegas, and we have ourselves a few problems, I'm thinking.'

'Not any more, Tu. I'm here to make your problems go away.' Spriggs pushed some papers across the desk. 'All of your problems, just by signing these.'

Hollis sighed mournfully over the papers, wincing slightly at the name on the bottom. Way too high up! 'Tim, at the least I'm obliged to impound the dog: it could have killed that kid. It's a potential threat to public safety. So are these friends of yours, in my opinion.'

Tim Spriggs stood up. 'Tu, my friend, I give you my word of honour that they are not vigilantes. I'll take them into my custody, usual guarantees and all that. And I don't think you need worry about the dog. I'd be awfully grateful if you could keep a sharp lookout for Douglas and Horatai. And of course, bring in that rotter Tomoana if you can.'

Hollis studied the letters, and reflected that he had no choice. He felt oddly relieved. 'You really do have some guardian angels in Wellington, don't you, Tim?' Hollis signed the papers quickly, and pushed them back to Spriggs. 'Okay, okay, take them away, and don't let me see them again. The Labrador's out the back with the police dogs. They seem to like him, funnily enough.'

'I should think so, he's a lovely fellow. Good evening to you then, Tu. Thank you, and don't work too hard, old bean.' They shook hands firmly, Spriggs's smile slowly infecting Hollis's lugubrious face.

Hollis shook his head as the tall Englishman went through into the interview room beyond, to be greeted by joyous exclamations from the young couple. Out back the dogs all began to bark happily.

Oh, to be loved wherever you go, he thought ruefully. *What normal policeman ever has that privilege?*

Spriggs took Wiri, Kelly and Fitzy to a private lounge of the famous, or infamous, Red Deer tavern in Aotearoa-Rotorua, in the smallish European part of the settlement. The Red Deer had a dodgy reputation for bad whisky and gunpowder smuggling. Although it was well after midnight, the tavern remained open and, judging from the noise from the taproom below, well patronized.

It was only the second time they had got together since they had aided Mat's flight north a year ago, but the prevailing mood was worry. Spriggs knew Aethlyn Jones better than Wiri and Kelly, and they drank a quiet toast to him.

'Mat thought Jones might be alive,' Kelly stated.

'He may not be dead,' Spriggs agreed. 'Judging from what you said Mat saw. I for one have learned to assume the best when it comes to Aethlyn Jones.'

'I hope so,' Wiri replied. Fitzy mewled softly from the floor — turehu weren't popular here so he was staying in dog form.

'I say, Wiri,' said Spriggs, 'I'm surprised at you bringing your lovely wife into this situation in her, ahem, delicate condition!'

'She's not so delicate, actually. I tried to insist she stayed in Wellington, and nearly found myself divorced over it.' Wiri glanced at Kelly, smiling slowly.

'He would have come alone, the thick-headed dork, and

then where would he have been, huh?' scowled Kelly. 'You men have such delusions of adequacy. Wiri thinks he's still immortal, and can charge a roomful of gunmen armed only with a patu and still come out the winner.'

Wiri looked at Tim as if to say 'See what I'm up against?'

Kelly took a swallow of orange juice with no enjoyment, and glared at her swollen belly. 'Sooner this bloody lump's out, the sooner I can have a long, glorious double brandy and feel human again.' She looked at the others. 'So, where's our Matty?'

'Hollis has the Rotorua police looking out for him on his side,' Spriggs told her. 'But we'll need to hunt in Aotearoa, too. I can enlist some Aotearoa constabulary to have a look round, but they will struggle to get anyone here 'til after sunrise.'

'Parukau spoke like he knew Mat,' said Wiri. 'He must've got outta that dog-binding when Puarata died. Last time I saw him was back in the 1890s.'

'Ahhh, the 1890s,' Spriggs sighed reminiscently. 'Good times.'

'Speak for yourself,' Wiri grumped. 'I was bodyguarding the tohunga makutu, remember? Grubby, nasty decade.'

'You're a pair of relics!' Kelly complained. She swirled her glass thoughtfully. 'So, who's Parukau?'

Wiri gave her a potted history, and Kelly thought it over. 'Why would Parukau want Mat? If Parukau took over this Tomoana-guy *after* his fight with Matty, then he wouldn't care about Tomoana's petty vendettas.'

'Also, they weren't prepared for serious resistance,' said Wiri. 'Apart from Parukau, they didn't have a clue what they were doing. They were amateurs.'

'They were morons,' agreed Kelly. 'I don't think they had any more idea where Matty is than we do. So, what's going on? Who is this Hine chick you mentioned, Tim? Any idea? I got a bit out of Mat when he phoned, but he was pretty cut-up over Jones.'

'I've no idea, Kelly my dear. If Aethlyn was sheltering her, then she must be someone of potential. Someone like young Mat, I suppose.'

'And Mat said that it was Donna Kyle behind the attack on he and his mother, and probably the second wave of attackers at Jones's cottage,' Wiri reminded them.

'I guess the theory that Matty and Hine are locked away somewhere making mad passionate love can be discarded,' Kelly joked half-heartedly.

The men half-smiled. 'Splendid thought, my dear,' said Spriggs, 'but, no, it doesn't fit the facts.'

Wiri nodded grimly. 'I think there is a crossfire going on here. Kyle, Parukau, maybe others.' He turned to Spriggs. 'What help can we get, Tim?'

Spriggs looked concerned. 'There's the rub, old boy. Puarata used to come here, and folk are afraid to get involved. There are not a lot of resources we can call on. The soldiery on this side are primarily mercenaries, and Venn has been doing most of the hiring. The only other manpower here are the local tribes and they're staying out of it. They've been burned by the warlocks too often.'

'There's no justice, there's just us, huh?' said Kelly.

'Well, maybe. I'll see what I can do. I'm going to see if anyone in the pa saw anything. I've booked you a room in the real world, and I'll be back to check on you in the morning.

Don't try ringing Mat's cellphone until morning, when we can rig up a few devices to trace any answer we get. Okay?'

They sat in silence, and contemplated their helplessness. Finally Wiri sat up a little. 'That sounds fine, Tim. I'll make a few calls, too, then we'll get some sleep, yeah?'

'It's not much of a plan, Stan,' rhymed Kelly, tiredly.

'It's all we can do for now,' said Wiri. He patted Kelly's belly. 'Let's all get some rest, and pick things up in the morning.'

Fitzy stretched. 'You can. I'm going to go and have a sniff around. Literally.' He padded towards the stairs. 'My nose can find things your dull human senses cannot,' he said smugly. 'I'll find Mat if anyone can.'

Bargaining points

Parukau liked Tomoana's body. It was muscular, virile, and Evan Tomoana was of a like nature to himself. It was a good alliance, a strong symbiosis. He wanted to keep it. *But, damnation, it hurt!* The shoulder was a mess, and he was bleeding dangerously from the bullet wound. The three-storey fall had broken ribs, a collarbone and his left ankle. He probably had concussion, too, judging by the double vision.

When he woke, he was amazed that his spirit had not been torn loose already from this body — anything and anyone could have slain him as he lay behind the buildings of main street Aotearoa-Rotorua. He had been lucky. Evidently people didn't venture out after dark for any reason around here.

He wondered dimly if Deano and Ronnie had lived or died, but he didn't really care. Another world-shift right now could just about finish him off. He was essentially a disembodied spirit, and psychic exhaustion was more dangerous to him than physical punishment. So he skirted the old town, limping along the lakefront, falling in and out of tepid mud pools until he was fouled and begrimed. He didn't know if anyone saw him, but no-one challenged him. Problem was, he got dizzier and dizzier. Finally the ground swung up and smacked him, and everything went black again. It felt final.

Parukau. Wake up!

He shook his head. *Damn, I know that voice …* Old memories rose, and a face … *Asher Grieve!*

Indeed, Parukau.

You're dead. The thought raised frightening implications. *Am I dead?*

No, Parukau, you parasitic worm. Whatever claim you have on life, you still retain.

All charm as ever, Asher … What do you want? Where are you, if you're not dead? Then he smiled, as he realized the truth. *No, wait … You're chained up inside Te Iho!*

Indeed. Well done, old chap. But then, Te Iho was as much your idea as the Master's. You're quite right. After my fall from grace, I was locked up with the rest of his enemies. We were the wind beneath his wings.

Parukau snorted without sympathy. *Tough shit. I got locked inside a dog for a century. So, what do you want?* He could picture Asher, the old Asher, primping and looking indignant.

I didn't choose to reveal myself to you for your pleasant conversation, Parukau. I have an offer for you. As it happens, I'm the only inmate here that knows about the other inmates. A couple have made contact with real-worlders, though. They don't know I can hear everything they say. I've learnt much, here in the darkness. I can help you.

The pain in his wrecked human body reminded Parukau of his predicament. But he remembered Asher Grieve, too. It had been the three of them, back in the day: Puarata, tying up the Maori side of things, Asher working the missionaries and whalers and settlers, and Parukau the wildcard, the bodiless spy. As nasty a triumvirate as any Roman politico-tragedy. *When I went after Puarata, you just looked the other way, you bastard*, he growled at the presence in his mind.

Yours was an ill-advised attempt. If you'd come to me we could have worked together. At least my coup had a chance, until my daughter betrayed me.

Ahh. So that's how that one went down ... *Did little Donna not play ball? Serve you right, you old fruitbat!*

No, she didn't. And I will make her pay for that. I have a proposition for you. I understand you may have one half of the puzzle that is defeating you and her: how to lay claim to Te Iho ... which as you now gather, means how to find me! Do you?

Parukau lay in the mud in his failing body and thought about that. In his present state it didn't take long. *Yeah. I do.*

Tell me. The mental voice was deceptively disinterested.

Like hell! I remember you, Asher: I don't give info for nothing.

My dear fellow, think about this. Currently either my vile daughter or that bastard Venn are poised to claim Te Iho. Will they release me? No! Will they let you live? No! So if either of us wishes to be free, we have to work together.

Damn! He had to think this through, but pain was clouding his reason. *Did you approach Donna?*

She hates me. What would be the point?

Makes sense ... Shit, what to do ... *Okay, yes: I have half the puzzle. But I need the other half.*

Then you shall have it! Tell me what you know, and I will reveal the other half ...

Despite the pain, he wasn't going to fold that easy. *Like hell — other way round, arsehole!*

Asher Grieve chuckled in his ear. *Parukau, my friend. You have a girl in your custody; you think she is the key. For my part, I know where I am, but not how the door is opened ... We each have half the puzzle. We have to find a way to work together.*

Damn you, old man! You gotta earn my trust before I tell you anything. He clutched his head with relief. *I was right! It's the girl, she really is the key ...*

Then let us exchange conditional pledges, Parukau. You will reveal the key, and pledge to free me when you have opened the door to Te Iho ... and I will tell you where the gate is.

He stared into the darkness. Somewhere, Donna Kyle was *winning*, and he was stalled, in a broken body and no way forward. *Damn it! Okay, okay. Let's do it, old man.*

Before dawn, in a haze of pain, he managed to recover sufficiently to shift back to the real world, close to his motel. It was almost too much. He avoided the eyes of the pedestrians, and slipped inside the motel. He hammered on the door until Ko let him in, glanced at the girl to ensure she was still there because she was his only ace, and then he collapsed across his bed, oblivious to anything else.

Friday morning

Riki didn't know how long it took him to fall asleep, but he did. The rasping voice of the Birdwitch haunted his sleep, half-rousing him time and again. The place she had brought him — *her nest* — stank of bird droppings and there were old bones in the corner of the cage. *Human bones.*

This was bad. The cage was damned solid. There was water in a plastic bottle she had left him, but nothing else, just a bucket for slops. It didn't look like she planned on keeping him for long.

Hatupatu's adventures had been his favourite stories when he was a kid. Hatupatu was the classic youngest son, and was full of clever tricks to fool his elder brothers and his tribe's enemies, like draping toitoi bushes in cloaks to make it look like they were crouching warriors. He had beaten up his evil brothers and become chief. Hatupatu was Riki's sort of hero, especially at a time when his own brothers all seemed pretty evil, although he loved them dearly now.

I just wish Hatupatu had killed this old hag properly!

Hatupatu had been kidnapped by Kurangaituku and held in a cage for food. But he had escaped, hid inside a rock, and then led her through the mud pools here in Rotorua until she had slipped, fallen in and been boiled to death. The way Granddad told it, she had seemed as much comic as frightening — but she didn't seem funny at all in the flesh.

The dawn chorus started before five o'clock, by his wrist-watch; there was no point in trying to get any more sleep. He felt battered and sore, and he was trapped in the Never-never with a carnivorous witch. *Now would be a good time to show up, Matty Douglas! Ain't that what heroes do?*

An hour passed in which nothing stirred in that gloomy room. It was utterly unfurnished, with nothing but his six-by-six cage in it. Nothing he could reach out and snag to help him escape. His experimental kicks at the door just produced a rattling that he was afraid would bring Witchy-poo, so all there was to do was wait and hope.

She came for him just after dawn, as sunlight gleamed golden through the shutters. The deafening chatter of the birds fell silent as she opened the door, and hunched inside. She was still wrapped only in her feather cloak and a small shift. Her crone face sat incongruously above that muscular body. She stared at him, licking her lips, her eyes nothing like human. 'Do you know my name, human?' she asked, eventually. There was a strange weight in the question, in the way she said it. It was ... *wistful* ... hoping for something she did not believe would ever happen.

He thought he knew — the obvious answer — but he didn't answer at once. Something told him that this was a riddle she asked all of her victims, like the sphinx did in Egyptian stories. *Damn, I wish I'd listened more to the old fellas around the marae ...*

'Kurangaituku,' he answered slowly, experimentally.

Wrong answer! She swelled in size, filling the room, hunched over the cage like a hungry beast. Her face contorted, her nose and chin growing together like the top and bottom of a beak, the eyes blazing with hunger. Her huge taloned hands reached out, and pulled the cage open. He fell back to the far wall, as she cawed like a crow and reached out.

He continued frantically: '—*is the wrong name! The right one is on the tip of my tongue!*'

To his utter amazement, she paused. A talon that could have crushed his skull clenched and retracted.

Her voice held a genuine longing. 'You have ten seconds, human, to find the right answer ...'

Asher's bargain

Friday, pre-dawn

All night, Donna Kyle stalked real-world Rotorua, throwing death-threat looks at anyone that glanced at her, until the night-time crowd simply vanished. Then she slumped onto a bench by the lake and stared across the waters.

Kurangaituku had sent a morepork, which had spoken in a harsh voice, telling her that Kurangaituku held Matiu Douglas's companion, whoever he was. *One morepork!* What sort of alliance of mutual agreement was that? There had been no further contact. *Damn her, this is betrayal!*

Had Matiu Douglas been there? Had he heard her words? Did he believe them? She didn't even know now if she had meant them, but she could hear them still, replaying in her mind.

She summoned the patupaiarehe, and sent them into Aotearoa. Stone, to bring the goblins to this shore; Heron, to find Kurangaituku and deliver her most urgent summons; Thorn, to scout for Parukau — only Rose she kept with her. The girl was singing softly to herself, pirouetting at the water's edge, lost in some fantasy. Together and alone, they waited out the eternal night. It came as a vague surprise that the sun rose. Donna had almost forgotten that such a thing happened. It hurt her eyes to watch that orb lift above the dark horizon, and see the shafts of light stab the darkness with brutal clarity.

Rose whimpered as the light grew. 'Go! Go and cower in a hole,' Donna snapped at her. The patupaiarehe quailed, but she didn't stay. Alone — finally, truly alone — Donna made herself watch the dawn. While she still could.

Where and what is Te Iho? If I don't get to it first, I'm worse than dead. Everything was slipping from her hands. *If I stop concentrating, I'm going to fly apart …*

A dry voice chuckled into her mind, and she didn't have the strength to banish it. *Daughter*, whispered Asher Grieve. *My little Donna, take courage. I can help you.*

She cringed, curling up inside herself.

Daughter, I feel your pain. It hurts me as it hurts you.

'Liar!'

He ignored her. *The clues are falling into place, Donna. Te Iho is within your grasp. It is in Rotorua. I remember the smell of sulphur.*

'You remember *what?*' she asked, her interest sparked despite herself.

Yes, he replied, in his baited tones, *it is in Rotorua, Daughter. Where you are! And there is a special, unique blood that opens the gates, and the path beyond. I remember it, floating through the air as if it were flowing through water. The Blood of the Swimmer, Daughter!*

'The Blood of the Swimmer? What does that mean?'

Think, Daughter! Lake Rotorua. A swimmer.

Omigod. 'An avatar?'

Yes, an avatar. Parukau has her.

'How can you know that?'

Parukau himself told me of it. His voice sounded eerily self-satisfied.

She felt herself chill. 'He *told* you?'

Indeed, Donna. Do you think you are the only one I can communicate with?

She almost swallowed her tongue. *'You're helping Parukau?'* she breathed, more frightened than she had ever been in her entire life.

Manipulating him, Daughter. I know his strings, and how to pull them.

'Why are you telling me this?'

To give you one last chance, Donna. Do you think I want that snake Parukau beside me when I rise anew? Of course, if needs must, then that is how it will be, but it is you who I truly want at my side.

She wondered how her heart kept beating. 'But I don't know where Te Iho's gate is. And I don't know where Parukau has the girl. You've got to give me more than this, Father!'

Do I have your Pledge then?

Damn this! Damn this! 'Yes,' she half-sobbed, 'I pledge to free you.' She put her face in her hands, wailing inside.

To free me alive and unharmed, and to kiss my ring and serve me, Daughter, he purred inside her mind. *To rule beneath me — my princess — in a new regime that will rule Aotearoa forever.*

'Yes. Yes. I so pledge.' She felt something tighten, like a chain twisting about her soul.

Ahhh. It is done, Asher sighed. She shuddered. *Do not despair. There is a way to prise the girl from Parukau. Remember the legend, Daughter! Seek the avatar that is her mate! He will be close at hand! Remember the legend.*

Suddenly he was gone. It was almost as if she felt his hand

on her head, but then his presence, almost tangible, faded away. She sat shaking, wondering what she had done. Then she realized that she was not alone. Only a few dozen metres away, a Maori man stood, his breath steaming in the cold air. He wore a police uniform beneath an overcoat, but she could see his other identity overlaying him plainly, if she concentrated. It felt so serendipitous as to be fate. Could it truly be him?

She walked towards him, as casually as she could. Before she could even open her mouth, he spoke aloud. 'It's a beautiful morning, isn't it?'

The effort of concealing her excitement and wonder was almost beyond her. But she managed. 'Yes,' she breathed, forcing the slightest smile while her heart leapt in her chest like a caged beast. 'Unbelievable.'

The Maori man smiled softly. 'I love this place,' he said, as much to himself as to her. He was, perhaps, in his forties, and had a kind of emptiness in his eyes, a loneliness he didn't know how to fill. 'I love the way the water catches the light.'

She stared at him. This wasn't any sort of chat-up line — he would have said the same things even if he was here alone. 'I'm Donna,' she said quietly, hoping it wouldn't break the moment. But she needed to know his name. 'You are …?'

'Tu Hollis,' he replied, half-turning. His face had a tired, disappointed cast to it, but unbroken. 'Tutanekai Hollis, actually. My folks named me for the old story.'

Yes!

She froze him in place with a smile, then smashed him around the temple with a fist that she infused with stone. He dropped like a pole-axed bull.

She took the prone Tutanekai Hollis through to Aotearoa, and was pleasantly surprised to see that Stone had not failed her — a waka of tipua goblins stood standing offshore, awaiting her. She waved them ashore, and they carried the prone policeman through the shallows and deposited him on the canoe. She took a position in the stern, and gestured impatiently. Within minutes, they were paddling across the dawn-flecked lake to the island. She sent out a mental call to the other patupaiarehe as they surged across the water.

Come to the island, immediately. The game has changed.

In the modern world, Mokoia Island is semi-deserted, a native flora and fauna reserve, a tourist site and, during the school holidays, a school for traditional Maori martial skills. It had once been inhabited, but no more, in either the real world or Aotearoa. They struck the south shore beside the hot pools, and dragged the waka ashore, under the canopy of the forest. The tipua hid themselves in the shadows, liking the sunlight little more than the patupaiarehe. Rose and Thorn arrived minutes later, flowing through the air like jets. But no Heron. Donna frowned, then realized in sudden panic that she no longer held the life cord that controlled the scarecrow-like being. She felt her heart flutter in alarm. *How had that happened? When?*

Father did it ... He must have ...

She banished the others to the shadows uneasily.

She had the goblins leave Tutanekai Hollis beside the very pool where the legends said Hinemoa came to Tutanekai. The policeman woke slowly, groggily, and stared at her. With her servants in the shadows she might have seemed alone, but he didn't try anything, just waited as the pale morning sun lit Aotearoa. They were in a grassy clearing, right up against the lake, where flat slate rocks bounded a pool of gently bubbling hot water that steamed enticingly in the chill morning air. A few metres away was a disused mission house established in the 1800s but gone now from the real world, although still present here in Aotearoa.

She had taken a crude flute from one of the tipua, and now she proffered it to Tutanekai Hollis. 'Play.'

He glared back at her with rebellion in his eyes. 'Go to hell.'

'I'm not a believer in heaven or hell,' she told him. 'Play the damned flute.'

'No!'

With an effort of will that made her shudder, she refrained from ripping his heart out. Instead, she bent over him. 'Listen, Tutanekai. You have two choices. You will play that flute, and finally get to meet the one woman who can make your lonely existence meaningful. I swear I will even let you both live, once I'm done with you.' *Maybe.* 'Or you keep refusing, in which case I will allow my servants to eat you, slowly, raw. You have around ten seconds to make up your mind.' She sat back and stared out across the water. 'Think of me as an unusual kind of dating service.'

Tutanekai Hollis faced her down for a few seconds, then capitulated. He slowly picked up the flute, raised it to his lips, and began to blow. He seemed surprised as a strange and eerie music arose, as much from the place about them as from the instrument he held. But she wasn't surprised at all.

Can you hear this, Hinemoa?

Prisoners in the darkness

Friday, pre-dawn

Mat dreamt, of Ngatoro.

They were in a darkened room, moonlight streaming through big windows behind him. The old man hung in the air before Mat, wrapped up in tubes that looked like veins, pulling and pumping fluids from his body and out into the darkness. His body was thin and hunched, his limbs twitching occasionally. His long, grey hair floated as if he were under water, and his eyes were closed, but his lips moved faintly. Bubbles formed at his lips and streamed upward and dissolved.

They weren't alone. To the left and right, in a circle fading into the shadows, there were at least a half-dozen others, male and female, all old, almost all of them Maori. The windows revealed a vista of moonlit rose gardens, oddly familiar.

Ngatoro opened his eyes. They were like two discs of slate, and they didn't seem to see Mat at all. 'Matiu?' Ngatoro whispered, barely audible. 'Are you dreaming or are you really here?'

'I think I'm asleep,' Mat replied. 'Where are we?'

'In my prison, where Puarata left me.'

Mat looked at the other captives. 'Who are these others?' he whispered, slightly awed.

'What others?' Ngatoro breathed. 'There are no others. They're all dead and gone.'

'Can't you see them?' Mat asked. 'They're right here …'

The old tohunga shook his head, making his silver hair ripple through the air. 'There used to be others. I am the last.'

'But … what is this place?'

Ngatoro sighed. 'This is Puarata's lair. He called it "Te Iho" — The Heart.'

'This is what all of his warlocks are looking for!' Mat stared about him.

Ngatoro nodded. 'Yes, this is the place. He overmastered me, with poisons and treachery, and he brought me here. I remember blood, a stream of blood that we followed through a dark shifting cave or tunnel: a shadow-maze. I was only half-conscious.' His voice became dreamy and faint.

'Where are we? Where in the real world?'

'I don't know.'

'I went to sleep in Rotorua! The warlocks are here. I think they're looking for Te Iho in Rotorua.'

'Rotorua? I don't know … I thought it was in the Ureweras, in a cave. They took me through caves, Parukau and Puarata, and then …' The old tohunga visibly fought to rouse himself. 'Mat, a shadow-maze is impenetrable without a guide. Without the guide, you will be lost forever. You must find the gate, and the guide!'

Mat bit his lip. 'I don't know what the guide is. And I don't know where the gate is. Is there some other way?'

Ngatoro thought for a time, going so still Mat almost

thought he had fallen asleep. Finally, he whispered, 'There is only one other way: primal fire.'

'Primal fire?'

The old tohunga nodded. 'Original fire. True fire. To burn the walls of shadow.' His head slumped again. Mat bent as close as he could. 'Mahuika,' the tohunga whispered, utterly exhausted. 'Mahuika. You must find her. Immediately! If you cannot find the guide, then you must gain primal fire from Mahuika, and then you must find the gateway ...' His head slumped forward. 'All else is secondary ...'

'Ngatoro!' Mat called him, a forced whisper. He tried to reach towards him, but found his hands passing through the old man. He jerked back, and looked left and right.

Every prisoner in that place dreamt on, oblivious.

Except one.

The next prisoner in the line, a grey-haired Pakeha with a hook nose and deep dissolute lines about his face, was staring at him open-eyed. 'YOU!' the man spat. He raised a hand, and pointed straight at him. 'GET OUT!'

A blank wall of force swatted him, and he spun and fell ...

... and woke.

Mat sat up abruptly, a cry half-formed on his lips, and blinked in the dim sunlight. Then he almost leapt ten feet as a wet tongue slopped at his cheek. *'Arghhh!'*

Fitzy chuckled darkly. 'Heh heh. Just me, Mat.'

He stared at the turehu, clutching his chest. 'Hell, Fitzy! Couldn't you have just barked or something?'

'Yeah, but that would've meant I didn't get to see you nearly wet yourself.' Fitzy glanced around. 'I suppose you know that we're under observation?'

They both looked up at the birds that sat silent on every branch. 'Yeah.' He rubbed his eyes. The first thing he remembered was that bizarre one-way conversation with Donna Kyle. He was still struggling to think his way through that ... Was she sincere? She had tried to kill him several times, and yet when she had captured him a year ago in Auckland what she really wanted was a way to escape Puarata's clutches. It was that desire to escape that had enabled him to turn the tables on her.

Then he remembered Riki, and that pushed all thought of Donna Kyle from his mind. He sat up, his eyes wide. 'Kurangaituku has got Riki, Fitz! She eats people — we've got to find him.' Even while speaking, though, he remembered Ngatoro's words: *Mahuika. You must find her. Immediately! ... All else is secondary ...*

Fitzy was sniffing about. 'I've already tried, while you were sleeping. But things that fly or can leap fifty or sixty feet at a go aren't so easy to track.' He hung his head. 'I lost them. I'm sorry.'

Mat hung his head. 'It's my fault. I dragged him into this.'

Fitzy didn't disagree. The turehu just padded up and nuzzled him. 'Blaming ourselves doesn't undo our mistakes,' he said softly. 'Come on, we've got to go back and join the others.'

Mat stood unsteadily, looking about him with unseeing eyes. *Mahuika ... find her ... all else is secondary ...*

How long would it take to find the others, and then to find Mahuika? And what was the Birdwitch doing even now to Riki?

215

All else is secondary ...

He would have to trust in Ngatoro.

'Fitzy,' he said slowly. 'Do you know how to find Mahuika?'

Fitzy looked up at him in puzzlement. 'That old bat? Why the hell would you want to find her?'

Everyone knew the legend of Maui and Mahuika — well, everyone Mat knew. It was a staple of kindergarten story-time. Mahuika was guardian of the fire, and she was also Maui's grandmother. Mankind had fire as a gift from her, but could not make new fire. Seeing this, Maui, the famous trickster demigod who had fished up New Zealand and tamed the sun, put out all the fires of the village. Then he went to Mahuika, telling her all the fires had somehow gone out, and asked for more. She believed him, and pulled out one of her fingernails, which burst into flame, and gave it to Maui to take back to his village.

But Maui went just a little way from her caves, and then stamped on the fingernail to put the fire out. He then went back, told her it had gone out, too, and asked for another. Because he was her grandchild, Mahuika let him have another, and he again doused it, and so on until she had no fingernails and only one toenail left. This she threw at him, and it burst into a great living fireball that pursued him as he fled. He ran for his life, even took hawk form, but the great fireball pursued him, and would have destroyed him and all the world, but he called upon the gods to save the world, and they did, sending rains to douse the fireball. These rains also fell upon Mahuika, and extinguished her fires. To preserve fire, she sent the last of her powers into the trees, into the mahoe, the totara and the kaikomako. This had been Maui's plan all along, because now anyone could make fire, just by rubbing splinters of those trees together.

'What happened to Mahuika?' Mat asked Fitzy.

'She's been sulking in her cave for centuries,' Fitzy told him. 'She has a tendency to throw fireballs around, so most people find her a little antisocial. Anyway, she's a bore — all she does is whine about Maui and what a bastard he was.' He stared out to the south. 'Do you know of the Pink and White Terraces, which were buried by the eruption of Mount Tarawera? Her caves are near there, in Aotearoa, where the terraces remain undamaged.'

'How far is that?'

'Twenty kilometres to the southeast of here.' Fitzy looked up at him. 'Why do you want to know?'

Mat told him.

Fitzy studied him anxiously. 'The others are going to be really worried if I don't come back. Why don't we go see them, and maybe catch a lift?'

'I don't think so. What Ngatoro said implied that Parukau has everything he needs to get control of Puarata's lair: he knows the location, and he has Hine — 'the blood of the swimmer'. He could get to the lair any time. I don't think I can waste even a minute.'

Fitzy exhaled. 'Okay. Okay! I guess I'll have to get you there myself then.'

Mat looked down at the turehu gratefully. 'Thanks. But it's a long way.'

'Yeah, but at least I know the way. Turn around,' he added.

Mat turned around. 'Why?'

'Just because,' the turehu answered a few seconds later, in a deeper voice, huffing in a most un-dog-like manner.

Mat turned and gasped. 'Fitzy! You're a horse!'

He was, too — a sleek chestnut with a lean frame and long thoroughbred lines. 'What decent turehu has only one shape?' he asked disdainfully.

Mat thought for a second, then grinned. 'A one-trick pony.'

Fitzy snorted. 'Hrumph! Get on, you cheeky sod, before I change my mind.'

Mat swung up hesitantly. He had never ridden before, except for a couple of walks on school outings to farms, and certainly not bareback. 'You mean you could have carried me all the way from Napier to Taupo last year?' he asked, a little accusingly.

'I couldn't carry all three of you, so why would I carry just one?' the turehu retorted. 'And anyway, I don't like being a horse. Gormless lummoxes! Now, hold the mane, and I'll try and make it easy for you. Grip with your thighs, and hang on!'

Mat had barely settled on Fitzy's back when the turehu erupted from a standing start, and suddenly he was clinging on for dear life.

Avatar

Friday morning

Hine awoke shaking from a dream about Evan: there was a serpent inside his mouth that kept lunging out at her when he tried to kiss her.

'Hush!' Ko was kneeling over her, holding a hand over her mouth. For a second she panicked, thinking Ko was attacking her, then realized that all she was doing was trying to muffle her.

She was on the floor of the motel bathroom, manacled to the piping beneath the handbasin. Somehow she had slept, even there, but with horrible nightmares. She felt grimy and desperately needed to use the toilet. There was still dried blood on her clothes and skin.

When Ko saw Hine was calm, she put a pudgy finger to her lips, and looked back over her shoulder into the bedroom. Hine peered past her. Evan lay face-down on the bed, covered in filth. She could smell mud and rottenness emanating from him in waves. Blood was running from his right shoulder. She felt a surge of hope. Then Brutal loomed around the corner, and looked at Ko. The kneeling woman held out a hand, and Brutal placed a small key into it. Ko unlocked the manacles, and then Brutal pushed in, bodily lifted Hine up and carried her out into the main room, through the adjoining door and into the unit Ronnie and Ko and their children were sharing. Brandi looked up curiously from a pile of newspaper she was playing with, then went back to her drawing. Brutal put Hine down in the bathroom of this unit, then turned back to Ko. She handed over the cuffs reluctantly, and he manacled Hine again to the basin pipes, exactly as she had been in the other bathroom.

'No more damned screaming,' growled Brutal quietly. 'Man can't sleep. You make a racket like that again an' I'll smack you one.' He straightened, then put a big hand on her right breast and squeezed it.

'Hey!' hissed Ko. 'Get your hands off her!'

'Piss off, Ko,' snarled Brutal, shoving her out, and shutting the bathroom door. He looked down at Hine with an empty, implacable gaze. There was nothing behind his eyes, nothing to reason with, as he knelt and placed a massive hand on either of her breasts, and groped roughly through the T-shirt.

'Brutal, don't do this,' she whispered. 'Evan will kill you.'

'Evan's stuffed. Two bullets in the shoulder. He'll be dead by nightfall.' His voice took on a whining quality. 'I hope he dies. Cos everything's gone to shit. I want to go home. I don' wanna die.'

'Where are Deano and Ronnie?' she asked, to get him thinking, talking, anything to make him stop.

He stopped mauling her. 'They never came back, Hine. He took them off with him, an' they ain't come back. He's got them killed ... an' they're my *friends*. He's killed the poor bastards.' He bent over, and started to cry.

She watched him in sick wonder. She had never thought to see this man cry in her life. It was beyond strange. 'Brutal, please let me go,' she whispered. 'Let's all go, back to Taupo! You and me and Ko and the kids.'

He looked up, wavering. It occurred to her that he had probably never done a thing of his own volition since he had met Evan. Maybe in his whole life. He was just muscle and appetite. He didn't know how to make a decision. 'I ... Can I ... uh ...'

She tried to sound calm and reassuring. 'We can do it, Brutal! We can leave him behind. We can get through this. Please, let me loose!'

His face wavered. Her heart hammered as he gave a faint nod, and—

The door smashed open behind him, and Evan stood there, swaying, his shoulder swathed in scarlet, the rest of his body filthy. A massive flintlock pistol was clenched in his left hand, the hammer primed, the long barrel almost touching Brutal's forehead. His face contorted into a demonic grin. 'Et tu, Brutal?'

The pistol roared. The explosion was deafening as the back of Brutal's head exploded outwards, bathing the room in hot blood and sticky lumps of bone and brain. Hine was beyond screaming, felt her mouth work soundlessly, her ears ringing silently, her whole body rigid with shock.

Evan ... *Parukau* ... was swaying. The pistol's recoil was enough to numb his weakened grip, and the weapon clattered to the floor. He clutched his bloody shoulder, and staggered sideways, smearing blood along the wall. 'Got you, you big bastard,' he rasped at Brutal, and then he slid down the wall to the floor. His face turned to Hine, his mouth opening. He said something unintelligible, then slumped sideways onto the floor beside her as blood pooled about them.

Ko appeared, her eyes round. 'Lovey! Are you okay? Omigod, omigod—' She began to shake. Behind her, in the lounge area, both children began to cry.

'Ko!' Hine interrupted, as sharply as she dared. 'Ko, you gotta get me outta these cuffs — please!'

Ko looked at her with bewildered eyes. 'Where's my Ronnie? Where's my Ronnie?' she repeated with mounting hysteria.

'Ko! Get me the key.'

Evan — *Parukau* — stirred.

'Get the key, Ko!' Hine pleaded. 'He's going to kill us — get the key!'

Outside in the room, she could hear shouting. The gunshot had been heard. Evan shook himself weakly. His eyelids flickered.

'The key!' she pleaded, trying to reach Ko. 'Ko — please!'

Something penetrated Ko's confusion and horror. She crawled into the pool of blood that was welling from Brutal's head, and fumbled in his pocket. She drew out the key, and clumsily unlocked Hine's right hand. Hine snatched the key and unlocked her other wrist, then scrambled up, hauling Ko to her feet. 'Get Filli! I'll get Brandi! We've gotta run, Ko — come on!'

Hine edged around Evan, and snatched up Brandi. Outside there was more shouting. Ko followed, slipping in the blood and almost falling. They tramped bloody shoe prints into the lounge.

'Filli!' She waddled to the bed, and picked up her baby.

'Hine!' growled Evan. His eyes were open and fixed on hers. 'Hine!'

Suddenly a strange sound penetrated the room. The thin call of a flute, barely audible, but carrying to her ear like a whispered promise, like the whisper of a mother. *No, not a mother ... a lover ...* She turned towards it, in sudden confusion. She saw a vision, of an island, and a man, and music that was winging across the surface of the lake, calling her home.

'Hine!' snarled Evan. 'Hine: block your ears — don't listen!' His face contorted with ... *was it fear?*

She wrapped Brandi in her arms and ran through the adjoining doorway, and then outside. An old man was peering out of his unit with a frightened face. He called out tremulously: 'What's happening? I thought I heard—' He saw the blood on her clothes, and backed away.

She looked back over her shoulder. 'Ko! Come on!' The big woman was scooping baby things into a bag. 'Leave them!' Hine screamed. 'Run!'

Ko looked up, took a deep breath, and stumbled towards her, tears streaming over her face. Filli was screeching in her big hands, the baby's tiny face red and furious. Ko rumbled past, but Hine lingered, hearing the song of the flute, feeling it shimmer about her.

Evan lurched around the door. 'Don't listen, Hine!' He tried to grab her with his right hand, but his arm wouldn't respond. His left hand held a handgun. She ran. The old man from the other unit stepped towards her, then looked over his shoulder in sudden terror. She ran past, clutching Brandi tight. A gun coughed behind her and she heard the old man cry in pain, and fall. She ran on, through the car park. The flute was even

223

more demanding here, rolling in waves across the water.

Ko looked at her helplessly, while Filli bawled. There were sirens in the distance, coming fast. 'What do we do?'

Hine looked past her friend, across the highway, across the houses and the fens, to where Lake Rotorua sparkled *so close* in the late afternoon sun. She saw the island, waiting. 'Tutanekai,' she whispered, speaking the word that whispered through the song of the flute.

Ko grabbed her shoulder. Evan's footsteps resounded behind them. 'Hine! What do we do?'

Hine knew. Somehow. She thrust Brandi into her mother's grasp. 'Go — go that way!' she said, pointing away from the lake, away from the island, away from that undeniable call.

'Hine?'

'Go!' she screamed at her friend, and then she ran, fleeing like a bolting horse. Down the driveway, out onto the highway, where car horns blared and tyres shrieked as they tried to avoid her. She never even saw them. 'Tutanekai!' She tore across the lawn of a house and leapt the fence, found herself in a ragged wasteland, soft ground sucking at her feet, growing deeper by the step, an expanse of water opening up beyond the reeds.

'Hine!' bellowed Evan, shockingly close. She threw a wide-eyed look back over her shoulder, and nearly collapsed in fear. He was right behind her, reaching, his face inhuman. She slipped and sprawled headlong into a muddy pool, scrambled up covered in green slime. His hand gripped the hood of her top and wrenched. She half-fell, but let her arms go limp and felt the garment come away. Overbalancing, Evan lurched to one side. She scrambled up, breathless and terrified, as he

224

tossed the hoodie aside and roared. 'Hine! Hinemoa! Stay! You are mine!'

She fled, pelting through the deepening pools, tripping and slipping, yet somehow staying away from him. The flute urged her on. A pale, cold light seemed to open before her, and she heard Evan cry out and his pursuit falter in a sudden splash. She pressed on, unable to risk looking back, until only open water lay between her and Mokoia Island.

'Tutanekai — I'm coming! I'm coming!' She waded into the water.

'Hinemoa, come back!'

She looked behind her. He was at the edge of the lake, clutching his shoulder, swaying. Behind him, the houses, the cars, the hotels and buildings — they were all gone. To her right, Rotorua was gone. Just like back in Taupo when Jones had showed her the view from his house, the modern city had vanished. Instead a few old-fashioned buildings were set back from some docks, and beyond them, the walls of a great pa. She was in Aotearoa again.

Evan stepped into the lake, raised his gun, and aimed it at her. It clicked impotently. He looked down at his limp right arm, and howled with rage.

She turned away, and blanked him from her mind. It wasn't hard, not with that flute calling. She walked into the deeper water. Her body thrilled to the sound of the little waves, lapping her thighs and then her belly with their cold, and to the texture of the water. Her element, washing her clean. The pitch of the flute's song was somehow different now, like an echo repeating over and over, urging her on. Her trackpants were heavy so she pulled them off before the floor of the lake fell away. *Maybe that's all they'll find of me.* The cold water caressed her skin. She plunged forward, and began to swim.

The sun climbed in the sky, but the lake, never warm, grew colder with each stroke Hine took. The water grew clearer as she drew further from shore, and she could see small fish, and larger ones, too, dimly outlined beneath the surface. Once she could swear something larger than her passed below her. *Impossible! There's nothing bigger than trout here ... right?*

Not in the real Lake Rotorua, her subconscious replied, *but what about here?*

She could still hear the song of the flute, echoing in her mind, but she was struggling to make out the island now, as mist and light rain wafted over the lake. She had been a good swimmer once, but that was years ago, when she was still the Golden Girl. Her muscles were tiring, and her confidence began to seep away. Freestyle became too sapping, so she switched to breaststroke. There were currents, too, and they didn't seem friendly. She was being pulled to the right, inexorably, away from the island. Her arms and legs felt heavy, and exhaustion crept deeper into her bones.

Keep going, girl.

She remembered her mother coming to watch her at swimming sports. She always seemed to be winning something then. She had felt so proud.

She also recalled her own thoughts from just a few days ago: *Some days I could just walk into the lake.*

The deep water called her. There were voices, audible when her ears were below the surface. She recalled dreams of sharks

circling below her. Cold things stirring, beneath the waters …
She heard them whisper: *Listen, Golden Girl! The flute has gone
silent. You are lost out here — there is just you … and us …*

But no, she could hear it still. That echoing refrain, calling
over and over, to the rhythm of each stroke.

Something cold and hard brushed her legs. She gasped,
and went under. Her mouth opened and filled with the deep
water, water that came up from far below, to pull her down,
to bloat her flesh and her eyes, and turn her skin to blue and
grey. The voices from below were loud now, accusing her of
betrayal, calling in her mother's voice.

Where are you, girl?

Why don't you come home?

You selfish little wretch, what haven't I done for you?

She felt the life drain from her arms, and she slipped deeper.
A huge shape circled in, a massive eel, and a huge saucer-eye
stared into hers. It opened its jaws …

… and the dark shapes circling her fled.

It's a taniwha.

Huge eyes fixed on her, and a huge body glided past her, and
writhed away. The wake of its passing cast her back towards
the surface, and she heard the music of the flute again.

Tutanekai!

Her legs jack-knifed, and suddenly she burst upwards, out
of the water like a leaping dolphin. She splashed and thrashed
on the surface, coughing up the deep water back into the lake.
The taniwha circled protectively. Her arms suddenly tangled
in ropes, tied to small buoyant gourds. She gathered them to
her chest and clung on, gulping sweet, sweet air. In a sudden
rush of white feathers, a gull swooped above her, calling. She

followed its gaze, and saw the bulk of the island, looming above her, suddenly close. Still the flute called.

She wrapped the gourds about her, and felt their buoyancy hold her up. New energy surged through her. She kicked out, ploughing her way freestyle towards Mokoia, the song of the flute ringing in her ears.

Cassandra walked Colleen O'Connor along the lakefront, on a day that had dawned bleak with a swirling wind. The waves were tipped white, and a light spray blended with the occasional showers that whipped Taupo. They both shivered inside their coats as they squelched beneath the willows.

At the old kauri, Cassandra led a sceptical Colleen around the tree anticlockwise — 'going this way round is called widdershins, you know' — and they emerged into a similar day in Aotearoa. Colleen looked nervy, ready to flee at the slightest strangeness, but she let Cassandra hold her forearm and pull her along the muddy path to Jones's cottage.

A black-clad colonial trooper was sitting on the porch, and he rose to his feet slowly as the two women approached. He didn't give either much of a curious look, as if he had seen stranger sights, or maybe he couldn't tell a strangely dressed real-world woman from a normally dressed one anyway. 'Wait here,' was all he said. They waited on the porch, and Cassandra examined the front door, which had been forced open — Mat had mentioned locking it.

A minute later, some kind of officer, if the braid on his shoulders was significant, came through the house. He had sideburns and a moustache, and a cap held respectfully in his hands. 'Ma'am, I'm Captain Blaise Duncan, Taupo Constabulary. With respect, what's your business here?'

He was looking at Colleen, but she seemed mute with fear and curiosity. Cassandra spoke up instead, introducing herself and resisting a sudden urge to curtsey. 'We're friends of Mister Jones, sir. We've come to help.'

Captain Duncan looked somewhat awed. 'Friends of Aethlyn Jones? Please, come on through.'

Colleen looked at Cassandra quizzically. Clearly she had been bracing for a curt dismissal. Being friends of Aethlyn Jones must carry a lot of weight. He probably thinks we're wizards or something, Cassandra realized with an internal smile.

There were no troopers inside the house, and her wiring and telephone gear were still on the table. Someone had been cleaning but there were blood traces, and she saw $R - O - T - O$ written in blood on the side of a cupboard. Out the back, a bunch of soldiers was loading bodies onto a cart — bikers from the Roadhawks gang and tipua goblins by the look of it. The stench of dead flesh permeated the yard, making both women gag.

'Widow Calder visited Jones yesterday, and found this mess,' Captain Duncan said. He indicated a grey-haired woman surveying the scene like a hawk watching over a road-kill possum. 'There is no sign of Mister Jones. Do you have any idea what happened here?'

'My son …' Colleen's voice trailed off.

'Your son, ma'am?'

Cassandra stepped in. 'This is Colleen O'Connor. Her son is Matiu Douglas.'

'Jones's apprentice? Where is he?'

Cassandra replied. 'He's okay. He went to Rotorua to seek the perpetrators of this attack.' She peered at Widow Calder, who was circling a piece of earth where all the grass had withered, and dark roots jutted from the ground. 'What's she doing?'

'I'm sure it's best not to ask,' muttered Captain Duncan. 'Ladies, I have to oversee the body tagging; if you will excuse me.'

Colleen slowly walked towards Widow Calder, who was leaning on her nobbled walking stick, making hand gestures over the circle of earth and chanting softly. 'Excuse me, ma'am?'

'Shush, Colleen,' the widow responded. 'I'm trying to find out what Aethlyn's gone and done this time.'

Colleen shuffled awkwardly. 'How do you know my name?'

'It's written all over you, child,' Widow Calder told her in a singsong voice. 'Yours, too, my sharp little tack,' she added, glancing at Cassandra. 'Hush. I'm sure he's here somewhere.'

Cassandra looked about her, trying to find some difference to the place she had seen last holidays. The only thing she could think of was … 'What happened to the ivy?'

Widow Calder frowned. 'He told me he'd cleared it.'

'Tough stuff to get rid of, ivy,' Cassandra replied, not really sure where she was going with the thought.

Widow Calder smiled at her suddenly, and walked back to the house. She dropped to her knees and nosed around until she found a single strand of ivy that rose from the ground, and beckoned Cassandra over. 'Look, girly,' she said in a sandpaper voice. The sprig of ivy was twined about some piling beneath the veranda, coiling upwards and then ... vanishing. It wasn't cut and it didn't end — it simply stopped. She tugged on it experimentally, and more appeared, as if she were pulling it through a hole in the air. 'Ahhh. He told me he had an idea about this.' She lifted her voice slightly, humming wordlessly, and then gave a smile of satisfaction.

The soldiers gave a collective gasp as a shadow fell across the yard. A tall, spiky shape formed, gradually solidifying into a spiny tree of a type Cassandra didn't recognize, which was wrapped in ivy. She looked up, and sucked in her breath.

Aethlyn Jones hung in the branches, his clothes torn, wrapped in ivy which held him up aloft and pierced his skin. The ivy was pulsing like a heartbeat.

'Omigod, is he—?' Colleen gasped.

Widow Calder raised a hand for silence again. 'Ahhh, I see. He's created a safeguard system for himself if he was injured in this place. He cleared the ivy, but has set up a mechanism for the memory of the ivy to return at his command, and take him away.'

Cassandra looked at her blankly. She wasn't the only one. 'Huh? Memory of ivy?'

The widow was examining the ivy. 'This is Aotearoa, a place built on memories. Because the ivy was here, in Aotearoa it has the potential to be here at any time. Jones as an Adept can cause it to return — he can shape Aotearoa. He must have been wounded, and to escape being finished off he has sent himself to another part of Aotearoa, where he had set up this ivy and tree as a kind of organic medical emergency aid.'

Colleen and the soldiers looked utterly at sea, but Cassandra could kind of get what the widow was saying. 'Earlier this year, in Wairoa, we were at the Aotearoa pa site, and then Jones did something that took us to a semi-modern Wairoa, so we could visit the bakery.'

Widow Calder nodded. 'Yes, you understand. Aotearoa remembers all these things. An Adept can influence which one comes to prominence.'

'So it isn't time travel — it's place travel.' Cassandra nibbled her lower lip. 'Aotearoa has linear chronology, but it is physically mutable.'

The widow smiled sideways at her. 'Aren't you the clever one?'

Cassandra preened slightly. Then Jones moaned softly, and all attention returned to him. 'Do we get him down?'

'Oh, yes!' Widow Calder turned to Captain Duncan. 'This is going to be very difficult, Captain. We must remove him without endangering him, and get him into proper care. All he has done is put himself into a limited stasis. He will still die unless we can get proper medical care.'

Like Scheherazade

Friday morning

*H*ine-manu!' Riki shouted desperately.
She froze. 'What did you call me?'

'Hine-manu,' he panted. 'Hine-manu — The Queen of Birds.'

Some of the fury left her eyes, but she still looked like a monster from some kind of Dali-esque nightmare. 'Hine-manu?' She seemed to be testing the name on her lips, her eyes struggling. 'Hine-manu?' She looked at Riki with doubt-clouded eyes. 'Are you *sure*? Where did you hear that name?'

'My granddad ... um ... he said Hine-manu was Queen of the Birds, all the birds, and daughter of the forest god, I think, back when the world was formed, and she was, um ...'

'Yes?' she asked with menace, her talons flexing.

'... beautiful! *Really* beautiful, with a feather cloak like the night sky, and a voice like a song, and the most lovely goddess of all ... ah, goddesses ...' he tailed off, flogging his brain for inspiration.

She paused, her talons just itching to rend him, but the rest of her waiting, ears cocked and listening, mind striving to recall.

Did she seem softer, somehow?

An eternity passed, as a sweat bead ran down his spine.

'Go on,' she breathed. Her eyes softly glowed as they faded from red through orange and yellow to white and violet and blue, a deep blue like water in the winter on a clear day. 'Go on. Tell me more about me. Remind me ...'

Oh, shit.

He took a very deep breath.

Who was that Arabian Nights chick? Scheherazade or something? Hadn't she had to come up with a thousand stories to postpone her execution? Riki had never really appreciated what she had gone through — but now he did. Right through the morning he talked as though his life depended on it, because it probably did.

In truth he knew nothing at all about the Queen of Birds but the name. Grandad had mentioned her *once*, in passing. There were no tales. She was a goddess no-one remembered any more.

That must hurt her. I bet that would drive her insane ...

But just because he didn't know any stories about her didn't mean he wasn't going to talk her hind legs off if it meant he would live long enough to see Mat come through the door with fire and musket and break him out.

So he told her the War of the Birds story, but he put her in it as a beloved peacemaker. He involved half the heavens and spun it out for almost an hour. Then he did Ruakapanga and the Moa, and had her bringing vengeance on Ruakapanga for killing the first moa. She seemed to like that one, and fed him water. His throat and mouth were as dry as, well, the bottom of a bird cage. He sucked the water down gratefully.

'More,' she told him. Or asked; it was hard to say.

So he gave her Pou-rangahua and the Flying Moa, only this time the moa that Pou rode was really her, and they were lovers and parted tragically, in circumstances no student of Maori folklore would have recognized because it was utterly made up from movies he had seen. She cried at the end of that one, while he sagged against the bars, mind whirling.

By this stage he had almost forgotten that he was talking for his life, he was so caught up in the performance. *Did Scheherazade feel that way, too, after a while?* He told her about Maui and the Goddess of Death, but in his version she was the little wagtail who prevented Maui from defeating Death, because in her wisdom she knew that immortality would be too much for humans to deal with. She was nodding in agreement after that one. 'It is so,' she murmured thoughtfully, in a voice that was younger and softer.

He stole a look at her, sitting side-on, hair curtaining her face. Her hair had turned black-green like tui feathers, and the skin on her shoulders was not leathery any more. Her face was lost in a curtain of hair. Was she smaller?

By midday he was desperately shoe-horning her into every story he could think of, from a bird-style *Romeo and Juliet* involving warring bird flocks to a weird concoction that owed most of its plot to *Watership Down*. Anywhere he could put a sympathetic *merciful* bird-goddess, he did.

His voice broke around three o'clock, and the water was all gone.

He stared as she slowly turned her face towards him. Her visage had changed utterly. Her eyes were like opals in the twilit room, her skin golden and clear as that of a young girl, and she was small and delicate. There were tears on her cheeks. 'You cannot know what it is like to be forgotten,' she whispered. 'You cannot know what it is to slowly go mad, as your powers fade, and your memories, too. The tohunga no longer chants your name. Offerings are no longer left. New gods take your place, and you fade into bitter shadows. You forget what you once were.'

'You're not forgotten, Hine-manu,' he told her.

Her eyes flashed. 'Liar!' She flexed her right hand, and it sprouted six-inch claws. 'Do you think I do not know my own history, poai? Barely a word you have spoken today has been true.'

He went totally still. *Oh no ...*

She laughed. 'You're a liar — but an entertaining liar, Riki. Very entertaining. I have not had such a pleasurable afternoon since ... hmm ...' Her voice trailed away as her voice drifted into silence. Then her face knotted into the face of Kurangaituku, lean and beaky and ugly. 'I am hungry,' she told him, while she could still talk.

She stood, scattering the bones of her past victims, and outside it seemed every bird in creation shrieked — then went silent.

Kelly put her hands on her belly to feel her child kicking furiously. She winced at the dull pain, and wondered if she was going to carry to term. She was due in twenty days. It didn't seem long. Not when the child had already turned, and was this active. 'You stay in there, little fella,' she whispered.

'We're too busy for you right now.'

She gazed out the hotel window at Rotorua, deep in thought. 'Where are you, Matty-Mat-Mat?' She murmured aloud, nibbling at her lower lip. 'And you, Fitzy? Where have you gone? Are you with him?'

Her cellphone rang. It was Wiri. 'Kel, we've got some news. There's been a shooting over at a motel on the east side of the lake. Tim's taking me over there. We're sending a car for you. See you soon, love.'

The knock on the door came even as she put down the phone. She got awkwardly to her feet, and waddled to the door. A young and eager-looking constable peered in uncertainly. 'Good afternoon, ma'am. I'm Constable Benham, Rotorua Police. Are you Kelly? Wiri's wife?'

'No, that's the other pink-haired pregnant woman in the next room,' she answered tiredly. 'Yeah, I'm her. Let's get going, shall we?'

They arrived to find ambulances and police cars and the press jostling for position around a wide perimeter that extended several hundred metres around a small motel on the Te Ngae Road. The sun was nearing midday, and the lake gleamed red in its reflected glow. There were Armed Offenders Squad officers present again. Benham's car was waved through by an unflustered policewoman at the roadblock, and they entered a quiet stretch of highway. Horns sounded in the distance as traffic backed up.

Tim Spriggs was arguing with a senior-looking policeman with grey hair and an impatient manner. For once, Tim's gentlemanly charm didn't seem to be making headway. Kelly sidled up.

'I fully understand, Dennis old man, I really do,' Tim was saying. 'And I certainly am not ... er, "muscling in" on your jurisdiction at all. We just need to have a quick look around. Really.'

The policeman's eyes flickered over Kelly, and he took in the huge belly and pink hair with a determined lack of reaction. Wiri put a hand on her shoulder and introduced her. 'My wife, Kelly. Kels, this is Commander Dennis Robson.'

Robson frowned, nodded irritably, and turned back to Tim Spriggs. 'I want Forensics in there first; there will be fingerprints. Evan Tomoana is still missing, and he's armed. You cannot — I repeat, YOU CANNOT — go in there.'

Wiri whispered in her ear. 'They've found one of the other men who attacked Mat on Sunday — John Makurangi, alias "Brutal". He's been shot dead, according to a witness. Another man, a guest who tried to intervene, was wounded. They've got a witness, a friend of Hine Horatai called Ko Symes, and she says Brutal was shot by Evan Tomoana. In other words: Parukau.'

She looked up at him and squeezed his arm. 'Is Matty here?'

'No, but Hine Horatai was.' He dropped his voice. 'A cop has gone missing, too. Tu Hollis, the guy who let us go last night.'

Kelly bit her lip, gazing towards the lake, as something in her subconscious shifted. 'Hine isn't here?'

'No. Apparently when Tomoana shot Brutal, this Hine and Ko took Ko's kids and ran. Then Hine yelled out "Tutanekai" several times, and sprinted towards the lake. Tomoana chased

238

after her, and that's the last time either of them was seen.'

'Tutanekai? As in Hinemoa and Tutanekai?'

'Yep. Tutanekai was this lovelorn kid who lived on Mokoia Island. He heard about this lovely chick called Hinemoa, and used to play love songs on his flute to her that carried across the waters. One night, to escape a man she didn't want to marry, she swam out to the island, met Tutanekai, fell in love, and they lived happily ever after.' He half-smiled. 'Aotearoa's own Romeo and Juliet. Apart from us, of course.'

'You sweet-talker, you,' she smiled distractedly, staring at the dim bulk of Mokoia Island.

Benham, who had been listening quietly beside her, suddenly leant in. 'Did you say she called out "Tutanekai"?' he asked, in a subdued voice.

'Yeah,' said Wiri, noticing him for the first time. 'Just like in the story.'

The police constable's face twisted slightly. 'Funny. That's Tu Hollis's full name.' He stared across the lake. 'His mother named him for that story. He goes walking by the lake every morning. He loves the lake.' His eyes were drawn to the island. 'He even had a girlfriend called Hinemoa, long time ago. She drowned while diving in Lake Taupo. Eighteen years ago, it was.' He shrugged. 'Weird, huh?'

Kelly looked at him wordlessly, thinking: *Hine Horatai is eighteen* …

Dennis Robson stomped away. Tim sighed. 'Sorry about this, chaps. Seems the old 1850s charm is having an off-day today.'

'That's okay,' said Kelly. 'I think I know where Hine is.'

Hinemoa and Tutanekai

Friday afternoon

Donna Kyle stared as a female form lurched from the silty shallows of the lake and flopped against a tree, right beside Hinemoa's pool. A girl clad only in sopping knickers and a crop-top. She was clearly exhausted. Hollis's eyes went from disbelief to wonder. Then he was standing, pulling off his jacket, holding it out to her as she stumbled towards him. He wrapped the coat about her, and his arms, leading her gently towards the hot pool. She was shaking, her teeth chattering and legs rubbery. But the girl's eyes, when they lifted to his face, shone.

Donna felt strangely envious, wondering what it would be like to feel, and to engender, the emotions she saw in their faces. It was beyond her how anyone could trust another enough to love, and so instantly. And why should it come so easily for these two? What right did they have to love? What had they ever done to earn it? Bitterness filled her mouth, and she palmed her gun.

Stone appeared, blinking in the light. 'What is happening, mistress?' he asked, something like wonder in his hard, jaded voice. 'I felt a strange thing.'

'I called for Hinemoa to come to her Tutanekai. I needed her to come, to open the way. She's the key to Te Iho. Puarata bound the gateway to a living soul. It is her destiny to come here, so I felt it likely if Tutanekai was the summoner that she could escape the clutches of anyone who held her. Puarata once told me that when an avatar's story is being fulfilled, Aotearoa is compelled to aid their destiny.' *And Father tipped me off*, she didn't add.

Stone turned his head away. 'You have asked Aotearoa to enact one of its great stories, so now you must let the story play out. Try to interfere and the land itself will rise against you. It will be as a curse upon you.' He touched the hilt of his sword as if it was a talisman.

She grimaced. 'I'm cursed anyway.' She rose, and followed the policeman, lifting her gun.

The stones about the pool poured heat up through Hollis's feet, and worked a soft warm magic upon his body. He felt a surge of energy and a sudden feeling of rightness, of gears engaging, of pieces falling into place. The young woman who rose from the lake was no-one he had ever seen before, but he knew her utterly. He had been waiting for her, ever since his lovely, wondrous Hinemoa had died in Taupo that awful day eighteen years ago. The shivering girl fell into his coat, into his arms, shaking and dazed. She swayed, but he held her up. Her skin was icy, leeching heat from him.

'Tu? Tutanekai?' she whispered, dream-like, her eyes unfocused.

His first-aid training took over. She was nearly frozen, in

danger of hypothermia. *I need to get her dry and warm.* Then footsteps stopped behind him, and he turned to see—

He stared down the throat of a gun. 'Please,' he whispered. 'She needs help.'

The blonde woman with the scarred face and hollow eyes looked him in the eye, and he thought she would pull the trigger, but she only nodded. 'Ten minutes.'

He dried her with his shirt while she stared at him helplessly, utterly spent. He sat her on the lip of the pool, but didn't dare immerse her in the hot water too soon. Instead he hugged her, and tried to tell her where she was and what was happening, although he knew little enough. Mostly he just looked at her, and knew, deep inside, that she had come back to him — his Hinemoa — and if they could survive this, life would be a blessing once more.

The time passed too soon. Donna Kyle stepped out of the trees with a face like flint, and scowled down at him. Pale shapes flitted behind her, people who looked like goths or emos or whatever they called themselves these days, but redhaired and feral-looking. Their eyes were like cold fire, and they flinched from the sunlight. Then movement beyond them caught his eye and he stared. He saw leering goblinesque things that tittered at him through shark-like teeth. He shook his head, but these nightmare creatures refused to vanish.

What the hell are they? What's happened to reality?

The tallest of the goths attending Donna produced a cord, bound Hollis's arms tightly behind his back, and dragged him onto the porch of a wooden building overlooking the pool.

The sun was setting. Donna eyed him and the girl uneasily, then spoke to the goth. 'Put him inside the mission house and stand guard! Keep him unharmed.'

'Let us feed on him, Mistress,' the tall man said, and bared fangs like Dracula.

Hollis stared in shock. His gaze flew to Donna Kyle, half-expecting her to recoil. Instead, she pursed her lips, as if she considered the request perfectly reasonable. She shook her head. 'No, Stone. I have too little information. I may need them both still.' She clapped her hands. 'Move! We must muster: I want the whole tipua tribe with me when we descend into the lair. If anything is there to oppose us, we must have overwhelming force.'

'It is here, then?' Stone asked.

'Yes, I believe it is,' Donna replied. 'Put the policeman in the house. I'll keep the girl with me.'

He struggled, but the vampire-things were immensely strong. As they hauled him into the mission house, he frantically tried to seize one last look at the girl's anguished face. Then they tied a sack over his head, and the half-burnt she-vampire knelt and whispered a promise: 'Tonight, I will drink you dry, mortal. We will keep your woman as a plaything, but you're just dinner.'

Parukau hid on the edge of the lake as the song of the flute faded. He was in Aotearoa, having followed the flute music across in his vain pursuit of Hine. He had passed out in a clump of reeds, and had been fortunate not to drown. Only by luck had he fallen with his head above water. Now he lay in a bundle, shaking and shivering, wondering how he could find another body then flee.

I've screwed this up totally.

This body had failed him. His right arm was near-useless. The girl was gone, and Asher Grieve must be laughing at him. *I gave my Pledge and the clue about the Swimmer for ... what? Asher, you bastard!*

Some rival — Kyle? Venn? Bryce even? — had known enough of the importance of the girl to use the Tutanekai and Hinemoa legend to steal her away. How had they known? Had Asher Grieve betrayed him? How long now, until a new makutu-master arose? How long did he have to run and hide before they came for him? *I should run* ... but he found himself paralysed by pain and fear as the sun fell towards the western hills.

Dimly, he became aware of a small rakish waka rippling through the waters, returning from Mokoia Island. The waka was clearly a tipua craft. He could see them hunched over their paddles. It was near-empty, but as he watched another left the shore, going the other way, laden with warriors.

The island — the island must be the gateway ... Whoever stole Hine Horatai must have also found the gate, and now they have the key, too. Donna Kyle, surely: Venn and Bryce didn't use tipua. Damn her!

A future as miserable as his recent past loomed, of being hunted — worse, of being found, and the horrors that would be inflicted upon him. *I've got to run.*

But he didn't. Instead he eyed the tipua waka. Calculating. Something an old soldier had once told him popped into his head. He and the veteran had just found a man dead of gangrene, after what had probably been weeks of agony. 'It's better to die with your boots on,' the veteran had said.

Perhaps I can somehow resurrect my chances ...

Slowly he nursed his wrecked body through the shallows, towards the goblin village. Had he not been close to collapse, he might have woven a hiding spell about himself, but he was beyond that. He walked openly, knowing he would be swiftly seen.

He felt and then saw them gather about him. Hairless, elongated skulls, leathery skin, vaguely reptilian little figures half his height. Each a perfect little nightmare come to life. Despite this, if led by an intelligent chief they were capable of friendship and trade; but they were mostly stupid and gullible and tended to believe whatever anyone told them — ideal foot soldiers for Puarata and his warlocks.

They crowded about him, herded him like prey, prodding and jabbing him with their weapons until he could barely stay upright. Finally, he found himself kneeling among a whole stinking crowd of them, mostly male. Squalid huts surrounded him. Everything stank of fish and blood — his own.

A larger tipua clad in a feather cloak stepped in front of him. 'I am Kotukutuku,' it snarled. 'I am chief here. Who are you, human?'

Parukau looked up at the goblin, and forced a smile. 'My name is a secret,' he said. 'Let me whisper it to you ...'

It was some time before the confusion died down. The man lay in several bloody pieces at Kotukutuku's feet. Something had happened, some dark serpent had seemed to envelop them both, until the bravest of the goblins had waded in and hacked the human to pieces. Now they circled warily, spitting on the remains.

Parukau looked out from Kotukutuku's eyes, ransacking the goblin chief's memories for names and words. When he thought he could deal with a conversation in the goblin tongue, he pointed to one of the sub-chiefs. 'Come! I know a place, not far away, where there are Pakeha fire-spears buried. Let us spring a surprise on the Witch.'

Two hours later, as the sun fell, he directed the final waka of tipua warriors across the lake. Each had one of Jones's muskets wrapped in a cloak, primed and loaded. There had been no time to train them, only to show them how to load the weapon. He would likely only get one shot each out of them, but maybe it would be enough to tilt the balance. They were sworn to conceal these new weapons until he gave the word. He could sense their excitement. *Tonight*, they whispered among themselves, *the arrogant White Witch will pay for all of the brother tipua she led to death.*

Parukau stared ahead, the waka thrumming with a music only he could hear, as they carved through the waves towards Mokoia Island. *I am not done yet.*

The Mother of Fire

Friday afternoon

Mat rode Fitzy at a steady canter along old hunting trails and through sun-dappled clearings. The distance wasn't great, but there were no roads and they had to be wary of who else might be traversing the Aotearoa back ways. He wondered if they shouldn't have rejoined Wiri and Kelly after all, but clung to the hope that he was doing the right thing.

He had few glimpses of what lay ahead or behind: the kauri and totara here were like tower blocks, and the undergrowth was dense with uncoiling ferns. He saw little other wildlife. The Birdwitch's creatures had driven all other life away. If that multi-hued flock did not have so sinister a purpose, he might have enjoyed watching them. Although there were dozens of sparrows and thrushes and mynahs and other common birds, there were other, more interesting, birds among them. Fantails flittered about him and kaka swooped, screeching whenever they had to move to keep him in sight, while the wind-chime tones of tui could be heard above the harsh chatter of the other birds. Woodpigeon wings throbbed. And there were vanished birds, too, like huia, no friendlier than the others.

He knew of no way of losing them. 'I guess I'm stuck with

you all,' he grumped out loud as they flapped about him. 'So Kurangaituku knows where I am, huh?'

Fitzy cocked his head. 'That's her big edge over the other warlocks. She usually gets any information first. But there are limits. She has to exert herself to utilize their senses, and they're not physically strong. None of the other warlocks trust her. If Puarata had been able to fully control her, he might have tracked us down last year. But she was AWOL, as usual.'

They rode on, their unwanted watchers swooping about. It was an eerie feeling. There was an unnerving intensity to that bank of unblinking black eyes and the rush of wings surrounding them. Mat felt hungry, having not eaten since lunch the day before. There were streams trickling through the forest, pools to sip from, but nothing to eat, and he had the feeling that catching and cooking a bird would be fatal. He felt depleted, too, of his magical abilities. The mere thought of trying to slip back to the real world was as exhausting as the twenty kilometres he had to walk either way. So he filled his belly with water at the next stream, and rode on, in a kind of fixed daze.

Hours later, as the sun sank in the west, they descended a narrow track towards a thin strip of glistening water. The path had become too tricky for riding, and Fitzy had gone back to dog form. His fur was damp and matted and he was panting heavily. Mat felt guilty for having tired him out so much.

The birds seemed fewer, and almost nervous, as if they too were being stalked. He half-sensed something larger in the deeper shadows, but couldn't catch a glimpse. It was almost impossible to see more than ten to twenty feet anyway. The ferns grew profusely, choking the ground between the great sentinels of totara. Glow-worms clung to the dank spots under the banks of a small stream they struck five minutes down the path. Apart from the occasional night-birds, all was silent but for their footfalls.

A dark bulk was growing before them, a low hill. Fitzy led him upwards, a climb of five minutes only, to a small ridge. He halted, panting a little, and lost the train of his thought in the beauty before his eyes as a new vista of Aotearoa was revealed.

They stood partway up a bare slope that led down to the shores of the small Lake Rotomahana. A series of shallow shelves cascaded past them to the lake. On each shelf, hot thermal water pooled in basins of glowing white residues of the sulphates and chemicals in the water. The slope was luminous, and steam flowed down the slope like a dry-ice show at a rock concert. The air was warm and thick and smelt sulphurous, but not unpleasantly so. The glow was magical, unearthly, surreal. He drank in the sight with pleasure.

'Otukapuarangi, they called it. "Fountain of the Clouded Sky",' Fitzy told him, emerging from the shadows in his goblin form and clambering onto a rock. 'In your world, it was destroyed when Mount Tarawera erupted, more than one hundred years ago. These are the White Terraces. The Pink ones are around the bay.' He gazed down fondly. 'Some folks called them one of the Wonders of the World. Sad they're gone now from your world, but at least we can come here.'

Mat could only peer about and nod his head slowly. The glowing slopes seemed part of a fairy paradise, not of this planet at all.

Fitzy slipped back into dog form, and they traversed the

White Terraces, stepping through steaming pools encrusted with mineral sediment like cake icing. They even glimpsed a few bathers: white settlers, quaintly attired in bathing costumes that covered them head to foot, alongside naked Maori. Fitzy told him most bathed at the Pink Terraces over the hill. They avoided those, however, climbing back into the trees, where a path took them into a dark cutting, and they lost the sunlight. Mat's eyes quickly adjusted to the gloom as they descended to where the slopes on either side of them became bare rock, and closed about them like a tunnel.

The cutting ended before twin pillars, carved wood dyed with red ochre. Twisted tiki faces and sinuous taniwha shapes piled one atop the other in the totems, paua inlaid into the eyes, catching the remaining light and glowing like opals. He sized it up while Fitzy changed again to goblin form.

'This is the gateway to Mahuika's Cave,' the little turehu said.

Mat inhaled nervously. 'So, shall we go in?'

Fitzy looked at him sideways. 'Um ... actually "we" won't. Just you.'

Mat felt a small thrill of surprise and fear. 'But —'

'Mahuika and I have a little past history,' Fitzy told him. 'My brothers and I had a dare over who would go in and bring something valuable out. She caught me, and told me if I ever came back she'd fry me and eat me.'

Mat peered, trying to see if he was joking. 'Really?'

'On my honour,' the little turehu replied, a little defensively. 'We turehu don't spend all of our time nobly defending the righteous, you know. Some of the time we just kid around.'

'So I have to go in there alone?' Mat winced at the sulphurous reek emanating from the cave.

Fitzy nodded. 'I'll wait here, I promise.' He squatted and pointed at the gateway. 'You have to knock, and call out to her.'

Mat swallowed. He had no weapons, and he was tired and starving. With a hesitant fist, he rapped on the gatepost, and called. 'Mahuika? Mahuika? May I enter? My name is Matiu Douglas, and I need your help … Please?'

His voice echoed through the narrow cleft. All other noises faded.

He felt something turn and regard him. He had a faint vision, of a shadowy head swivelling, and a sightless white eye like a boiled egg fixing upon him. A whispered female voice echoed from the depths. *'Enter.'*

The walls of the cave ran with a coppery glow, so that no torch was required. The air was warm and wet, and he was soon sweating profusely. He wished he had some weapon, but nothing confronted him. The walls were unadorned initially, but then he began to see carvings, twisting shapes that seemed to move when his eye was not on them. Many of taniwha and tiki, turehu and kehua, even bird-like manaia. But the primary design was a coiling tongue of fire. The carvings became more and more prominent, until every surface held them, and he could clearly see the faces turn and look at him with paua-blank eyes. The air stank like rotten eggs, and his skin ran with perspiration, as if in a sauna. He began to feel dizzy, needing to put his hands on the walls for balance, always careful to avoid the carven mouths of the beasts. The strain of being awake for hours and the constant battering his body and mind were taking were beginning to sap him to the core. He longed to just lie down, but there was too much at stake.

Finally the tunnel opened onto a small sandy beach. The way forward was blocked by steaming, bubbling hot pools of mud which burped and slopped before him, assailing his nose with the hot reek of sulphur. He gagged, and held a hand to his nose. Dimly he could make out a thin path winding between the pools, and he teetered around their steaming edges. He felt a rising faintness running like a slow current to his brain, and he dropped to his knees before he fell. His senses reeled.

The air here … poisonous … I have to do something …

He grabbed at a memory of pure, clean air, and clung to it. Clean air, heavy with rain, tangy on the tongue. He called that wind, tried to bring its cold purity to this foul place. It seemed to take forever, as he panted, feeling energy ebb from him in waves, then suddenly, gently at first but then stronger, a cold breeze wafted over him. He sucked it in, and then gasped as tongues of fire ignited over the pools — some combination of the heat and gases of this place and the oxygen from outside. A near silent *whoof* sounded all about him as he pressed flat, and a boiling ball of flame washed over the carved ceiling. The fire seared his eyes, and in that flash of light he saw that dozens of bleached skeletons lay all about him, men who had succumbed to the deadly air of the cavern. Then everything went dark again.

A high laugh echoed around the chamber. An old woman's cackle.

Mat looked up, but his eyes couldn't pierce the gloom.

'Come ahead, boy. In a few more metres you'll come to a pool. Swim it — you can swim, I take it?' The old woman still sounded vastly amused.

'I can swim,' panted Mat. 'Thank you, Mahuika,' he added.

'Hmmm, a polite young man ... and handsome, too, although a trifle pale.' She tittered to herself. 'I might just keep you.'

Mat refused to think about that. He peered ahead, and saw a copper-coloured pool some ten metres in front, frothing like a freshly poured beer. Beyond lay a stair emerging from the water, climbing up into darkness. The old woman's voice floated from that darkness.

'Come on, boy. Whilst your little breeze maintains the breathability of the air down there.'

That spurred him onwards, and he darted between the mud pools, and poised above the pool, dipping in a toe. It was hot, very hot, but not enough to scald him. The water was clear, now that he was above it, and he could peer down a long way, as the red-copper glow radiated down the walls of the pool, like the inside of a tube. He couldn't see the bottom, and dark shapes moved, down below in the depths. Big long shapes, lots of them.

'Swim quickly, boy. The eels are hungry tonight,' came Mahuika's voice from above.

His clothes weren't ideal for swimming, but he saw no choice. He took a deep breath, and dived. The heat of the water was a shock, stinging his eyes when he tried to open them. Warmth burrowed into his pores, and he felt his muscles loosen, but he did not tarry to enjoy the sensation. Not with those eels below ... He groped for the steps, and clambered up them, blinking furiously. They were coated in mineral deposits and slick as oil, but he scrabbled onto them as swiftly as he could, sensing more than seeing a dark mass of shapes flowing upwards. No sooner was he clear than the water boiled with writhing bodies, a thrashing tangle of snapping mouths, and he had to scramble further to be clear of their lunges. The largest, a horror with a foot-long skull, snapped its jaws closed just centimetres from his face as he clambered away backwards.

Mahuika chortled merrily from above. 'Well, you were just quick enough, boy!'

He looked down at the thrashing eels and went cold, despite the heat. He hurried up the slick stairs, water running from him. He ran his hands over his hair and face, and cleared his vision. Then he saw her, and froze.

Mahuika sat on a ledge above him, looking down with gleaming white eyes that had no iris. He realized with a shock that they were completely sightless, but she seemed to perceive him regardless. She was huddled beneath an old cloak of feathers, and a rank smell rose about her. 'Come here. Let me look at you properly,' she rasped cheerily.

He climbed hesitantly to the small flat space before her, and not knowing what else to do, bowed as if to a queen. She laughed, and climbed to her feet. She was small, hunched, and her mouth was toothless. She clutched a wooden stick, unadorned but for a small clutch of feathers at the top. The fingers that grasped it had no nails, just bare, pulsing pink flesh that seeped wetly. She hobbled up to him and stuck out her nose. Belatedly realizing what was expected, Mat touched his nose to her, a traditional hongi. The woman smelt unclean, and she was as bony as a starving cat.

'Sit, boy. What a handsome child you are! What is your name?' She sat on a mat, cross-legged, and pulled the cloak about her. She indicated a place on the flaxen mat opposite her, and he sat, their knees nearly touching.

'Matiu Douglas, grandmother.'

'I'm not your grandmother, boy!' she retorted tersely. 'Although I was grandmother to that wretch Maui. What do you want here? Nothing good, I'm sure.' She laughed, slapping her thighs as she wheezed. 'You are here to steal fire, like that sly dog Maui. Did he whisper in your ear: "Go to Mahuika and steal fire"? Ha! Well, he stole all my fire. I have nothing to give any more. So your journey is wasted.'

'It was Ngatoro who sent me. And he didn't tell me to steal fire. He said to ask for it.'

She looked at him with her white orbs and shrugged, huddling into her cloak as if she had taken a chill. 'Ngatoro is dead and gone. And I told you: I have nothing to give.'

He opened his mouth to speak, but she stuck out a nail-less finger and placed it against his lips. 'Silence, boy! I can hear without ears, and see without eyes.' She leant forward and put her hands to his temples. She crooned something, and he immediately felt a dreamy distance, and a torrent of images flowed from his mind. He felt no sense of invasion, but no sense of control either. And he couldn't seem to marshal his thoughts enough to stop it.

'Don't fight me,' said Mahuika. 'Let me see ...'

He fell into a vague dream, a random re-run of the last few days. Riki and Kurangaituku ... Hine gone ... Jones caught in that tree ... the attack on himself and his mum ... And then she was prying into Waikaremoana, and then his flight to Reinga last year. He couldn't say how long it went on, but when he came to, clutching his head dazedly, Mahuika was

255

sitting opposite him again. She bobbed her head and smiled.

'So, I had heard that Aethlyn Jones had taken a protégé … I have even heard your name. Now here you are, determined to play the hero. Ngatoro thinks I will just give you what you want, does he?' She didn't seem at all surprised at the revelation that Ngatoro, and others, had been imprisoned by Puarata. 'What do you hope to gain, boy? Power? Status? The love of this girl Hine? She is a pretty thing, isn't she?' She looked at Mat thoughtfully. 'You are even a little in love with her — but she isn't for you.'

'I know that,' he told her. 'I'm just trying to help her.'

She put her finger to his lips again. 'Hush, boy. I know you know. I've seen inside your head. Your motives are clear to me. You are that rare thing: a selfless person. Although you want things for yourself, you are prepared to put those wants aside for the sake of those you love, even a little.' She bared her gums. 'Oh, I know about love, although I'm just an old crone in a cave. Love is a kind of fire, made of belief. Love lasts as long and shines as bright as you believe it to. You can ignite it with a single glance, and douse it with a single doubt. It burns, and flickers. You must feed it, or it will turn to ashes. But no flame burns forever, boy. Not even the sun, or the fires that well up from beneath the stone.' Her voice was bleak and faintly regretful.

He felt a pang of fear, that she would not aid him after all. 'Please, Mahuika, will you help me? I must save Hine and Ngatoro! I must return with your fire!'

'Must you, must you? Why? Why should I care? The world outside means nothing to me. Why should I help you or anyone else?'

He couldn't think of a reason that would sway her, if she cared so little about the world. He took a deep breath, and met her sightless eyes. 'What must I do?' he asked her, as humbly as he could. 'I would do anything, give anything, to rescue Hine and Ngatoro.'

Her blind gaze seemed to look through him. 'Would you indeed, boy? Anything?'

'Yes — yes, I would.'

She regarded him for a long time. Finally, she opened her mouth again. 'Did Aethlyn Jones tell you how to win power from the powerful?'

He shook his head.

'You must give to receive, Matiu Douglas. That is what he would have told you, had he been here. I was guardian of the primal fire, until I was tricked into relinquishing it. I have languished here ever since. Few come any more, and most end up feeding my slippery friends in the pool. I have grown sick of men and their taking. If you wish for fire, Matiu Douglas, then you must give. You must sacrifice.'

He looked down, and into himself. Then he looked up.

'What must I give?' he asked in a small voice.

She leant towards him, so he could smell her poisonous breath. 'You must give yourself, Matiu Douglas.'

He felt a shiver of fear, and a slickness on his brow. 'What do you mean?'

The blind crone cackled low and mirthlessly. 'You must give me your Pledge. A Pledge can take many forms. Puarata demanded one of loyalty of his warlocks that was linked to their power — if they broke with him, their powers were lessened for a time.' She reached out and clutched his face in hands that felt like heated metal clamps. 'You will pledge me your service, Matiu. Pledge me that, and I will aid you. Betray that promise, and my wrath will find you.'

He stared at her ruined face, and her horribly seeing blind orbs. He nodded slowly, and she felt the movement through her hands. She dropped them, smiling gummily. 'Good,' she purred. 'Good. Your service is accepted.' She pulled him towards her, and kissed his cheeks with burning lips. 'I will aid you.' She added, cackling, 'I never liked that arrogant bastard Puarata or his pustulent minions.'

He nodded slowly, frightened as to what he had just committed himself. What might she demand of him? A thousand horrible fates flashed before his eyes. She snickered as if she read them there, flashing her gums. 'Your promise is given and heard. Violate it, and this little flame in here' — she tapped his chest — 'will go out. You hear me? Break your oath and you will die inside. Now, give me your hand.'

He held out his right hand. She shook her head, and then took his left hand instead. 'You are right-handed, are you not?' she asked. He nodded. 'I thought as much,' she replied, and then gripped his little finger. 'This will hurt,' she said cheerily. 'It will hurt a lot.'

Then she pinched the fingernail on the little finger of his left hand, and ripped it off.

The pain was excruciating — a liquid, acidic fire that tore through his hand and arm and racked his body as he threw back his head and howled. All he could see was fire; red agony that shook him uncontrollably. He snatched back his hand, and gasped over it, as the pain subsided slowly.

When he opened his eyes, a tongue of fire danced in his

gaze. It lay in the palm of Mahuika's hand. It was his tiny fingernail burning with a tiny flame that didn't consume it. The flame burned with a purity and brightness unlike any he had seen, captivatingly lovely.

'Aethlyn Jones told me that a foreign god with the strange name of Odin sacrificed the sight of one eye for the gift of prophecy,' Mahuika told him. 'A strange choice, in my view; but then, I gave two eyes, and gained less.' She thrust the burning nail at him. 'Take it and go, and rejoice that you are only the third man to leave this place alive. Go, Taker! Go before I change my mind. And do not forget your oath!'

He sat there, and looked at her. His little finger felt as if it was being cut in half slowly with a blunted knife. But he felt a sudden surge of pity for the old woman. He reached out with his right hand, and took the nail tentatively between his forefinger and thumb. The heat was searing, yet it did not seem to damage his hand. He reached out, grasped the right hand of the old woman. He turned it over, and fitted his burning nail into the puckered flesh of her forefinger as her mouth fell gently open.

'Here, grandmother. Take this, as a gift from me to you.'

She sighed, bent her head, and shook gently. The carven moko of her face seemed to flare softly to light, like rivers of lava coursing her cheeks. She blinked, and the milkiness drained from her eyes, revealing copper irises that focused intently on his face. She seemed younger, somehow.

Wordlessly, he screwed up his courage, and offered her another finger of his left hand.

The heron and the Birdwitch

Friday evening

Mat climbed the path from out of the caves, both hands wrapped in blood-soaked rags, every movement agony. But cupped in his right palm, he cradled his prize — a tiny piece of fingernail that glowed, a tiny whisper of flame playing on it. True flame, to burn away the shadows.

I did it …

He tried not to think about what he had given away, to gain this tiny thing. Nor what the Fire-Queen might eventually demand. The old woman had seemed to grow younger with each new nail; when he left, she was more like a thirty-year-old than the ancient crone he had first beheld. Her eyes remained ancient, but her body was fuller, her skin more youthful. She had a frightening type of beauty, the sort that hurt the retinas. Burnished eyes that smouldered and fingers that seared. In some ways she frightened him more, not less.

Outside, the daylight had gone, and only the tongue of fire lit the path, like a little piece of a setting sun. He stepped through Mahuika's gate, cradling the tiny flame, and looked about him. 'Fitzy?'

Then he froze.

A scrawny, ageless man sat on a rock above him, kicking his feet like a child. He had white skin and colonial-era clothing, and his chin was smeared with blood. His orange hair, piled like a windblown haystack, shimmered in the half-light. He held a Labrador on his lap, breathing in wet rasps. Fitzy's eye rolled towards Mat, and his limbs twitched.

'Turehu blood,' the pale thing smirked, licking his lips. 'My favourite.'

Another patupaiarehe ... Mat stared up at the pale thing, his heart pounding. 'Put him down!' He brandished the Fire-Nail, although even moving his hands sent screaming pulses of pure agony through them. 'Put him down or I'll burn you alive.'

The patupaiarehe curled his lip. 'Will you just, my pretty little boy? Then I certainly won't put him down, will I?' He sat up, kicked off, and floated through the air, down to the bare rock before the gate, about ten feet from Mat. He held Fitzy in front of him, as a shield, clamped effortlessly in one arm. 'What is it you've got there, boy? Something of value?'

All about them, the birds in the trees sat watching and waiting, a silent audience. He didn't know how to answer. Fitzy whimpered in the patupaiarehe's grasp. Mat's brain seemed to seize up, like a jammed machine.

'What is it?' the patupaiarehe insisted. 'Is it something of hers? Is it a fire-nail of Mahuika?' He grinned ferally. 'Yes, of course it is! How fascinating.' He cocked his head, as if listening to an unheard voice, then licked his lips. 'I must take it to my mistress. It will please her, make me her favourite. Give it to me — give it to Heron!'

No! He bowed his head, trying desperately to think.

'Give it to me or your little friend here dies,' Heron wheedled insistently. 'Give it to me.' He held out Fitzy in one skinny arm, holding thirty kilos of Labrador effortlessly. 'Exchange ...'

He could see no way out of it. Defeat seemed to lurk at every turn and it now seemed that all he could hope for was to keep himself and as many of those he loved alive as he could. Starting with Fitzy.

He slowly stepped forward, holding out both hands; the Fire-Nail in his right hand; and his left hand ready to pull the turehu to himself. His bandaged hands throbbed with merciless waves of pain, and he gritted his teeth.

The patupaiarehe's hands blurred, snatching the Fire-Nail and stepping backwards. But Mat reached desperately, gasping in pain as his bandaged fingers grasped the turehu. Fitzy twisted suddenly and bit at Heron, forcing the patupaiarehe away. He snarled as he backed from them, cradling the Fire-Nail in his hand.

Mat held Fitzy against him protectively. 'Fitzy?' he whispered.

'I'll be fine,' Fitzy muttered. 'Caught by a patupaiarehe. Damn, that's embarrassing!'

Heron smirked in triumph. The flame lit his eyes. 'Got it!' he crowed. He cocked his head again. 'I must take it to her.' He turned back to Mat. 'But first I must kill you, and now there is nothing to prevent me.' He raised the hand holding the Fire-Nail, as if to smite him with it.

Mat stepped in front of Fitzy to shield him. There wasn't time for anything else. But as Heron gestured with the Nail, his own hand burst into flame, and the patupaiarehe screamed in agony, his back arching and face contorting.

Mat gaped in sudden hope, which died as another shadow fell over them, a vast shadow with massive wings.

'My children told me you would be here,' rasped Kurangaituku.

Mat looked up, his heart in his mouth. Kurangaituku stood beyond Heron on a rock, her dirty grey hair fanned about her head, falling over the thick cloak of feathers that covered her shoulders. About her waist she wore a piupiu, a flax kilt. Her dark tattooed face was expressionless. It looked like etched leather.

Heron turned, cradling his burning hand, his eyes glazed with pain. 'Witch, the mistress must have this. It is commanded.'

Kurangaituku's eyes glittered. 'Commanded by whom, Heron?'

The patupaiarehe's voice faltered. 'By ... er ...' He shook his head, then nodded again. 'It is commanded!' His face was drawn with pain from handling the Fire-Nail.

Mat watched the Birdwitch's hands sprout claws a foot long. 'You have been subverted, Heron. Another has stolen command of you.' She stalked closer. 'Place the Fire-Nail on the ground, dead thing.'

Mat flexed his hands painfully. The bloody rags were like clumsy mittens, and he felt nauseous from the pain and blood loss. Beneath them, he had no fingernails left, and no weapon. He glanced at Fitzy, but the little turehu looked weak and his throat glistened with blood. They were helpless. Their only hope was this apparent division in the enemy ranks.

Heron backed slightly, looking about him. 'Don't come near me, Witch! I have primal fire. I am patupaiarehe. I will rip you apart and burn the remains.'

Kurangaituku hissed and stalked closer, flexing claws that would have made Freddy Krueger blanch. 'Put the Nail down, Silas.'

Silas. The name dropped into the silence like a stone into water, and rippled over Heron. He gave a small sob, and tried to run.

'Hold, Silas!' the Birdwitch rasped.

The patupaiarehe jerked like a puppet on tangled strings, and suddenly couldn't move. He wailed in terror as the Witch pulled back her right hand. Mat stared, then looked away as the talons plunged like some mechanical tool into Heron's chest. He gasped, a sound that died as it began, as with a wet, tearing sound he slid backwards off the Witch's claw, leaving a pulsing organ in her grasp, connected by a tangle of blood vessels to the hole in his breast. The vessels tore and snapped as he fell. The Nail dropped from his lifeless hand and fell smouldering to the dirt, but it didn't go out.

Mat gaped as the Witch gulped down the still pulsing heart, then turned her head towards him. 'Don't move, poai.'

Winged shapes swooped from the sky behind her, and the birds closed in.

The mission house beside the pool

Friday afternoon

It was late afternoon before Tim Spriggs could get a launch to take them to the island. They packed their antique weaponry into kitbags and stowed themselves in a small cabin.

'You don't have to come,' Wiri patted Kelly's belly. 'Maybe if you got some rest … ?'

She looked at him with tired yet determined eyes. 'Nice try, mate,' she drawled. 'I snatched a few winks while you and Tim were sorting out the boat. You're not getting rid of me that easily.' She didn't tell him that she was having light contractions every fifteen minutes. Part of her knew this was probably foolish, but Matty was out there somewhere, and it was her idea to go to the island. It would be fine.

The pilot of the launch was a friendly-faced man called Gavin, with curly dark hair tucked beneath a stained naval cap, and filthy overalls. He wasn't the regular pilot, he told them, just a mechanic doing some maintenance on the engine. 'May as well give her a run out,' he said laconically, but Kelly could see that his interest was pricked. She felt another contraction coming and sat hunched over, keeping her face serene. *You're not keeping me out of this*, she told the lump in her belly.

Wiri waited until they were chugging out over the water, and Gavin was busy in the wheelhouse, before opening the kitbags. Tim Spriggs had gone shopping in Rotorua-Aotearoa earlier and purchased three muskets, three powder pouches and three dozen balls of lead, which he had then soaked in melted silver. Wiri had a mere with a rope on the handle looped about his wrist, and Mat's taiaha was propped in the corner of the cabin. Tim was screwing bayonets under the muzzles of the muskets.

Kel's cellphone rang. It wasn't a number she had programmed. 'Hello?'

'Hi. This is Cassandra Allen — I'm a friend of Mat.'

'Yes, I remember you, Cassandra. You were the only one at the wedding better dressed than me! How are you?' She dropped her voice. 'Any news on Jones?'

'Yes! We've found him!'

A huge swell of relief bubbled through her. She turned her gaze forward to the island, and hoped she was right about all this. 'That's wonderful, Cassandra. Tell me all about it.'

Gavin deftly steered them into the small steel-and-concrete wharf on the southeast tip of Mokoia Island and moored the launch. He would stay with the boat. The taiaha school Riki had attended was over, so they would be alone on the island. If Gavin was alarmed at the odd weaponry of his passengers, he gave no sign; in fact, it looked like he wanted to join them. Wiri shouldered his musket and carried Mat's taiaha. Spriggs held another musket, and Kelly the third, cradling it awkwardly as she waddled in the men's wake.

Fantails darted around them, a reassuring presence. Somewhere out of sight a bellbird chimed. They took the short path that wound from the docks to Hinemoa's Pool. 'It's nice here. We should come again, when baby is born,' whispered Kelly in Wiri's ear.

He looked back at her and flashed his teeth. 'Yeah, we could work on number two.'

'You betcha, big boy.'

Wiri grinned, then looked at Spriggs. 'I'll go ahead and scout the clearing. Back in five.' Then he stole into the forest and vanished.

Kelly felt another contraction, and closed her eyes, wincing slightly. When she opened them, Tim was looking at her with concern on his face. 'Are you well, Kelly, my dear?'

'Yeah, I'm fine. Just getting kicked a little, that's all.'

'He picks his moments, doesn't he?' the Englishman smiled sympathetically. He was a father several times over, his family in Hamilton-Aotearoa. 'When is he due?'

'In about three weeks.' She forced a smile as the contraction eased and passed.

Tim looked uneasy. He probably knew as well as she did that babies could very easily come early, especially in situations of stress or physical activity. He didn't look at all convinced by her protestations.

Wiri jogged back. 'There are a couple of tipua in the clearing, but they aren't on alert,' he reported briskly. 'You okay, love?' he added to Kelly, his eyes narrowing as he took in her pallor.

She stood awkwardly, holding her distended belly. 'Yeah. Let's get it over with.'

Kelly watched Wiri nod and look at Spriggs; something passing between them, about her no doubt. 'We need to go over to Aotearoa,' was all her husband said, though.

Spriggs nodded and pointed up the forested slope. 'There's a partly fallen tree up there. If you walk under it, you can come out in Aotearoa if you wish to.' He inclined his head. 'Shall we?'

Wiri looked at Kelly. 'I'd prefer you stayed with the boat.'

'Like hell, lover-boy. I'm going right where you are.' She fixed her eye on him and put her hands on hips. 'Or else the biggest fight tonight is going to happen right now. And you won't win.'

They eyed each other, and then Wiri sighed heavily. 'Just be careful.'

'Aren't I always?' She flashed her most winsome smile. 'I love my husband,' she told Spriggs. 'He understands me perfectly. Now, let's go find Matty.'

They wound up a small path and then branched onto another barely deserving of the name, and had to almost crawl to pass beneath the toppled tree Spriggs had identified. There was a faint prickling sensation, but that was all, and the only noticeable change was in the taste of the air: cooler and damper, richer and more pungent. The first stars gleamed through the forest canopy, twinkling faintly in the darkening sky.

Wiri gestured for silence. They crept after him down the slope and filed around the southern walkway, almost identical to the real-world setting, until they reached the clearing about Hinemoa's Pool. There was a building, an old mission house; just beyond the pool which bubbled enticingly. Kelly peered about warily, until Wiri touched her shoulder and pointed, and she realized that they weren't alone.

Sitting in the shadows beside the mission house were half a dozen or more tipua goblins, their reptile-like skin pallid. Kelly looked at Wiri, who merely shrugged, tapped Spriggs on the shoulder and stepped into the open.

The tipua gaped, then snatched up their small weapons in skinny hands, and snarled. For a few moments they all looked at each other, then Wiri strode forward. The largest of the tipua bellowed, and the goblins pelted across the clearing towards them. The two men stepped in front of Kelly, raised their guns and fired. The muskets coughed explosively, and two goblins cartwheeled backwards. The rest momentarily vanished behind a cloud of stinging smoke. Kelly blinked furiously and raised her musket, but the men before her and the smoke obscured her view. Then a goblin launched itself out of the smoke, screeching a war-cry that died in its throat as Wiri's taiaha whipped across and cracked its skull. Dark fluid splattered, and it tumbled away. Spriggs's bayonet speared another, and then Wiri danced forward, smashing skulls and arms in a series of flashing blows. He was a one-man front-line, a barrier the tipua could not pass. One tried to edge around him, and Spriggs slammed the butt of his musket into its skull with a wet crunch. The remnants fled.

Wiri and Spriggs edged through the gun smoke which hung heavily about them. The sudden silence jarred the senses, the only sound the panting of the two men. Then the mists shifted as more shapes emerged. Two tall, pale figures strode through the powder smoke into the glade. They were human-sized but lean and wiry, with matted red hair and feral eyes. The male held a broadsword, Celtic knot-work decorating the guard and hilt. The smaller was female; she had no weapon save her nails and teeth. *Vampires*, was Kelly's thought, her mind flashing to the B-movies an old boyfriend used to make her watch. The creatures stank of rotting meat and soil.

'Patupaiarehe,' Wiri breathed, and then they were on them. Tim Spriggs yelled and staggered as the female seized his gun before he could align it, while Wiri exchanged blows with the male. The creature's broadsword sliced about with sight-defying speed, and Wiri was forced to defend desperately, wood chips flying with each parry; all the while, the sword-fighter hissed like an angry snake. Kelly lifted her musket, trying to find a mark in the dancing figures.

Spriggs was trying to wrench his musket from the female's grasp, but she held it effortlessly with one hand while raking at him with her other hand, forcing him inexorably back-wards. Then she shrieked and wrenched, and Kelly heard the Englishman's right arm snap. He shouted and fell, and in an instant the feral thing was on him. Time seemed to slow as Kelly levelled her musket with its gleaming bayonet. She shrieked, and lunged. Something in her belly tore, and a curtain of red agony flashed across her eyes, but she felt the bayonet of her musket plunge into the patupaiarehe woman's chest. The creature shrieked, and Kelly found herself staring into her mad eyes. The vampiress sniggered and began to pull herself off the bayonet slowly, staring at Kelly murderously. 'Wrong weapon, girl,' she snarled.

'How's this one then?' and Kelly pulled the trigger. The musket roared, and blew the vampire woman off Spriggs and onto her back, her chest blackened and burnt, the smell of hot, rotting meat mingling with the smoke. A look of disbelief stole across her face, becoming terror as she felt the silver ball bite. Her face emptied and her eyes rolled back in her skull. She sagged, and lay unmoving.

The male patupaiarehe howled in shock and disbelief, leaping away from Wiri and staring at his fallen companion. Wiri interposed himself, crouching in readiness for a renewed attack, breathing heavily. Spriggs crawled to his feet, but all Kelly really saw was the face of the male patupaiarehe, contorted by shock and malice. She thought it was going to fly at her. But instead, with a desolate cry, it turned and was gone, a dark shape that the bush swallowed up in an instant.

She staggered and fell. Wiri gasped and ran to her. 'Kel! Are you—?'

'No. I'm fine. You were right about bringing silver,' she added, barely able to think coherently through the pain in her stomach. She looked up dazedly. 'Honey, can you see if the midwife is ready?'

Then another contraction tore her, and everything went scarlet and black. She heard herself cry out, and fell to her knees. She heard Wiri gasp, and then he was half-carrying her. For a while, all there was was pain. But it receded at last. They were in a dark room that smelt of mildew and rot. A lamp flared, and she blinked. She realized they were inside the mission house that stood in the clearing. It was a mess, the few wooden pews pushed over, prayer books and oddments scattered about. In one corner, though, a dark shape huddled; a man tied up. Tim helped her sit, his arm hanging at an ugly angle, and then he too slumped against the wall, cradling the broken arm gingerly. Wiri darted over, and removed the sack from the prisoner's head. She had hoped it was Matty, but it wasn't. It was the missing policeman, the man who had released them after the hotel shooting: Tutanekai Hollis.

Wiri untied Hollis, and the policeman stood shakily, stretching his limbs, taking in their antiquated weapons without reaction. 'How did you get here?' Wiri asked him.

'There was a woman, she called herself Donna,' the cop answered. 'And there were ...' He ducked his head as if embarrassed. 'Things like orcs or something from the *Rings* movies. And ... uh, vampires ...' He looked at Tim Spriggs. 'What the hell is going on, Tim? And who are you all really, anyway?'

Tim Spriggs began talking to him in a low voice. Filling him in on a new version of reality, no doubt. Kelly looked at Wiri, who was still breathing hard. 'What *were* they, love?' Kelly asked.

'The woman was patupaiarehe, and the male was Sluagh Sidhe. Vampires, if you want a reference point. But don't try waving crosses or garlic at them. Creatures from myth.' He was still panting. 'Damn, he was fast.' He showed Kelly the taiaha: it was almost in splinters.

'They don't like silver,' Kelly observed.

'No. But you still need to pierce the heart or brain to kill them. Otherwise, you've just got to hit them so hard they can't take it.' He looked at the taiaha ruefully. 'This thing wasn't up to it.' There was a new sound in his voice she had never heard. It wasn't fear, exactly. But it was respect and, almost, apprehension.

'Next time, just shoot it,' Kelly told him.

Wiri looked at her. 'I knew the dead one,' he commented in a low voice.

Her eyebrows shot up. 'You knew her?'

'Yeah. She used to be a warlock, among the first settlers with such powers. Eventually Puarata poisoned her with patu-paiarehe blood, and she degenerated until she could no longer even think properly. She became patupaiarehe herself, and fled to the wilds. Last I heard she had met others, and had a nest on Mount Tauhara. Her name was Shonagh.'

'What was she like?'

'A warlock. Don't feel bad about her, love.'

She snorted. 'I'll try and restrain my sympathy, then. What about the guy with the sword?'

'Col, we called him — not his real name. He was Irish, a Sluagh Sidhe, a malign Irish faery who fled his homeland. He took up with Puarata when he came here, but fled with Shonagh, who was his mistress, after Puarata infected her. He was considered invincible with that sword.' Wiri looked reflective. 'I kind of liked him, way back when. He wasn't all bad, just angry.'

'But you'll shoot first and look sad afterwards next time, won't you, darling?'

He half-smiled. 'Yeah. I promise.'

By the door, Tim Spriggs was still talking quietly and urgently to Hollis, his voice pained. She could guess the content: a quick rough-guide to Aotearoa. Hollis seemed to be taking it fairly well, all things considered. She breathed hard through the next contraction, and opened her eyes to find Wiri holding her hands with concern written all over him.

'Where's Mat?' Kelly wondered.

Wiri shook his head. 'I don't know. This was our best guess.'

They sat for a while, and she felt a little peace, until the next contraction began. It was the worst so far, and she felt another thing — a hot, wet flooding that poured from her loins, soaking her knickers and the crotch of her overalls in dark fluids. She met Wiri's eyes. He was as pale as she had ever seen him.

'Your waters have just broken, Kel,' he whispered. 'Our son is on his way.'

Kelly lay on the altar as the room came in and out of focus. Time was floating away, disjointed visions between bouts of searing pain. She was naked apart from her T-shirt, her skin slick, and she felt ill. The air stank of sweat and blood. Hollis was with her, flannelling her belly with warm water from Hinemoa's Pool, which fortunately was only a few short steps away. They had found two buckets in the broom closet; they were coping. She couldn't say if it was going well, because it hurt too much to think.

Tim Spriggs was beside the door, peering out with a musket cradled in one arm, his other bound against his chest in a temporary sling. Wiri had gone to see about getting them back to the launch, but returned quickly and whispered something urgently to Spriggs. Now he was outside again.

Hollis was proving a godsend. He had actually delivered babies before, twice. It was one of the hazards of being a cop on the beat, he told her, and he was dealing with every-thing calmly, although he was clearly still taking in all the strangeness that had overtaken him.

Wiri arrived with another bucket of warm water. 'About bloody time,' Kelly told him. 'Here comes the next contrac— *Shitshitshit!*'

They were getting even worse, if that was possible.

What brought her awareness back to the here-and-now was a cold voice, calling from outside the building.

'Wiremu, this is Donna Kyle! We must talk!'

'Matiu Douglas,' said the Birdwitch. 'You are needed.'

Mat stared up at her, wondering if he were hearing things. This was Kurangaituku, the Birdwitch, one of Puarata's warlocks, an ally of Donna Kyle. She had attacked him in Rotorua. What was happening?

Then a second winged figure stepped into the remaining light, and he almost choked. 'Riki?'

His friend stared down at him, then glanced at the fallen patupaiarehe and the heart in the Birdwitch's hand. He visibly shook. 'Hey, man.' He grinned weakly, 'Surprise!' He was clad only in jeans and a feather cloak which clung strangely to his arms, as if pinned there. He had a taiaha in his right hand. 'Sorry I couldn't get here sooner, but I'm still getting the hang of flying.'

Getting the hang of flying? Mat blinked and looked about him.

There were birds all around them, every type he could imagine, staring at him. The Birdwitch reached down, and pulled him upright with leathery hands. She peered at his bandages curiously, but said nothing. He looked at her, met a measured, glinting stare that reminded him of an emu he had eyeballed at Wellington Zoo, unblinking and slightly insane. It wasn't a gaze one could meet comfortably. He sought Riki's instead. 'What's going on, man?'

Riki looked at Kurangaituku, and shook his head slowly, as if he didn't really trust his own recollection. 'This is Hinemanu. The Queen of Birds. She has remembered herself. She wants to help us.'

Mat gaped. 'But she's—'

The towering woman half-turned. 'Yes, I was Kurangaituku. The Eater of Men. But that was after ... after I forgot all that had been. Puarata trapped me, and changed me. People forgot me; they gave praise to new gods, and forsook me. The tohunga makutu said he could restore me. He lied. He changed me instead, made me into Kurangaituku.' She put a hand on Riki's shoulder. A possessive hand. 'This poai remembered me. So now I am his. And he is mine.'

Mat stared at Riki, who gave a weak smile.

'His coming has given me hope,' the Birdwitch whispered. 'Hope of redemption.'

Mat looked at Riki, who leant in and whispered in his ear. 'Jus' go with it, man. She jumped me, and made me tell stories for half the day, then announced she was hungry. I thought she was gonna eat me. But she let me go, and gave me smoked eel and kumara instead.'

Mat shook his head in disbelief. 'Only you could talk your way out of that, man.'

'Yeah, I know,' Riki acknowledged with a smirk. 'So, what's up, doc?'

Mat bent and picked up the tiny nail, cradling it in his bare palm, carefully keeping it from his bandaged fingers. The

Nail smouldered brighter at his touch. 'Primal fire,' he said. 'Ngatoro says we can use this to get into Te Iho even if we lack the key. I think Hine is the key to the door, but this is like a sledgehammer. If you've got a big enough hammer, keys and locks cease to matter. We need to get back to Rotorua and find Hine, or the gate.' He looked at the Birdwitch. 'I guess that means finding Donna Kyle.'

Kurangaituku — he couldn't think of her by another name yet — nodded her head. 'My children will find her. Come!'

He turned back to Fitzy. 'Are you okay?'

The turehu shook his head weakly. 'I'm not good, sorry. I'll live, but I can't shape-shift right now, and I need to rest. I'll stay here, and follow when I can.' His dog eyes looked utterly mournful.

Mat and Riki stroked his fur, and carried him to a small rivulet running through the cleft so he would have water. 'We'll come back for you as soon as we can,' Mat promised.

'Just go already. I'm embarrassed enough as it is,' the turehu complained weakly.

Kurangaituku handed Mat a cloak of black-and-white feathers. 'Wear this, poai.'

Mahuika had told him he could suppress then reignite the Nail, so he doused and pocketed it, then let Kurangaituku wrap the cloak around his shoulders. It gripped his arms to the elbow, and suddenly it was as if a million needles were stabbing him. He lifted his arms and the cloak swept about him like angel wings. Beside him Riki did the same. They looked at each other, sharing a moment of wonder.

Riki grinned. 'This is how I got here, man. It's not hard, you just gotta go with it.'

Kurangaituku — or Hine-manu — lifted her vast wings. Her blank, insane eyes fixed on him, and she beat at the air. He did the same, or rather the cloak did, as if it knew the moves, and he leapt into the air. All around him the birds surged about, and they streamed up, out of the gully, and flowed towards Lake Rotorua in a cloud.

Hidden hands

Parukau watched with hooded eyes as a tall man hurried towards Donna Kyle, who was with her tipua on the southern shore of the island. There had been a settlement here in the real world, and for a while longer in Aotearoa, but both were long abandoned. All that remained were a few old kumara beds beneath a rock that served as a kumara god.

The tipua called the newcomer 'Stone', but Parukau knew him by another, older name: Col, the embittered Irish Sidhe. Parukau's face mottled with fury and despair as Col spoke to Donna Kyle. So close, and neither suspected his presence, but how to take advantage, and when? For now, he bided his time, and watched Hine Horatai. The girl's head was bowed, but he could see her big, scared eyes. He licked his lips.

The news went around quickly: the patupaiarehe Thorn was dead. Col's mate. There was no sympathy among the tipua, but there was fear. If someone had slain a patupaiarehe, then no tipua wanted to encounter the slayer. Parukau saw that Col was devastated by the loss of Thorn, which meant that Thorn was Shonagh — he recalled her too, and with no liking. There was only one other patupaiarehe: the waif-like Rose, who seemed lost in a dream world. She did not even look at Col nor try to comfort him.

A runner brought orders to form up and march to the pool clearing. As always with tipua, it took time to organize them. Parukau played his Kotukutuku role and aided the muster, whilst staying close to Kyle and the patupaiarehe. It was almost half an hour before they set off, on the ten-minute walk to the clearing by the pool. Parukau held his secret gun-squad aside, hidden in the trees with more than forty muskets. When to use them was the question. They were eager to strike, but he counselled patience. Too soon, and all would be lost; the gateway to Te Iho would remain unrevealed. Wait, he commanded them, then he slipped away to rejoin the main body of warriors. They were nervously sniffing the air and whispering among themselves.

At the edge of the clearing, Donna Kyle and her minions were staring at the mission house that overlooked Hinemoa's Pool. There was no-one to be seen, but several dead tipua lay on the grass, beside the contorted body of Thorn. Already it looked like a centuries-old corpse. The tipua eyed the scene nervously, and Parukau made calming gestures while staring intently at Donna Kyle.

The blonde witch hailed the mission house. 'Wiremu, this is Donna Kyle! We must talk!'

Wiremu is in there? Then burn it down, Parukau silently exhorted her. *Burn him!*

There was a long silence. Finally, a voice called out. 'Alright. Let's talk. You and I, alone.'

Donna Kyle nodded grimly. 'Five minutes!' She ordered the goblins away. Parukau tried to linger, but even he, as chief, did not have the rank to stay; nor did he dare come too close to her, lest she realize just who now inhabited the goblin's body. He slunk back into the woods, to ponder his next move.

Donna Kyle licked her lips, feeling her heart beat like a bass drum in her chest. She waited in the tree-line, only twenty metres from the door of the mission house, maintaining a stasis shield in case one of Wiremu's company shot at her. Not that she thought they would. *They're the 'good guys' after all*, she thought, with a sneer that somehow tasted bad in her mouth.

The door opened a slither, and a musket barrel tipped by a glittering bayonet poked out at her. But what struck her more sharply was the muffled cry of a female voice inside. *What's going on in there?*

Wiremu slipped out of the door and glided into the deepest shadow, in the lee of the building. She caught a glimpse of his chiselled features and curly hair, and then he was somewhere in the darkness. She caught her breath a little. He could still move like a ghost.

'No closer,' he said, from within the shadows.

'I'm alone,' she replied, aware that he probably knew. 'And I'm unarmed.' She showed him both her hands, stepping into the open. 'I don't want this to be overheard. Come closer. I'll stay in the firing line of that gun if it makes you feel better.' They both knew she had ways to avoid bullets.

He nodded, and stepped out. They stalked each other, until almost in touching distance. Up close, he was still the man she remembered. She had begun her servitude in 1956, by which time he had been Puarata's servant for hundreds of years. She had always fancied that he regarded her with pity, something she both resented and craved. For a time, she had fantasized that he would free her and they would fall in love, back when she still thought she might be able to feel such emotions. He had been her most secret hope. Then Puarata had lost him, in the 'sixties, when she was still a teenager. At the time it had crushed her. Seeing him again, the first time since he struck her down a year ago, made her tremble.

'Wiremu,' she blurted, feeling as nervous as a girl. 'You know, if Matiu Douglas had not ruined things for me in Auckland last year, you would be my servant, and I would already have won this war.'

He gave a small, wary shrug, as if this were of no consequence. The scar on his forehead, the death blow inflicted by Tupu all those long ages ago, caught the half-light. It only made him more beautiful to her.

'You would be at my side, immortal still,' she went on. 'Perhaps even my lover.'

'I might have been at your side,' he acknowledged, 'but there would have been no love.'

'Oh, I'm sure I'd have won you over,' she told him, trying to infect her voice with a knowing irony to mask a growing sense of emotional vulnerability. He didn't bother to answer that, which cut her. 'You would have been my tool, to play with how I wished,' she insisted angrily.

'You failed, Donna. Might-have-beens are irrelevant,' he reminded her evenly.

'I used to think that you and I were kindred spirits, Wiremu. We were the unwilling disciples, the decent people made to do evil. We know each other's histories. We've been through the same things. You had no choice, and neither did I. No-one understands what we've been through except us.'

He stared at her for a few seconds, and then said, 'Is that really how you remember it, Donna?' There was not a hint of mockery or judgment in his tones. Just a faintly surprised sadness — which was worse. The way he said it undercut everything else she might have said, and made the whole ground beneath her seem paper-thin.

'How dare you?' she flared, her mouth flooding with bile. 'I was just a girl when he took me, and I *suffered*. He made me do everything I've done. I had no option!'

'I remember a woman who took pleasure in others' misery. I still see her.'

She swallowed angrily. 'Then you're blind. I have no choice — I never had!' She felt her skin moisten. 'You had the excuse of having no autonomy. No choice, so no guilt! I didn't have that! I had to damn well love my work or die. He butchered my conscience — but it's growing back! How do you think that feels?' She felt something beginning to fray inside, and tried to reel in her emotions. 'I'm his worst victim.'

He seemed unmoved. 'Perhaps. But until you walk away from this war, you're still his victim.'

'Walk away? You think I can walk away? I'm the most wanted woman in Aotearoa.'

'Then leave it. It won't miss you.' His eyes flickered to the patupaiarehe on the far side of the clearing. 'If Col can cross the seas, you can.'

'I can't! You think Sebastian Venn can't track me anywhere? You think Parukau couldn't? There's nowhere to run. Nowhere to hide. No-one's protection I can claim. I either win or die!'

His face remained unmoved. 'Then you believe yourself incapable of the redemption you pretend you want.' He met her eyes. 'Surrender yourself to me, and I will vouch for you before Governor Grey.'

'That old fox won't show mercy,' she spat. 'He's wanted my head for decades.' In Aotearoa, New Zealand's most famous and powerful governor still enjoyed nominal authority over the north of the North Island through complex arrangements involving aspects of the Treaty of Waitangi that were adhered to in Aotearoa. Governor George Grey had put a price on her head bettered only by the bounty on Te Kooti, Hone Heke, John Bryce, and Puarata himself. 'He's not so keen on you, either.'

'I have a pardon now, as I'm sure you know. Surrender yourself to me, and I will speak for you. If your life is so bad, then accept imprisonment.'

She looked at the ground. 'You understand nothing! I'm on the verge of gaining control of Puarata's secret lair — I can't step out of the game now.'

'Then you certainly won't if you triumph,' Wiri replied. 'Which only leaves trying to hide behind me if you fail,' he added with a touch of irony. From inside came those muffled cries again, and he glanced anxiously over his shoulder.

She recognized the tone and rhythm of the cries and guessed what they were. 'Your woman is in there! She's giving birth!' *Good grief!*

He looked at her, then nodded shortly. 'It is quite advanced. We can't leave here even if we want to.'

She scowled. *Damn this!* 'I have more than one hundred

tipua and a nest of patupaiarehe. If I order them to attack, you will all die. You are in *precisely* the wrong place, Wiri.'

He never flinched. 'Then we are in your hands,' was all he said, rocking back on his heels slightly.

They've already killed Thorn. They have silver. I could lose the patupaiarehe — and without them perhaps the tipua will rebel. And I can't afford to damage the mission house until I know how the gate to Te Iho works ... which means I can't burn him out. He'll be defending a confined space. And it's Wiremu: I'm not even sure we'll win.

Then an answer occurred to her that might serve — but it involved doing something she had never done before: show mercy. She bit her lip and tasted her own blood. It made her feel shaky and hollow. 'I need you all gone, as soon as possible. Will you accept my word that you will not be harmed if you depart?'

His eyes widened, then narrowed. 'What's the catch?'

'No catch. I just want you gone. This isn't your fight.'

'Where's Mat Douglas? Where's Riki Waitoa? And Hine Horatai?'

'I have the girl. I don't know where Matiu Douglas is, or the other person. Nor do I care. Just take your woman and get out of here.'

'She's in full labour. She can't be moved.' Wiri glanced over his shoulder, his normally dispassionate face gnawed by worry. 'We have the only defensible place on this island.'

'I could torch it in minutes. As you know.' She felt like she was walking a tightrope between portraying threat and weakness. 'Damn it, Wiri, wouldn't you rather it was me controlling Te Iho than Parukau or Venn?'

'Frankly, I see no difference.'

'Then you're a fool! I'm ...' she trailed off, too desperate and angry to continue. 'Let me take you all across — let me get you out of there! Let me move you across!'

More cries of pain came through the door. She saw him flinch, and consider. He nodded. 'Very well.'

She exhaled, in sudden relief. 'Agreed!' She offered her hand, because she wanted to touch him.

He ignored it. 'Await me here,' he said. He withdrew, and she heard a few heated words inside. All the while the musket was trained on her. A few minutes later, he opened the door. 'Come in. Move slowly and predictably.'

She entered the mission house, where the tang of blood was overwhelming. They were using the altar as the birthing-table, which struck her as odd until she saw what poor repair the rest of the building was in. The pink-haired girl on the altar turned her face to her with a look of blank hostility.

How could he prefer that fat ugly freak to me?

The policeman Hollis glared as he trained his musket on her. The Colonial Constabulary man, Spriggs, was the other occupant of the room. An old adversary. His right arm was in a sling, but the musket in his left was steady.

'Do they understand why I'm here?' she asked Wiremu.

'We know,' the pink-haired girl, Kelly, said in a hard voice.

'It's for your own good,' she snapped back. 'Perhaps if you have a girl you'll name it after me,' she added in a sarcastic voice.

'I wouldn't name a rabid dog after you,' Kelly shot back.

She looked at Wiremu. 'Darling, let's get this over with so she can piss off back to her goblin buddies.'

Donna clenched her teeth to stop herself lashing out. Slowly, she walked towards the altar. 'I'm sure you know how this works,' she said, looking at the clown-girl with her most disdainful look. 'You have to touch me when I'm making the transfer.'

They gathered with clear reluctance, and laid hands upon her arms. She felt suddenly vulnerable, suddenly afraid. Wiremu looked at her, and she at him. 'Your skin is cold, Donna. Unnaturally so.'

'I know,' she whispered. 'It's just another reason that I have to win.'

He stared and then nodded.

She took them across.

They appeared in the evening-cool glade beside Hinemoa's Pool. Spriggs immediately shoved Donna away from them, his bayonet centimetres from her breast. There was no trace of his normally habitual politeness. 'Over there, ma'am,' he told her in flat tones.

Wiremu walked towards her. 'You know that Shonagh was a servant of Puarata, just as you were. He gave her fairy blood to heal her, and gradually she degenerated.'

She hadn't known this at all. It took all her discipline to hide the fear this titbit sent through her.

'Now go,' he said. 'I will not wish you luck.'

She smiled tightly. 'I will not need it.'

'Aren't you tired of all this, Donna?'

Yes, yes I am. 'I have no choice,' she told him, and stepped back into Aotearoa.

Donna called the two remaining patupaiarehe and the tipua chief, Kotukutuku, to her side. The tipua watched them confer. She disliked all these eyes on her, when she was still uncertain how to proceed. She might have the girl Hine, but what was she supposed to do now? Her mind frantically explored the possibilities. She had the girl, but she needed to know where the gate was. She still needed Father ... and she had given her damned Pledge.

As if summoned by her thought, Asher Grieve's voice filled her mind. *Daughter, have you obtained the Blood of the Swimmer?*

The fact he had to ask reassured her that her actions and thoughts were still somewhat cloaked from him. 'I have her. You were right about Hinemoa and Tutanekai. But what do I do now?'

Try dribbling some of her blood into the pool, and watch for unusual effects. It is associated with the legend, so it is the logical place to start.

'Try? You mean you don't actually know?'

He seemed unmoved by her doubt. *Of course not. But it is the logical place to start.*

What kind of future will I have, at his beck and call? How will I deal with being always afraid of what he knows and what he will do? She carefully masked her fears, while her subconscious began to work on a new problem: how to extricate herself out of her bargain with Asher Grieve.

'I must proceed,' she told him.

Then bonne chance! *I will see you soon, Daughter-dearest.*

'I am trusting you, Father. Why should I do that?'

Because I have always been on your side.

'You have never been on any side but your own.'

You are wrong, Daughter. I am proud of you, and I have always been for you. I put you in the forge that was Puarata to temper you, to make you purer and stronger. Everything has been done for you.

'You old liar! You self-serving lying bastard! You cared nothing of what I went through!'

What do you know of what I cared for? What would you be now if I had not come for you? A wrinkled, forgotten pensioner at the end of a sad and bitter life. Think of all you have now. All the opportunities I gave you.

'Oh, so it was all "tough love", was it?' she sneered. 'I went through purgatory and I'm still there.'

Daughter, I feel your pain. But just a few steps more, and the task is done. The war will be won, and then you can be the person you have always wanted to be. Weakness is a luxury you cannot afford yet.

She hung her head. 'I know.'

You may be in purgatory now, Daughter, but when I am free, we will create our own paradise.

She wanted to tell him that she believed no such thing, that life under his thumb could only ever be hell, no better than life under Venn or Bryce or Parukau. But what was the point? She had given her Pledge. A wave of utter despair threatened to engulf her, but she fought it down. 'Farewell then, Father.'

See you soon, Daughter.

She wondered if he were responsible for the loss of control over Heron. Could he do such a thing, trapped where he was?

Her fears told her, yes he could. *I must resolve this quickly.*

She took the girl Hine and walked her to the pool, where she pulled out her Swiss army knife and cut the girl's thumb. The girl was so numb to all that was happening that she barely flinched. A tiny drop of the girl's blood dripped into the water. The water hissed, and then all of a sudden it evaporated. With a rumble, the bottom fell away, revealing a stairway that descended into the darkness. Only the drop of blood remained, hovering in the air, then flowing like a flying snake down the stairs, like red ink on an unseen page.

Omigod, this is really it … Te Iho.

Distantly, she could feel a heartbeat emanating from the earth. Or perhaps her chest. She clutched her left breast, vaguely surprised that she still had a heart at all.

Within minutes she had led Hine, the patupaiarehe and the tipua down into the earth. Although the water was gone, they moved as if underwater. It was an eerie thing, to see their hair swaying like waterweed, and her throat clenched, until she took an experimental breath and survived. After that, breathing became second nature once again.

At the foot of the stairs, normal gravity reasserted. Some sort of maze began. She made a deeper cut in Hine's arm, and watched the blood flow out into the air in a thin thread, like a guiding arrow through the twists and turns of the maze. Behind her the column of goblins filed in, exclaiming in awe. She wished somehow she could send them away, but was afraid to go without warriors into the maze. Who knew what traps and guardians Puarata might have left here?

She ushered the tipua past, noticing the wall beside the doorway. It held a map of New Zealand, carved in wood relief, a dozen feet high. A needle jutted from the middle of Lake Rotorua — right here on Mokoia Island. She smiled, realizing what this was: the device that determined where this gate emerged in the real world.

Ahhh … now to ensure there is no pursuit. She waited until all of the goblins were inside, barely noticing them. The tipua chief, Kotukutuku, edged closer, staring up at the map. She nodded to him. 'Do you know what this is, Kotukutuku? This controls where the gate emerges on the real world. Now that everyone is in, I shall shift it. That way no-one can follow us into this place.'

She pulled the needle out, and with a sucking sound, the gate vanished. She chose a new gateway: her own manor here in Rotorua — it would do until she returned these tipua to their village.

'There! Now no-one can get in: Te Iho is mine!'

A hammer clicked, and a circle of steel pressed into her breast.

'Surprise, Donna!' breathed Kotukutuku. 'It is I, Parukau.'

He reached out, and with a swirl of power pulled the cords that controlled the patupaiarehe from her grasp.

Warrior's choice

Friday night

Kelly pushed and pushed. Nothing else mattered but to expel the alien from her belly before it came through her stomach. A part of her knew she wasn't rational right now, but it wasn't the part that was in control. The alien was ripping her in two; it was too big. She was bleeding everywhere. She was burning up. She clung to hands and fought through the next wave of pain. Foul smells clogged her nose. Faces came and went. Tim ... Tu Hollis ... Then Wiri was holding her, his mouth moving, and she could feel him willing her through this, so she forgave him the agony and gave just a little more, to bring life to their little boy. Push again, push again.

The stars glittered above, and the lake water murmured. A breeze stirred the trees. It felt utterly primal to be outdoors, the only light coming from the oil lantern they had brought with them from the mission house. To be giving birth beneath the stars. If she was more of an Earth Mother type she would have been in her element, but right now she would have traded it all for an epidural and a hospital bed.

Then came a tearing feeling, and the men all whooped and

pounded each other's backs. Wiri blinked damp eyes, and then came a high, thin noise as her baby began bawling its tiny lungs out. Hollis splashed warm water from the spring over it, and then the tiny, angry, ugly, precious thing was pressed to her chest. She felt an incredible feeling of wholeness and relief as she lay panting in exhaustion.

Wiri beamed down at the little bundle. 'A boy,' he confirmed. 'Our son. Born on Mokoia Island.' He sounded as if he couldn't believe it. She was drenched in perspiration, but nothing mattered now except for the child at her breast. She pulled up her tee and helped the little mouth find one of her swollen nipples. After a minute of frustrated failures, he latched on, and greedily slurped. It kind of hurt, but it was good, too. She gave a contented, relieved sigh.

'I thought it went well,' Hollis said in a tired but warm voice. 'An easy birth, very quick. No complications. The other two I did were much worse than that.'

Kelly looked at him in mute horror. 'But that was unspeakable!' she gasped.

The cop smiled wryly. 'Toughen up! Wiri told me he wants enough kids for a rugby team.'

She caught Wiri's eye, and the warrior shook his head. 'Never said any such thing, love,' he grinned.

Kelly smiled tiredly. 'You're having the rest of them if you do, kiddo. No way am I going through that again.'

For a few minutes, all was calm. Wiri told her it was only just over an hour since they were brought back across to the real world. She was stunned — it had felt like at least a day. 'Any news on Mat?' she whispered to Wiri.

He shook his head, shrugging. 'Tim went back to scout

293

the clearing half an hour ago. We'll know more when he gets back.' He sounded slightly worried that the Englishman was still gone.

'You want to go after her, don't you?'

He grimaced. 'If I had enough men, yes. But it would be suicide. There is only Hollis and I fit to fight. Tim has a broken arm and you're ... well, obviously ...' He scowled. 'There's just us, and we're not enough.'

She nodded in possessive relief that he wouldn't go off on some errand, no matter what was at stake. Let someone else sort it all out. He was hers, and now he was a father. He was too precious to risk. In her arms, the infant nuzzled her breasts and burped contentedly. She felt a sense of peace and happiness unlike any she had ever felt before.

Then Tim Spriggs hobbled out of the woods, with a familiar face behind him.

'Mat?' She stared as Mat Douglas stepped out of the shadowy bush. He was wearing a feather cloak about his shoulders, and looked very solemn. His hands were wrapped in bandages. Wiri seized Mat in a bear hug. Then Mat saw Kelly lying on the ground, clutching a bundle in her arms, and his eyes went round. She grinned up at him, whilst noting that he looked wrecked. Still she felt her heart swell with relief and joy.

'You look like crap,' she told the boy. 'What've you done to your hands?'

'Yeah, I know,' he said. 'They look a mess, but they don't hurt any more ... umm ... much.'

Riki appeared behind Mat, high-fived Wiri and nodded around the group like this was all his doing. 'Hey, it's my crew,' he drawled. 'So, my peeps, how's it goin'?'

'We are not your crew, brown boy,' Kelly growled. 'Where've you been? Draft-dodging again?'

'I was rescuing Mat's ass — as usual!' Riki smirked. 'It's my super power.' He bent over Kelly and peered at the baby. 'It's a boy? You could name him Riki, I reckon.'

Wiri cocked his head. 'We'll consider it,' he said, in a tone that suggested they wouldn't. He looked at Mat and Riki properly. 'Where'd you get the feather cloaks?'

Mat glanced guiltily over his shoulder. The gathering fell silent as a tall Maori woman stepped from the forest shelter, a leather-faced giant with bristling grey hair. Wiri gripped a musket, but Tim Spriggs put a hand up. 'Wait, Wiri. There is more going on here than you know.'

Mat stepped between Wiri and the Birdwitch, raising his bandaged hands. 'She's on our side now,' he said urgently. Wiri and Kelly looked from him to Kurangaituku, their faces astonished. Tim Spriggs still looked that way, and they had already told him.

Wiri spoke first. 'Mat, she sat at Puarata's council. I have seen her there, many times. She served him for centuries. It's impossible.'

Riki lifted his chin. 'Nah, she's okay, man. She wants to help us. She wants to get free, get outta the game. Like in *The Godfather*, man, when Al Pacino tries to go straight.' He winced a little, regretting the analogy. 'Although that didn't turn out well, I hear you saying. But she's, like, remembered who she is now, and she wants to earn her way back to the right side. It's kosher, man. I'd know.'

Wiri looked at him with disbelief. '*You* would know? Riki,

the only creatures that have ever trusted her have feathers, and brains the size of peas.'

'Which describes Mat and Riki perfectly just now,' Kelly threw in. But something in the witch's face seemed sincere. 'Come on, Wiri, she's clearly helped our boys out.' She looked past the two young men and fixed her eyes on the Birdwitch. 'At least let her have her say.'

Kurangaituku looked hunched and uncomfortable. She glared at Wiri and rasped, 'Who are any of you to judge me?' Then she hung her head. 'Proud, too proud ...' She looked down. 'Little enough reason do I have for pride, after all I have done. I must find humility.' She stepped behind Riki's shoulders and gripped them in her long, talon-like hands, making him wince fractionally. 'I am with this boy. He reminded me of who I once was, when the world was new. A goddess, not some hunched and shrunken thing such as you see. He reminded me of things I have forgotten, like friendship and loyalty and companionship and trust. Laughter and simple conversation. Simple, small things that make life bearable.' She looked at Wiri again. 'Hearken, Wiremu the Undying. Kurangaituku seeks redemption. I am filled with remorse, and wish to atone.'

Wiri stared. 'Donna Kyle told me much the same, but she's still at war with us.'

Kurangaituku bobbed her head. 'This I know already. Donna Kyle has entered Te Iho. If she gains the power that is there, we will all be undone. She will become a new Puarata.' She visibly shuddered. 'I will not serve her or any other. I wish to pursue — and fight.'

'So do I,' Mat put in. Riki nodded agreement. 'Te Iho is

where Ngatoro is being kept. There are others, too. We've got to do something!'

Wiri shook his head, standing up. 'Mat, I would love to — but Donna Kyle claimed to control more than a hundred goblins. I know they're small, but they're still a match for any man when they're in numbers like that. And then there is Donna herself and the patupaiarehe.' He raised both hands. 'You know me, Mat: I don't shirk a fight. But we have three guns, two unhurt men, you and Riki, and Kurangaituku. And with respect, her strength is not in battle. It wouldn't be a fight, it would be suicide.'

Kelly saw Mat bite his lip. 'But this could be the only chance—'

'Mat, there are five of us. It is insane.'

A new voice broke in. 'What if we could even the odds, brother?'

A Maori man with a tangle of long curls sprouting from beneath a battered top hat stepped from the trees. He wore ragged European settler clothing, with a battered old frock coat and a pistol in his belt, and he was holding a musket. Although she knew and liked him, Kelly's heart sank.

Wiri's face lit up. 'Manu!' He strode across the lawn and threw his arms about the scruffy Ngati Maungatautari scout. From the bush behind them boiled more and more men of Wiri's tribe, until a cloud of warriors in piupiu filled the swathe, grinning broadly. They eyed Kurangaituku warily, but they had clearly been listening from the trees for a while before revealing themselves — they offered no objection to her presence. Several bobbed their heads respectfully to Kelly. She recalled many faces from the visit to the village last year, and another more social call five months ago after the wedding. She felt a strange surge of excitement and despair.

'I've brought a war-party from the village, brother,' Manu smiled broadly. 'We left the same hour that Tim's pigeon arrived. How does forty of the whanau sound? All armed to the teeth, and eager to kick some tipua butt.'

Riki whooped loudly. 'Man, that aces everything! We gotta go now!'

Wiri looked at Kelly.

She could already see what he wanted to do, written plain across his face. 'You don't have to do this,' she told him. 'You're a father now. I accept that Kyle needs to be stopped — but can't you leave it to the others? Please? Just this once?' She hated the selfishness she heard in her voice, but she couldn't bear to lose him. 'You're a father now,' she whispered again.

Wiri stroked her hair. 'You're just sore that you can't come on this one,' he murmured. His mind was already calculating, his muscles already flexing in readiness.

'No: I'm scared you won't come back.'

He smiled. 'It's me, lover. I always come back.'

'But you're not immortal any more! And that patupaiarehe with the sword is still out there! I've already almost lost you. I never want to go through that again. We're parents now!'

He shook his head and straightened. 'I'm sorry, love, but I have to go. There is no other choice.'

She glowered up at him. There were any number of other choices, she wanted to scream, but his mind was set. He was not the sort that let others accept danger for him. It was part of what she loved in him. *But, damn, it makes things like this hard!*

'If you don't come back, I'll kill you,' she growled without a trace of humour. She hugged their infant close, while her eyes drank Wiri in. He was her warrior. Of course he would fight. She had to quell a surge of resentment that she could not go, too; that she had to let him go.

Wiri looked at Mat. 'What're we facing, Mat?' he asked. He signalled silence as Manu and the Ngati Maungatautari gathered. They all knew Mat, but only as a frightened boy who had come through the village a year ago, and wielded strange powers. Now Mat looked about with level-headed confidence. He stood up tall, and when he began to speak she saw them nod at his growing maturity.

'Well, it's like this: Ngatoro-i-rangi and many others are chained up in a place Puarata built. It's a magical makutu power-plant. But Puarata's dead now, and this place is the key to succeeding him. If we can get there before Donna — or maybe a close second before she consolidates control — then we can wreck it, rescue Ngatoro and the others, and prevent anyone from using it again. I think that's worth it. If Donna Kyle or anyone else gets control of it, they will come down hard on all of us, in both worlds. Let's take it down, and make everything better.'

He stopped for breath and looked around. 'Maybe this sounds strange to you, but maybe not. I just know that I believe. If we're going to put an end to these warlocks, this is the place to start.'

For a few moments everyone took in his words, and then the warriors began to nod their heads. Manu grinned. 'We're in, ruanuku. Lead us to them.'

Kelly rolled her eyes in a resigned way. Riki dropped down

beside her. 'We'll be okay, Kels,' he said, in what he seemed to imagine was a reassuring way.

Wiri pulled off his shirt and hefted his musket. His chest rippled and his tattoos danced in the afternoon light that streamed through the window. The war-party grinned as Tu Hollis did the same.

Mat saw Wiri and Tu look at each other, and slowly nod. He didn't know the policeman at all, but Tim Spriggs had vouched for him in their conversation on the way here from the Aotearoa gateway. Plus he looked determined and handy in a fight. And he wanted to rescue Hine — that went without saying.

After that, it was all preparations and logistics, priming muskets and readying themselves. They were too many for Mat to take across, but the way between worlds was well known. 'Don't you make a widow of me,' Kelly whispered in Wiri's ear as they parted. Tim Spriggs was going to take her back to the launch. He had already spoken to the engineer, Gavin, and apprised him of her labour and childbirth. Spriggs wore a wan expression, his shattered arm preventing him from 'fulfilling my duty as an officer', as he put it morosely.

Kelly met Wiri's eye one last time, and then they were gone, into the trees, going to war.

She looked at Spriggs, who came and sat beside her, cradling his broken arm. 'Being left behind sucks.'

Spriggs exhaled heavily. 'Yes, Miss Kelly, it does indeed, ahem ... "suck",' he acknowledged. He peered down at the baby. 'You have a fine young son. What will you call him?'

Kelly looked down at the sleeping bundle. 'We don't know yet. We haven't even had time to discuss it.' She felt tears well up. 'We'll talk about it if … when … if …' A tear rolled down one cheek.

'When!' said Spriggs firmly. 'When Wiri returns, victorious as always.'

'He's not immortal any more,' whispered Kelly. 'He thinks he is, but he's not.'

'But he is a warrior like no other. And Mat is resourceful, and the match of these warlocks. Tu Hollis will move mountains to rescue his Hinemoa. Kurangaituku is fighting for her very soul, and she will look out for Riki too, I fancy. These are powerful things they each bring to the fray.' Spriggs sighed, and patted Kelly's hand. 'They'll be back, old girl. You'll see.'

The exhilaration of the decision to pursue and fight lasted around ten minutes. That was all the time it took to steal through the gateway into Aotearoa, and creep through the bush to the clearing on the south side.

It was empty. Donna and her allies were gone. They all watched Manu and Wiri examining the grass about the pool, now trampled in a column leading right to the edge, as if a herd of beasts had vanished into the waters.

Mat glanced at Tu Hollis, whose face was clouding over in despair.

Kurangaituku put a hand on his arm, leading him to join Wiri and Manu. 'My children watched from the trees,' Kurangaituku told them. 'They saw Kyle drip Hine Horatai's blood into the water.'

Mat closed his eyes wearily. 'Ngatoro told me that if we couldn't regain Hine, then we would be able to get in with primal fire.' He went to the pool and experimentally immersed the Nail, praying it wouldn't wink out. The water sizzled, and a cloud of steam rose, but nothing else. He pulled the Nail out slowly — it still burned as bright as ever. But nothing else happened.

'I don't think there is a gate here any more,' he told Wiri. 'We've lost the race.'

The Information Age

Mat sat on a boulder beside the lake, in the real world. Gavin, the launch engineer, had taken Spriggs and Kelly to hospital in Rotorua. They seemed to be the only ones going anywhere. He sulked morosely. It had seemed so right, and now they were stonewalled. His fingers were throbbing, and the bandages were scratchy. He stared across the water at Rotorua, and phoned Cassandra, using the cellphone awkwardly with his wrapped fingers.

She responded immediately. 'Mat? Hi!'

'Hi! Where are you?'

'Taupo hospital. Jones is okay. We're with him, your mum and me.'

'Mum's there?'

'Yeah. She was with me when we found him. He's getting the best attention possible, Mat. Widow Calder found him,' Cassandra went on. 'He had a defence mechanism, totally organic, that dragged him away into some kind of niche in time and space.'

'What?'

'You know how Jones can alter Aotearoa sometimes, so

303

that places change? He used that to have the ivy he cleared reappear and take him into a different part of Aotearoa — same place but different period, kind of. The principle seems to be that if you're unaware of that memory, you can't get there.'

Mat had seen Jones cause Wairoa-Aotearoa to alter to his whim, but had never really thought about it — it had been just another minor miracle on that day when bigger things had happened. He found himself nodding as Cassandra spoke. It was good to have something else to focus on, to lift him above the heartsickness that had descended when they had found that Donna had escaped them.

'So, what's happening there?' Cassandra asked.

'We're screwed,' he told her desultorily, while his mind picked over this question of memories of places.

'What do you mean?'

He tried to keep the defeat from his voice, but couldn't. 'Cass, we're mostly okay, but Donna Kyle has got into Te Iho.' He rapidly filled her in on the state of play. 'So basically, this Te Iho is the ultimate power, and it's where Ngatoro is. Donna is going to own it, unless we can follow her, and it looks like she's blocked the only gateway in. There is nothing we can do.' Back in Aotearoa, the Ngati Maungatautari were alternately pacing or sitting, frustrated. Everyone was feeling low. He had left them to it, needing to talk to someone.

He heard Cassandra exhale, and could picture the way she would be frowning, her eyebrows almost touching, as they did when she confronted a puzzle.

'Is Jones awake?' he asked hopefully. Maybe he could give them guidance.

'No, he's unconscious. It's not a coma and the doctors seem confident, but they say it'll take time.'

He nodded. He tried to picture the scene in the hospital, but instead the image of Ngatoro and the other prisoners intruded. He wondered who that evil old man beside Ngatoro was, and at what he had seen through that window, the moonlit garden …

He flicked his eyes open. 'Cass, have you got your laptop with you?'

'Duh! Of course — it's me!'

'Sure. You're surgically attached to your laptop.' He frowned, trying to piece together his thoughts. 'Well, there was this thing that happened tonight, when Riki and I were flying over Rotorua-Aotearoa.'

'Flying?'

'Yeah. I'll explain later. Anyway, we were flying over Rotorua-Aotearoa, and I saw the whole place change all of a sudden. The big pa disappeared, and the Aotearoa village reverted to almost modern. Really weird.'

'Yeah … and?' She paused. 'Hang on! Maybe it was like what Jones did to Wairoa-Aotearoa, or the ivy, but large-scale!'

'Yeah, that's what I'm thinking!' He smiled wryly at being a step ahead of Cassandra for once. 'It can't be coincidence. I figure the change must have been when Donna Kyle entered Te Iho, near enough. It must have been that: her entering Te Iho.' He nibbled on his lip as he put his ideas into order. 'We know that Te Iho is a prison for Ngatoro and maybe others. It must *physically* exist somewhere! But somewhere that doesn't normally appear, otherwise people would find it. Maybe even *can't* appear unless someone is actually already inside Te Iho.'

'Like Jones's ivy! A place in Aotearoa that's locked off except when it's needed, and only then is it accessible.' In the background he could hear her typing. 'Go on, I'm getting your drift, Mat.'

'Well, I dreamt a conversation with Ngatoro the other night, and in it I saw gardens: rose gardens, really big ... Aren't there some rose gardens by that museum place — you know, the one that's in all the Rotorua postcards?'

'The Bath House? Yeah, I've been there. Who hasn't? It's a museum, and there's still big gardens. But it's really famous, Mat. Surely it's *always* present in Aotearoa?'

'Yeah ... but Ngatoro and other prisoners were on what looked like old-style hospital beds. Was there ever a hospital or something similar in the Bath House gardens?'

The typing sound that carried down the phone became frenzied. 'Hang on,' Cassandra whispered. 'Ahh! The Bath House ... it was built in 1908 ... Mat! *It was the first hospital in Rotorua!* But they shut that part down in, um ... 1966. The hospital wing has been demolished. Hang on, though — wasn't Te Iho constructed well before 1908?'

Mat paused, but his mind made further connections. 'Yeah, but listen! Ngatoro said that the others imprisoned with him were dead. He was oblivious to the other bodies. What if all the earliest prisoners started dying, so Puarata moved them to a hospital ward to keep them alive? But to conceal it, he chose a hospital ward that existed only in a certain space and time, then put protections around it so no-one could find it. Remember: each death of a prisoner would have reduced the power he gained from them. A real-world hospital is traceable — but not one that is in a forgotten corner of Aotearoa. Especially if that period is overshadowed by more famous ones.'

Cassandra sucked in her breath. 'That's awfully tenuous, Mat,' she breathed. 'Too many ifs.'

'Not impossible, though,' he replied. 'And get this: when we flew over, there was a dense, low cloud-bank right over the Bath House area. It's still there — I can see it from here!'

'Mmmm. Then maybe you're right. The only way to check would be to go and look, while this 1960s incarnation of Rotorua-Aotearoa holds.' She tsked in frustration. 'I wish I was there.'

'Sorry. But thanks for staying with Mum. And for helping just now. You're a magician yourself, you know.'

'Yeah, well, it was mostly you. Surprisingly smart for a boy, if you're right.'

He felt himself smile. Cassandra never called anyone smart, because her own standards were so high and she didn't believe in false praise. 'Thanks for looking it all up.'

'Donchya just love the Information Age?' she laughed.

He smiled back down the phone. 'Yeah. I owe you.'

She giggled. 'Promises, promises.' Her voice turned serious. 'Good luck! And be careful — don't get yourself killed.'

He felt mildly euphoric, despite this admonition. 'I'll be fine — Wiri's here! Hey, gotta run, if we're gonna be in time. See ya!'

'Bye! Take care!' Her voice was anxious. He suddenly wished he could hug her, and reassure her.

'I will. See you soon.' He thumbed off the phone painfully with his bandaged fingers, leapt to his feet, and shifted to

307

Aotearoa. Heads turned as he appeared beside Hinemoa's Pool. 'Wiri! I've got an idea!'

Five minutes later, the Ngati Maungatautari were in their waka, paddling furiously as they tore through the water, and trying not to gape as the giant war-canoe rose into the air. Kurangaituku stood in the prow, her arms extended. The warriors paddled the air as if it was water, and somehow the paddles bit and propelled them forwards ever faster. The craft glided gracefully into the sky.

In the prow behind the Birdwitch, Wiri, Manu and Tu laid plans for the disposition of the warriors. Above them Mat and Riki soared, their winged cloaks spread, feeling the exhilaration of renewed purpose. Thousands of birds rose in their wake as they soared towards a dome of dark cloud that shrouded the night cityscape of Rotorua-Aotearoa.

Through the shadow-maze

Friday night

The firelight behind Donna failed to leave any impression on the shadow-walls about her, but at each intersection, the thin trail of floating blood led her deeper into the maze. She stared after it with forlorn eyes. The gun pressing into her back jabbed insistently, and the tipua snickered to see her brought low by their chieftain. They clearly didn't realize that Kotukutuku was inhabited by Parukau. They openly brandished guns and taunted her and Hine.

On her forehead, Parukau had carved a sigil, a magical symbol, with his knife, and poured a spell into it. The pain of the cut had taken her breath away, and then abruptly she was shut off from her powers, as helpless as an ordinary woman. She knew the spell — she had used it on others — but that knowledge wouldn't save her. She was at Parukau's mercy, of which there would be none. She knew him by reputation, and there was too much at stake. Only one hope remained: her father. But she could no longer speak to him.

Parukau seemed exultant as he prodded her along beside Hine Horatai. The girl seemed lost in despair and wouldn't meet her eye, but her knuckles were white, as if she concealed a seething fury. Or perhaps it was just blood loss. The girl's blood trail wove through the air eerily as they went deeper and deeper into the darkness.

Parukau had to lash Stone and Rose more and more often. They had become increasingly rebellious, and when he had enquired of Stone, he found it was because Stone had sensed the death of the missing one, Heron. He had been slightly shocked himself to only take two heart-strings in his grasp when he took command from Donna. Doubts gnawed him — killing a patupaiarehe was no casual feat. Who had done it? Another warlock, lurking secretly? Wiremu and his allies? Even Matiu Douglas?

But we're inside and the locks have been changed ... I'm safe, I must be! My only enemies are here ... or awaiting me at the heart of this maze. He licked his lips. Soon he would have to deal with Asher Grieve.

'Are we close?' he called mentally to the old wizard, wondering if he would hear.

He sensed Asher smile. *Yes, Parukau. I sense you. You are very close. Now silence, I must gather my energies.*

He nodded, exhilaration growing. He pushed Donna Kyle along before him. 'I am in conversation with your father, Donna. Soon I will free him from Te Iho. And you will take his place there. He is not happy with his recalcitrant daughter, not at all.'

Her face was so bleak he almost thought that she would try to flee, just so that he would kill her. But she didn't try anything. Yet.

Was it minutes or hours? Who could tell in this place? The girl Hine was losing blood slowly, and looked shaky. Donna staggered every few steps as Parukau drove her on. Then, abruptly, they were through the maze.

At last! Parukau could not contain himself from roaring in excitement. His cry of triumph was echoed by the tipua, as awe lit their faces. At last, they all beheld Te Iho.

Green light pulsed from the centre in time to a huge heartbeat, and the colour washed over their pale skin and shone in their eyes. Even Parukau was forced to stop and stare at this place he had helped create all those centuries ago, yet scarcely recognized now. Puarata had been busy.

From the inside of the shadow-maze, they appeared to be inside a dome of darkness, perhaps half a kilometre wide, and two hundred metres high in the centre. The gap between the ground and this 'roof' grew towards the centre, where a rocky floor opened out on, of all things, a neat and orderly rose garden. Set amongst the garden, miracle of miracles, was the quaint architecture of the Rotorua Bath House, with all of its wings. The Bath House: an iconic Rotorua building constructed between 1906 and 1908 as a spa, with black timbers framing whitewashed walls, and huge sloping roofs of terracotta tiling. In the real world it was a museum, but in Aotearoa it was still a health spa, with a fine restaurant on the ground floor.

But the Bath House had another, seldom seen, incarnation. Right now, because Te Iho had been opened, it was a hospital, and an additional wing had reappeared. From within, this wing pulsed with the same deep emerald light that washed over the gardens. The whole building seemed empty but for that lurid throbbing glow in the lost wing. Parukau stared. The place he remembered had been much more primitive. No wonder Puarata had so much power. *I was lucky not to end up here too, being leeched for all eternity.*

His eyes were inexorably drawn to the hospital wing, where the prisoners presumably lay. Where Asher Grieve waited, at the centre of the web. But was he fly or spider?

I will be the spider here, and I'll eat him alive.

He raised his hand to order the advance, but the words died in his throat.

A roar of noise reverberated from high above, and the shadowy dome of cloud was shot through with scarlet like a sunset. Then a fiery hole was blasted through it, a hole in the sky that roared with a blast of wind. The tipua howled in disbelief and fear. As did he, when a waka flew through the jagged hole and swooped towards him, a thousand smaller shapes pouring behind it, shrieking in hatred.

Rotorua-Aotearoa opened up panoramically to Mat, the sparse street-lighting glistering beneath a diamond-studded sky. To his right, Riki was grinning with the sheer joy of flying, but Mat was already peering ahead. Before them, a dome of shadow cloaked the lakeside just east of the main city, the only blemish on an otherwise clear night. It was the shadow-maze, if he was right, visible because someone walked in Te Iho.

Mat's arms grew steadily colder as they flew, fortunately numbing his fingertips, which still stung. His arms were not built for flapping, but thankfully the feather cloak did most of the work; he just had to keep his arms spread. The air rushed by and the thrill of speed was exhilarating. He met Riki's eyes and grinned.

'Damian is going to be gutted at missing this!' Riki crowed.

'So's Cass!' Mat shouted back. Cassandra had parachuted; she would have loved this. He peered forwards at the mound of shadow. 'Is it a complete dome or can we fly over it?'

'Don't think so. It curves over.'

I thought so. What would happen if he flew into it: disorientation and a messy landing? Or would they simply rip straight through it? *I bet it's the former, but I've got the Fire-Nail!*

He swooped over the waka, shouting to Wiri: 'I'm going to try it!'

Wiri raised a thumb in acknowledgement, then spoke in Kurangaituku's ear. The Birdwitch tilted her head slowly towards Mat, her eyes flashing madly. Riki might vouch for her, but she looked demented right now, her arms spread, carrying the waka aloft by her powers alone. The Ngati Maungatautari warriors were singing a rowing song, the cadences rising and falling as they ploughed through the air, the wave of birds above blocking out the stars.

He pulled out the Nail, and thought about fire, remembering all Jones's lessons, and pouring his waning energies into the flame. It began to flare and the bandages started to smoulder and burn away. He felt nothing, and his fingers suffered no harm.

He spread the cloak's wings, his right fist before him, and plunged towards the shadow-maze, calling the others behind him. For a few seconds he thought he might splat on the surface of the dome like a bug on a windshield, but in the last seconds he realized that it was misty and indistinct, like clouds viewed from an aircraft window. 'Mahuika!' he shouted and the Fire-Nail burst into incandescent light, punching a hole in the shadow, a hole that kept growing and widening as he plummeted through.

'Woohoo!' hollered Riki behind him, but Mat kept his eyes fixed ahead, blazing a trail through the darkness, through the mists — and in!

All about them, the dome of shadow became riven with multiple seams of fiery scarlet, and shrivelled. Mat shouted and pointed as the Bath House appeared below. Before it was a swarm of tipua. The Ngati Maungatautari warriors responded with renewed paddling, scooping at the air as the waka nosed into a dive.

Kurangaituku threw out a huge call, and suddenly the air above beat with countless wings. Her children soared above in a wall of feathers and claws and beaks. It was impossible to even guess how many. She threw her hands dramatically forwards, and they dived through the shredding darkness.

The tipua only had eyes for the air above them now. Their leaders screamed orders, but they were staring upwards in awe as a massive wall of birds plummeted towards them like a tidal wave. Panic was written over every tiny goblin face. Worse, among the birds flew a waka full of warriors, diving towards them with the maniacally grinning Kurangaituku at the prow.

That snapped Parukau out of his sudden paralysis. 'Cootface! No way!' He strode back to the tipua ranks. He saw Stone, holding Hine's tether. 'Stay beside me!' he shouted

at the patupaiarehe. 'Keep the girl safe!' *I've got plans for her.*
Then he turned to the tipua war-leaders. 'Form up, form up!
Get them into a line!'

The tipua milled, squalling. Sporadic fire opened up, at too
long a range; ineffectual and, worse, the tipua musket men
barely knew how to reload. Parukau swore in fury. But then
the banshee wail of Kurangaituku filled the air, and Parukau
saw a wave of darkness swell above his ranks of tipua. Birds,
shrieking down on them. By sheer weight and momentum
alone, the birds were going to rip through his goblins. Many
of the birds were swooping over the top — straight at him.

He took one look at Donna Kyle's white face to know this
wasn't her doing, either. Stone and Rose looked at him blankly,
and Hine Horatai's face was disbelieving.

The old disciplines of leadership rose inside him. He rapped
out his orders furiously. 'Stone, stay with me! Keep the girl
close. Rose, keep hold of Donna Kyle. If she runs, rip out
her heart!' *I might need hostages.* 'Asher!' he shouted. 'Asher,
hear me!'

Parukau.

'I've got your daughter, Asher! I know you want her back —
she's yours, if you can help me! We're under attack, right outside the Bath House.'

Are you? How unfortunate. What is your price?

'I've no time for this! It's Cootface and Wiremu and a
bunch of warriors, and they're going to *dismantle* us if you
can't help me!'

I see, purred Asher, seemingly unhurried. But there was
a tension in his voice. *Reach out for me, Parukau, with your
mind …*

315

There was about six seconds before the first birds struck: he had no choice. He reached out, like a fuse seeking a spark. His inner eye saw an outpouring arise from the phantom wing of the Bath House, a jagged emerald branch like slow-moving lightning, and he grasped it without thinking.

His eyes flashed verdant power, his chest filled to bursting. He felt like a god, yet also like a bug caught on an electric pad, as the full strength of Te Iho jolted into him, through him …

… and out of him, in a wave of fire that erupted into the sky above.

The waka glided in on the power of the Birdwitch, swooping low until its keel almost skimmed the turf. 'Get us down,' Wiri called anxiously in the witch's ear. 'If anything goes wrong, I want to drop two feet, not two hundred.' He pushed his open palm down, signalling a slowing of the paddling.

Behind him, Manu muttered, 'Why didn't we fit this waka with landing gear?'

The birds swarmed past, obscuring the tipua ranks. Kura-ngaituku lifted her arms slightly, and the keel carved the turf while the nose of the waka lifted, and gently slid into a skidding, twisting landing. The men inside it cowered beneath the rim of the waka, in case the canoe flipped. It didn't. The Birdwitch kept the waka steady until it halted some hundred metres from the tipua, and tipped lightly to one side.

The warriors whooped, and weapons clattered as they leapt from the canoe hull. 'Form up!' Wiri shouted. Above, the vast cloud of birds dropped, and Wiri tried to anticipate the impact of this wall of flying bodies upon the tipua. *They're going to rip the goblins apart* … He almost felt sorry for them.

Suddenly, from behind the tipua, flame washed in a burst of molten light. It carved through the birds as if through paper, and in that single instant they ceased to exist. The cries of the swooping avians were extinguished in a concussive roar of heat. Wiri heard Kurangaituku scream and saw her fall to her knees, her arms raised in despair as every death among her children tore through her senses. The warriors staggered to a halt, as they lost all vision in a falling cloud of smoke, burnt feathers and falling bodies.

Great Tane, what was that?

Mat and Riki dropped beneath the flow of birds, and found themselves only a few metres above the waka. They hit the ground running, and staggered to a halt. A second later, the air above them exploded in fire.

Mat threw himself down, Riki beside him, as heat swept over them and the air was suddenly a whirlwind of searing, unbreathable smoke. He buried his head in his arms, sucking oxygen from ground level in gasps. Burning winds whipped at them, and his lungs felt like the inside of an oven.

For long seconds, he could see nothing but the smoke and ash, and there was nothing to breathe. Then the hot air swirled away, and cool air whooshed about him.

Before them, unseen, the tipua howled triumphantly, while the desolate cry of the Birdwitch wailed amidst the ash and spiralling feathers.

The Ngati Maungatautari scrambled to their feet, sucking in a sweet flow of oxygen, grabbing at their weapons. All were armed with muskets as well as their traditional Maori weaponry. The air ripped open the smoke clouds, revealing the enemy shockingly close. Wiri peered forward. *If that happens again, we're toast. We gotta hit them fast.*

'Close formation, boys! We volley at fifty metres!' Wiri raised a hand and signalled the advance. *I can't let them dwell on that firestorm. We've got to get among the enemy before whatever makutu did it gives us a repeat dose.*

Wiri saw Mat and Riki scramble to their feet and join them, and breathed a sigh of relief. They trotted past Kurangaituku, who was on her knees, a broken figure.

Tu Hollis ran behind him, fiddling with the lock of his musket. In front of them the tipua waited in thick, layered ranks. Wiri glanced at Manu. He had never seen such a thing before: a tipua defensive line. Tipua did not crouch in lines — they boiled forward in berserk assaults, screaming and frothing at the mouth.

This is all wrong.

He peered through the gloom, trying to see what was going on. The shadowy massed ranks were only silhouettes, and if he didn't know better, he would have said they had—

He spun. 'Fan out! Fan out! They've got guns!'

Mat heard Wiri's call about the guns, and saw them, too. Rank upon rank of gun barrels fell into line, right down the tipua lines. The rational part of him began to calculate: *Maybe half the goblins have guns — we could lose half our men in one go,*

and then they'll roll over the top of us. And what if that firestorm happens again?

The Ngati Maungatautari were trotting forwards, and he kept pace, caught up in the flow, but his mind was desperately looking for something he could do, some 'magic bullet' to prevent carnage. *God knows how many guns, and only forty targets ... What are the odds?* The Fire-Nail barely flickered in his palm, all but drained from breaking into this place. Could he make it ready in time?

'Drop and take aim!' Manu shouted, and the Ngati Maungatautari fell to one knee. But already the tipua were aiming. It was too late — they were still too bunched, impossible to miss even for untrained goblins.

I've got to do something ...

Only one thing sprang to mind. He dropped his taiaha and lifted both hands, shouting as he summoned and sent the only thing he could think of towards the array of glinting *metal* gun barrels.

Electricity, just like Cassandra had showed him, but more than he had ever attempted before. To fail would mean disaster ...

He nailed it perfectly.

White sparks blazed, forked spasmodically, and leapt towards the tipua guns. A frightened howl erupted from the goblins as lightning danced among them. Virtually every gun fired as trigger fingers convulsed at the sudden pain stabbing through the hands of their wielders. But the shock of the electricity had ruined all aim. Instead of a level volley into the ranks of Maori warriors, there was only an erratic burst of fire. Lead balls whined through the air, but only a handful of men

319

shouted in pain, and none went down. Mat swayed as the effort hit him. Then Riki dragged him flat as Manu shouted. 'Ngati Maungatautari, *fire!*'

Forty guns barked in unison, and the front rank of the goblins was blasted apart. The whole body of the enemy staggered backwards, howling and thrown into confusion. It was as if a giant machete had scythed through them as they stood.

Manu lifted his hand, assessing, then grinned viciously. 'Reload! Let's give 'em another lick!'

It made sense. The tipua had been thrown into chaos, and were incapable of charging. Mat looked past the goblins, searching in the shadows for greater threats. On the steps lurked taller figures, and something that glowed green like a classroom chemistry experiment. He pointed them out to Riki. 'We've got to stop that fire from happening again!'

Riki nodded. 'Right with you, bro.'

They ran three steps towards the enemy, spreading their arms and letting the feather cloaks pin their arms again, shouting through the tingling pain, and then they were soaring into the air and over the tipua.

Parukau backed away as his goblin war-party disintegrated into chaos. The current of power that had jolted through him receded, releasing his limbs. He could still feel how good it had been to unleash that energy and release such destructive power. Had even Puarata done such a thing?

'I need more, old man!'

Asher's mental voice, when it came back, was shaky. *Wait ...*

you must wait … You've exhausted me. I can't channel more, not immediately …

'DAMMIT, GIVE ME MORE!'

Wait! The source is infinite, but I am not.

'How long?'

Not long … half a minute.

Half a minute. 'HOLD THE LINE!' he screamed at his captains. 'HOLD THE LINE!'

His heart pounded as two man-size shapes leapt into the air, and soared high above.

No! No-one must get inside before me!

A second volley crashed through the tipua, and the goblin lines burst apart. Suddenly the line of warriors was terrifyingly close. He leapt down the stairs, desperate now to rally this remnant that protected him, to buy some last precious seconds.

'Attack! Attack!' He menaced the tipua with the traces of green fire that still played about his fist. They responded fearfully, staggering forward towards the enemy guns with little conviction, caught between two terrors. 'We have the numbers!' he implored. 'Attack!' They streamed away from him, those that could still move, or would. Many fled. He had to resist blasting at them — he had to harbour the rekindling energy. *Damn this!*

Instead he spun and gestured at Rose, who hovered behind Donna Kyle, licking her neck. 'Bring her!' He turned to Stone, waiting at his side with his broadsword in one hand and Hine Horatai in his other. 'Follow!' he commanded the patupaiarehe, and sprinted towards the Bath House, his eyes searching the night sky above for those two fliers.

Wiri spun his taiaha as the warriors beside him drew into a loose skirmish line. From out of the carnage before them staggered a wave of tipua, howling in fury. He saw Manu thrust his smoking pistol into his belt and draw a sabre — Manu had preferred European weaponry for decades — but most of the warriors pulled a patu or mere from their belts, or lifted long taiaha from the ground beside them. They had been lucky, virtually untouched thanks to Mat's burst of electricity. But they were still outnumbered. There had to be close to sixty tipua swarming towards them over the bodies of their fallen comrades, howling for revenge.

Momentum is the key in close combat. Years of war had taught Wiri this. The man going backwards loses his footing, has one eye behind him, and is already defeated mentally. Size and power can only be used off the front foot. 'Maungatautari, advance!'

Manu gently wove a pattern in the air with his blade. He had a wide smile on his face. 'Don' s'pose we have time for a haka?' he remarked laconically. About them, the Ngati Maungatautari war-party rose and broke into a slow run, as the enemy boiled closer.

Wiri bared his teeth. *'Charge!'*

The Bath House

Friday night

Rose's hand clamped on Donna's forearm like steel, and her eyes held no more intelligence than a child. Strange to think she had pitied the girl, but the sharp teeth that had teased her throat offered no release except death. 'When will he let me drink?' Rose fretted. 'I'm thirsty.'

All semblance of control and order was gone. There was only chaos now. The firestorm — *how?* And now Kurangaituku — how had the Birdwitch enlisted such aid? What had she promised them? How had she corrupted Wiri and his allies? *Or had she?*

She cursed the sigil on her brow. With it there, she was helpless; a loser no matter how this turned out. Only years of pitiless training under Puarata kept her upright. She harboured her remaining strength. There would be a chance, she had to believe that.

Rose hauled her up the stairs to the wide double doors of the Bath House. Beside them, Stone guarded Hine, sword in hand. Hine's face wore a look of sullen anger — and readiness to act. The girl was a gang moll, Donna recalled. She had to be tough. Self-preservation would force her to resist. She tried to meet the girl's eyes, to establish some kind of rapport. 'Hine,' she whispered. 'Be ready. Follow my lead—'

'Quiet!' Rose casually slapped her, a wafting blow that almost shattered her jaw. Stars exploded behind her eyes and she reeled, but the patupaiarehe's hand kept her upright. 'No words, Mistress. We have a new master now, and he will let me eat you soon.' She smiled dreamily at the thought.

Her eyes watered and her cheek stung. She blinked, seeing Parukau at the foot of the stairs, staring out over the battlefield. 'Asher — now!' Parukau called.

Father is aiding him … Something else died inside her.

She sucked in a breath as two figures dropped out of the skies and landed before Parukau. Matiu Douglas and Riki Waitoa, wearing cloaks of the Birdwitch. They looked incredibly young, and, in that instant, vulnerable and noble and foolish and beautiful.

Parukau cried aloud, and raised his fist to strike again. The air about him boiled with emerald fire.

Parukau reached the steps of the Bath House; Stone and Rose hauling the prisoners on ahead. He turned as a whir of wings reached his ears. Spinning, he saw two shapes swooping from the skies towards him. A skinny youth with a taiaha, and Matiu Douglas. He snarled in fury. *You again!* He gathered the emerald current from the hospital wing as it forked towards him again, feeling its power about to peak. He raised his fist.

'Stop!' Matiu Douglas called.

'Asher — *now!*' Beyond the boy the goblins and the Maori

warriors fought, and the wails of the tipua told him that they were folding. He had minutes at most. But one burst, aimed at ground level, would be all he needed. Men and tipua, they would perish together.

He pointed his burning hand at the boy to let the flames surge. 'Burn!'

'No!' The young Adept threw up his hands, and suddenly they were fighting, mind to mind.

Fire! The gift of Mahuika to the world. He held it in his hand, that tiny fingernail. He felt it stir to life again, and begin to slide up his forefinger. It gripped and seemed to root itself into the puckered open wound at the top of the finger. It hurt, like tipping antiseptic on a cut, but it rooted into his fingertip like a normal nail, only blackened and full of menace. He lifted it, felt its power swell. Maybe he could strike, just as the goblin had, and incinerate all before him: Parukau the goblin, Donna Kyle, the two patupaiarehe ... Then he saw Hine Horatai among the enemy, held in Stone's fist.

No, not her!

Instead of attacking with the fire, he reached out desperately with his mind, and threw it like a spanner into the machinery of destruction that was brewing inside Parukau. As he opened himself up to it, he saw the current of power flowing from the hospital, and realized that what he was doing was suicidal. He was making himself the circuit-breaker on a line of power that dwarfed any he had ever experienced. But it was too late.

The moment he locked horns with the goblin, a flash of

recognition passed between them. *Parukau!* The centuries-old body-snatcher against a partly-trained youth. He knew within seconds that there could be only one result. He felt the force confronting him shift and solidify, felt the gleeful triumph of Parukau, heard taunting words as unseen hands wrapped around his throat. His vision swam, and the flames grew in the goblin's hands.

'Yes, boy, it is I,' Parukau purred. 'Say goodbye!'

The past couple of hours had been a nightmare, but Hine was waking now. She was dragging herself from a walking stupor of blood loss and fear. She was recovering from the array of shocks, from seeing the horror of death close up, and the nightmare creatures of this Ghost World. Part of her wanted to crawl away and hide, but she refused. *I'm stronger than this! I can rise above this!* And the need to see Tu Hollis drove her on, to face the world again, however crazy it had become.

For the past half-hour, she had thought only of how she might escape. When Mat Douglas appeared, she saw her opportunity. She could see he was fighting, somehow, some unseen struggle. His hands burned with the same flame as that in Parukau's goblin hand, but it was purer somehow. She could almost sense what they were doing — and she realized that Mat was losing.

She knew that she had to act. Parukau was going to use that hideous fire again, and this time Mat would burn, and Tu and all the others. Then after that she would be at Parukau's mercy. She felt the blaze mount, the light growing hotter and hotter. The goblin was feeding that flame, and it was going to burn Mat and Tu and the others to ash. She felt Mat flounder, and so she did the only thing she knew.

She called on water to counter the flames.

She could see no physical water here. But this wasn't a physical battle. And she was an avatar, of a legend entwined with a whole lake full of water. Water that filled her dreams, that soaked her soul. She swam through it all her life, the deep water that wanted to swallow her. She called it, called it to douse the fire, and protect those she cared for. She called in desperation, but with total conviction and belief.

And the deep water came.

Mat staggered, lost his link to Parukau's mind, and almost fell. The flame in Parukau's hands burst into a ball, and the goblin pulled back his arm to hurl it. But with a sudden roar, water exploded from the very ground around them, as if every geyser in Rotorua had come *here*, right *now*. The windows of the Bath House erupted. Walls shook, and fountains of scalding water tore through the earth. A multitude of massive geysers gushed from the ground and from the broken pipes of the Bath House itself, in a torrent that scythed them all down.

Perhaps the primal flame protected him — he felt no pain.

But the others about him did, as torrents of boiling water slapped them off their feet.

Water and steam billowed about him. He could no longer see Parukau. Riki staggered beside him through the steam and fountaining water, his face buried in his cloak as he stumbled towards the Bath House doors. Mat followed, and he saw

Hine Horatai, on the landing, roped to a taller shape holding a sword. *Water ... She is an avatar of water ... She did this!*

He didn't question this miracle. Parukau reappeared, silhouetted in the Bath House door, and then was gone, the swordsman dragging Hine with him.

He leapt past Riki and ran after them.

The ground bucked, and the lower floor of the Bath House seemed to explode outwards in sheets of boiling water and clouds of steam. A geyser erupted at Donna's feet and threw her sideways, tearing her from Rose's surprised grip. She found herself flung sideways along the steps, landing on her ankle and going over on it, the pain wracking through her. All about her, water flew. She saw Parukau lifted by a geyser that burst up through the ground at his feet. She had no strength to resist, nor even the will to do so any more. The steam and gushing water rendered everything a blind grope through wet darkness, then it dissipated and vision returned.

The first thing she saw was Parukau, upright again, but drenched and no longer holding verdant fire in his grasp. His goblin face was contorted in rage. She saw his teeth flash as he roared fresh orders. 'Stone, bring the girl!' Then he saw Donna, lying alone on the stairs. 'Rose!'

Rose emerged from the mists, her dress plastered to her body, her livid face full of teeth. 'Master?' she mewled.

Parukau's finger stabbed towards Donna. 'Rip her apart — I don't need her any more!'

Riki had always believed there was good in everyone. It was something his granddad liked to say, and Riki generally thought he was right. Which was just as well because some of the guys who hung around his family were pretty bad eggs by society's reckoning. Ex-crims and street toughs, the sort of guys who ended up being defended in court by Mat's father. If Riki had not believed in his granddad's wisdom, he would have been too scared to leave his bedroom every day.

But Puarata's warlocks were a different class of being, and he didn't think of them as human. Not after the things he had seen at Waikaremoana, and the stuff Jones and Mat had told him. They weren't people; they were hollow things who had emptied themselves of normal feelings to make room for something darker.

The mercy shown him by Kurangaituku had changed his view on that point slightly. He had been forced to see her as a being trapped by circumstance, lured and tempted by a dark life that promised everything and delivered little more than fear. Power, too, but a false kind of power — the sort that permitted inflicting pain on others, but failed on delivering peace of mind and security and happiness. A devil's bargain. It reminded him of a drug dealer who used to be friends with his brother, until some rival shot him in the spine and left him paraplegic.

So when he saw Donna Kyle sprawled on the stairs, and some vampire girl in a wet floral dress looming over her with bared fangs, he didn't hesitate. While Mat turned left and ran after Hine and her captors, he went right, swinging his taiaha as he shouted to distract the thing from its prey.

The girl spun and reared back like a snake, swaying from

his blow. She hissed and then sprang before he had even completed the follow-through, his whole weight off-balance and his weapon askew, leaving him utterly exposed. Her mouth widened into a jagged fence of teeth as she uncoiled and sprang. She hissed exultantly, in her mind already feasting on him.

The taiaha looks like a wooden spear, but it isn't. It's a long wooden club, held two-handed just above the pointed tongue. Which makes it a two-ended weapon. And Riki wasn't top of his taiaha class for nothing. Even as the patupaiarehe leapt, he was moving his left hand up the shaft, spinning the weapon like a bandmaster twirling his staff, bracing and thrusting.

The taiaha punched through the girl's chest and burst out her back. A thin splatter of blood sprayed down the shaft as her weight settled. He twisted the weapon and drove her down, slamming the tongue further through, and into the wet earth. Her body thrashed blindly, her talons raking, but he rolled clear, and came up on all fours, staring at the hideous sight of the young girl dying. She convulsed and jerked to stillness as he tried and failed to look away. Her face turned towards him.

She smiled just like his little sister did, and died.

All at once the horror of the moment struck him, and he felt a gorge of bilious food rise up his throat. He had sagged to his knees and vomited over the steps before he could stop himself.

Damn, I'll never get used to this.

By the time he thought to look for Donna Kyle, she was gone.

When Rose loomed above her, Donna didn't have the strength to move. But someone shouted, and the girl turned and leapt at a youth — Mat Douglas's friend Riki.

Rose moved so fast it seemed he would be torn apart, but somehow he turned a missed blow into a hidden thrust, and Rose went down with a wooden stake through the heart. The boy moved the way Wiremu did. He looked only seventeen, but she was suddenly scared of him, even when he went down and spewed like a child who has had too much cake.

She suddenly didn't care about winning any more. Or even escaping.

She had lost. It wasn't her fault.

Donna lay back on the wet stone, listening to the gushing water slow. She felt utterly out of her depth. The world had turned on its head, and the only familiar thing left was the distant but familiar sound of a tipua war-party disintegrating in confusion.

Perhaps she could crawl away …

Daughter!

She groaned.

Daughter — come!

She wanted to block him out. But some kind of silvery cord, like that with which she had bound the patupaiarehe, appeared, sprouting from her chest.

'No, Father! Please!'

Edith Madonna Kyle: I summon you! Come to my aid!

She sobbed as she rose to her feet, tried to resist, but the cord at her heart jerked and she flew through the air like a toy, towards a bank of broken windows lit from within by vivid green light.

Mat raced through the Bath House doors into a beautiful, deserted lobby, with polished marble floors, oil paintings and furniture of deep mahogany. A stairway curved upwards, and on it was Parukau, his goblin body hunched, his hand about Hine's wrist. His face was contorted by pain and desperation. Mat stormed after them even as his brain screamed a warning: *Where's the swordsman?*

From above him something cracked, and a chandelier, with the patupaiarehe riding it, snapped from its moorings and plummeted towards him.

He threw himself aside, diving and rolling as half a ton of steel and glass smashed into and through the tiles with an almighty crash. Glass fragments and stone slivers ricocheted about him. The swordsman erupted instantly from the tangle, emerging from the dust and splinters as fast as sight, with a blur of steel in his fist. The sword flashed, and Mat twisted and threw himself sideways. The blade scoured his back and he fell against the balustrade, lifting his taiaha one-handed, just in time to parry another slash. Steel jarred on wood, and the pale face snarled at him from beneath lank hair. The sword in his fist looked huge.

Mat gripped his taiaha and beat away another blow, but was forced to give ground. He tried to bring the weight of his taiaha to bear, but the blade that met his blow was thick and heavy. Wood chips splintered from his weapon as he parried a series of blinding attacks. He could barely see the blows he was parrying, and knew he was outmatched.

He desperately blocked, and then shouted as the tip of the blade left a bloody trail up his left forearm. He had to give more ground, until his foot caught in the wreckage of the chandelier, and the world tipped. He crashed to the floor amidst the twisted metal, half-winded and gasping for air.

He couldn't move.

The pallid thing licked his lips, and thrust downwards.

Parukau dragged Hine up the stairs, threw open the doors and pulled her deeper into the building. They burst into what she realized with shock was a hospital ward. And yet it was much more: in the centre of the room on a stone dais was a ghastly thing that drew the eye and appalled it. It appeared to be a giant heart which pulsed in emerald splendour. A giant heart carved from pounamu. It hung above the room like some alien squid, a distended sac of stony, translucent flesh from which spread a tangle of tentacles that became veins, which gripped and punctured the skin of at least a dozen patients on life support in the hospital beds. There were no doctors, no nurses, but there were beeping machines and diodes everywhere.

As she stared at that great alien leech, she saw that one of its chambers was darkened, the same chamber through which a taiaha handle had been thrust, piercing the flank of the organ. Viscous black fluid ran down the flanks of the organ and pooled in an overflowing stone bowl. A gold chalice sat beside the bowl, as if on an altar.

The men and women imprisoned here lay on hospital beds,

pierced by the tubes that ran from the life-support equipment, and the veins that distended from the giant heart. Those veins were fixed to their flesh like huge, sucking worms. Most of the prisoners were Maori. They gazed out sightlessly, their chests rising and falling slowly.

Parukau turned to her, his goblin face eerily reminiscent of Evan Tomoana's shaven skull. 'Welcome to my parlour, little fly. Two avatars will make a potent addition to my little coterie. You and Tutanekai, joined forever in my service. And the Adept boy, too. You will all feed me, Hine.' He jabbed a finger at her. '*Stand still!*'

She felt herself locked in place, her limbs frozen. She could not even scream.

He went first to the chalice and drained it thirstily, licking the spillage on his chin and inhaling deeply, as if it were the finest of wines. 'You cannot imagine how good this feels, Hine,' he told her. 'It's better than anything I've ever tasted. Like booze and drugs and sex and murder all rolled up into one.' His eyes were glazed. 'If only I had more time to savour it. But unfortunately my tipua outside are falling apart, and my enemies will be here soon, although with luck Col will slay the leaders. And there is one thing I need to do here before I can wreak full havoc upon them.' He turned to a male patient, a Pakeha. 'I must fulfil my Pledge to this man, so that my powers will not be hampered.'

Hine didn't comprehend. All she could see was that horrible beating heart, to which he was going to bind her forever. She tried to call the water again, but her mind was as locked up as her body. All she could do was watch as Parukau removed the old man from the huge heart. The newly detached veins swayed like worms. He made a gesture, and they all moved in unison: towards her, snaking slowly with their maws widening.

The patient was an ancient white man with long, grey hair and a hook-nosed face. Parukau leant over him, chuckling softly. 'See, old man: I keep my bargains; I've freed you. But I've a wee surprise for you, Asher.' He pulled open the man's slack mouth, as though about to administer rescue breathing. 'You see, I won't need to let you rule over me as agreed — *if I am you!*'

His parasite soul slid from his mouth, just as she had seen it do at Taupo police station. It began to slide from his mouth and into the old man's. She gaped, while those detached tentacles writhed through the air towards her, readying to latch on. She opened her mouth to scream as they lunged.

But it was Parukau they seized.

The mouths of the giant veins clamped on Parukau's back, and he howled in sudden terror. The mocking, knowing eyes of Asher Grieve looked up at him, the mouth curving with wicked glee, and then the world turned to liquid pain. Some kind of tongue stabbed into him, entrails from each vein, and all he could do was scream. He could feel those rasping proboscises inside him, ripping, tearing; and fluids were pouring into him, acidic, burning. He thrashed in their grip, feeling the darkness closing in.

He tried to leave this body, tried to flee, but it was as if some kind of vacuum cleaner were inside him, sucking his soul, and instead of escaping he was drawn deeper, into the mouths that bound him.

Something tore. His soul.

A swirling, sucking oblivion shredded him.

His last perception was of Hine, watching motionless. Without pity.

Then nothing.

She saw the old man on the hospital bed flicker his eyes knowingly, and realized then that it was he who was commanding the tentacle-veins. The hideous appendages struck Parukau, clamping over torso and head and limbs. He screamed once, and then one engulfed his head. She saw his serpent-spirit try to free itself, thrashing out of his mouth, but it was sucked back inside. All the veins turned black as the soul of Parukau was torn from the goblin body, ripped apart and digested. The goblin sagged, and was pulled into place beneath that huge, pulsing heart.

The old man coughed once, and slowly sat up. His rheumy eyes swung about. Except for a loin cloth, he was naked. There was no muscular degeneration despite his imprisonment.

She found she could move, and speak. She staggered towards him. 'Don't get up, sir! I'll get help—'

Too late it dawned on her just who it was who needed help.

Two cold eyes pinned her in place. 'Hold,' he croaked softly, and she found herself frozen again.

The old man stood slowly, brandished his right hand, and conjured clothes about him, long velvets in an antiquated style. An ebony cane appeared in his hand. He shook slightly, and peered at her. 'You will be the avatar,' he said, musingly. 'The Hinemoa. So nice of you to come.' He turned, waved his left hand, and fresh veins coiled from Te Iho, towards her. 'My name is Asher Grieve, and I will be your god for the rest of eternity.'

Wiri hacked a path through the fleeing goblins. It wasn't a fight; it was a slaughter. They had begun to run before contact was even made, the assault falling apart in the final volley Manu ordered. From then it was brutish and nasty. Warriors bashing the skulls of goblins as they turned to flee — there was no glory, just butchery. But he had to get through fast. Mat was somewhere ahead, and the enemies he faced would be beyond him.

A small part of him worried that he wasn't horrified enough by all this. Had all those years in Puarata's service killed the part of him that felt remorse? Maybe it had, but now wasn't the time to think about it. He dispassionately stabbed and bludgeoned, running through the disintegrating mob. All of a sudden the steps to the Bath House were in front of him. He passed a dazed-looking Riki, kneeling and vomiting beside a dead girl. There was no time to wonder. He took the steps three at a time, stormed through the open doors, and bellowed as he dived, whipping his taiaha at the steel blade that was poised above Mat Douglas's chest.

Col hissed, and his sword snaked at Wiri, but he was already rolling, sweeping at Col's legs, making him dance aside. He came up gymnastically, thrusting and shuffling his feet, seeking a clear patch in the smashed glass and tangled metal.

Wiri saw Mat roll away, throw him a look, and then run for the stairs. The pale swordsman went to follow, but Wiri blocked him, shoving him away with a surge of strength. He spun the taiaha and poised to counter, three steps above the pale thing.

'Wiri,' Col breathed. 'The former Immortal. I always thought you were overrated.' His blade levelled at Wiri's chest. 'I am commanded to prevent pursuit.'

'Then you'll have to come through me,' Wiri panted.

'Perfect. *En garde*, human!'

The wizard and the tohunga

Friday night

Mat tore up the stairs, following the pulsing, green light through rooms filled with steam bursting from broken pipes, skidding over wet floorboards, before bursting through into the ward. The greenstone heart hung like some kind of hideous parasite above the lines of hospital beds, and he saw Ngatoro at once, right beneath the heart. Hine stood as if stunned and unmoving, but he burst past her, blocking a lordly man he recognized from his vision. *Asher Grieve!* He swung his taiaha at the man's skull in a killing blow.

The blow struck the man's head and the taiaha splintered — but the wizard never even flinched. It was as if the weapon had been made from polystyrene. His eyes swivelled and he gestured coldly. Mat felt himself picked up and flung aside like a doll. He skidded into the stone platform that held the heart, and two veins bunched above him. Hine gasped, and he saw her try to move. And fail.

Asher Grieve drew a blade from his cane and walked towards him. 'Ngatoro's pet,' he sneered. 'You can feed me, too, you half-trained mongrel.' He gestured, and the two veins plunged towards Mat.

With a desperate twist, Mat rammed the broken remains of his taiaha into the gaping maw of the nearest vein, caught the other in his left hand, and pulled. The vein was slick to the touch, but its instinctive retraction jerked him to his feet. He gripped the taiaha that was stuck in the side of the giant heart, and pulled. It came out with a sucking noise, and the whole heart pulsed. Every patient jerked, and opened their eyes. Black blood washed the taiaha, making his grip slick, but he twirled the weapon and dropped to a guard position.

Asher Grieve lunged, but Mat's blood-wet taiaha swept the sword-stick aside. Mat leapt into a counter, leaping and striking. For a few seconds they thrashed at each other, until the heavy taiaha snapped the sword-stick in two.

The old wizard snarled as he staggered back, but he palmed a tiny derringer pistol, and placed it against Hine's temple. 'Halt!' he commanded Mat.

The command was on two levels. One level was threat — 'Move and I'll kill the girl' — but the other was a sorcerous command that, if he succumbed to it, would hold Mat immobile. A double-bind: move and his enemy would kill Hine; fail to move and he would be held prisoner.

Jones hadn't trained him rigorously for nothing. He solved the dilemma almost without thought, stepping away, but not holding immobile. He felt the magical energies reaching to bind him fail. He eyed the wizard warily.

Asher Grieve half-smiled. 'Maybe a little more than half-trained,' he acknowledged. He ground the pistol into Hine's temple. 'No closer, boy.'

Mat's eyes met Hine's as blood trickled down her throat.

There has to be a way ...

Footsteps echoed from behind him, and he backed away. Donna Kyle lurched from the shadows, limping badly, her face drawn. Mat swivelled to keep father and daughter in view. The look on Donna's face was murderous — and directed at her father.

Asher Grieve jerked his hand, and Donna was thrown against the heart-platform, where Mat had fallen a few seconds before. 'Daughter,' he breathed, 'bring me the chalice. I must drink, and restore myself.'

Mat saw her give a soft sob, and thought he recognized what was happening. He extended his senses and perceived a cord of silver light running from her heart to the wizard's hand. She looked at him mutely, and he could not honestly say what he saw in her eyes.

He stepped aside, lifting the taiaha, still dripping with heart-blood — and swept it through the silver cord.

She gave a small cry and fell against the stone dais, right in the shadow of that grotesque green heart, while Asher roared in sudden pain. Hine twisted and slammed her elbow into the wizard's face, as if this were a bar-room brawl. His nose broke audibly, but he shoved at her, and she staggered towards Mat. Blood streamed down his face as he gestured towards Donna Kyle, who had lifted the chalice, black blood running down its side. He still held the pistol.

For a second everyone froze as the blonde woman lifted the chalice to her lips.

Asher's voice rang out. 'Yes! Drink, Daughter! Heal yourself! Then we will crush this pair of insects, and rule together.'

It took less than a minute of desperate defending for Wiri to realize two things: one, Col was faster and better than anyone he had ever fought; and two, his taiaha was going to splinter inside a minute. Perhaps when he had been an Immortal he could have beaten Col, but as it was he had only seconds left to live.

Except that winning was a habit. He had never lost, not since Tupu that first time. There would be a way. Parry, slash and retreat. Block, withdraw. Half-counter and jab. Lose slowly. He crabbed backwards up the stairs, keeping the Sluagh Sidhe from going after Mat. He took a slash to the shin when he was too slow with one disengage, but every second he bought gave Mat a chance.

The front doors burst open, and Tu and Manu and a cloud of warriors ran into the lobby. Col glanced sideways at them, then back at Wiri, his face suddenly resigned. 'Ex-Immortal,' he hissed, spreading his arms, 'you're going down with me.'

Two guns cracked from below, and Col staggered sideways at the impacts. His flesh splashed scarlet.

Wiri thrust. The Sidhe gurgled, staring down at the haft of wood that stuck from his chest.

Wooden stakes don't really kill vampires. Well, they do, but the fact that they are wooden is irrelevant. Big, sharp things stuck through hearts kill vampires, and Sidhe and patu-paiarehe and everything else.

But some beings die more immediately than others.

Col howled even as he began to crumple, and swung that huge sword as another fusillade of bullets hammered into him. Wiri literally saw the Sidhe torn apart before him, but still Col swung, even as he fell. With his only weapon stuck in Col's chest, Wiri was helpless, but the Sidhe's swing went awry even as it came. Steel sliced into Wiri's thigh instead of his chest. He scarcely felt it, but his leg gave way in a spray of blood.

The magical hold that her father had had over her had been shattered by Matiu Douglas's taiaha blow. How a mere taiaha could do such a thing she didn't know, but maybe the blood it had soaked in for centuries had given it some supernatural power — one could only guess. But now Asher's sorcerous binding over her was broken. She was free ... whatever that was.

Donna stared at the chalice, every eye on her. Hine was beside Matiu Douglas, both of them ready to strike. Others burst in. Tu Hollis first, striding towards Hine. When their eyes met, love shone amidst the grotesque evil of this place. Asher Grieve's derringer swung about, unsure where the true threat lay.

'Drink, Daughter!'

Wiri appeared at the doorway, his left leg hastily bound, held erect by a ragged Maori in a hat and trench coat. The wound was clearly serious, but he was here. Ngati Maungatautari warriors followed, faces shining with fierce love and loyalty to their leader.

Loyalty ... Now there's a big word. And love ... There's another one.

She felt a pang of envy. *Have I ever commanded actual loyalty? Has anyone loved me? Has there ever been someone I could trust out of love and respect and loyalty, not fear and compulsion?*

No, no-one.

She felt the familiar, bilious taste of being excluded, being the outsider, the enemy. Not even the wicked thing that called her "daughter" would mourn her death. She measured her father out of the corner of her eye. *My God, he looks utterly unchanged* — and yet, she could tell he was exhausted. Until a few seconds ago he had been just another prisoner of the bloated heart above them. Perhaps he had aided Parukau by channelling the power of the Heart, but he wasn't attached to that any more. He was spent, she realized. She was his only real hope.

But Wiri and his allies were similarly stricken. Wounded, tired, taken to the edge of mental and physical endurance. Few held a gun. Probably none could stop her if she drank.

I hold the balance of power here. What I choose decides this whole damned war ... A sip of this blood and I can burn away the sigil, and I'll be whole and free, and more powerful than I've ever been.

And still the Enemy.

The reek of the heart-blood stole over her senses. Unpleasant, oily and full of menace. She realized another thing: that if she drank it, it might tip her irredeemably down the path of the monsters — to be patupaiarehe, to be a monster, finally and forever.

But if I don't drink, I lose everything.

'Drink, Daughter,' Asher Grieve repeated. 'Drink. Heal yourself, and destroy these people. Then you will have won. Victorious, after all your suffering. The prize you have always sought.'

The prize.

What was this prize? Power? But what is that really?

Influence? Dominance? The ability to command? Wealth and luxury? Safety?

No, this 'prize' would bring none of those things. Dominance would happen only by force; wealth, by theft. And safety would be a myth. There would never be safety — whether she was under Asher's thumb or free of him, there would never be safety. There were always rivals and enemies. How many assassination attempts had she seen upon Puarata even in the relatively short period of her service to him? Dozens, and he had lived centuries before she met him.

It was an illusion. There was no victory, and therefore no prize. There was only sacrifice of all the things she would never have: friendship; laughter that wasn't scornful or derisive; affection that was not bribed or compelled — and love.

'Daughter,' Asher's voice took on greater urgency. 'Drink!'

She met Wiremu's eye, realizing she had never seen him damaged before. She thought about what he had done: exchanged an eternity of servitude for a mortal span of weakness and vulnerability — and done it for love, yes, but also for honour, and to be free.

Freedom. The hardest word of all.

Was freedom possible? Could it ever be, when she was wanted dead or alive throughout Aotearoa?

But I'm so damned tired of all this …

It would be so easy to just drink, to turn into the monster her father wanted her to become. She could let the beast do all the thinking, and never have to take responsibility ever again. Blame everything on someone else and never acknowledge any complicity. To be a victim, a murderous victim, from now until someone finally knifed her in the back.

Wiri met her gaze, as if he knew exactly what she was thinking. 'Donna, you can't go on blaming others for your acts. You have to make your own choice, and be judged by it.'

She looked back at him, his face strained, pain written all over him, but his eyes trained like lasers on her. She looked at Matiu Douglas, so like a younger Wiri, his young face pure and determined, on the verge of everything her life would never be. She knew he wouldn't even have to think about this. She yearned for that kind of childlike clarity.

Something strange and unknown bubbled up inside her.

I'm doing this for you, she mouthed silently at the boy.

And emptied the chalice over the floor.

Mat stared in disbelief as Donna Kyle poured the black fluid to the floor. His brain refused to interpret her silent words.

An apoplectic roar burst from Asher's throat. The wizard's eyes bulged in fury, and his arms rose. Several warriors fired, but the balls froze and shattered before impact. He cast the derringer aside as fire leapt into his hands. It bloomed to a purplish-yellow conflagration in an instant as he shaped it, his arms spreading as he roared. Musket balls shattered around him, and the warriors tried to reach him, seemingly swimming through the air in slow motion as their deaths took shape before them in flame and shadow.

Mat did two things at once: he thrust the heart-blood-stained taiaha into Ngatoro's hands, and he stepped in front of Asher Grieve, lifting up his right hand, shielding the others with his body. There was no plan, just the echo of a conversation with the Goddess of Fire. Her words echoed in his ears: *You have learnt how to give and take, poai. Fire is yours, to conjure or shape it.*

To shape fire.

The wizard stabbed his fingers at Mat, and the ball of fire billowed towards him. The heat filled his senses, as he called 'Mahuika!' and stood directly in its path.

His right hand, with its one black fingernail, met the wall of fire, and stopped it. As he shouted, four other fingernails, like chips of flint, grew on his hand. From them poured a shield against the fires of the wizard, which threw the flames aside. A curved wall of air rose about him, and the fire battered against it. He felt a furnace-like gust of wind wash over him, felt his skin go slick then dry instantly. But behind him his friends, and Donna Kyle, crouched, safe for now.

The curtain of flames fell away, and Asher Grieve stared at him, thwarted. 'How did you ...?' he muttered, then fell silent, baffled. He sagged and wobbled, his blood-streaked face a mask of disbelief.

Ngatoro rose slowly to his feet, and the veins holding him fell away. He was clad only in a loin cloth and Mat could see his physique repairing itself. He gripped the bloody taiaha in strong hands. 'Asher Grieve,' he said in a rusty voice. 'Surrender yourself.'

The wizard took a step away. 'Surrender? I, Asher Grieve? The man who brewed poison for the Borgias, and burned London? Surrender to native scum like you? Who do you think you are?' He tottered backwards down the ward, his eyes wild, beginning to fade into the shadows.

'Halt, Asher!' Ngatoro commanded.

For an instant, an unseen struggle was apparent on both

faces, two terrible old men striving for mastery. Every facial tic, every tiny gesture was a clue as to the flow of the forces. Mat sought a way to help, but the forces were bewildering. To intervene was too dangerous. Instead he gripped Donna Kyle's shoulder, holding her in place. 'Don't move,' he whispered. 'He doesn't own you any more.'

She turned her hollow-eyed face towards him, the dark twist of moko stark against her white chin. She looked incredibly young, a frightened child. Somehow he could see it in her: the dread and exhaustion, the self-loathing, the surrender. The woman who had haunted his nightmares was gone, no longer a threat.

Something she saw in him made her cower, but she pulled closer, not further away, ducking her head, trembling. The desperate gratitude in her eyes when she looked up at him was almost alarming.

He looked away, straight into Asher's eyes.

The wizard's face was bereft, his only child stolen. In that split second, he was vulnerable.

Ngatoro struck. A small gesture, but Asher reeled as if punched, and crumpled.

The blonde witch at Mat's feet began to weep uncontrollably.

Good for the heart

Saturday morning

They cleansed Te Iho, under Ngatoro's direction. Each prisoner was carefully detached from the veins distending from that mighty greenstone heart. Most, Ngatoro scowled over, and traced a warding, a sigil that would prevent the newly freed tohunga makutu from using their arcane powers. Then they were bound to their beds, and wheeled outside. Asher Grieve was among them, lying as still as a corpse.

'Who are they?' Mat asked, his eyes still struggling to take in the fact that his hidden mentor was before him, alive and free. He wasn't tall, and had been horribly weakened by his term in Te Iho, but he had a strong frame and there was every sign that he would recover strength quickly. For now, Mat and Riki were taking turns helping him walk.

Ngatoro-i-rangi smiled grimly. 'They are tohunga makutu. Many old enemies of the people of Aotearoa, Matiu Douglas.' He gripped his bloody taiaha like a walking stick, and exhaled with satisfaction. 'We will transport them to the Maori King for judgment.'

Mat's eyes strayed to where Donna Kyle sat, unbound, a sigil on her forehead. 'What about her?' he asked, feeling an odd empathy for the woman who had prowled his nightmares. She seemed to have shrunk somehow, but she still made him uneasy. She hadn't spoken since Asher was taken.

Ngatoro looked him over. 'Neither she nor her father are tangata whenua. We will send the Pakeha prisoners to Auckland, to Governor Grey, if he is still in charge there.'

Governor Grey has sworn to hang her, Mat remembered.

Wiri limped up, catching the end of the conversation. 'Grey is still in charge there. Donna Kyle and I have a bargain, which she has honoured. I will speak for her before the Governor.'

They saw her listening, turning her head to catch their words. But she didn't acknowledge them.

There were only two of the prisoners of Te Iho whom Ngatoro did not imprison. They were tohunga ruanuku: a revered old tohunga and his younger daughter, a girl who barely looked Mat's age. They were shockingly weak, but they had a chance at life. They were taken away reverently to obtain better care. Miraculously, the Ngati Maungatautari had not lost a man — by the time they went ploughing through the tipua ranks, the goblins had lost their will to fight. Several had been wounded, but Wiri's leg was among the worst injuries. 'Kels won't give me a second of peace over it, you'll see,' he muttered in Mat's ear.

The Birdwitch had vanished in the confusion. Riki seemed uneasy, but Mat was relieved. He wasn't sure how Ngatoro would react to her, and he thought she needed time to be free in the wild, and remember herself fully. But already she had forged one new legend for the storytellers to recall her by.

Before they left, Ngatoro sang a low chant that made the timber walls of the Bath House sprout branches. They grew rapidly, entangling with the veins of the greenstone heart. The outflow vein pumped a thick black sludge — the last of the poisonous blood that had sustained Puarata — into the ground where it sank and was gone. Something seemed to change in the air. The stale, bloody reek of the chamber vanished, replaced by something cleaner and more wholesome.

'Puarata and Parukau did not create Te Iho,' Ngatoro told Mat. 'They usurped it from me. It was once a force for good. I shall make it so once more.' He closed off Te Iho again, restoring the shadow-maze. Mat didn't ask him where he had repositioned the gate. He didn't want to know.

They then simply walked back into the town of Rotorua-Aotearoa, wheeling the prisoners and patients on the hospital beds. Rotorua-Aotearoa had reverted to its more usual aspect of pa and colonial town. The locals had seen the conflagration about the shadow-maze, and gathered to witness this strange procession. They kept their distance at first, until the news that Ngatoro-i-rangi was here spread, and then they flooded forward, to see for themselves, and to help.

Sunday evening

The pain in his hands woke Mat, and he lay with his eyes closed. The smell of clean sheets enveloped him, and the warmth of deep soft fabric embraced him. Everything ached, but his skin was clean and soapy smelling.

Slowly images surfaced from memory. Hine and Tu smiling as they left the Bath House in each other's arms. The way

Kelly had cried as she greeted Wiri on Saturday morning, having discharged herself from hospital when she learned that the party had returned. Tim Spriggs brought her across to Aotearoa, baby cradled in her arms. She tried to look reproachful, but relief overtook her and she flew into her husband's arms and all but knocked him off his feet.

But the thing Mat remembered clearest was the look in Donna Kyle's eyes as she tipped the blood of Te Iho from the chalice.

I'm doing this for you.

He shuddered and opened his eyes. He was in a colonial-era hostel in Aotearoa. The light at the edge of the curtains was vividly bright. Somewhere a clock chimed briefly. He stared at the open-beamed ceiling, and listened to horses whicker and wagons roll past. He examined his hands, where ten flint-like nails tipped his fingers, shining like black marble. The magical feather cloak hung over a chair beside the bed, and a blotchy-stained taiaha was propped against it. Ngatoro's taiaha, soaked in the blood of Te Iho. The old tohunga himself had given it to Mat on Saturday morning before the whole tribe in Rotorua-Aotearoa. 'I'm too old to wield such a thing any more, Matiu Douglas. And I owe you my life. It is yours by right.'

Ngatoro had left that morning with the Ngati Maungatautari, taking the prisoners to the Aotearoa Maori King in Ngaruawahia without delay. Two of the prison wagons would go further: all the way to Auckland, with Asher Grieve and his daughter chained inside. Donna Kyle had stared out at Mat as her coach lurched into motion that morning. She still looked like a lost child. He wondered if he would ever see her again. He hoped not. But he didn't wish a hanging on her any more. She had rejected her father, and saved their lives. Whether that meant she could ever be a better person it was impossible to tell, but perhaps she deserved a chance to find out.

It's out of my hands. He felt both guilty and glad at the thought.

There was a soft knock on the door, and it swung open with an awkward thump, allowing Wiri to lurch through on crutches. Kelly followed, holding their baby boy to her chest. He realized she was breast-feeding, and frantically tried to find something else to look at.

'Kia ora, chief. How're you goin'?' Wiri propped himself in front of a large armchair and then literally fell back into it, wincing heavily. Kelly perched on the side of the bed, the baby suckling noisily. She giggled at Mat's averted eyes.

'Get over it, Matty-mat! I'm going to be hanging my boobs out for the next six months, minimum, and there won't be anything sexy about it. It's just feeding time at the zoo!' She had dark bruises around her eyes and looked as exhausted as Mat felt. 'The little bugger wants a drink every three hours.'

'What are you gonna name him?'

'Aethlyn,' said Wiri promptly.

'Anything but Aethlyn,' said Kelly at the same time.

They both looked at each other and laughed.

Mat put his hands behind his head. 'Matiu is a good name,' he suggested.

'But then we'd get confused over who we're talking about, you or him,' said Kelly. 'Otherwise it'd be our first choice, honest.'

'Liar. You keep telling me that "Mat" means "flat and lacklustre".'

'No, that's just you. The name is fine.'

'Cow.' He laughed. 'Dairy cow!' She began to protest, so he put his hands over his ears and went *Moo, moo*, until she flicked him a rude gesture and poked out her tongue.

'And I was about to compliment you on your new-found maturity,' remarked Kelly caustically, when he fell silent. 'Anyway, what we really came to tell you was that it's after five in the afternoon, and everyone else is up and hungry. So you can bloody well get your arse up, and join us for dinner.'

Hunger suddenly washed over him at the mere thought of food. 'Sure!' After seeing the wagons off yesterday morning, he had gone straight back to bed and slept thirty hours straight — the price of his exertions, both physical and magical.

Kelly waved her hand grandly. 'I shall now hand you over to my husband for a status report.'

Wiri gave an ironic half-bow from where he sat, and coughed. 'Yes, status report ... Well, Tu is fine, just a few bumps—'

Kelly immediately interrupted him. 'How's your leg, sweetie-darling?'

Wiri coloured, grimacing.

'Manu carried Wiri out,' Kelly went on.

Wiri frowned. 'He just helped me walk — I was on my feet,' he insisted.

'Wiri got cut up by a nasty thing,' said Kelly caustically. 'First wounds in how many centuries, darling? *Because he's not immortal any more.* In fact, he's promised to be *much* more cautious from now on, haven't you, *darling?*'

354

Wiri flashed Mat a 'gimme some sympathy' look. 'I think I'm healing up pretty quick.'

'How's Tim?' asked Mat.

'Broken arm. Wounded pride. And Fitzy is okay, he got back at midday.'

Kelly leant in. 'And Hine is fine.' She looked meaningfully at Mat. 'She's just outside.'

Mat looked up at the door, then down at the bedclothes. 'I better get dressed first.'

'Sure,' Kelly replied with a magnanimous gesture.

He looked at her and Wiri, who put on patient expressions. 'Ah, I said "I better get dressed", so I guess you'll want to leave?' Mat told them.

'Yep, got that. Go for broke, Matty-Mat.' Kelly continued breast-feeding with a bland look on her face. 'You've got nothing I ain't seen before. Including last night, I might add, when we decided you might sleep better out of your clothes.'

'Oh.'

There was an impatient knock on the door, and Hine popped her head around the door.

'Are you guys done already?' she said, and grinned at Mat. 'Hey!' she said. She looked anxious. She was wearing another colonial-era dress, like the one she had had on at Jones's place. Her hair was pulled back in a ponytail. She looked beautiful.

He thought he might feel jealousy or something, but in fact he found he didn't. She hugged him, and he breathed in the smell of shampoo and perfume. No cigarette smoke. He squeezed her shoulders, and then pushed her away. 'You okay?' he asked.

She nodded slowly. 'Yeah. Look, I just wanted to say thanks,

355

for coming after me. You really are my knight in armour. That's twice now. You're probably the second most wonderful guy I've ever met.' She measured him with his eyes. 'But I've also met the first most wonderful guy. You okay with that?'

He realized he was. 'Yeah, sure. Tu's cool. He'll look after you.' He put on a *Star Wars* voice: 'It is your destiny.'

She rolled her eyes, 'Not you, too.' Then she smiled shyly, 'Yeah, he will look after me. And me, him.' She put her hand on his. 'I know you fancied me, and I kinda fancied you, too. I want you to know that.'

He nodded slowly, aware that he felt both bereft and happy.

'You'll make some chick really happy one day. One day soon, possibly,' she added with a twinkle in her eye. She leant over him, kissed his forehead, and then she was gone in a swirl of cotton skirts and rose-scented perfume.

Kelly grinned at him, and Wiri nodded slowly, his face approving.

They gathered in the upstairs lounge of the Red Deer: Wiri and Kelly and their still unnamed child, Mat and Riki, and Tu and Hine, wrapped up in each other — despite the age difference, they clearly belonged together. Fitzy was there, too, fully recovered, but still in dog form because Tu and Hine found his turehu form 'just too weird'.

Cassandra was also there. She had driven up from Taupo that morning, peeved at missing the action but grateful to have been able to contribute. She had to put up with being centre of attention, as only Mat had seen the beginnings of her latest transformation of appearance. Her hair was now buzz-cut, she was wearing stylish clothes that didn't look like op-shop rejects, and of course no braces or glasses. She looked utterly different.

'I'm thinking Natalie Portman after she shaved her head,' Riki whispered in Mat's ear. 'Quite hot, actually.'

'So, what do you think?' Cass asked them, preening slightly. 'This is the new look.'

Riki gave a nodding thumbs-up, while Mat searched for words. *Not one of the boys. Still kinda kooky ... No: unique.* Not ordinary in the slightest. He suddenly realized something he should have known all along: that 'ordinary' didn't really exist. Everyone was extraordinary in their own way. Especially Cass. 'You look entirely like ... yourself.'

She gave him a thoughtful look, then smiled. 'Good answer. Ten points.' She raised a glass in salute.

'Do *you* like it?' Mat asked.

'Yeah, I think so.' She stroked the spiky down on her scalp tentatively. 'When I look in the mirror, I still get surprised, but it feels more ... honest. Although it makes me feel kinda naked. I'm still getting used to it.' She reported that Jones was awake, fully functioning and clamouring to be released from hospital. 'Oh, and he and your mum are getting on like old mates,' she added to Mat.

Mat blinked at that. 'Mum and Jones?'

'Yeah. He can make her giggle like an eight-year-old.'

'Mum? Colleen O'Connor?'

Cassandra smirked. 'Totally. She brings him baking.'

Very, very strange.

Kurangaituku had not reappeared, and Riki confessed to being a little worried. 'She's a goddess, right? She'll be okay?'

His friend looked years older. Adventures in Aotearoa seemed to do that to people. Although 'adventures' seemed the wrong word — *they're more like ordeals*, Mat thought ruefully.

'Has she promised you a date or something?' Cassandra teased, but for once Riki didn't rise to the bait.

'She needs to remind herself who she is. She'll be okay, I'm sure.' Mat said.

It seemed to be a gathering of the walking wounded. Wiri was still hobbling, and Tu Hollis was moving gingerly, too, from a cut to the chest and bruised ribs. Hine looked haunted and relieved. Tim Spriggs's broken arm would take weeks to mend. Fortunately there were waiters to do the serving and carve the meat. Kelly looked exhausted, the worst of them all, even though she had not been in the fight. 'Giving birth is far worse than being in any silly battle,' she told them in a dismissive voice. When the men demurred, she grinned evilly. 'Which would you boys rather do then?' It clinched the argument.

They toasted Aethlyn Jones and Ngatoro-i-rangi. They compared wounds. They ate venison and sipped a majestic red wine that Tim Spriggs ordered. Mat had one glass, for Jones. He could picture the old man lecturing him about the health issues involved.

They all fell silent for a time, lost in their own thoughts. Then Fitzy jumped onto the table to help himself to more venison, and sparked a round of laughter that seemed to never stop. Tim Spriggs teased Hine about her clothes, and Kelly threatened to tell them all about her labour all over again, until a thin, plaintive cry came from the corner where the baby boy was lying in a bassinet. They passed the little boy around; a naming competition ensued, but few of the suggestions were serious. Mat sidled in beside Cassandra and clinked glasses. 'Thanks for helping me find Te Iho.'

'It was nothing. You did most of the thinking ...' she grinned slyly, '... for a change.' She squeezed his hand softly under the table, suddenly looking extraordinarily lovely.

Everything was very nearly perfect ...

He met Hine's eyes. She was leaning into Tu Hollis with a contented look on her face, and smiled back at him. But he found himself thinking of another set of eyes, one that would be staring out from the bars of the prison carriage winding its way north. He no longer knew if Donna Kyle deserved death or not. He just knew he didn't want to be the one who decided.

He wondered about Mum and Dad, then put it aside. It was up to them. His happiness didn't depend on them reconciling, and maybe their happiness didn't either. There seemed nothing left to worry about, so he didn't. He sipped his wine and joshed with Cassandra and Riki. Wine and laughter ... weren't they supposed to be good for the heart? Maybe he would have another glass.

Author's note

Most of the characters of this book are fictional. Ngatoro and Puarata are figures from legend, and tales of their doings can be found in most New Zealand mythology collections. The tales of Maui and Mahuika, Hinemoa and Tutanekai, and Peha can likewise be found in most collections.

Glossary

There are a few Maori words used in this story and its prequels. Most are explained in the text, but here they are with a definition.

Please note that there are subtle variations of Maori usage in different regions of New Zealand. The definitions, below, are based on those given in P. M. Ryan's *Dictionary of Modern Maori* (Heinemann, 4th edition, 1994; republished as *The Raupō Dictionary of Modern Maori*, Penguin, 2008).

Aotearoa: The traditional Maori name for New Zealand, although it did not assume wide usage until the Europeans arrived. It roughly translates to 'Land of the Long White Cloud'. In the story I have used the word to signify the 'ghost world' of New Zealand mythology, history and spirits.

Haere ra: 'Farewell.'

Haka: A traditional Maori dance. We mostly think of it as a war-dance, which is a sub-type of haka called a peruperu and is performed by warriors as a challenge to enemies prior to battle. However, a haka can also be performed in celebration or to entertain, and not just by men. Different tribes have their own haka.

Hangi: A traditional Maori cooking method in which fire-pits are dug and filled with large stones, which are then heated by fires for around two hours. The food is placed in baskets, wrapped in soaked cloth, and placed on the stones and covered over, trapping the heat and moisture for a gentle slow cooking of the fare — primarily meat and root vegetables. The cooking phase takes three to four hours, and results in a smoky, juicy meal that retains all the natural flavours of the ingredients.

Hau Hau: A branch of the Pai Marire, a Maori religion that fused Christian and traditional beliefs. It was strong on the East Cape of the North Island. The militant branch of the Pai Marire was known as Hau Hau, and fought in the 1860s for the return of land. They were infamous for the slaying of a reverend in 1865. This set them as 'bogeymen' in the colonial settlers' psyche, with the result that they became synonymous with cannibalism and savagery.

Hongi: A traditional Maori greeting where the two participants rub noses. They are thereby symbolically 'sharing breath', and the visitor becomes one of the people of the tribe for their stay. The god Tane is said to have created woman by moulding her from clay and then breathing into her nostrils, and thereby gifting her life.

Iwi: A tribe or race of people.

Kai: Food.

Kapa haka: A traditional display of Maori dance and song.

Karani-mama: Grandmother (an adaptation from English).

Kawa: Protocol, especially the protocol of the local marae. This covers who may speak and who may not, who is welcome, etc.

Kehua: One of the many terms for a fairy or goblin in Maori mythology. For the purposes of this story, 'kehua' denotes spirit-goblins that can animate earth or wood, appearing as clay-like goblin creatures. Only about sixty centimetres tall, they are more mischievous than evil, but might be enslaved by a tohunga makutu for evil purposes.

Kia ora: A universal greeting that can mean 'Hello' or 'Thanks' or even 'Good health' or 'Best wishes'.

Korerorero: A chat, a discussion.

Koru: A carved spiral pattern based upon the unfurling fern frond. It symbolizes new life, growth, strength and peace. The koru is a common motif of Maori art.

Makutu: Evil magic.

Mana: Prestige, or charisma, or honour, or dignity, or all of these virtues; mana encompasses the personal qualities of leadership and pre-eminence within a tribe and people.

Manaia: A sea horse, and a common motif in Maori carving. In the Aotearoa of this story, I have used the word to denote sea-taniwha.

Maori: A Polynesian race that settled New Zealand, probably from around 800 years ago (the timing is unknown and somewhat controversial). They settled primarily in the North Island of New Zealand, and on adapting to the cooler lands, thrived and multiplied until the coming of the Europeans after Cook's journeys in the late eighteenth century. The ninteenth century saw increasing European settlement and conflict, until Europeans dominated numerically, and colonized the country.

Marae: The central place of a Maori community. In a pre-European settlement, it was the central area of a village, and contained the meeting halls and central courtyard where social gatherings and events would occur. In the modern world, a marae is often in the countryside, and will contain a meeting hall and lawn outside for gatherings on special occasions and the funerals of noted community members.

Mere: A traditional Maori club, which could come in many forms and be made from stone, bone or wood. The term **patu** also means club. For the purposes of this story, I have used the word 'mere' to denote blunt, heavy clubs which would be used to bludgeon an enemy, and I have used 'patu' to denote lighter-edged clubs which would slash an enemy.

Moa: A flightless bird of New Zealand, extinct before Europeans arrived — though some say there might yet be some in the wilds of Fiordland in the South Island.

Moko: A traditional Maori tattoo. Maori have a strong tradition of tattooing and this can cover much of the body, including the face. The patterns and motifs are strongly traditional. The carving of moko was a very painful ordeal, and part of the rites of passage of a young man or woman of rank — the more moko one had, the more mana and rank was implied.

Pa: A fortified village. Pa were normally found on hill tops, encircled by several rings of wooden palisades and, once guns became widespread, also entrenched.

Pakeha: Traditionally a Maori term for foreigners, although these days it has come to mean New Zealanders of European descent (primarily British, but also Continental Europeans such as German, Dutch and Scandinavian).

Patu: A club — see 'mere'.

Patupaiarehe: One of the many terms for fairy or goblin in Maori mythology. For the purposes of this story, 'patu-paiarehe' denotes pale-skinned, red-haired vampire-like creatures, which are dangerous to men.

Piupiu: A flax kilt.

Poai: Boy.

Pohoi: An earring — these might be made of stone, bone, or even cured hides of birds. A pohoi from a rare bird like the huia was highly prized.

Ponaturi: One of the many terms for fairy or goblin in Maori mythology. For the purposes of this story, 'ponaturi' denotes pale-skinned, man-like sea-fairies who prowl the coasts, occasionally glimpsed by men.

Pounamu: Greenstone — a jade found in New Zealand, often used for the most precious ornaments.

Rangatira: The chief of a tribe.

Ruanuku: A wizard; as in 'tohunga ruanuku'.

Ruru: The native New Zealand owl, or morepork.

Taiaha: The traditional Maori long-club. A taiaha looked a little like a spear with a carved point, but this was deceptive. It was not a spear, and never thrown. In fact the 'point' was the handle, and the thick haft of the weapon was the striking part. It was used more like a two-handed sword, and had a tradition of fighting moves associated with it. In combat, the pointed end was often used to apply the *coup de grâce* to a stunned opponent.

Tangata whenua: The People of the Land. The term can take a wide meaning such as all Maori, or a narrower view such as the people of a certain region. It implies a right to dwell upon that land.

Taniwha: A taniwha is generally seen as a protective spirit, associated with (especially) waterways, but also with other natural landmarks like caves and hills. They commonly appear in tales as giant lizard-like creatures, or massive serpents. They are also associated with great white sharks (mako-taniwha). They are sometimes hostile, sometimes protectors of a village or place.

Tapu: Sacred. The term can apply to a place or a person or a thing. To break a tapu — by entering a place without the appropriate ritual actions, for example — was to court misfortune, and to pollute oneself spiritually.

Tikanga Maori: Maori customs.

Tiki (or **hei-tiki**): A tiki is a carving of a primal human form, usually male. Tiki are worn as a neck pendant, and can be made from wood, bone or stone. They have a great deal of cultural significance and mana, and are often treasured artefacts passed down through the generations.

Tipua: One of the many terms for fairy or goblin in Maori mythology. For the purposes of this story, 'tipua' denotes small, wiry, pale-skinned, goblin-like creatures, about a metre tall, with primitive weapons, living in wild places and mostly hostile to men.

Tipuna-tane: Grandfather.

Tohunga: A Maori priest or wise man (they were always male), similar to a druid or shaman. The tohunga preserved tales and legends, genealogies, and were the cultural repositories of their people. They were also looked to for guidance in astrology and as intercessors with the gods, and appear in legends as powerful 'wizards' with magical powers, some good and some evil. The term can also cover experts in skilled traditional fields like carving, navigation and canoe-making. The term **tohunga makutu** denotes a tohunga who uses black magic.

Tuatara: A native lizard-like reptile of New Zealand, typically up to a metre long from head to tail. (They are, in fact, a relic of the dinosaur era.) They are associated with boundaries in folklore, and women were forbidden to eat them. They were held to be found at the boundaries of tapu places.

Turehu: One of the many terms for fairy or goblin in Maori mythology. For the purposes of this story, 'turehu' denotes shape-shifting creatures, who appear goblinesque in their natural form. They are mischievous, and might be dangerous if antagonized, but friendly if respected.

Wahine: A woman.

Waiata: A song. Maori was not a written language in pre-European times, so songs and stories were an important part of retaining cultural identity.

Wairau: Spirit. In the context of a 'tohunga wairau' it designates one who acts as an intermediary with spirits, and is synonymous with 'tohunga ruanuku', except that a tohunga wairau is one who would not use makutu in any form.

Waka: A Maori canoe, generally a large canoe whose hull has been carved from a single tree trunk. Waka ranged in size from small unadorned river and fishing vessels to forty-metre war-canoes used by war-parties for water travel.

Whanau: Family; both immediate and extended family.

Whare: A house. The meeting house at the centre of a marae is generally termed the 'whare runanga', and is adorned with traditional carvings at the entrance and inside.